ABOUT THE AUTHOR

Richard Watson has written for magazines including *Hip-Hop Connection* and *Total Film,* during which time he's interviewed artists from Ice Cube and Eminem to Idris Elba and Eve. He's also written for a couple of television shows that went off the air not long after he came onboard, but that's probably just coincidence, right?

Hanging Out With Jessica George

Richard Watson

58 Kings

First published in Great Britain in 2009 by
fifty eight kings press
3 Mayfield Road, Southam CV47 0JX

Copyright © Richard Watson 2009

Richard Watson has asserted his moral rights in accordance with the
Copyright, Designs and Patents Act of 1988.

ISBN 978-0-9561250-1-9

Cover design and artwork by Robert Jones

To Cagoule Girl

"I'll say she looks as clear as morning roses newly washed with dew."
   William Shakespeare

"I can't cope / 'Cos that girl is dope."
   Bell Biv Devoe

CHAPTER ONE

'OK, guys,' she said, grinning as she fastened a stray lock of chestnut hair behind her ear and peered over her thick black frames. 'Who's next?' I was next. I knew it and so did my pounding heart. So, too, did the man sat a metre to my left, who casually nodded his tousled head at me from over his battered newspaper. I rose to my feet and, trying hard not to show my nerves, walked across the room. I lowered my body into the black leather seat and tried to maintain composure while she wrapped me in red nylon fabric. 'What are we doing, then?' she asked.

'Um, seven on top, two at the back and sides, please,' I said. As she fixed up the clippers, I studied her features in the mirror and came to the conclusion that they were equally beguiling in reverse. Was it possible that her face was perfectly symmetrical? What, I wondered, was a drop-dead gorgeous girl with a perfectly symmetrical face doing working in a dingy barbershop which still had faded photos of its most requested, least Ozone-friendly 1980s styles lining the walls?

'Just finished work?' She pushed the clippers over the top of my head.

'Yeah,' I replied. Lord, I hoped I had more than 'yeah' in the tank.

'Lucky you. What do you do?'

'I'm a writer. A television writer.' Her hazel eyes lit up from behind her sturdy-but-really-rather-sexy specs.

'Really? Anything I might have seen?'

'Oh, probably not.' I was making an assumption, of course, but Zoe (I knew her name was Zoe because it said so above her mirror) didn't seem like the sort of girl who'd stay at home watching *Disc Heads*, the epic saga of life in a beleaguered DVD rental store, and at any rate, it wasn't a credit I was particularly proud of.

'Go on, try me.' She leant in, pursed her minimally made-up lips and gently blew a sprinkling of hair off the bridge of my nose. Her breath smelled of chocolate. I like chocolate a lot, so it struck me that we already had that in common.

'Well, I'm mainly developing ideas of my own,' I said, which was true in the sense that I had a pile of (mostly half-done) scripts I'd written lying on my bed at home. 'In fact, we're shooting a pilot tomorrow over in Lewisham.' This was true in the sense that ... Well, it was true in a fictional sense.

'What's it called?' asked Zoe.

'It's called, er ...' My eyes darted across the shelf in front of me, moving over a half-eaten bag of chocolates and landing on a tube of hair gel. 'It's called *Firm Hold*.' Zoe switched off the clippers.

'*Firm Hold*?' she echoed. 'What's that about?'

'Um, it's about a guy born with the mysterious power of being able to grip things ... really tightly.' (Yeah, I know. But give me some credit – had I based my premise on the *very* first thing to meet my eyes, I'd have found myself attempting to put a positive, post-ironic spin on face paint-intensive variety show *A Pack of Minstrels*.)

'So what does he do with this power?' asked Zoe.

'He fights crime,' I explained, before clarifying, 'he's a crime-fighter.'

'Oh.' Zoe sounded suitably unconvinced as she changed utensils and started tidying up the back of my neck with a razor. 'It doesn't seem like a particularly helpful power. I mean, it's not like being able to fly or see through walls.'

'Well you say that,' I countered, 'but if you were hanging off the back of a speeding car you'd probably be glad of the ability.'

'I suppose ...'

'Not to mention if you were trying to climb up a cliff face while vultures clawed at your head or dangling off a helicopter above a volcano ...' Zoe stared incredulously at my reflection.

'You're filming all of this in Lewisham?'

'Well, yeah, but, er, you know, there's gonna be a lot of

CGI in it,' I qualified. Before my runaway tongue had time to commit George Clooney to the project, we were interrupted by the telephone ringing from over by the till.

'Will you excuse me for a second?' asked Zoe.

'You've got a razor blade held inches from my neck,' I pointed out. 'I'm hardly going to say no.' Zoe laughed, put down her weapon and walked over to the phone. Meanwhile, I quietly breathed a sigh of relief. Saved by the bell. Time, now, to compose myself. It seemed I'd finished the first half of this thing on a positive note, but if I was to make my mark with Zoe in the second, talk of fictitious, styling product-inspired TV shows was going to have to be kept to a minimum.

'No, sorry,' said Zoe to the person on the other end of the phone. 'He's not in. No, they all left half an hour early. They're meeting up with a girl who used to work here ...' I snuck a glance over at her. She was rocking a funky kind of ensemble that comprised a raspberry-coloured cardigan, a black miniskirt, black-and-charcoal hooped tights and slightly worn brown suede boots. I looked back at my reflection. It was a markedly less attractive sight (not least because I had a load of hair clippings stuck to my face and looked like a werewolf) but an entirely necessary one as I challenged the floundering lupine fool in the mirror to dramatically step his game up. 'OK, will do,' said Zoe to whoever it was she was talking to. 'No problem at all. Bye.' She hung up the phone and walked back over, while I resolved to steer the conversational spotlight onto her, or at least away from myself, vultures and volcanoes.

'So you're new here ...' I observed astutely while Zoe got back to work with the clippers.

'Yeah, I just moved down to London from Bristol two weeks ago.'

'Oh, wow. Well, you know why they hired you, right?'

'Why's that?'

'You've only got three letters in your name.' I looked up at the Z, the O and the E above Zoe's mirror. 'If you're rubbish and they have to get rid of you, they've only wasted three of

11

those stickers.'

'If I'm *rubbish*?' Zoe switched off the clippers and placed her fist on her hip in a pose of exaggerated outrage.

'Plus they probably had a surplus of Zs they needed to use up. So in fact they'd really only be wasting *two* stickers.'

'Mister,' intoned Zoe, squeezing two millimetres of air between her thumb and forefinger whilst staring me down from over her specs, 'you're *this* close to walking out of here with a Mohawk.' Our reflections laughed with each other.

'So are you enjoying it?' I enquired.

'Enjoying what?'

'Your job. D'you like it here?'

'It's alright.' Zoe screwed up her almost-certainly-symmetrical face just slightly. 'I wouldn't be saying this if my colleagues were here, but I'm hoping it's a short stay. I'd rather be working at, you know, like, a salon.'

'OK, well, I wouldn't be saying *this* if your colleagues were here, but you probably don't have enough facial hair or bad enough breath to be working in this joint anyway.'

The banter continued apace, but with my low-maintenance haircut (long enough not to scare elderly women; short enough to intimidate cocky twelve-year-olds, or at least those not packing heat) rapidly reaching completion, I realised that my window of opportunity was narrowing. To recap, Zoe was sexy, funny, down-to-earth and, as someone new to London, probably in need of new acquaintances, not least acquaintances that were also relatively recent transplants to the city (I'd moved down from the Midlands six months earlier) and who shared her interest in chocolate. Besides, even if I fell flat on my face, the only other person within earshot of us was Tousled Guy, whose messy head was buried in his red-top. No doubt about it, this was a gift-wrapped opportunity if ever I had one, and so, as the object of my instant affection put down the clippers and lifted a mirror up to the back of my head, I steeled myself for action.

'How's that?' asked Zoe. I jolted up in my seat, a look of

horror plastered across my face.

'Oh, God. That's terrible. No. You're going to have to glue it all back on.' Zoe laughed and lifted the mirror up higher, as if she intended to smash it over my ungrateful, freshly shorn head.

'Seriously.'

'Seriously? You're great. I mean *it. It's* great.' Shit. Had she heard that? She was smiling as she lowered the mirror and hung it back on its peg beneath her sink. That was a good sign, right? Unless she was smiling in a pitying, 'God, this guy's pathetic' kind of way. That would be bad. No, actually, either way this was good. Zoe had seen my hand. I mean my metaphorical hand of cards, not one of my actual hands, both of which were – beneath their hair-strewn, red nylon cover – clenching the armrests like I was the hero of *Firm Hold*. I swallowed hard and went for it.

'Can I ask you something?'

'Sure.'

'I mean, I hope I'm not being cheeky in asking this, but I'd love it if you would, er ...'

'If I would ...' The smooth, chiselled faces on the wall tried to shake my nerve by ganging up and staring me down from beneath their chemical-saturated eighties quiffs and curls. After what seemed like an eternity, and with my finger nails damn near pushing through the leather and into the foam beneath, I brushed off their intimidation tactics and finally got the words out.

'If you would put some gel in it.'

Upon leaving a barber's, it's pretty routine for even the least vain of customers to check out the hairdresser's efforts in a shop window or two, but I was too ashamed to look at my own reflection – and not just because I had a head full of sticky sludge. Apparently, I wasn't the only one who couldn't bear to look at me, either. On the pavement, a trendy-looking lad indiscriminately handing out trendy-looking flyers for a trendy-looking club night looked away from me as, hand open in preparation, I walked past. What? I was supposed to be avoiding eye contact with *him*. Clearly, this guy could smell the pungent stench of lameness the way a dog sniffs fear, and I was oozing lameness out of every last lame pore.

What a disaster. I tried to tell myself that I could pick up where I'd left off next time, but who was I fooling? Next time, I probably wouldn't be sat in Zoe's chair, especially if her chair was in a fancy woman's salon somewhere on the other side of town. Nope, I'd royally messed that one up. I'd let slip a golden opportunity and now there was nothing I could do about it. Or was there? I stopped in my tracks and belatedly went eyeball-to-eyeball with myself in the nearest shop window (although I still couldn't bring myself to survey the sticky mess on top of my noggin). Time to show some stones, I thought to myself. Time to seize control of the situation and be a fucking man. Realising that my reflection was wearing a wedding dress, I called time on my internal monologue and headed straight back to the barber's.

'Hang on a sec, I'll just get it out,' said Tousled Guy, fumbling about under his bib or whatever the hell those things are called. Before I even had time to recoil in terror at the thought of what I'd walked in on, he whipped out his mobile and flipped it open. 'Fire away and I'll give you a call sometime before Satur ...' He trailed off as he saw me.

'Oh, hi,' murmured Zoe, looking surprised while the pretty boys on the wall looked smug.

'Hi.'

'Watch out. I think he's come for a refund on his wet look haircut,' cracked Tousled Guy. Great. Not only had this prize knob beaten me to Zoe, he was taking the piss out of me, too.

'I think I, er, might have dropped my, um, keys here,' I lied, pointlessly scanning the seats by the door. This was now beyond the realms of regular lameness. In years to come, this would be remembered as the day I pioneered my Spector-esque 'Wall of Lame' approach. 'Nope,' I concluded somewhat inevitably, 'must have dropped them on the street.'

'Hang on,' said Zoe. 'Maybe you dropped them on my chair. Have a feel about will you, Rob?' Flipping heck, she already knew this guy's name. Tousled Guy, sorry, Rob, shifted about in his seat.

'It doesn't feel like I've got anything hard up my arse, so to speak,' he sniggered. Realising that I was getting close to putting something sharp in this clown's eye, I decided it was time for me to make a miraculous discovery. I plunged my hand wrist-deep into my pocket, fumbled about for a second, then rolled my eyes skywards as my fingers came up clutching the keys.

'Sorry,' I sighed. 'I've just realised that they're actually in my pocket. And that I'm an idiot.'

Slouched on a hard plastic seat at the bus stop, I shook my head at my own ineptitude, my own cowardice. Despite my desire to sulk in solitude, though, it wasn't long before I felt someone watching me. I looked around to discover American R&B sensation LaMont fixing me with his smouldering gaze as, fingers cradled beneath his goateed jaw, he hawked his new album 'The L Word' from the side of the bus shelter. I wondered if LaMont had *ever* had trouble sealing the deal with women and concluded that it was an unlikely scenario for a young man who probably moonwalked his way down the birth canal and popped out of his mum screaming in perfect falsetto. Hell, even the cream-coloured fabric of his cashmere sweater seemed to cling to his sculpted frame as much out of lustful adoration as good tailoring. As the bus pulled up to the kerb, I thought I saw a sly smirk flicker across LaMont's well-balmed lips, as if word of my pathetic antics up the road had reached him. Fucker. What sort of arrogant prick needed two capital letters in his first name anyway?

Back at my house, sorry, back at my flat, sorry, back at my pokey little Finsbury Park bedsit that evening, grisly footage of The Barbershop Massacre was still playing on a continuous loop in my head. Nonetheless, as I placed the last of the washing-up on the draining board, I consoled myself with the knowledge that at least I wouldn't have to explain to Zoe why *Firm Hold* hadn't been commissioned as a series (although for the record I would have cited spiralling production costs). Besides, perfectly symmetrical faces were overrated anyway – you wanted variety in a visage. I was just about to turn off the light in my compact (read: 'shoebox-sized') kitchen when the phone rang. I took two steps over to the sideboard opposite the sink and picked it up.

'Hello?'

'Hello, Rich,' said a familiar voice. I hauled my arse up onto the work surface.

'Hi, Mum.' We talked for about half an hour. About my mum's work and my dad and my sister and the family that had moved in next door to my mum and dad. My mum asked how work was (I said 'not bad') and how I was eating (I said 'good') and she told me that, although she hadn't seen last week's episode of *Disc Heads,* she'd recorded it, and was going to record tonight's episode and watch them both back-to-back at the weekend while she did the ironing. I told her she shouldn't feel obliged to watch the programme, let alone two episodes in a sitting. She said she didn't; that she enjoyed it. I was enjoying speaking to her. We spoke some more, then we wound it up and, as always, I told her I loved her.

'I love you too,' said my mum. 'Remember to take care of your wallet.' I promised her I would, then said goodbye and put the phone back in its base. My mum always told me to take care of my wallet. I was certain she still envisaged London as a grim and gritty Dickensian world in which grubby-faced, fleet-fingered pickpockets waited to deftly relieve you of your valuables before scurrying like rats over the cobbles and through the fog into the shadowy back alleys. Little did she know that the greatest danger on London's generally not-all-that-foggy, increasingly less cobbled streets wasn't the Artful Dodger and his undernourished posse of thieving urchins, but rather the Capital's impressive supply of delectable, distinctly non-Dickensian women, ready to lift your heart as quickly and effortlessly as one of Fagin's pocket-picking protégées would swipe your shillings.

At this point, I would have gone and sat down in the lounge, but I didn't have one, so instead I trundled into my bedroom. Deciding some relaxation was in order after a hard day making an arse of myself, I cleared the debris off my dark red-and-terracotta duvet cover. First to go was that pile of (mostly half-done) scripts, after which I picked up the box for the broadband kit I'd recently hooked up to my laptop. On it, and set against a spotless white background, a beautiful, vivacious-looking black girl with a halo of bouncing curls and a spearmint-coloured roll-neck tilted back her head and flashed her pristine pearly whites as, latte in hand, she enjoyed the chrome laptop perched on her powder blue suede sofa and laughed ecstatically at the tremendous good fortune that had brought broadband internet access into her life. I looked longingly at the woman and wished that I could take the place of the laptop on that sofa – if easy installation and wireless connectivity were enough to get her shaking orgasmically, imagine what some flirtatious patter and a friendly foot massage could accomplish.

It suddenly occurred to me that I was developing feelings of jealousy for an internet package, and so – letting the two lovebirds get on with their cosy good time – I placed the box face down on my carpet, flopped onto my bed and pointed my remote at the TV that, thanks to the wonder of the wall bracket, overlooked me.

I was greeted by the omnipresent Hannah Thornwell presiding over her new talk show. While critics had savaged Thornwell's nascent star vehicle, *Hannah* was, it seemed to me, almost scientific in the way it exploited its host's complete array of skills. Forged over her extensive career in reality TV presenting and hair dye adverts, these skills were, specifically, grinning, gurning and feigning empathy with idiots undeserving of oxygen, let alone feigned empathy. One such character, pretty boy youth TV presenter-slash-DJ Brett Scott, was, at that moment, knee-to-knee with Hannah, exhibiting all the wit and charisma of breaded plaice (oh, and a customary, overpowering smugness fuelled by years of off-camera laughter from sycophantic production runners) and giving my finger extra impetus, if any were needed, to hit the remote.

Over on the next channel, the popular detective series *Thrust and Parry* was underway. Clad in his signature tan suede jacket, moustachioed, maverick detective Thomas Thrust was bickering with his balding, by-the-book partner Geoff Parry as the two of them sped to the scene of that week's crime in their trademark black Land Rover.

Not my cup of tea at all, so, in search of something completely different, I flipped channels once more and found cross cultural detective series *Art and Kraftz* in full swing. Clad in his signature skullcap, bearded, by-the-book Jewish detective Arthur 'Art' Goldstein was bickering with his blonde, maverick German partner Hans Kraftz as the two of them sped to the scene of that week's crime in their trademark silver Mercedes (Kraftz' choice, presumably). Realising that I was going to have to make my own entertainment, I reached for the pen and spiral bound notepad that lay on my bedside table (lest nocturnal inspiration should suddenly strike) and set to work brainstorming some new fictitious TV cop duos. I'd come up with crime-crushing *Pestle and Mortar*, Cotswolds-based sleuths *Wattle and Daub* and zero-tolerance hard men *Noel and Void* by the time the pen dropped from my hand and I drifted off into a slumber.

I was awoken by a Geordie man taunting me with his blandly quirky recital of some strangely familiar words. Opening my eyes, I realised that the screen above me was awash with another thrilling real-life vignette from the senses-shattering world of DVD rentals:

Geordie Man: 'It's fifteen minutes 'til closing time, but the drama's just beginning for branch manager Sean. The shop's only copy of *Cocoon* still hasn't been returned and Brenda, who has booked the film for her husband's birthday, is at her wits' end.'

Brenda: 'No, I won't settle for *Cocoon: The Return*! It's a lazy retread and you know it!'

Sean: 'It's got Courtney Cox in it. You know – her off *Friends*.'

Brenda: 'I don't care if Jesus Christ himself makes a cameo appearance. This is a yearly tradition for me and my husband.'

Sean: 'Maybe you should think about buying a copy. It would save disappointments like this, and it would probably work out cheaper in the long run.'

Brenda: 'Oh. Well, yeah, I suppose it's a thought ... Do you have a copy in your DVDs to buy section?'

Sean: 'Um, actually we don't.'

I clicked off the TV. Watching this made me wonder if maybe I should, in fact, get started on *Firm Hold*.

'*Firm Hold*?' repeated Eddie, his eyebrows – one of which was augmented with a metal hoop – reaching up to touch the most adventurous tresses of his shaggy brown hair. 'Why didn't you just tell her you write *Disc Heads*?'

'Because it's a steaming pile of shit,' I reasoned, 'much like everything we do.' There followed about ten seconds of silence as Eddie, a researcher and one of my two best buddies on the Red Button staff, scoured the walls of our shabby, first floor Docklands office for an argument. Being as his eyes were greeted with lurid posters for such televisual gold as *Prang! Britain's Most Annoying Automobile Scrapes* and *Hedge Your Bets: High-Stakes Topiary,* none was forthcoming.

'Oh, forget about her. You'll meet someone you fancy more next week.'

'That's the problem,' I observed. 'I probably will, and I'll let *her* slip through my fingers too.'

'If you want my advice …' offered Eddie. I wasn't sure I did – Eddie's last words of advice to me had been that, should I decide to trim my downstairs hair, a gradual, 'feathered' cut would minimise painful prickling against the inside thighs. 'When I believe that something feels right,' he continued unsolicited, 'I go for it.'

'Like what?'

'Like my animal rights stuff.'

'That lasted about a fortnight,' I pointed out. Eddie was well known for showing passion in a new cause, pursuit or impractical facial decoration before abandoning it a couple of weeks – or even days – later in favour of something fresh. For instance, that eyebrow piercing was brand new and I hadn't even bothered to comment on it yet.

'Ah, yes, but the point is I went for it all guns blazing.'

'If by that you mean you got yourself arrested ...'

'I got myself arrested for expressing my beliefs. I don't regret throwing red paint on those fur coats.'

'They were fleece jackets. You were the only animal rights activist barred from entering Millet's.'

'Well, if it looks like fur, it's promoting fur,' argued Eddie, his voice taking on a note of exasperation. 'That's the way I see it.'

Before Eddie could expound upon the chilling evils behind the warm fleece, the debate was interrupted by another insulating outer garment. The sound of swinging arms brushing against padded polyester alerted us to the arrival of our colleague Joy, whose slender frame was wrapped in a new, army green body warmer with a faux fur-trimmed hood that scooped up the serpentine black braids which swerved over her head and wandered absently down the back of her neck.

'Aww, isn't that sweet?' cooed Joy, glancing at the soft, pale blue jumper I was wearing. 'A real live Care Bear.'

'Well I never,' I retorted. 'A runner bean with braids.' Joy flipped her middle finger up at me, leaving it to catch up with the rest of her body, which was heading off to her desk at the far end of the room. This was pretty much the way we began every day, with an exchange of prickly but good-natured insults. In fact, it was also the way we continued each day: the first exchange of the morning was always a curtain-raiser, a sneak preview of the savagery that was to follow. The next blows were struck about five minutes later, when Joy would go to the vending machine – situated in the break area, right behind my desk – for her first cup of Indiscriminate Beige Slop. Fully aware of this timetable, Eddie wheeled his chair in closer to mine, scanned the room for potential eavesdroppers and, content that the coast was clear, seized his chance to offer me a further helping of his questionable wisdom.

'You know,' he began in hushed tones, 'I really don't know why you're giving this hairdresser chick another thought when you've got Joy there for the taking. It buggers belief.'

'OK. Firstly, I think the phrase is *beggars* belief.'

'No,' insisted Eddie. 'You're taking belief and buggering it. Right up the arse.'

'Fine – but how? What's all this about Joy?'

'True or false?' queried Eddie, pressing his fingertips together in a manner he obviously thought typical of a psychiatrist, 'You're madly in love with her.'

'Um, I *like* her,' I admitted, looking down awkwardly at the blue carpet tiles beneath my feet. Well, I say 'blue', but 'blue with sporadic, abstract splashes of brown' would be more accurate. The area around my desk – leading as it did into the partitioned-off break area – was something of an accident black-spot (or rather brown-spot), with various tea, coffee and hot chocolate stains serving as grave reminders of fatal collisions past.

'Well,' said Eddie, callously refusing to join me in a moment's silence for all those hot beverages cruelly cut down before they'd had a chance to be sipped (I would have poured out a little coffee in their memory, but it seemed to somehow defeat the point), 'she's head over heels for you.'

'Head over heels?' I echoed. 'What are you basing that

on?' Eddie rolled his eyes and smacked his forehead in a manner not typical of a psychiatrist at all. At least not one whose services I'd pay for.

'She goes on about you all the time. After you left last night she came over to my desk and started talking about you.'

'Really? What did she say?'

'She asked whether I'd heard that you have Syphilis.'

'Oh, yeah, she's crazy for me.'

'Don't you see?' asked Eddie. 'It's playground stuff. You're like two eight-year-olds calling each other names and pulling each other's hair because you're desperate to have sex.' He paused for a moment, mentally replaying his words before adding, 'The sex part is separate from the analogy about the eight-year-olds.'

'Thanks for clarifying. I did wonder.'

While Eddie needed to pay closer attention to his phrasing, his 'playground' theory was, from my end at least, on the money. I knew the reason I constantly took the piss out of Joy was because I fancied her – I'd had a crush on her since the day I'd arrived at Red Button; since the moment I first saw her, in fact. You know how in movies, when the hero sees the love of his life for the first time, they show her gliding across the screen in slow motion? Well, the very first time I laid eyes on Joy moving across the room towards me, it was just like that; as if her every step had been slowed down eight times. Alright, you would hardly say Joy was gliding – she simply had an excruciating attack of pins and needles in her left foot – but for some reason the effect as she dragged her slumbering hoof across the floor was no less seductive, and, as I sat peering over my newly allotted computer monitor, I found my movement severely impaired, too. I was unable to shift my eyes, which were glued to Joy's bundled-up brow and endearingly pained grimace. At that moment, our malfunctioning bodies conspired to throw us together, as Joy clocked me clocking her, bent her grimace into a smile and uttered those seven little words that I'll never forget: 'What the hell are *you* looking at?'

22

By popping that question, Joy set in motion a bickering, bantering relationship for the ages. When we weren't exchanging quips face-to-face, the two of us were bouncing them back and forth via e-mail. Indeed, there were times when using my keyboard to actually bang out some pithy narration seemed merely like a way to fill the seconds as I waited for a little envelope bearing Joy's latest put-down to arrive in the corner of my screen (the day we discovered a system-wide cache of clipart containing donkeys, clowns and myriad other unflattering images was a highlight, with a real visual edge being added to our electronic diss wars). In amongst the insults, though, Joy and I had increasingly taken the time to find out about each other, and a few months and several hundred cups of IBS later, we each knew a lot of funny-but-quite-personal things about the other. For instance, Joy had once related to me a story about how, after receiving the advice 'must try harder' on a school report card, she'd made an anonymous phone tip-off to the police that her teacher was going to be contravening copyright laws by screening *Labyrinth* for her class the next day. Perhaps inevitably, the dramatic SWAT team raid that she envisaged failed to materialise, and Form 2H's end-of-term treat passed by without the interruption of armed, copyright-savvy frogmen smashing through the window and wrenching the rented 1986 David Bowie fantasy movie from the school's clunky, top-loading VCR. Nevertheless, I thought, this bizarre tale gave a perfect insight into the psyche of a girl who, even back then as a youngster, you didn't want to mess with.

The one thing I didn't know was whether Joy's barbs were coming from the same place as mine, or whether she simply enjoyed a verbal workout with a fellow big-mouth. Still, it was academic anyway as Joy had recently acquired a boyfriend, an infuriatingly decent and affable guy called Matt, who, having worked as a cameraman at Red Button for a few months, had graduated to ply his trade on, you know, proper respectable programmes and stuff.

That said, it wasn't as if I myself didn't have a special

someone in my life; a person to whom I was totally and wholeheartedly committed. I switched on my computer, reclined in my chair and looked around my desk at the gallery of pictures devoted to the only woman in my life I could truly count on; the one girl who was always there for me when I needed her – Jessica. One picture, a particular favourite of mine, showed Jessica sporting a pink-and-red, thick-striped polo shirt that clung perfectly to her small but athletic frame. Another captured her laughing it up on holiday, an inflatable crocodile tucked under her arm. Clinging to the corner of my computer monitor, a small, passport-sized picture found Jess in playful form, sticking her tongue out from beneath the brim of a baby blue bucket hat.

Once upon a time, this unassuming, modestly sized snapshot had been the only picture of Jessica at my desk. During my first few weeks at Red Button, I'd chosen to keep our relationship private, but I soon realised that I needed Jess's photogenic features to help me get through my days of writing drivel. Before long, that one little picture, tentatively and discreetly Blu-Tacked to my PC, had grown into a proud, sprawling celebration of my girl spanning both of the blue, fabric-covered partitions separating my desk from those around it.

And then there was the centrepiece of my exhibition. My monitor stirred into life and the screen filled with my newest picture of Jessica. Clad in a simple yellow T-shirt, she'd had highlights put into her thick dark hair since the holiday snap and looked, in my opinion, more beautiful than I'd ever known her to be.

Still, the best thing about my special girl wasn't her hair, her tongue or even her admirable lack of self-consciousness in the company of ridiculous inflatable reptiles. It was the fact that she was completely out of my league. She was unattainable, and thus I would never have to worry about not having the guts to ask her out. Jessica, you see, was Jessica George, the bubbly host of bustling, brightly coloured Saturday morning children's

TV show *The Hangout*. She was beautiful. She was intelligent. She was charismatic ...

'She's a slag who has unprotected sex with tramps and one-armed drug addicts.' Indiscriminate Beige Slop in hand, Joy had reappeared to offer her considered opinion.

'Oh, don't be jealous, Joy,' I mock-pleaded. 'I like you too.'

'No you don't. You only like women you'll never ever get the chance to speak to.'

'That's not true,' argued a voice from a few feet away. It belonged to Mitch, the producer of *Disc Heads* and, indeed, most of Red Button's dubious canon. Despite rumours from some of the production staff that he hailed from Lowestoft, Mitch, a small guy with a round, shaven head, generous black eyebrows and a neatly groomed goatee, spoke with a fiercely Cockney accent. 'I've told 'im, if he wants a job on The Hang-aht I can get 'im in there. I know the producer, Kam, and she's always looking for new writers.'

'And I've told *you*, Mitch,' I reminded him, 'that while I appreciate the offer, I'd rather stay here and help make *What Lies Beneath: True Tales of Britain's Worst Haemmoroid Sufferers* than risk embarrassing myself in front of the goddess Jess.'

'Pathetic,' observed Joy. She placed her cup (which itself was aggressively beige) down on my desk and uprooted a small blob of Blu-Tack from the top of my monitor before stretching it out with her fingers and attaching the resulting elasticated strand to my screen so that a formidable blue bogey appeared to be hanging from Jessica's left nostril. 'So tell me, Rich,' she began, proudly surveying her low-brow handiwork. 'When's the last time you went out on a date with an actual, real-life girl in the actual, real-life world?'

'For your information, Miss Bennett, I'm seeing a girl at the moment.'

'Bollocks!' scoffed Joy. 'What's her name?' I caught sight of a newspaper sports supplement peeking out from the magazine rack on my desk. The Williams sisters were on the front cover.

'Seren ... us,' I ventured. 'She's called Serenus.'

'Serenus,' grinned Joy. 'Hmmm ... She sounds like she's sporty.'

'A little bit,' I winced, vaguely miming a backhand.

'Sad.' Joy grabbed her drink and trooped off to her end of the office, where she sat next to Beth, her and Eddie's fellow researcher. If there was a certain spark between myself and Joy, then Beth and I had all the chemistry of two damp towels in an airing cupboard. I didn't dislike Beth, a blonde-haired, jagged-faced girl who did most of her 'research' on holiday web sites and internet handbag emporiums; I just didn't seem to connect with her, something that had become apparent to me fairly early on in our working relationship.

I remember once sitting on the end of Joy's desk and talking about superheroes. As I recall, the topic came up because Joy had been invited by a friend to a superhero-themed fancy dress party and wanted my opinion on who she should go as – I suggested Storm from The X-Men, if only in the secret hope that I'd later be rewarded with photos of her in form-fitting black leather and a long white wig. Anyway, after pontificating over whether fine-textured hair was the deciding factor in Bruce Wayne and Peter Parker becoming Batman and Spider-Man (a thicker texture would have meant telltale 'hat-hair' – or rather 'mask-hair' – thus putting their secret identities at risk), we turned to the time-honoured question of what superpower we'd most like for ourselves. Joy selected telepathy, so she could hear which of her friends were slagging her off. I settled for a type of super-hypnosis in order that I could make any woman I desired fall in love with me, regardless of whether she was patently too hot for me – actually, *especially* if she was patently too hot for me. Looking to include Beth in the banter, I asked her what her ideal superpower would be, to which she replied 'touch typing'. Assuming that this was a joke (and, I thought, a pretty funny one), I started laughing, only to be met by a pissed off look. Thinking that she was merely being deadpan, I suggested that her name could be Keystroke and her outfit could feature a giant 'QWERTY' emblazoned on the chest, at which point her maximum strength stoneface alerted me to the fact that she wasn't being deadpan, she was being insulted. Beth, it seemed, genuinely felt that X-ray vision and the ability to leap over tall buildings in a single bound were small fry compared to hitting one hundred and thirty words a minute.

I was sure that Beth, too, knew – or at least suspected – that I liked Joy, and I was equally certain she disapproved. Unlike my own immediate neighbour Eddie, who right now was working feverishly to get myself and Joy bickering and bantering our way up the aisle.

'You *have* to make a move on her,' he remonstrated. 'You know when you should do it? Next week at the wrap party.'

'Right,' I agreed, nodding attentively. 'But the question is *how exactly* to make a move on her. Hmmm, I know who I could ask for tips. Her boyfriend.'

'Who, Matt?' Eddie screwed up his face disdainfully. 'I don't think they're even official these days. Besides, even if they're still clinging on for dear life, you don't have to actually ask her out – just tell her how you feel.'

'There's a difference?'

'It's like making a preliminary enquiry; putting forward a tender for your services. You're giving her a choice.' I couldn't believe I was listening to Eddie, but with just ten days left until the wrap party, I knew I had a choice to make myself.

Laid belly-up on my bed, I wiped the sleep from my eyes, then looked up contentedly at the face looming over me and wondered why I'd never found a silver-haired woman in bifocals this sexy before. Up on my TV screen, Jessica George had slipped into the role – and, by extension, the wig and stern, old-fashioned spectacles – of Judge Jessie, tireless provider of justice in all matters concerning viewers of *The Hangout* and their irritating parents, siblings, mates or teachers. On this particular Saturday morning – one on which the late spring / early summer sunshine forced its way through the crack in my curtains and washed across the room – Judge Jessie had just heard the rather pitiful case of a dad who kept pilfering his daughter's Beyonce CD without asking her permission. It was a decision that was to cost him dear, as, with a bang of her gavel, Judge Jessie decreed that he entertain the audience with the fruits of his illicit listening by portraying the bootylicious Miss Knowles in a live performance. To help him get into character, Jessica's co-host Liam Barton arrived in frame proffering a long blonde wig. The dad, a beefy, bespectacled, bald-headed fellow, laughed gamely as he slipped on his new thatch, but for my money neither it nor Jessica's legal locks looked as ridiculous as Liam's 'do, an übertrendy style best described as, well, I'm not even sure *how* to describe that mess. It was kind of spiked at the back, with a flattened-down, jagged fringe and all manner of other shit going on too. I wondered if Liam was so vain, so petrified of being five minutes late for a tonsorial trend, that at any given time he kept half a dozen different hairstyles on standby. Certainly I could think of no other reason why he covered his scalp with a collage of dizzying rosettes, soaring wisps, slicked-down patches and rampant, spiky thickets, all divided up like farmer's fields by sharp, scratchy tramlines and violent, out-of-nowhere partings.

My musings on Liam's 'do were interrupted by the rattling of the letterbox, and so, with Old Man Knowles gearing up for his musical debut, I got out of bed to investigate, accidentally kicking my laptop, which, despite its black screen, was still on following a late Friday night writing session. Yeah, I know – rock and roll, eh? Having overcome this obstacle, and ignoring my desperation for a wee, I headed down the stairs to see what awaited me. There on the doormat was a white envelope bearing a big red thumb print, the logo of TV comedy production company Sore Thumb. I knew what this was about. A few weeks earlier I'd sent them a script for the pilot episode of *Crushed* (a quirky comedy series following a young man's attempt to track down his unrequited love – a girl he never plucked up the courage to speak to at university), and this, it seemed fair to assume, was either a declaration of interest or another addition to my small but growing collection of thanks-but-no-thanks bog-standard brush-offs. I walked back up the stairs clutching the letter. I was even more desperate for a wee now but it would have to wait. I stood in the hallway in my T-shirt and boxers, tearing open the envelope. The letter – printed on thick cartridge paper and folded into thirds – wasn't halfway out of the envelope when my eyes landed on the phrase 'we are sorry to inform you ...' I dropped the letter to the floor and scurried into the bathroom. I'd risked the onset of a kidney infection for *that*?

Back under the duvet after almost *deliberately* kicking my laptop (the fourth episode of *Crushed* was the project I'd been fine-tuning the night before), I felt as deflated as one of those cheap, garage-bought plastic footballs after a brush with a rose bush. I'd thought that Sore Thumb, of all companies, would surely be in tune with the accessible yet intrinsically oddball sensibilities of *Crushed*. Maybe they were. Maybe when I eventually picked that half-opened letter up from the hallway floor, I'd open it up fully and read it properly and find out that, while the standard of my work had impressed them, the project simply wasn't something they were able to commit to at this time. And maybe they meant it. Maybe they'd been sincere when they'd opened up the 'fob'emoff.doc' template on their screen and printed my copy along with nineteen others. Actually, maybe I was being too cynical. During the brief time in which it had remained in my hands, the letter had felt like maybe, just maybe, it was more than a one-page thanks-but-no-thanks job. Maybe someone in Sore Thumb's script reading department had attached a few useful notes of constructive criticism to help me improve upon the work which had nevertheless impressed them. Maybe. Or maybe I was deluding myself to even bother beavering away on these scripts. Maybe writing docusoap narration and gags for little-seen sketch shows was as good as it got for me. A lot of maybes, then, but amongst them there was one definite. Sore Thumb weren't going to be greenlighting *Crushed*. Just like Corkboard Productions, Suction Cup Productions and A Funny Thing Happened. Now I thought about it, there were actually quite a lot of definites, too.

I looked up at Jessica. She wasn't Judge Jessie now, those bifocals banished from their prior perch atop her impressive cheekbones, the wiry silver rolls replaced by her own, glossy dark locks and her scarlet robes removed to reveal a black t-shirt emblazoned, in gold foil print, with the words 'HIGH MAINTENANCE'. Nope, now she was just plain (or rather not-so-plain) Jessica George, enthusiastically congratulating the eagle-eyed viewer who'd blessed the show's *Faces in Foodstuffs* segment with a prawn cocktail crisp that, thanks to either God, mystic forces or – just possibly – uneven baking at the crisp factory, bore the apparently unmistakable face of Justin Timberlake. She was having fun, but then the thing with Jessica was that I couldn't really recall a time when it seemed like she wasn't.

'Pick it up, pick it up,' I murmured. After a few more rings, a woman on the other end of the phone granted my request.

'Good morning, Sycamore.'

'Hello, can I speak to Lianne Learner, please?'

'Can I ask who's calling?'

'My name's Richard Westbrook. I sent Ms. Learner a script about a month, a month and a half ago ...'

'OK, hold on one second please and I'll try to connect you.'

'Thank you.' The line went quiet. Actually, on this particular morning, ambient noise was at something of a premium in the Red Button nerve centre, with many of the company's already meagre workforce elsewhere as they prepared for the upcoming UFO-themed programme *Gross*

Encounters. Joy and Beth were present and correct at the opposite end of the room, leaving Rohini, a pretty production runner with a sleek bob haircut, the only colleague within chin-wagging distance. What better time, then, for me to check up on how, if at all, the pilot script for *Crushed* had been received by the script-sifters at Sycamore? True, it wasn't really a correct observation of protocol to pester production companies, but maybe by politely touching base I could at least move my comic masterwork to the top of the 'to read' pile. Besides, a little bit of over-the-phone charm surely wouldn't hinder my already slim chances of success with Sycamore, a company which specialised more in twee sitcoms and Sunday night dramedies – if, that is, their resident script-reading supremo could actually be persuaded to bless me with a moment of her time.

'Hello?' ventured the same female voice I'd just been speaking to. 'Ms. Learner's line is busy at the moment. Would you like to hold, or shall I take a message?'

'No, that's OK, I'll hold.' It wasn't like I had anything better to do.

If Sycamore's list of in-house hits (including scone-centric sleuth series *The Teashop Mysteries* and divorcee abroad ratings stalwart *Costa Del Sal*) suggested a certain lack of cutting edge credentials, then their choice of hold music drove home the point in definitive style. It took me a couple of seconds to place it, but the uplifting ditty flowing into my right ear was the song 'Yes' by Merry Clayton, from the soundtrack to *Dirty Dancing*. Smiling at the selection, I grabbed a pen and added it to the track listing for 'Now That's What I Call Hold Music', an imaginary album I'd been compiling over the course of many patience-testing phone calls and which already featured such stalling-for-time classics as 'Easy Lover' by Phil Collins and Philip Bailey, 'Crockett's Theme' by Jan Hammer and an exclusive panpipe version of 'Wicked Game' by Chris Isaak. As an appetiser for this future chart-topping collection, I couldn't resist putting the music on speakerphone for Rohini's benefit.

'Ooh, *Dirty Dancing*,' she noted approvingly. 'You can't go wrong.' Rohini spoke the truth, and as the mighty Lianne Learner continued to keep me waiting, I looked around my gallery of Jessicas – the one in the white vest; the one with the baby blue bucket hat; the one with the inflatable crocodile – and realised that my phone was cranking out the perfect soundtrack for a celebration of my number one pin-up. It started as a soft murmur, but, holding the ear-end of my receiver to my lips like a microphone, I was belting out my own custom-constructed version of the chorus as, clad in a black T-shirt, tan work boots and baggy camouflage combat pants, Joy strode over in her usual purposeful manner: '*Ohhh, Jess! We're gonna fall in love, and it feels so right ... Ohhh, Jess! We're gonna make love, it's gonna be tonight ... I can just imagine, huggin' and teasin' and lovin' and squeezin' all* – Hello? Ms. Learner?' Rounding the corner of my desk, Joy shook her head and sniggered at me, disappearing into the break area while I struggled to regain my composure with the receptionist who'd abruptly pulled the plug on my impromptu concert.

With my call proving to be something of a non-event (Lianne Learner, it transpired to no great surprise, was yet to review the *Crushed* pilot script but would undoubtedly be in touch at such a time as she did), I put down the phone and stepped into the break area. Now I *did* have something better to do. At the not-particularly-far end of the small, rectangular space, Joy, who obviously fancied something a little bit classier than her regular IBS, was ferrying a plastic cup of hot water from the vending machine to the top of the fridge directly opposite, where a proper mug and a herbal teabag were waiting to take receipt of the liquid.

'G.I. Joy!' I exclaimed. 'Loving the trousers. The camo really makes your bum look a bit less enormous.' Joy scowled at me, but her scowl couldn't camouflage the smile that was bubbling up underneath it. 'Yeah,' I continued, 'it's like an optical illusion or something. The pattern really draws your buttocks in.'

'Piss off.'

'I'm joking,' I pointed out, even though Joy was well aware. 'Seriously, I like them.'

'My trousers or my buttocks?'

'Your trousers. You already know I like your buttocks, Joy. I've always been completely transparent about that.' I zeroed in on the machine for a cup of IBS, only to find my camo-clad colleague stepping in to block my path.

'Uh, excuse me,' intoned Joy sternly. 'I'm not finished.' I tutted and rolled my eyes. Joy pressed the '2' and '9' buttons and, while the machine gave birth to another cup of hot water, I stepped back over to the small, circular table laden with Red Button's regularly updated supply of trashy, celeb-saturated periodicals. On the cover of omnipresent, market-leading gossip rag *Gab*, a menagerie of female pop stars and reality show nobodies flashed their overpaid and apparently overexposed crotches (obscured, thankfully, by yellow stars) as they clambered in and out of taxis, limos and thundering great people-carriers.

'You know what separates celebrity women from normal women?' I asked. Joy raised the water level in her mug to the desired point, then pushed her latest plastic cup inside its two predecessors.

'Celebrity women can afford *not* to listen to you singing?'

'Nope. Celebrity women shoot out shining yellow stars when they open their legs.' Joy pressed down on the foot pedal of the bin that stood next to the fridge.

'How do you know normal women don't?' She dropped the stack of cups into the bin and let the slam of its lid punctuate her quip. I had to admit, it was a good one, not least because there was an element of truth to it. I hadn't had sex in six months. Actually, to be specific, it was more like six months and eighteen … months more. I wasn't sure I even remembered what to do or how to do it. Then again, I'd recently gone bowling for the first time in a decade as part of a Red Button night out and actually hadn't embarrassed myself, guttering the ball only twice and even racking up a strike en route to a scrappy but ultimately satisfying victory. Five bowling years were, I was pretty certain, the equivalent of one sex year, so by that reckoning I might still be able to put in a respectable if unspectacular performance in the sack if, by some strange twist of fate, the opportunity arose. That said, with the exception of Rohini, who'd turned out to be something of a surprise package, the other members of our bowling party hadn't been up to much either, and in the currently unlikely event of a nice, right-minded girl getting naked at the same time as me without cash up front, I couldn't necessarily rely on her having the same level of carefree inexperience as my alley-mates, one of whom I now confronted with a voice full of pretend pain.

'Why must you always try to hurt me, Joy?'

'I don't know,' she shrugged, a mischievous grin sneaking onto her face. 'Because it's fun?' I chuckled and opened up *Gab*, landing on a full page picture arguably even more grotesque than the star-studded, underwear-free front cover. It showed the ever-irritating Brett Scott stumbling out of a night-club with a cigarette balancing on his lip and a satsuma-skinned blonde hanging off his arm.

'Well,' I said, holding aloft the picture, 'if you really want to upset me, tell me you like Brett Scott.'

'Urghh.' Joy screwed up her face. 'No way. He's vile.' I put the magazine back down on the table and flipped through page after page of the usual celebrity suspects (most of whom were currently on at least 14:38 of their allotted fifteen minutes of fame) before eventually landing on *Famous 'Fits*, the style pages that helpfully informed readers how and where to acquire the latest celebrity-approved looks. This week, Charlie Carter, the blonde, girl-next-door star of soap *Tachbrook Park* was modelling the latest, must-rock leg wear.

'You know, Joy, camouflage combats are all well and good, but it says here that if you want to look current this summer, you're going to have to invest in a pair of culottes. If they're good enough for five eighths of Charlie Carter's legs, they're good enough for five eighths of yours.' Joy stirred her pink drink nonchalantly.

'I'll wear 'em if you do.' I laughed quietly before making an effort to broaden the intellectual parameters of our conversation.

'Have you ever worn something specifically because you saw a celebrity wearing it?' Joy looked at me suspiciously.

'You mean other than the TLC thing?'

'Ah, yes, of course. The TLC thing. When are you going to let me see that photo?'

'How about the twenty-first of Neverwary?' sighed Joy. 'For the last time, you're not seeing it.'

'You've already told me what you looked like,' I pointed out. Using her plastic spoon, Joy lifted her dark pink teabag out of the water, then plunged it back in again.

'Well then you don't need to see the photo, do you?' This was tough, but the snap we were bickering about was the stuff of legend and I wasn't giving up that easily.

'What would you say if I told you that I had a photo from 1993 showing me and three friends dressed up as Jodeci?'

'I'd say, DeVante, that at no stage in your life have you ever had three friends.' Joy had me there, and so, opting instead for an appropriately TLC-centric tack, I interlocked my fingers, squeezed my palms together and lifted the resulting ball of knuckles up underneath my chin.

'I ain't too proud to beg.'

'So I heard from one of the cleaners.'

'Damn it!' I seethed, separating my digits into two clenched fists. 'I thought I told Jurgen that our two minutes of passion were between us and the industrial-sized pack of jay cloths in that store cupboard.' At that moment, Beth steamed into the break area. I flashed my fashion-forward reading matter at her.

'Whaddya think, Beth? Would I look good in culottes?'

'Nope.' Beth walked straight past me and my culottes and

shovelled a handful of coins into the chocolate machine that stood between its drinks-dispensing counterpart and the magazine table. She poked a couple of buttons and the machine emitted its familiar high-pitched whizzing noise, but crucially failed to deliver the satisfactory dull thud that usually signalled the end of a cash-for-snacks transaction.

'Shit,' muttered Beth, eliciting a discreet exchange of half-amused, half-vaguely unsettled smirks between myself and Joy. She rolled up her sleeves, positioned her feet shoulder width apart, then grabbed both sides of the machine and started rattling it with every agitated ounce of power in her flustered little frame. Her frenzied assault sent tremors through the break area and beyond, but did nothing to dislodge her defiant snack of choice from behind its metal loop.

'Beth, Beth, let me,' I insisted, stepping into the breach before she rammed her face, by now as rosy as Joy's herbal tea, through the glass and wrestled her elevenses out with her teeth. Beth, who was staring furiously through the pane whilst clouding up a small patch of it with the breath being violently expelled through her flared nostrils, reluctantly relinquished her spot, allowing me to survey the job at hand.

'What are we looking at?' My eyes quickly picked out the stuck-in-situ source of Beth's frustration. 'Ah, the classic four-finger Kit-Kat. Its large, flat surface, combined with its ill-advised positioning at the edge of the machine, makes it the most notoriously temperamental of all the vending machine's inhabitants. That said ...' I grabbed both sides of the machine and slowly but firmly rocked it back and then forward again. As the front of the glass-and-metal box touched down on the carpet, the Kit-Kat jumped free from its shackles and landed with an even more satisfying dull thud than normal at the bottom of the machine. I leant down, slid my hand through the flap and pulled out the stubborn slab of confectionery.

'There you go,' I said, proffering the unharnessed snack to Beth. 'See, you've just got to have the right ...'

'Thanks.' Beth took her chocolate and walked off. I

waited until her quick, tense footsteps faded out before resuming conversation with Joy.

'Beth's in a good mood, I see.'

'Go easy on her,' implored Joy. 'She's having a rough day. She just found out her cardigan has fibre fatigue.' She pursed her lips and fluttered her eyelids as if blinking back tears. I laughed, but I couldn't help thinking how cute she looked. In fact, it's possible I may have descended into some sort of minor trance had my brain not butted in to remind me that I still had a cup of coffee to cop. I motioned towards the drinks machine.

'*Now* am I allowed?'

'I suppose so.' Joy lifted her finely brewed mug of herbal tea from the top of the fridge. 'But first, aren't you going to congratulate me?'

'Congratulate you on what?'

'Don't you notice anything different?' I studied her for a couple of seconds.

'You trimmed your sideburns?'

'Very funny. Look harder.'

'Where am I supposed to be looking?'

'Why don't you try the general vicinity of my hand?' My eyes darted to Joy's left hand, which she was resting demonstratively on her jutting hip, supermodel-style. Without warning, an ominous sinking feeling overtook my stomach as I scanned Joy's fourth digit. Surely not … She hadn't … She wasn't … She couldn't be ...

'Yes, it's official,' beamed Joy. 'I'm the world's greatest aunt – look … My right hand, you dopey twat.' I diverted my gaze to Joy's other mitt and the mug that she was proudly holding aloft. Sure enough, there on its side in pink bubble letters and accompanied by a funky female character was the legend 'WORLD'S GREATEST AUNT'.

'Ohhhhhhh,' I exhaled. 'That's cuuuute.'

'I know. My niece Constance gave it to me.'

'Wow. I'm really happy,' I enthused, before adding, 'For

you.' Joy looked at me through narrowed eyes.

'OK. Now you're just being sarcastic.'

'Bonita!' I exclaimed, speaking the word in a tone that asked – sarcastically, of course – 'Would I do such a thing?' Bonita was a nickname I often called Joy and which derived, albeit rather tenuously, from her surname Bennett (sometimes I stretched the name to Bonita Applebum in reference to A Tribe Called Quest's beguiling muse; she of the impressive 38-24-37 measurements and general prophylactic-worthiness).

'Arseface!' responded Joy, mirroring my gently scorned tone. Arseface was a nickname Joy often called me, and which derived, pretty directly I was led to believe, from my face and its allegedly arse-like appearance (sometimes she stretched the name to Effing Arseface or Arsefaced Idiot, which, to my knowledge, weren't specific references to the beguiling muses of any fondly remembered 90s hip-hop act).

'No, really. That's brilliant news,' I insisted as she disappeared into the world outside the padded blue partition, the middle finger of her non mug-wielding, blessedly naked left hand the last part of her body to leave. Well, it made a change from her right one.

I put my three five pence pieces into the slot, hit '6' and '1', then rested my forehead against the vending machine and poured out a huge sigh as IBS with sugar and extra milk gushed into the corrugated plastic receptacle. I couldn't believe how nervous I'd felt scanning Joy's ring finger – or how relieved I'd been that the porcelain handle of a gaudy novelty mug was the only shiny new thing encircling any of her digits. Joy didn't know it, but she'd rattled me just as surely and forcefully as Beth had rattled the vending machine – now it was up to me to make sure I coughed up a Kit-Kat. You know, metaphorically speaking. There, in the coffee area, I'd been given a wake-up call, and the message was clear: If I kept sitting on my arse, Joy was going to be sipping future herbal teas from a 'WORLD'S GREATEST WIFE' mug. Eddie was right. I was going to have to make a move. Soon.

'Twas the night of the wrap party and, try as I might to remain calm, I was shitting breeze blocks. The hot water of the shower had relaxed my muscles but done little to prevent my heart from bumping against my chest as it anxiously reminded me of the evening's mission. I didn't need reminding.

I pulled back the shower curtain and grabbed the towel hanging over the side of the sink. Was I mad? I wondered, drying off my shoulders and chest and rubbing the towel over my head. Was I out of my mind to even entertain the idea of revealing to Joy how I felt about her? Even allowing for the dream scenario of Joy feeling some spark of attraction towards me, she was a colleague. A colleague with a boyfriend. She was therefore off-limits and, while that certainly frustrated me, there were times when I actually looked upon this state of affairs as something of a blessing. In fact, I'd long since come to the realisation that in many ways, what I had with Joy was perfect. Staging our interaction in short, sparky bursts undimmed by the mundane, everyday burdens that accompany any real romantic relationship, it was like we saw each other in trailer form as opposed to sitting through the whole movie, in which the funny, exciting bits we'd previewed to each other with fast cuts and a gravelly voiceover were lost amidst interminable stretches of unfunny, unexciting material.

Still, maybe this trailer was particularly well edited, because for a while now I'd been asking myself, what if it *was* merely a tantalising appetiser for a full-length movie that was indeed funny and exciting, romantic, heart-warming and all the rest of it; one that in years to come might even be labelled a classic? True, it was a gamble. But the more times I saw that trailer, the more I wanted to buy a ticket and wander into a darkened auditorium to see for myself.

I stepped out of the shower and pulled on the pair of clean boxers that lay on the floor. Was there a chance that I was making too big a deal – too big an *ordeal* – of this? The things in life that seem the most dreadful or difficult seldom turn out as tough as we imagine. I dropped my towel onto the toilet seat.

Maybe opening my heart up to Joy was the relationships equivalent of getting up for the toilet during the night. You know how it is: you wake up in the (pun intended) wee hours, your bladder swollen up like a basketball. The choices are simple: get up and relieve yourself or remain in bed suffering excruciating pain. The journey to the bathroom is, for most people, not a long or arduous one – even less so when you live in a bedsit and the total distance from bed to bowl is about seven metres – and yet, *and yet*, when you're snuggled up under your duvet in the dark, that seconds-long trip across the carpet and over a few tiles seems like a hell-and-high-water expedition to the ends of the earth. It's a heavyweight clash between cosy arse and painful bladder, but in the end you drag both of them off the mattress and, back in bed a minute later with your eyelids drooping, you're glad you did (unless, due to impatience, you failed to thoroughly empty yourself the first time around and thus require an immediate second visit, which can happen on occasion). I wandered into my bedroom, unconvinced and still nervous. Tonight's mission certainly felt trickier than a nocturnal toilet trip, but no way was I backing down now. That said, there was one thing I knew I needed to do first.

I knelt down at the side of my bed. I knew this day would come. Somewhere in the deepest, darkest recesses of my mind I think I'd always known that, if there was any chance that my relationship with Joy was to progress, I'd need to take this extra – if slightly dodgy – preliminary measure.

Hand trembling slightly, I pulled up my valance (what? It was a bedsit, not a disused railway siding) and slid open the drawer beneath my bed. I peeled back a pile of bed sheets and a fleece blanket and there it was: The Box. A red-and-beige shoe box, slightly battered around the edges and with the words 'FOR EMERGENCY USE ONLY' written ominously on the lid in permanent marker. Placing one hand at either end, I slowly and carefully hoisted it out of its chamber and placed it down gently on top of my bed. Pausing to take a few deep breaths, I let my eyes trace those indelible, jet-black letters. No question about it, this *was* an emergency. Besides, even if it turned out I *didn't* need the contents of the box, it wouldn't hurt to go into this evening with a little extra insurance; a confidence booster of sorts.

I pulled off the rubber bands holding down the lid and pressed my palms down flat on the thick cardboard. This was it, I thought, curling my finger tips around the bottom of the lid. No turning back now. If I was to emerge victorious at the end of the night I was going to need confidence, I was going to need stamina and, most importantly, I was going to need unwavering strength in the face of immense nervousness and potentially huge embarrassment. I breathed in, breathed out and lifted the lid ... There they were. My soft rock CDs.

'It's gonna take a little time, take some time to think things over.' Twenty minutes later and, following choice selections from Toto, Cutting Crew and Mr. Mister, the inspirational words of Foreigner were travelling across the hallway from the stereo in my bedroom. I was still in my boxers, but now I also had a fresh white bath towel draped over my head. Mouthing the words into the bathroom mirror, I felt like a prize fighter ready to let loose a whirlwind of jabs, hooks and uppercuts at the sound of the bell. Instead I heard the sound of my door buzzer. I stepped out into the hall and spoke into the intercom.

'Who is it?'

'It's Tom Bosley, star of *Happy Days* and latterly *Father Dowling Investigates*.' I pressed the button to let Eddie in and returned to my bathroom-based singing session.

'I want to know what love is ... I want you to show me ...'

'What the hell is this?' asked Eddie, clomping up the stairs, 'Foreigner?' Bypassing the bathroom, where I was now delivering my words into a plastic cylinder of toothpaste, he followed the fluffy-haired sound to its source and found the contents of my emergency box scattered across my duvet.

'My God,' he exclaimed, sounding like he was surveying

a grisly, blood-soaked murder scene rather that rifling through a stack of CD cases. 'This is power ballad Heaven. Or Hell. Chicago, Journey, Starship ...' Eddie's stock-take trailed off and I assumed he was simply immersing himself in the track listings or perhaps pondering whether his next image change might involve generous quantities of stonewashed denim. Instead, he appeared at the bathroom door, a look of alarm on his mirror-reversed face. 'Oh, shit,' he murmured. 'I know what's going on here.' He tapped his temple with his finger. 'I know how your mind works. This music ... It's an inspirational tool. You're psyching yourself up. You're going to ask Joy out.' I peered out from underneath my moisture-absorbent head-dress.

'Nope. I'm going to tell her how I feel.'

'There's a difference?'

'According to you. Something about a preliminary enquiry. Or a tender.'

'What if Matt's there?'

'Joy and Matt aren't that serious. Again, according to you.'

'I did say that, yes,' conceded Eddie, tugging at the generous collar of his brown-and-orange, seventies-style floral shirt, 'but the thing is ...' I put down my minty-fresh microphone and turned to face my friend.

'You said that I should go for it and you were right. It's not even about whether Joy feels the same way. It's about me not being afraid to risk humiliation with a girl I really like. I should have done this a long time ago ... Just like I should have put all this great music on my iPod. You gave me the inspiration, buddy, and tonight I'm going to do you proud.' Eddie absorbed my words (or perhaps those of Foreigner, whose 1985 monster hit was now reaching its gospel choir-powered climax) for a few moments before speaking.

'Alright, Soft Rocky,' he sighed. 'If you want to make me proud, maybe you could start by taking that towel off your head and putting some clothes on.'

42

The doors swung open and I stepped into the arena. Yeah, I know I'm labouring the whole boxing analogy but that's how it felt as, heart pounding, I heard the roar of the crowd – or at least an enthusiastic 'Wheeeyy!' from Mitch, who, over at the bar, raised his bottle of beer to celebrate our arrival at this lively West End haven of chrome and lacquered wood. If not quite jumping, The Willow was at least bouncing gently up and down on the balls of its feet as Eddie and I made our way through assorted web site designers and ironic T-shirt models towards our leader (who himself was helpfully wearing a heather grey sweatshirt with 'Mitch' screenprinted on the front).

Flanked by Red Buttoners Rohini and Jonty (a VT guy who fancied himself the next David Fincher) and with his wife Nat in tow, Mitch bought bottles of beer for myself and Eddie and, presumably, thanked us for our sterling efforts on *Disc Heads*. I say 'presumably' because at this stage I was already nervously scanning the room for Joy. For a split second I almost didn't recognise her. She'd undone her braids and her hair cascaded down the sides of her head in thick, lustrous black waves that bounced against her dangling, feather-shaped earrings before crashing against her bare shoulders. Sufficed to say, it – or rather she – looked stunning. And not just from the collar bone up, either. Her torso was wrapped in a crinkled, emerald green camisole which hung over her cropped jeans. If I sound like I'm speaking in rather florid detail about Joy's outfit, then I guess I assimilated terms like 'camisole' during a brief fixation with a girl in the Grattan catalogue. Still, maybe the cheap paper stock had put her at a disadvantage (it certainly never stood up to the rigours of bathtub reading) but Grattan Girl had never looked as good, as hot, as sexy as Joy did now, standing across the room talking to Beth.

Excusing myself from the (presumed) backslapping, I took a swig of beer and moved in on my target. The sound of punchy modern dance music had pummelled into submission the eighties rock that had, until that moment, still been whispering last-minute tactical advice in my ear. No matter, I thought, cutting across the dance floor and through its loose-limbed inhabitants. The untimely death of my grizzled but worldly-wise coach may have left me to think on my feet and fend for myself, but honouring his legacy would only give me greater incentive to deliver the knockout blow. That said, it was Joy who landed the first punch as I rolled up alongside her and her blonde bodyguard.

'Serenus couldn't make it, then?'

'No,' I sighed. 'She pulled a hamstring.' Noticing that the top of Joy's camisole was beautifully embroidered with beads and sequins, I decided to offer a compliment before we became locked in the familiar cycle of playful insults. 'I like your bits,' I said, rubbing my inwardly-turned palms against the air around my own chest. Joy stared at me; Beth tutted. 'I mean your beads,' I stammered. 'I like your beads, your sequins and stuff.'

'Oh.' Joy looked at me suspiciously. 'Well, you can look but don't touch.'

'Joy, can I speak to you for a second?' I asked. 'In private?'

'I don't know,' mused Joy, raising an eyebrow. 'People might think we're a couple.' She hit me with her best spoilt diva face, rolling her eyes and clamping her lips around the straw in her drink. Great, she was going to love this.

I knew from extensive past experience that it was imperative I made my move immediately, before I lost every ounce of the confidence that my body was already starting to haemorrhage and watched another missed opportunity affix itself in my increasingly thick and vividly illustrated scrapbook of all-time bitch-outs. It was now or never, and my first task was getting rid of Joy's flinty-eyed guard dog.

'Beth,' I said, holding aloft a crisp twenty pound note, 'any chance you could get the three of us some more drinks?' Beth met my enquiry with a slow shake of her head.

'Nope. But you could go and join the queue yourself.'

'Queue? You won't have to queue,' I contended, going for

44

flattery. 'That bartender's been eyeing you up all evening.'

'Like you're eyeing up Joy, you mean?' sneered Beth. Now she was beginning to irritate me.

'Can you hear that, Beth?' I asked, cupping my hand to my ear. 'Someone's trapped in a collapsed building and they need a rescue letter typed up very quickly. Looks like a job for Keystroke! Go, go, go!' Beth whipped the cash from my hand, gave me a withering smile and strode off. OK, that was the easy part over with; time to get to work. I turned to Joy – bloody hell, she looked sexy. She looked sexy like Nick Nolte looks grizzled – and cracked straight on with it.

'Um, OK, Joy,' I began. 'The thing is ... Well, first of all, you look gorgeous. Your hair looks gorgeous; your outfit looks gorgeous ...' Joy raised an eyebrow and unwrapped her lips from around the straw, instead assigning them the duty of a resigned smirk.

'OK, so what, then? It's a shame about my face?'

'No, that looks, um, gorgeous too.' Gorgeous, gorgeous, gorgeous, gorgeous. I wondered if Joy was docking me points for repetition as she stared back at me. Shit. I should have at least said 'lustrous' for her hair.

'Are you drunk?' she asked. In fairness, I could see how it was a question she probably needed to ask.

'No. I kind of wish I was, but ...' Hmmm. This *definitely* felt tougher than a night-time toilet trip.

'Well, um, thank you,' she responded cautiously. 'Is that what you wanted to tell me?' The next words I heard took me by surprise. Which was a little odd considering they came from me.

'Joy, I'm in love with you.'

It was as if my mouth had said exactly what it wanted to without getting clearance from my brain first. Maybe that was what happened when your bloodstream contained five times the legal limit of soft rock. Joy's jaw dropped and she pressed her hand against her beaded chest. She parted her lips as if to say something, but either her brain was doing its job and reigning in

45

her mouth's more maverick tendencies or both of them had packed in altogether, because nothing came out. I got the feeling that perhaps, having introduced this topic, I was going to have to expand upon it a little. 'I know this announcement is a little sudden,' I admitted, 'but didn't you suspect something? I mean, every insult I've ever fired at you, it's because ...'

'We have a classic playground relationship.' Joy, not a moment too soon, had found her voice.

'Yes!' I exhaled.

'All the teasing is because we're totally obsessed with each other.'

'Exactly! That's just what Eddie was ... wait ... You mean?' Joy looked deep into my eyes.

'I'm so in love with you it's not even funny.' As soon as the words left her lips, the music stopped and everyone in The Willow – on the dance floor and over at the bar and probably even in the toilets – went quiet. Or at least that's how it seemed to me. I couldn't believe it. This couldn't be happening. I felt like I'd entered some strange parallel dimension. That was surely the only explanation, unless ...

'Are *you* drunk, Joy?'

'This is such a relief,' she continued, ignoring my question. 'When we're not at work I'm thinking about you constantly. It's like weekends and evenings are just time to be endured until I see you again.' She grinned at me. Joy had a slim diastema between her two front teeth, and I'd always wondered how a thin glimmer of even thinner air – nothing, effectively – could be so sexy.

'Wow. I mean, that's exactly ... Wow.' Suddenly, reality cut through my elation. 'But ... what about Matt?'

'What about him?' Joy raised her hand for what I thought was going to be a nonchalant air-swat, but instead she placed it gently against my cheek. Freshly lifted from her bottle, her palm and fingers were cold and a little damp, but even warm and dry, I'm certain they would still have sent those same tingles roaming down my neck and back and all through my

46

body. She stared at me with her deep, dark brown eyes and a smile played on her soft, sumptuous and – yes, OK – gorgeous lips. Not a diastema-baring grin this time, but something subtler; more contemplative and wistful. 'I can't believe it,' she marvelled. 'All this time.' I couldn't believe it, either. Part of me wanted to ask Joy to slap me in the face, just to prove that I wasn't dreaming, but her hand felt too good against my cheek and besides, provided I wasn't dreaming, there was a very real possibility that it was the only thing holding me up.

Sound started to leak back into the world around us – first the laughter and chattering of the punters, then the music from the speakers. Then Joy removed her hand and I stayed standing. I stayed standing and I felt incredible. I mean, I felt *incredible*. As incredible as I felt, though, the sight of Matt appearing from nowhere suddenly made me think it might not be the end of the world if Joy and I kept our feelings under wraps just a little bit longer.

'Speak of the devil,' exclaimed Joy. 'Matt, you don't mind if I run off with Rich, do you? We've just discovered that the reason we've been such arseholes to each other for the past six months is that we're madly in love.'

'There's no need to run off, babe,' insisted Matt, as my heart went into freefall. 'Rich can move in with us. You two can have the double bed and I'll take the spare room.' He paused to swig on his beer before adding a proviso. 'All I ask is that the pair of you don't scream too much when you're shagging. The walls are pretty thin.' I tried to emit a laugh, but what came out was more like the final, dull murmur of someone who'd just been fatally riddled with lead.

'Me and Matt are moving in together,' beamed Joy, wrapping her arms around Matt's robust frame as tightly as the extra-medium, white-and-blue striped polo shirt already clinging to it. Matt raised his bottle and proposed a toast.

'To you having sex with my girlfriend, night in, night out,' he announced, jovially clinking his bottle against mine. He had a playful sense of humour; I had to give him that. Looking away from the heartbreakingly happy couple, I caught sight of Eddie, who, from his vantage point across the room, nervously averted his eyes.

'Will you excuse me, guys?' I asked. 'I've just seen someone I need to punch in the face.'

Walking across the room, I felt like someone was stabbing me repeatedly in my heart. And not with a *Psycho*-style sharp, gleaming carving knife, either. Nope, this was a blunt bread knife that kept getting stuck on the way out. Suddenly finding the strength to overpower the bar's in-house sounds, the strains of soft rock returned, belatedly and without invitation, to my ears, with Cutting Crew tweaking their lyrics to inform me that '(I Just) Died On My Arse Tonight'. As I approached Eddie, he reluctantly cut off the conversation he was having with a red-headed, arty-looking girl and put his arm around my shoulder.

'You know, I once went to a job interview with my flies undone,' he offered sheepishly.

'Not as bad,' I said grimly.

'I didn't have any underpants on.'

'Still not as bad. Nowhere near as bad.'

'Neither I nor the lady interviewing me would have noticed my lack of underpants were it not for the fact that I fancied her, if you know what I mean.' I didn't say anything, instead hoovering down the remainder of my beer while Eddie reached into his memory banks and tried again. 'Then there was the time I rolled up at a bad taste party dressed as an aborted foetus. To my horror, the attire of my fellow partygoers quickly informed me that the bad taste theme actually just meant clothes with clashing colours and patterns.' I placed my empty bottle down on a nearby table.

'Pretty bad, but while you did go a little over the top, the wording *was* ambiguous.'

'She'll get tired of him when they're living together,' speculated Eddie. 'It'll expose the cracks in the relationship.' I let out an anvil-heavy sigh. Listening to Eddie's advice in the first place had exposed the cracks in my head.

'Oh, great. So you knew about that.'

'I had an inkling,' winced Eddie.

'Do you have an inkling about what I feel like at the moment?'

'At least you went through with it and told her how you feel,' reasoned Eddie. 'You've got to feel good about that.' I fixed him with the most expressionless, unflinching stoneface and wondered if the evening could possibly get any worse.

'Don't Joy and Matt make a cute couple?' asked Beth, materialising from nowhere to hand me a bottle of beer and a fistful of change.

CHAPTER TWO

I woke up feeling like shit. Then I remembered my failed attempt at romancing Joy and I felt like shit festering on the pavement on a sweltering hot day. I hung my arm over the side of the bed and trailed my hand through the pile of plastic debris littering my carpet, my fingers fishing for the TV remote. Instead I came up with the CD case for 'The Best of Foreigner'. I squinted at the band – all beards, big hair, denim and leather – through my bleary, sleep-encrusted eyes, then smashed the case down hard on the corner of my bedside table. Those bastards had put me up to the whole thing.

No, fuck that. The embarrassment, heartbreak and, well, alcohol-induced nausea I was feeling at this moment wasn't the fault of any MOR eighties rock outfit. Nor was it Eddie's. It was my own, and I needed more than my pounding headache and churning stomach to distract me from that cold hard fact.

Finally getting hold of the remote, I pointed it up at the TV. Even in my current state I knew that it was Saturday morning, and that meant *The Hangout*. On screen, a young girl had just opened her front door to a surprise visit from the feckless but wildly popular boy band 6 Appeal. The girl shrieked hysterically while the action momentarily cut back to Jessica in the studio.

'Don't hold back,' she laughed, clamping her hands over her ears. 'Show us how you really feel.' As the girl continued to shriek, I took Jessica's advice myself, bolting out of my bed and violently emptying the contents of my misbehaving stomach into my waste paper bin. The girl kept screaming and I kept emptying until, after a minute or so of turbulent upheaval, it was over. Slumped on the floor amidst a loose mosaic of CD cases, I slid my palm over my wet, glistening face and looked up at the TV screen. We were back in the studio now, the boy band-inspired hysteria apparently over. Jessica smiled down at me. 'And remember,' she concluded, 'if there's someone *you* really, really want to meet, maybe we can make it happen.'

As Jessica's words rang in my ears, I felt like Joseph must have done on that fateful night when the Angel Gabriel showed up, told him that his wife was expecting God's child and suggested that the two of them haul arse to Bethlehem, pronto. Alright, there was arguably a greater surprise factor in what Joseph had heard, and it's hard to say for certain whether he was wiping a trace of sick off his bottom lip as he soaked it all in (I didn't recall The Bible mentioning it, but then maybe it was cut for length), but the comparison still felt valid. Jessica was even surrounded by a yellowish aura that shimmered brightly as she imparted these words from up above, although admittedly this may have been because the contrast on the TV was buggered.

'Someone you really, really want to meet ... make it happen.' The more I thought about it, the more it made a gloriously bonkers type of sense. In one fell swoop I could atone for my entire, woeful history of shocking romantic cowardice by trying my vomit-stained hand with the girl I desired beyond all others. The time had come to break open that glass case. I had to accept Mitch's offer and get on board *The Hangout*. Nothing could stop me as I embarked on my quest.

Rising to my feet, I peeled the sweat-drenched T-shirt from my body and hurled it dramatically to the floor. This (the quest, not my sweaty T-shirt) was for Cagoule Girl, my university crush. Building painfully over two years, my growing infatuation with this girl became full-blown, incurable love when, staggering sleepy-eyed out of bed one rainy morning, I opened my curtains to see her at the pillar box underneath my second story bedroom window, posting a letter from her slightly wobbly perch atop the seat of her trusty bicycle. Usually she wore a black leather jacket, but on this occasion she was dressed for the elements in a turquoise waterproof, the hood of which was pulled tight around her face and beneath a cycling helmet. Watching her pretty features emerging fresh into the world from inside their nylon, polystyrene and polycarbonate cocoon, I was simultaneously struck by both her beauty and complete lack of vanity. It was a combination that completely floored me; a combination that dared me to open my window and call out to her, to tell her that I'd seen her countless times on the top floor of the library, studying, like me, into the night, and wanted to approach her. To tell her that every time she passed me going to, from or through campus on that bike of hers, I felt as shaken as if a juggernaut had just thundered by an inch from my ear. To tell her that I was sorry if I was freaking her out, but could she please stay where she was, down there by the pillar box, while I ran down the stairs and out into the rain to speak to her properly? To tell her, by way of a warning, that she was probably going to be freaked out a little more when I emerged through the front door in a T-shirt, boxers and – only if I could find them quickly enough – slippers. Of course, I never opened my window, much less ran out half-dressed to express my adoration to her in the pouring rain. I never spoke to Cagoule Girl (as I henceforth knew her) there on that rainy morning or at night on the top floor of the library or at any time or any place on campus for the rest of my student career. If I had, maybe I'd be able to refer to this enigmatic cutie by her actual name. If I had, maybe I'd be *addressing* her by her actual name these days. Every day.

This was for Cagoule Girl, then, but for a few more people besides. This was for the Kerry Washington lookalike who intrigued me so much when she boarded my bus one Saturday afternoon that, vowing not to let her slip away, I got off six stops after my destination and followed her into a camping store before saying precisely nothing to her and instead spending one hundred and forty pounds on camping equipment I had absolutely no prospect of ever using.

This was for the girl in the camping store who sold me one hundred and forty pounds worth of camping equipment I had absolutely no prospect of ever using.

This was for the good-humoured, latte-sipping woman in

the spearmint-coloured roll-neck on the front of my broadband box. Alright, so I'd never actually had the opportunity to approach the woman currently lying face down on my bedroom carpet alongside the gentlemen of Toto and Journey, but there was no doubt in my mind that I'd only have chickened out with her as well.

This was for Zoe the hairdresser, in spite of her fondness for tousled-haired innuendo specialists and her general scepticism regarding the perfectly serviceable – and quite original, if I did say so myself – premise of *Firm Hold*.

This, most of all, was for Joy.

I had to make that call to Mitch and it couldn't wait another second. Well, it could wait until after *The Hangout* had finished and I'd had a shower and disinfected my wastepaper bin. An hour and a half later, then, I picked up the phone, dialled Mitch's number and was greeted by Nat, who didn't sound thrilled to be hearing from one of her husband's colleagues on a Saturday morning. Still, as she went off to find Hubby, I knew that a little bit of attitude from her indoors was a worthwhile price to pay for the course of events I was about to set in motion. In fact, my only worry was how much smugness Nat's worse half was about to inflict upon me for belatedly accepting his offer.

'Rich, geezer,' croaked Mitch, 'I know why you're calling.'

'Really?' I hadn't even asked the question and already the smugness had begun.

'Yeah, and before you say anything, I have no intention of going on about it.'

'I appreciate that, Mitch.'

'Nat's got too many shoes as it is, so don't even worry about it. Anyway, the patent leather should wipe clean, I reckon.'

'Um, Mitch. I'm phoning to ask if you can get me that gig on *The Hangout*.'

'Oh.'

'What did you think I was phoning about?

'Er, yeah. That.'

While I never found out exactly what I'd done to Nat's shoes (at any rate, I wasn't sure I wanted to know, especially given her curtness with me), the conversation yielded an assurance from Mitch that he'd get me a few weeks on *The Hangout,* and that afterwards I'd gladly be welcomed back at Red Button as the company entered the scripting stage of *Gross Encounters* and its other new schedule-papering projects. In the meantime, he wanted to know whether my Jessica pictures could be taken down so that my desk would provide a more comfortable / less psychologically disturbing base for a young girl who was going to be popping in for work experience.

'Yeah. Fine,' I said. 'In fact, you can get rid of them. I'm gonna be getting to know the 3D version.'

I ran my hand over the rich brown leather and wished I was able to enjoy it. While Latte Girl would have been in Suite Heaven the second her perfect posterior hit the sofa's plump, luxuriously upholstered cushions, I might as well have been sitting naked on a bed of stinging nettles for all the comfort I felt. Making accidental eye contact with the immaculately groomed receptionist, I hoisted a heavy smile up onto my face and wondered what the hell I was doing there. Well, actually I knew exactly what I was doing there, 'there' being the lobby of Fresh Coat Productions on New Oxford Street. I was waiting to begin my four-week tenure on a children's TV programme based on the crackpot assumption that I could win the affections of its gorgeous celebrity host, a woman clearly out of my league. I'd set this as a realistic goal for myself based solely on my complete inability to seal the deal with a catalogue of women who could actually be considered (albeit, in some cases, at a considerable stretch) *in* my league. Oh, and I'd pulled the trigger on this decision whilst emotionally battered and half-drunk. So yes, it was starting to occur to me that maybe, just maybe, I hadn't really thought this thing through as thoroughly as I might have.

While my cushy first day start time of 10.30am was presumably designed to ease me into my new surroundings, it had instead merely served to ratchet up my nerves. I felt like a death row prisoner (wrongly convicted, of course) whose execution had been pushed back an hour while my defence team desperately, fruitlessly scoured their books for a hitherto neglected legal loophole and, just for kicks, dead-eyed prison staff upped the voltage on the electric chair.

In an attempt to keep myself occupied, I'd spent the previous half-hour pottering around the shops. Well, I say 'pottering', but in addition to browsing the newsstands and watching a Kamikaze cycle courier narrowly avoid delivering a package direct to the Pearly Gates, I'd also dropped into the nearest office supplies shop to embark on a second, spiral bound print run of the *Crushed* pilot. With my masterwork having so far failed to spark a ferocious bidding war, it was time to widen the net to include, well, those production companies I hadn't deigned to include in my overconfident first phase of attack. If, somehow, someway, circumstances and the stars above conspired to offer me some slim chance of hooking up with Jessica, whose beaming face currently stared up at me from the latest edition of *The Hangout*'s official spin-off magazine, I imagined it would probably help my cause to have some sort of future beyond writing child-friendly Saturday morning banter. If, however, as currently seemed more likely, I gave into my impulses and fled before I'd even been assigned a desk, at least I could fill the afternoon doing a mail shot.

Of course, simply walking out on a job I hadn't even started was rude and cowardly, regardless of the nuttiness of the circumstances that had led me there, and if I wasn't going to honour my four-week commitment (the result, lest we forget, of Mitch having pulled in a favour at my short notice request), I needed a legitimate reason for my literal no-show. I was, therefore, contemplating walking over to the receptionist's desk and strangling myself with her telephone cord when my planning was interrupted by the arrival of a thirtysomething Indian woman in running shoes, combat trousers and a tight-fitting white vest. Handsome rather than pretty, she was short of stature but athletic of frame and with her hair bundled up at the back of her head, she looked so ready for action that if I hadn't just seen her step out from between the lift doors, I'd have assumed she'd abseiled down the side of the building on a fire hose to greet me.

'Hi, you must be Richard,' she deduced. 'I'm Kam.'

'Hi, Kam. Good to meet you.' Kam gave me a warm and welcoming handshake that nonetheless suggested she could rip my arm off if the need ever arose, then escorted me into the lift, hitting the button marked '2' while I checked the floor for the bodies of German terrorists whose necks she'd snapped on her way down.

'So,' said Kam as the lift passed Floor 1, 'Mitch told me you'd probably seen the show a few times.' I nodded in confirmation of Mitch's estimate.

'I've caught a couple of episodes here and there.' The lift stopped and the doors slid open to reveal a wall-mounted cut-out of the Fresh Coat logo, a bright purple duffel coat with drips of paint oozing down from the hem and left sleeve.

'Here we are, then,' announced Kam, leading me out of the lift and along the pristine white corridor surrounding the dripping purple coat. 'First things first: the place where it all gets started.' She ushered me into a small but perfectly formed kitchen filled with blonde wood cabinets and a heavyset, burgundy-haired girl eating colour co-ordinated red grapes and fleshy pink melon cubes from a Tupperware container. 'Allow me to introduce you to my best friend,' said Kam, placing her palm on the top of a gleaming hot drinks dispenser perched on the faux marble sideboard. Flanked by orderly columns of china cups and saucers, it was clearly several steps up the vending machine evolutionary ladder from Red Button's phone box-sized swill fountain. 'He never asks for anything,' continued Kam, stroking the machine's curves, 'but he's always there for me when I need a pick-me-up.'

'We really need to get you a man, Kam,' observed Tupperware Girl through a mouthful of melon.

'Yes, you do,' agreed Kam with a sarcastic smile. 'You need to get me Danny Waters confirmed for this Saturday's show. Today.' She turned to me. 'This is Kate, by the way. Rumour has it she's our guest booker.'

'Hi, Kate. I'm Richard.'

'Don't talk to her,' hissed Kam in mock disapproval. 'She's got work to do. And so have we. Come on, let's get you situated.'

Kam led me out of the kitchen and through a set of sturdy wooden doors onto the office floor, where fresh-faced, funky staff sat at slimline, sexy computer monitors and a fresh-faced and funky plush turquoise octopus spread his reasonably slimline if not particularly sexy tentacles over the sides of a water cooler. I recognised this denizen of the deep as 8-Ball, a character from *The Hangout*'s aquatic American animation *The C-Syde*, although as I navigated my way around a stack of humungous pump-action water guns and side-stepped a young woman in a multicoloured bobble hat, I started to think that the whole office had something of a cartoon feel to it.

'Here's your base,' said Kam, pulling up at a desk halfway across the room. She patted the partition behind my computer. The padded green fabric was mottled with a rash of lighter patches where wads of Blu-Tack had been wrenched off.

'Sorry about the state of this. Dan, the guy who's just been writing for us, used it as a shrine to Scarlett Johanssen. Bit of a psycho, that one.'

'I know the type,' I murmured, looking up at the huge photo of Jessica and Liam overlooking my new desk. They were stood back-to-back, arms folded as they grinned into the camera. I'd always loved to hate Jessica's pretty boy co-presenter for two reasons – one, he was a pretty boy and two, he was Jessica's co-presenter – but as I looked at the girl with her back to his and refocused on my mission, I realised the time had come to stop resenting the easy rapport Liam shared with Jessica. It was his job to concoct a chemistry with her and besides, as someone who'd begun his celebdom as a failed runner-up on televised talent show *Find Me an Icon*, the poor lad had doubtless already endured more piss-taking than his cocksure but mercifully short-lived pop career actually deserved. In fact, as one of the principal piss-takers during my stint on late-night comedy show *TTP* (as in *Taking The* …well, officially it was *Proverbial*), my first TV gig, I probably owed him a debt of gratitude. All told, it was definitely time to stop calling him a knob and start calling him a colleague. And maybe still a knob depending on how I found him.

'I'll just get you logged on,' said Kam, tapping away at my keyboard, 'and then I'll see if I can rustle you up a security tag. Make yourself at home, but not *too* at home, 'cos we're going to be having our Monday morning meeting in a few minutes.' A meeting already, I thought as I walked over to the water cooler. I'd almost forgotten that, like giving Liam the benefit of the doubt, the actual writing of a children's TV show was a vital and unavoidable part of wooing Jessica George.

'Wish me luck,' I whispered to 8-Ball as I pushed back the lever and cold water filled my cup.

'Good luck,' replied 8-Ball. Actually it wasn't him at all, the message coming instead from over my shoulder and sounding distinctly female. Female and human. I froze, teeth clenched in embarrassment, then turned to see who the voice belonged to. Its owner was a young black woman, short and chunky with friendly, open features and short, twisted hair.

'I know,' I conceded with a pre-emptive shrug. 'It's the first sign of going mad.'

'What is?'

'Talking to yourself.'

'Oh,' she noted, a smile slowly pushing her round cheeks upwards. 'What about talking to stuffed, eight legged fish?'

'Yeah,' I conceded, feeling like a proper twit. 'That's the last sign. That's the point of no return. Padded cell time.' Part of me wanted to point out that the octopus was, in fact, a cephalopod mollusc, but having just been caught attempting to initiate conversation with, well, a plush cephalopod mollusc, it clearly wouldn't have been a particularly hefty victory.

'I won't tell,' grinned the woman. 'I can be pretty bonkers myself sometimes. I'm Denise, by the way.' She stuck out her hand and I shook it. Her warm, slightly clammy grip was a lot softer than Kam's.

'Hi, I'm Richard. Good to meet you. What do you do on the show?'

'The dirty work, pretty much,' summarised Denise. 'But that job description includes sorting out tickets for the audience, so if you've got any young relatives who want to come down and be a part of things ...' I gave a covert but deliberate glance at my mate on the water cooler.

'Not really, but I know an octopus who would love to come along. You know, him and a couple of squid, maybe a starfish ...' Denise giggled and I took a sip of water just as Kam, whose trainers really seemed to give her an edge when it came to sneaking up on people, reappeared at my side.

'Richard,' she began firmly, 'you've really got to stop chatting up the staff or we're not going to have a show this week. Luckily, I'm about to lock you away in the meeting room, so grab yourself a pad and a pen and we'll be off.' Stepping back over to my well-stocked desk, I grabbed the required writing materials and followed Kam. Halfway across the carpet I heard Denise quietly calling my name, and looked around to see her holding 8-Ball up to the side of her face whilst she waggled one of his tentacles back and forth in a waving motion and mischievously mouthed the words 'good luck'. Ideally, I would have liked to respond by flicking up a good-natured V-sign or, alternatively, expending the energy of just one finger by either raising it through the air, holding it to my lips or perhaps even using it in a throat-slitting gesture (again, strictly good-natured, of course). As it was, my hands were completely full, so I simply took the ribbing on the chin and smiled back at my first friend in the Fresh Coat family. Well, second if you counted 8-Ball.

'First of all, that was a good show on Saturday, so well done everyone.' Kam paused to look around at the select group of Fresh Coat soldiers seated at the long rectangular table. 'Secondly,' she continued, 'the more observant among you may have noticed that there's a new face in the room. This is Richard and he's going to be our writer-in-residence for the next four weeks.' I put down my cup of water and dispensed a collective 'hello' (with a vague, upwards head flick thrown in free of charge) to the characters assembled in the otherwise rather characterless white meeting room. Characters to who Kam then proceeded to introduce me.

'This is Nina, our Series Producer,' she said, motioning to a set of pristine but oversized teeth sat to my left and bordered by a fortysomething woman with bottle blonde hair and a super-smooth forehead. 'Kate you've already seen slacking off in the kitchen, which only leaves these two chancers.' I looked down the table to the guys sat at its far end. One was small and shaven-headed, the other a man-mountain (six foot seated, I estimated) with thick, shoulder-length chestnut hair and an unruly beard that flowed down six inches past his hulking jaw. 'This is our dynamic duo, Greg and Yeti. They do our outside broadcasts and a lot of the pre-recorded inserts.' I gave the boys an understated 'Hiya' to share, thus bringing an end to the introductions. Or so I thought until, two seconds later, a girl in a lemon bonbon-coloured cardigan walked through the door.

'Sorry I'm late,' said Jessica. Jessica George.

'Don't worry,' replied Kam, 'Liam won't be here at all, as he's still in Paris with the girl from the sanitary towels advert. Besides, we've only just started. I was introducing everyone to Richard, our new writer.'

'Hi, Richard.' Jessica lifted her hand and sent a gentle breeze through her fingers. At such short notice, it was all I could do to bear my rigid, flattened palm and return a toothless smile, basically extending to her the same gesture I would a motorist who'd stopped to let me cross the road. 'I acknowledge that I'm at your mercy,' it said, 'and that if you wanted to, you could knock me down, drive over my face and render me utterly incapable of motion. But thanks in advance for not doing that.'

With my life spared but my nerves going haywire, I trained my eyes down on the uppermost page of my notepad while Jessica pulled out the chair opposite mine. In hindsight, I'm not sure how I'd expected our introduction to play out (none of my extensive catalogue of JG-related fantasies had covered this moment, assuming, as they invariably did, an, er, intimate familiarity between the two of us, forged, presumably, over our many prior moments of intimate familiarity), but I'd certainly taken some degree of advance warning as a given. Instead, here I was, suddenly and unexpectedly sat opposite the girl I'd faced in glossy photographic form every day at Red Button. I mean, I was, wasn't I? That *was* Jessica George seated across the table from me, right? I slowly counted the lines on my brand new, spiral bound pad (there were, it transpired, twenty-two of them), then looked up. Yep, there she was, less glossy but every bit as attractive as she rummaged through her cream leather handbag in search of something or other.

A crease ploughed through the soft, gently tanned skin of her forehead while her brown, almond-shaped eyes scanned the bag's contents from behind thick charcoal lashes and her full lips (which *were*, actually, quite glossy) parted slightly to provide an inaudible commentary on the search. Clinging to her crown, a thick, plaited white headband gently coaxed her dark tresses away from her high, sculpted cheekbones while, taking advantage of Jessica's preoccupation, the yellow fabric of her cardigan surreptitiously made a break from her left shoulder.

'Gotcha!' breathed Jessica, fishing out a pink mobile phone before switching it off and returning it to her leather-swathed lucky dip while Kam got down to business.

'So, *Judge Jessie* is looking interesting this week. We've

got a girl whose brother collects magazine sticky.'

'Magazine sticky?' echoed Nina. Her brow, I assumed, would probably have furrowed if the Botox hadn't denied it permission (it also occurred to me that she was probably a formidable poker player).

'You know, the adhesive they use to stick CDs and other free gifts to magazines.'

'Oh, the stringy, tacky stuff?' Nina screwed up her nose. That, at least, appeared to have retained its factory settings.

'Exactly. Apparently he's got a lump of it the size of a bowling ball.'

'Good Lord,' muttered Nina, running her hands over a suitably sized imaginary sphere of stringy glue-type stuff. Kam nodded.

'Indeed. But said lump gets a little bit smaller every time he flicks a stringy, tacky bit of it at his sister, so the question now is what sentence we're going to hand down to him.'

'Make him eat it,' suggested Greg. I couldn't place his accent but it sounded like it might be Russian.

'He'd eventually die,' reasoned Kam.

'Is that a bad thing?' queried Kate.

'Not the dying part, no,' responded Kam, stabbing her notepad with the end of her official Fresh Coat purple pen, 'but with the size of this thing it's likely to be a slow death and I'm wary of the time factor.'

'How about this?' offered Nina. 'We could get everyone in the audience to fire a bit of this sticky stuff at him.'

'That's undoubtedly a fitting punishment,' pondered Kam diplomatically, 'but I'm not sure little scraps of translucent plastic flying through the air would really register on camera. What we need is something big; something visual.' Doodling nervously on my pad, I took heed of her criteria and, fuelled at least in part by sheer nervous energy, had a crack at justifying my presence in the room.

'We could make him walk up and down the street with a giant magazine stuck to his back. Maybe a giant copy of *The*

Hangout's official magazine.' As the last word staggered off my lips, I brought the nib of my pen to a halt on the paper and braced myself for the reaction. At first, there was nothing. Then, an approving snort of oxygen from either Greg or Yeti gave way to a chuckle from Nina, and, confidence lifted just slightly, I looked up tentatively at Kam.

'Well, it's certainly big,' she admitted, raising an eyebrow while a wry smile pestered her lips. 'And visual. I'll get someone to run it by props today.' She paused, mulling over the image in her mind. 'Yeah, that could work, actually. Good little advert for the magazine, too.'

Kam's approval was nice, but it was instantly blown away by the smile Jessica threw me from across the table. She'd smiled at me several times in the past, but on each occasion I'd been forced to share her smile with a cameraman and a couple of million viewers. This one was different, though. This one was an exclusive; mine and mine alone. Speaking of all things mine, Kam made a written record of my genius idea on her notepad, then addressed Greg and Yeti with the next point on her agenda.

'So, guys, how are the pre-records looking?' she asked. I couldn't have told you the answer that came back, though. In fact, for the next ten minutes or so, the only information I could possibly have imparted was that Jessica George, separated from myself by only a metre and a half of resin-coated wood, had just smiled at me, knowledge that proved no help to me whatsoever when Kam suddenly dragged me back into reality and, apparently, the 'Any Other Business' portion of proceedings.

'Richard, you've been fervently scribbling away there with a big smile on your face,' she observed. 'What have you got for us?' I looked down at my pad. What I had, it turned out, was Jessica's name written in a seemingly limitless variety of styles (from frenetic graffiti wildstyle to elegant cursive), all of which I hastily buried under my forearms while I opened my mouth and attempted to make an intelligent contribution from off the top of my otherwise engaged head.

'I like Jessica,' I announced. Just to reiterate, this *was* off the top of my head.

'Pardon?'

'Er, I like the idea of Jessica ... and Liam ... um, the idea of the two of them doing some sort of weekly sketch thing. You know, like a spoof serial of some kind.'

'OK. Did you have any specific ideas?'

'I'm really just thinking out loud here,' I stressed, stalling for a few seconds' more time, 'but what about a spoof detective series? Jessica and Liam would be trying to solve a crime going on backstage and you could, um, get the guests involved. You know, it would be like *Thrust and Parry* but you could call it ... I dunno, *Cash and Carrie* ...' I tailed off, looking down at my sleeves and wondering why my sophomore contribution to *The Hangout* couldn't have exhibited the flair and creativity of the idiot savant scribblings concealed beneath them.

The silence that reigned for a few excruciating, elongated seconds was broken by the sound of Kam slowly tapping on her notepad with her pen, like a referee in a boxing match slapping the canvas whilst counting a punch-drunk pugilist out of the contest. As the purple, show-specific biro repeatedly hit the paper, I waited for her to call a TKO on both my hastily conceived idea and my short-lived credibility within the room.

'I quite like it,' she mused, cutting the count short at seven. I looked up and, to my surprise, saw Jessica nodding in apparent agreement.

'Yeah. I do, too.'

'We could have them in the car with some really cheesy back projection,' suggested Greg, throwing another unexpected 'yay' into the mix.

'OK, good. Well, Richard, that's something you can occupy your mind with today,' said Kam, little knowing how occupied my mind was already.

I was still in something of a daze when, a few minutes later, Kam called time on the meeting. Somehow, someway, I'd managed to punctuate my time at the table with two improbably well-received ideas, no mean feat considering the way Jessica – who was now checking her pink phone for messages – had, through her mere presence, had my heart rattling at my ribcage. Shuffling round the table, I watched as Kam, Nina and Kate filed out of the room and reflected on how I was now an official member of the Fresh Coat family. Hell, even the thus-far inscrutable Yeti now stood holding the door open for me.

'Thanks, Yeti,' I beamed.

'*I'm* Yeti,' corrected the doorman's diminutive, shaven-headed sidekick. I stopped inside the door frame, the look of confusion on my face earning me further explanation. 'Gary Yetinov. My dad's Russian.' He looked up at the man holding the door handle. 'Which makes *him* Greg.'

'Oh, er, sorry. I thought it was a nickname.' Yeti, no, Greg, stared down blankly at me, the only sign of movement in his face the gentle swaying of his abundant nostril hair as he pushed a solemn gust of air through his nose. 'You know,' I continued, 'playing on the whole beard and long hair and huge, intimidating build thing ...' I gave Greg a friendly pat on his boulder of a biceps, but his face remained as expressionless as it was hairy. 'And I realise now it would have been better not to offer that explanation,' I conceded, 'not least because of the aforementioned huge, intimidating build thing ...' I searched Greg's face for mirth, forgiveness or any flicker of human emotion, but his blue eyes remained unblinking and his mouth continued to plough a perfectly straight furrow through his field of facial hair. By contrast, I noticed that Jessica – up from her chair now, texts duly checked – was struggling to resist a smirk at my moniker mix-up. 'Alright, well, thanks,' I said, edging nervously out into the corridor. Ironic that, in a confrontation between me and someone resembling Bigfoot, I was the one heading for the hills.

Up in the hills, or rather back at my new desk, I tried to compose myself and assess the potential fallout of The Disaster in the Doorway. I was already half-resigned to living with the day-to-day threat of having my head ripped off by Chewbacca's less articulate cousin, but the thought of receiving a steady stream of sniggers, rather than smiles, from Jessica already had me nervously second-guessing our next encounter. As it happened, I didn't have long to wait.

'Feel free to do whatever you want with me,' offered Jessica from the end of my desk. Well, I hadn't factored that one in.

'Uh, how d'you mean?'

'In this *Cash and Carrie* thing. Don't worry about making me look stupid.'

'OK, great. It's good that you said that, actually, because it means that now I can concentrate on not making *myself* look stupid.' I glanced over the room at Fresh Coat's resident freak of nature, who was busy crushing a soft drinks can in his hand. 'I think Yeti's going to kill me.'

'No, he's not,' Jessica assured me. 'Greg is. *Greg*.' I slapped my head in exasperation.

'Oh, yeah. *Greg*.'

'On the off chance that he doesn't, though, I'll see you on Friday for rehearsals.'

'Alright. See you.' As Jessica's perfume lingered in the air, I looked over at 8-Ball, who had a big goofy smile on his face. At that moment, I probably would have benefited from being sat on a barrel of cool water like my tentacled friend, but instead I sunk into my chair and slowly swivelled around, surveying the ground beneath me. Maybe those sturdy china cups weren't as easily dislodged from one's hand as their flimsy plastic cousins over at Red Button or maybe Fresh Coat simply employed cleaners who actually fulfilled their remit, but, for as far as my eyes could see, the sky blue carpet at my feet remained untroubled by ominous brown coffee clouds.

'Is that the reason you wanted good luck in there?' asked an already familiar voice. I turned around to see Denise, and couldn't help wondering if she was always going to insist on addressing me from behind.

'Is *what* the reason?'

'Nothing,' she replied innocently, walking over to the water cooler and helping herself to a glass of the cold stuff. She had her back to me but I was certain she was smiling – at any rate, I was sure 8-Ball would let me know. Denise walked over to her desk while I looked up at the picture overlooking my own, Blu-Tack-stained work station. The picture didn't even do Jessica justice. I stared at it for a few seconds, trying to work out why before deducing that, as captured by the photographer, her beautifully formed features suddenly appeared too ... static. Don't get me wrong, though. I was more than happy to recline in my seat and look up at this picture, regardless of its lack of motion or, indeed, the presence of Liam, whose shit-eating ear-to-ear grin, scrunched-up eyes and fake tan lent him the aura of a human Jack O'Lantern. Without that picture, I might not have believed where I was or what had just happened. To recap, I'd just met the woman beaming down at me from above. I'd just met her, and, without making a particularly conscious effort – or, at times, even being particularly conscious – I'd come out of the encounter, all things considered, in pretty decent shape. Satisfied, if only just, that this was reality (certainly my Jess-centric fantasies seldom involved run-ins with The Abominable Snowman), I spun slowly around in my chair just in time to catch Denise shiftily averting her eyes from the all-new revolving idiot across the floor. She smiled at her screen, aware that she'd been caught in the act. Just like me.

When lunchtime came, I threw my newly allotted security tag around my neck and made my return visit to the office supplies shop, where, it appeared, my work hadn't exactly been fast-tracked by the lad I'd left it with. If only, I thought, his service could be as slick as his hair, whose black-as-ink tresses were greased down into the type of centre parted style favoured by 1930s mobsters and chimps. In fact, between his protruding ears, slouched shoulders and the curved facial furrows that formed two large brackets around his thin lips, there was definitely something of the primate about this chap. I looked at his name tag. Simeon. Of course.

'Sorry, could you give us two minutes?' he requested. 'My colleague's just binding your documents now.'

'No problem.' I didn't mind spending a few minutes mooching around this veritable Aladdin's cave of foolscap wallets, flip chart markers and lever arch files of the two and four-hole varieties, least of all whilst feeling as buoyant as I did. Unfortunately, I'd only got as far as putting one of those pimpled, orange rubber thimblet things on each digit of my right hand when the fun was unceremoniously wrenched from my browsing experience. There, on the other side of the aisle, was a face I knew all too well, even though I hadn't seen it in a while. It belonged to Nicki, my ex-girlfriend.

Suddenly I felt a bit hot and anxious. It was the first time I'd seen Nicki since a terse, bristling stand-off brought our relationship to an end roughly two years earlier (for the record, my final, point-of-no-return crime was petulantly refusing to wear a French collar shirt she'd bought me, while hers was buying me a French collar shirt – even now she still seemed like the worst offender). While the passage of time had done much to smooth out my more prickly feelings towards Nicki (and really, at the end of the day we'd just been wrong together, like, say, the plain white collar and sky blue body of that putrid French collar shirt), the idea of making small talk with her was still about as enticing as grabbing some giant-size bulldog clips off the shelf and fastening them to my nipples. With my scripts still on the production line, however, I didn't have the option of bolting. Instead, it appeared, I had no choice but to lay low amongst the stationery until I was able to discreetly grab my goods and split. Making use of the resources at my disposal, I grabbed a box of premium inkjet paper off the shelf (opting for my left hand when my thimblet-equipped right proved impractical) and held it inches from my face, studiously researching the specifications of its contents in an attempt to distract my mind from the potential disaster I was trying to avert. Alas, I'd ascertained that this particular variety of paper weighed 270 grams, had a high-gloss coating and was suitable for everything from company newsletters to family pictures when I realised that my A4, cardboard-encased cover was blown.

'Richard?' ventured Nicki.

'Oh ... Hi,' I chirped, lowering my disguise (perfect, apparently, for delivering crisp, sharp images with excellent contrast and maximum colour saturation; not so perfect for averting awkward encounters with ex-girlfriends). 'I didn't see you there.' Clad in a tight-fitting black tank top and a starchy, open-collared white shirt that showed off what, to my surprise, seemed to be a natural tan rather than her usual Cuprinol coating, Nicki smiled a narrow, tooth-concealing smile.

'I'm not surprised. Your face was glued to the back of a box of paper.'

'Yeah, it's a struggle,' I winced, returning the paper to the shelf and surveying its vast array of imperceptibly different rivals. 'I never know whether to go with the gloss or satin finish. So, er, anyway, how are you?'

'I'm good,' grinned Nicki. 'So are you living in London, now?' This, I sensed, was a loaded question, as my reluctance to move to the Capital had been something of a sticking point towards the end of our relationship.

'Yeah. I finally made the ...'

'How about this one, hon?' A tall, well-scrubbed guy interrupted my banalities to wave a chunky photo album under Nicki's nose. I couldn't help but notice he was wearing a French collar shirt.

'Oooh, how many does it hold?' asked Nicki, brushing aside a lock of hair (dark brown, but tinted red since I'd last seen her) to examine the sticker on the faux-leather front cover. 'Four hundred? Great, we can get all three weeks in there if we're selective.' She looked lovingly at the man who – all by himself – had made this genius selection, and who right now was beaming back proudly at her from beneath his rigid, flicked-up fringe. 'This is Connor. Connor, this is Richard.'

'Not Richard as in *your ex,* Richard?' checked Connor.

'Mm-hmm.' Nicki gave Connor a gentle nudge in the ribs.

'Oh, right.' Connor seemed to be suppressing a smirk as he shook my hand. 'Great to put a face to the name, Richie.'

'We've just got back from Cuba,' announced Nicki.

'Excellent. You look really ... Well, you look like you had a good holiday.'

'You could say that.' Nicki held out her hand to reveal a ring as big and shiny as the smug, self-satisfied grin on her sun-smacked face.

'Oh, wow! Congratulations! To both of you.'

'Thanks mate,' said Nicki (I suspected that the 'mate' bit was intended as a stinging reminder of what I'd thrown away). 'So are you seeing anyone?' She raised her diamond-adorned hand to her mouth. 'Sorry, that's nosy of me.'

'No, don't be silly,' I assured the nosy cow. 'Actually, I *am* kind of seeing someone.'

'Oh, OK.' Nicki raised her eyebrows as high as she could manage. 'Good for you.'

'Yeah, I mean, it's not super-official or anything; not yet. It's early days, but so far we're getting on really well, so ... watch this space, I guess.'

'Hmmm,' pondered Nicki. 'That's great. I must admit, I thought you were probably stalking Jessica George.'

'Heh.' I offered up a laugh as transparent and plastic as the shop's plastic concertina files (which were two for the price of one, as it happened) while Connor stifled a genuine one.

'The children's TV presenter?' he sniggered.

'Uhhh ...' I began.

'Yeah,' confirmed Nicki. 'He always fancied her more than me. It's difficult to get much action going on a Saturday morning when your boyfriend's more interested in the woman on the telly.' This wasn't a hundred percent accurate: though it gave me no pride to do so, I could recall at least two occasions where Nicki had, I like to think, actually benefited from me being more interested in the woman on the telly – but this wasn't the sort of riposte that needed airing, least of all in the presence of her fiancée. At any rate, Nicki was ready with another question.

'Still doing the writing thing?' To my chagrin, Nicki had always referred to my chosen profession as 'the writing thing'. This phrase, I was certain, was designed not to make my work sound arty and freewheeling, but rather abstract, insubstantial and the vocation of a deluded daydreamer who'd never have a conservatory or personalised registration plates.

'Yeah.'

'Cool,' responded Nicki, her intonation betraying the fact that, by 'cool', she actually meant 'pathetic'. 'Connor's a Financial Advisor.'

'Great stuff,' I remarked (and by 'great stuff', of course, I meant 'shut the fuck up'). That bulldog clip / nipple interface was now genuinely looking like a pleasant alternative to this.

'Where are you working these days?' probed Nicki. Before I even had time to formulate a fake answer, Connor leant in and flicked my security tag.

'Somewhere with good security, by the look of it.' How nice that a complete stranger already felt comfortable enough with me to take the piss, I thought, zipping my track jacket up over the apparently hilarious piece of rectangular, computer-encrypted plastic. The action was more difficult than it should have been, only because my right hand remained festooned with thimblets. My two inquisitors exchanged glances.

'Oh, these?' I asked. 'It's important to try them on before you buy. I've lost count of the number of times I've had to bring them back because the fit wasn't quite right.' I wriggled my digits about before consulting Nicki for her opinion. 'Be honest. Does my thumb look big in this?'

'So where did you say you were working?' asked Nicki, ignoring my joke. I hadn't seen her this tenacious since I reluctantly accompanied her to the Boxing Day sale at House of Fraser.

'Uh, a little production company round the corner. I'm just brainstorming a few ideas with them at the moment.'

'What programmes do they make?' queried Connor. Clearly, Nicki had him well trained.

'Um, magazine programmes. Magazine programmes kind of geared towards the youth market.'

'And your scripts?' pestered Nicki. 'Still plugging away?' There was something about her choice of the phrase 'plugging away', or at least her decision to deploy it so soon after using the phrase 'the writing thing', that flipped a switch inside me. Specifically, it flipped the switch that made me prone to slightly embroidering the truth.

'Yes, one of them just got picked up as a pilot.' Alright, I wasn't so much embroidering the truth now as appliquéing over it altogether.

'A pilot? So there's a possibility that it might one day become a proper programme?' That was it. I had no choice but to respond to Nicki's condescension the only way I knew how. By lying some more.

'Well, I say it just got picked up, but I mean earlier this year. It tested really strongly and now they've ordered the full six episodes.'

'Really?' asked Nicki. I couldn't decide whether surprise or disappointment was the overriding emotion audible in her voice.

'Yep. Just signed the contract the other day. Who knows – maybe if things keep taking off like this I'll need your man Connor here to advise me on my finances.' Nicki smiled weakly.

'Well, I suppose all your pestering people had to pay off sometime.' She placed a hand on Connor's sturdy upper arm. 'I used to stand around in shops like this while he got twenty copies of his little scripts done. It used to cost him the earth.'

'It did, it did,' I admitted, casting my mind back to those bygone bad old days before test audiences lapped up my every written word. 'But thankfully I can take a break from all that now. Besides, these days the agency I'm with get all my new material printed up and, you know, generally do the dirty work.' There was a thud from over at the desk as Chuckles the Photocopying Chimp slammed down a hefty stack of spiral bound scripts.

'Mr. Westbrook, your photocopying is done.'

'Contracts,' I grimaced. 'You can never have enough copies. Well, it was nice seeing you, Nicki.'

'You too.'

'And good to meet you, Collar. I mean Connor.' Nicki's fella squinted suspiciously as, leaving the two of them to fawn over their photo album, I headed back to the front desk, where Simeon was stuffing my stack o' scripts into a plastic bag.

'Thanks,' I said, putting my right hand down on the counter whilst using my left to reach for either my wallet or a bag of peanuts, whichever presented itself first. Simeon looked down at my pimply orange fingertips. 'And, er, I'll take these five thimblets,' I informed him. He nodded his greasy, centre-parted head and tapped the buttons on his till.

'Do you want to wear them out or shall I put them in the bag?'

Alright, so I'd needed that chance encounter with Nicki and her French collared fiancée about as much as I needed my freshly purchased fistful of thimblets, but as I stepped outside the shop, the warm rays of the lunchtime sun melted away all traces of aggro, leaving me once again at peace with the world. If anything, I felt even better now than I had before. In another reality, I might still have been trudging drearily through the motions with Nicki (or, for that matter, any girl who stirred in me little beyond mild irritation). Instead, I was now officially acquainted with the girl I fancied more than any other. Gladly surrendering myself to the river of bodies flowing over the Oxford Street pavement (not to mention those bodies stood in place every few metres dishing out flyers), I unzipped my jacket and let my Fresh Coat security tag swing, the plastic rectangle banging against my chest while the sunlight glinted off the metal fastener linking it to the fabric neck-strap. Except that in my mind, there was no fabric and there was no plastic. In my mind, the item around my neck was an ostentatious piece of hip-hop jewellery and I was a charismatic, braggadocious rapper representing to the fullest in a handsomely shot video.

This video wasn't short of the requisite eye candy, either. Forget inkjet paper (satin *or* gloss) – the women on London's busiest shopping thoroughfare were combining to provide all the crisp, sharp images any man could ever wish for as sexy business women in trouser suits mingled with bohemian babes in pretty summer dresses and high street hotties in snug-fitting jeans and tees. And you know what the best part was? None of them had any power over me. On any day prior to this, any one of these women might have been capable of ruining my day; of casting, with one smile or even a split second of accidental eye contact, a dark, rumbling thundercloud over even my brightest, most upbeat of moods. Today, though, they were little more than pleasant distractions from the inevitable mob of flabby, pallid and frequently furry male midsections that had come out, uninvited, to play in the warm weather. They were as plentiful but insignificant as the flyers being thrust into my palm every few yards by Oxford Street's paper-purveying foot soldiers.

My ice-flooded Fresh Coat medallion lay down on my chest as I stopped at a pedestrian crossing. Turning to gauge the steady flow of black cabs and motorbikes preventing my passage across the narrow road, I noticed that I was sharing the kerb with a drop-dead gorgeous Indian girl in a clementine-coloured T-shirt. Aided by the heels on her sandals, she was close to my six feet but approximately 84,000 times more attractive, with long, lithe limbs that placed her emphatically on the sexy side of lanky and jet black hair whose thick, wavy tresses meandered languorously down past her pretty face as if deliberately taking the scenic route towards her shoulders. Beneath a slender right wrist hula-hooped by an assortment of bracelets and bangles, an art shop bag dangled from her beautifully manicured fingers. I smiled to myself. See, I knew full well that normally, that bag might have been the kicker; the detail that convinced me, there on the spot, that this beautiful woman in clingy, citrus-coloured cotton was my perfect love match if only I could summon up the courage to make a move, or even, in the first instance, some type of sound. As such, it was also the detail that, ordinarily at least, would compound my heartache when, seconds later, I inevitably let this woman, eye-catching T-shirt and all, become swallowed up by the sea of nondescript shoppers washing over the concrete. Our eyes – hers smouldering from behind light brown lenses – met and she smiled a slight but nonetheless friendly smile at me. There it was: the fatal shot to the heart. Except that the bullet must have ricocheted off my security tag because, as the light changed and the woman stepped off the kerb, I felt fine. I felt better than fine. The thing was, there was nothing Orange Crush or any of the potential heartbreakers strutting their stuff on this or any other street could do to hurt me. I'd just introduced myself to Jessica George and I was letting my plastic rectangle-slash-diamond-drenched pendant swing like a muhfucker. Watching the sexy, stylish, stunning, immaculate and intriguing – oh, and arty – object of my indifference disappear into the crowd, I felt so happy about my new found immunity to beautiful female strangers that I'd gladly have skipped the rest of the way back to my new place of work if only skipping was socially acceptable. Although even if it *was* socially acceptable, it would have been somewhat ill at odds with the rap video aesthetic I'd conjured up for myself.

A couple of yards from the Fresh Coat front door, I stopped at a bin in order to ditch the handful of useless paper I'd returned with (the flyers, not my scripts). Amongst invitations to learn jujitsu, pole dancing and English, I noticed that I'd also been handed two babe-covered bits of glossy card touting forthcoming club nights. Trendy forthcoming club nights. I dropped the flyers into the bin and nodded contentedly to myself. No doubt about it, I was back in the game.

Downtime. It was the reason I'd decided not to become an assassin. Sure, lodging a bullet in a complete stranger's cranium from thirty stories up *sounded* like a laff riot, but on closer inspection, the thrill of the kill seemed to be vastly outweighed by the tedium of perching in wait on a rooftop with only your scopes and hollow-points for company. Alright, so if you got good at your trigger-pulling choice of profession it enabled you to travel the world, but being in an exotic land surely didn't count for much when you were stuck polishing your rifle in a nondescript hotel room.

Downtime, it seemed, was very much in abundance at the Friday rehearsal for *The Hangout*. It was 10am, and since arriving at Wembley's Artemis Studios at eight, I'd eaten seven slices of toast, drunk three 500 ml bottles of sparkling water, urinated prolifically and – whilst trawling through the morning papers – discussed with a sports-mad camera man called Graham whether a 'rout' was less or more decisive and / or embarrassing than a 'drubbing'. Having failed to reach a satisfactory conclusion, I was just lifting a fourth bottle of bubbly to my lips when Kam – who, black coffee coursing through her veins, had been zipping in and out of the production office all morning – zipped in again.

'Alright, people,' she announced. 'Our leading man has deigned to grace us with his presence, so we're ready to go.' She knocked back a mouthful of the hard stuff and turned to me. 'Speaking of leading men – Richard, we're going to need you to be an eighteen-year-old pop star. Follow me.'

Puzzled by this brief, but glad that things were finally getting going, I followed Kam out of the door, down the photo-filled corridors and through a set of double doors into Studio Five.

'It's just so that Jess knows what she's doing and the crew know their marks,' Kam explained as we walked past the small, peripheral stage on which the show's musical guests did their thing. 'There's no need to go method, just answer Jess's questions and have fun.' I rewound Kam's words and played them back in my head. Yep, there it was. I was about to have a one-on-one with Jessica.

As the show's title implied, the whole feel of *The Hangout* was intended to evoke the type of place where youngsters would congregate to socialise. However, as the Saturday morning time slot prohibited mocking up the studio to look like a vandalised children's playground covered with obscene graffiti, dirty needles and used condoms, the elected ambience was more cosy coffee shop meets laid-back basement den. A spiral metal staircase led up to a railed platform, both of them used each week to accommodate those members of the audience not nestling in the plump beanbags that sprouted from the studio floor like multicoloured mushrooms. Meanwhile, the set's bare brick walls were adorned with spray-painted murals, shelves of funky bric-a-brac and posters of the hottest pop stars, all of whom would regularly sink their rear ends into the centrepiece of the set, a spacious purple sofa positioned behind a knee-high table and in front of the giant plasma TV screen used for clips, live outside broadcasts and pre-recorded segments.

Five minutes later, the sofa was accommodating my very own rear end. Except that in this instance, my buttocks were portraying those of Danny Waters, a teenage pop star whose unfaltering sway over the nation's schoolgirls was rivalled only by the unfaltering reediness of his voice. Following a warm reception from a modest audience of laddish cameramen, caffeinated runners and various and sundry Fresh Coaters, I had sat down and, after experiencing nerves uncharacteristic of a precocious pop prodigy and TV talent show winner, settled into some small talk with Jessica whilst – out of shot and arse in a beanbag – Liam made up for lost time by scouring the latest issue of *Gab*. Most probably, I couldn't help thinking, for any mention of himself.

'So, Danny, the viewers have been e-mailing us in their hundreds,' gushed Jessica, brandishing a couple of flimsy, scribbled-on index cards. Her hair was bundled up at the back of her head while her petite frame – smaller than it had seemed from the vantage point of my bed on countless Saturday mornings – was swallowed up entirely by an oversized maroon sweatshirt. 'First of all,' she said, her brown eyes scanning the fabricated missive from behind a pair of frameless, rectangular glasses that, frankly, I found extremely alluring, 'Asha from Watford wants to know what you do to relax when you get a rare moment of free time.'

'Well, Asha,' I began, enjoying my growing confidence by reclining on the sofa and peering into the lens of Camera One, 'I'm just like any other young lad, you know? I like to play computer games, listen to music and explore every exciting inch of my body with my hand.'

'Whooo!' exhaled Jessica, fanning herself with her cue cards. There was an assortment of laughs, chuckles and the odd gasp from the floor.

'Quick! Somebody give this boy Asha's e-mail address!' implored Kam.

'Idiot,' I thought I heard Liam mutter absently. I looked over at him, wondering if he really was aiming some bile at me this early in our working relationship, but, as he had *Gab* open on a full page picture of Hannah Thornwell jogging, I decided to give him the benefit of the doubt.

After flippantly fielding a few more fictitious e-mails, I was spared the task of lip-synching to Danny's new single, the poignant, texting-themed break-up anthem 'Message Deleted'. Instead, I sunk into one of the beanbags and watched as the screen behind the sofa filled with the latest episode of *Lawrence Learns*, in which the eponymous third member of the show's on-screen team was picking up some funky fresh manoeuvres from a young troupe of elastic-limbed, tracksuit-clad breakdancers in a Portsmouth shopping centre. Despite his questionable co-ordination, Lawrence was taking to his assignment with customary vigour, so when his attempt at busting a windmill saw him collide with an obtrusively placed popcorn stand he was barely fazed.

A free-roaming, anarchic counterpoint to his cool and controlling studio-based colleagues, Lawrence was also an adept physical comic who surveyed the chaos he invariably triggered with an unflinching deadpan demeanour worthy of Buster Keaton. Right now, in fact, Lawrence's countenance remained entirely static as he picked himself up and used his chunky grey paw to brush the popcorn from his fur. About six foot five with his head on, Lawrence was, to the best of my knowledge, the only ring-tailed lemur with a presenting gig on British telly, and as his pre-recorded antics came to a close and the plasma screen filled with the show's logo (a jaunty affair with perky cartoon versions of Jessica and Liam sat on the bar of the 'H' and inside the curving tail of the 'g' respectively), the man himself arrived alongside the full-sized, flesh-and-blood versions of his co-presenters to practise the head nodding and shoulder shrugging I had painstakingly laid down on paper for him. As a memento of his latest learning experience, Lawrence came bearing old school hip-hop gifts, but while Jess gamely donned her Kangol bucket hat and clunky gold rope chain, Liam petulantly snubbed his head wear for fear of messing up his hair. I noticed Jess, from beneath her floppy, terry towelling brim, roll her eyes at her co-presenter's lack of enthusiasm. Kam, too, seemed less than impressed.

'What time is lunch?' she sighed before downing the hot black contents of her latest Styrofoam cup.

When lunch *was* called, I decided that my first order of business was to properly introduce myself to Liam. Seeing him buried in both his beanbag and his magazine at the start of rehearsals, I'd pegged him as moody, arrogant and aloof, but now I was coming to the conclusion that I was the one whose attitude was suspect. So what if Liam wasn't all sunshine and light outside of the camera's viewfinder? It would take quite a toll on anyone having to be as relentlessly chipper and cheerful as he did every Saturday morning, which, after all, is when it really mattered. And so what if he hadn't wanted to put on a prop hat for a run-through? *The Hangout*'s hair and make-up team already insisted on him sporting that product-packed, multidirectional 'do that apparently drove the preteen girls wild – you couldn't blame the lad for not wanting to make the area north of his forehead look any more ridiculous. Nope, in hindsight it was clear to me that, despite my best intentions to the contrary, I'd rolled up to rehearsals intent on disliking the fella who, for over a year already, had held down *The Hangout* sofa with Jessica, reading links, sharing laughs and generally exhibiting an easy-going interplay with my favourite gal. Well, now that I was a part of the show (and, by the look of it, a sporadic cohabitant of the sofa), it was time for me to grow up and exhibit a bit of class, a bit of professionalism. Above all, it was time for me to at least offer a friendly 'hello' before he had *me* down as moody, arrogant and aloof.

Liam was stood in the corridor when I caught up with him. He was speaking to somebody on his mobile, though, so I made myself busy by slowly inspecting the large, framed photos that lined the walls, showing the famous faces that had, at one time or another, worked their variable degrees of magic there at Artemis studios. Hearing Liam winding up his call, I sauntered over to where he was stood and noticed that Hannah Thornwell was gurning away from behind his shoulder. Remembering his critique of her – the 'idiot' comment that, in my paranoia, I initially thought had been directed at me – I realised that I had at my disposal the perfect icebreaker.

'God, I can't stand the woman,' I muttered affably, nodding at the photo and letting my eyes do a weary loop-the-loop. Liam turned round for a look at the offending showbiz moron.

'I really like her,' he said with a disapproving frown.

'Yeeeaah, she's alright,' I backtracked. 'Well, anyway, I'm Richard. I'm the new ...'

'Yeah, the new writer, I know,' interrupted Liam. 'Listen, mate, you couldn't do me a favour and squeeze some of my lines down? I mean, I'm not knocking your stuff but it's a bit of a mouthful.'

'Well, I suppose I ...'

'Try and remember the show's for kids, yeah?' he advised sagely, and I tried to forget that I was actually older than this fresh-faced font of information by about seven years. And that I suddenly wanted to slap those six strands of wispy bum-fluff off his chin.

'I'll definitely keep that in mind,' I promised as Liam's phone began to chirp. 'Well, anyway, good to ...'

'Hello, babe,' cooed Liam to his caller. 'Sorry, can I call you back in five minutes? I'm just gonna have a chat with someone ... Yeah. Five minutes ... Alright, cheers.' He slid his phone shut and I opened my mouth to have a second crack at uttering an entire pleasantry.

'Oi, Marcus!' Liam yelled down the corridor. 'You coming out for a fag?' I turned to see that Marcus was in fact the talented thespian behind (or, more accurately, inside) Lawrence the Lemur. I knew this because beneath his doughy, stubbled face, he still had Lorro's body.

'Yeah,' Marcus called back. 'Give us a minute to get changed, though. I'll get another bollocking from Kam if I light up like this.' He body-slammed his way through the double doors at the end of the corridor and I too decided it was time to part ways with Liam. What a moody, arrogant, aloof twat.

Arriving inside the studios' canteen, I wasn't overly excited about the prospect of lunch. Despite the friendliness of everyone (well, everyone bar Liam) on *The Hangout*'s production staff, I hadn't really fallen in with any crew, camp or clique yet, so I was quietly contemplating a meal spent in quiet contemplation as the woman behind the counter ladled some Thai chicken and rice onto my plate.

'Mmmm ... I'll have some of that too, please.' I turned to see a tray-wielding Jessica pulling up alongside me. No longer behind glasses, her eyes caught mine and we exchanged smiles before I calmly slid my tray along to the dessert counter. Today was going surprisingly well, I thought, selecting the most enticing banana from a pristine-looking bunch on top of the fruit counter. No need to force anything here. Just be cool. Just be relaxed. I felt a tap on my cool, relaxed shoulder. 'You might want to try a real one,' suggested Jessica.

'Beg your pardon?'

'A real banana. It's just a thought, but it would probably taste nicer.' I suddenly realised I was wrestling with a lump of yellow plastic.

'Oh, right,' I said, blushing. 'Thanks for the tip.'

'No problem,' grinned Jessica. 'Here you go, try this one. I know it hasn't got the same waxy texture or resistance to bruising ...' She handed me a banana from the shelf below. The one containing actual fruit rather than decorative plastic replicas.

'Thanks.'

'Don't mention it. But I think you'd better sit with me. With the real ones, you have to peel them. I might need to show you how.' I smiled. Perhaps being an idiot had its advantages after all.

'So, I was just speaking to Liam,' I began, as, seated together at a circular table on the periphery of the canteen floor, Jessica and I tucked into our matching meals.

'Oh, yeah, don't mind him,' advised Jessica. 'He's in one of his moods today.' Swivelling her neck, she quickly scanned the canteen floor before leaning in and lowering her voice. 'You know why, don't you?'

'No. Why?' Jessica pierced the air with her fork.

'He hates Danny Waters.'

'Oh, of course,' I exclaimed, pausing a chunk of chicken in mid-air as I remembered how my erstwhile alter ego had beaten Liam to the *Find Me An Icon* crown before adding insult to injury by actually sustaining a pop career.

'He loathes him,' continued Jessica. 'One of the few mementos he has from his pop career is his own card in Pop Star Top Trumps. And Danny Waters beat him in every category. I mean, obviously number of hits, dance moves, style sense ...'

'Sure. Those are givens.'

'Yes they are,' agreed Jessica, grinning broadly. 'But what *really* riled Liam is that Danny had a Phwoar Factor of ninety-one percent compared to his seventy-nine percent.'

'Ouch. So *that's* why he was so off with me. He knew he couldn't touch my Phwoar Factor.'

'You *were* pretty convincing,' noted Jessica. 'You made a good eighteen-year-old pop star.'

'Well, I was drawing on personal experience,' I joked. 'Not many people remember this, but for a brief period back in the mid-nineties, I was an eighteen-year-old pop star myself.' Jessica scrunched her brow and looked upwards, pretending to scour her memory banks.

'Nope. Doesn't ring any bells.'

'I supported Take That at a couple of schools and the odd gay club.'

'So why did you quit?' asked Jessica, slicing into a bit of chicken while I swallowed a mouthful of rice and wrestled with the question.

'I guess I was sick of being treated as a sex object, you know? I had a lot of deep, personal thoughts I wanted to share with the world, so I decided to concentrate on my writing.'

'Really?' pondered Jessica, clearly relishing her own newfound role as a probing investigative journalist. 'So what deep, personal work of art were you writing before this?' I looked down at my plate, coyly pushing the food about with my fork.

'I was writing the narration for *Disc Heads*.' There was a clank as Jessica dropped her cutlery onto her plate.

'No way! I love that programme!'

'Come off it.'

'No, honestly. It's hilarious. The episode where that woman asked if they had the Freddy McKreuger movies ...'

'Ah, yes,' I reminisced, wiping the corners of my mouth

with my napkin. 'Freddy McKreuger, the evil Scottish child murderer who lured the local kids into his Glasgow chippie with the promise of deep fried Mars bars. When a loophole in the Scottish law allowed him to walk free, the bereaved, rage-filled parents murdered McKreuger by throwing him into his own deep fat fryer ...' Jessica was laughing. I continued: 'They thought they'd seen the last of him until, some years later, the neighbourhood's new batch of teens realise they're all being haunted in their dreams by a hideously burnt man in a tartan kilt and Tam O'Shanter, and with bagpipes for fingers.' At that moment I caught sight of Kam, sat at a table across the canteen floor, looking over at myself and Jessica. Our eyes met fleetingly before Kam returned to whatever conversation she was having with Nina, Greg and Yeti while Jessica, now sufficiently up-to-speed with Mr. McKreuger's origin, delved gently into my own, somewhat less remarkable back story.

'Well, obviously you like writing ... hmmm ... creatively. Have you written any stuff of your own?'

'Yeah, a few scripts. Some finished, most of them not. Stupid comedies, mainly.'

'I guessed that,' said Jessica, not clarifying whether she meant the 'stupid' part, the 'comedies' part or both. 'So, then, what made you want to do this show?'

'It's a good show,' I answered (which, if not the actual impetus for my involvement, was at least an opinion I could just about say I honestly held). 'It doesn't talk down to children, but at the same time it's still good, clean fun. Oh, and I wanted to work with Lawrence. I wanted the chance to really get inside him and help him discover his voice.'

'Well,' pondered Jessica, 'those are good reasons.'

'You must enjoy it,' I ventured. Jessica took a sip of water before answering.

'Yeah, it's cool. I'm at the stage where I want to do other things, though. I mean, in addition to this, at least ...'

'I bet you get a lot of offers ...'

'What makes you say that?'

''Cos you're good. I mean, you're very ... watchable.'
Jessica looked down at her plate.

'Thank you. Well, actually I've been asked to audition for
a new travel show called *Wow! Voyager*.'

'Oh, nice title. That would be fun, though. You'd be good
at that.' I prodded at my food before making a surprise
discovery. 'Hey, can I get a mention on *Faces In Foodstuffs*?
This piece of chicken looks like Dane Bowers.' Jessica peered
over at the remainder of my meal.

'Where? Let me see.' I pushed a random piece of chicken
across my plate. In reality, it didn't resemble the former
Another Level vocalist as much as it did, well, a piece of
chicken – a fact that Jessica was quick to pick up on.

'You liar!' she laughed. 'Like our audience even knows
who Dane Bowers is, anyway.'

'Rubbish! Bowers and his music transcend the boundaries
of age.'

'Yeah, right. They wouldn't know Dane Bowers from …'

'From a piece of chicken! Exactly!' There was the rattling
of cutlery as our trays were joined by another.

'What have I told you about keeping it professional, Jess?'
asked Kate. 'That means no romantic dinners with the pop star
guests. Besides, he's in his teens, you sicko!'

'Relax,' grinned Jessica. 'I just want him to autograph my
breasts.' The mouthful of water I'd just taken immediately
embarked on a spur-of-the-moment detour through my nostrils.

Late that evening, I switched off my laptop having done
absolutely bugger-all on *Crushed*. It had been a futile task from
the get-go, as the only thing my mind wanted to do was
constantly replay the day. I could hardly believe how well
things had gone with Jessica. I reflected on the minutes we'd
spent on that purple sofa, then on our time at the dinner table,
during which we'd talked and laughed and gotten to know each
other a little better. God, she was gorgeous. Really gorgeous. I
wanted to run out into the street and swing from the lamp posts,

singing to the world about how I'd eaten Thai chicken and rice with the really gorgeous girl of my dreams (in the end, I decided against it – it was no use hurrying the lyrics, and at any rate, the infamous, pre-wrap party soft rock session had already earned me a not-so-soft complaint from Mrs. Quinn, the rather crotchety old lady who lived underneath me).

More than simply speaking to my inner Gene Kelly, though, my giddiness also brought with it a strange sense of clarity, the things I was feeling for Jessica suddenly pulling into sharper focus the things I'd felt – or *thought* I'd felt – for Joy. Before, I'd felt hurt and humiliated that Joy had taken my declaration of love as a joke. Now I felt as if her reaction had gifted me with the greatest escape in the history of great escapology. I mean, *love*? Seriously, what the hell had I been thinking?

This, I reflected, was what happened when you combined a non-existent social life with daily exposure to an attractive colleague. Just as my grudging tolerance for Red Button's vending machine coffee – which would have been nigh-on unpalatable before nine in the morning or after five in the evening – had evolved into a near clinical dependence on it, so my crush on Joy had surreptitiously spiralled into an unhealthy, uncontrollable, wholly unnecessary infatuation.

With Jessica, though, things couldn't have been more different. I'd already had an unhealthy infatuation with her *before* I met her. The laws of the real world dictated that by now, my illusions should be lying in pieces. I should have discovered that, despite her dazzling good looks and vibrant on-screen persona, Jessica was conceited or shallow or someone who ate egg-mayo sandwiches (in truth, I'd yet to check on the latter, potentially most damaging character flaw). If any illusion about Jessica had been shattered, though, it was the idea that she was unattainable. No longer was she just a face on my TV screen or all over my work station. Now she was an actual, factual, living, breathing person in my day-to-day life.

Until now, I couldn't believe how ridiculous that whole

wrap party episode with Joy had been. Now, though, I realised that an unseen hand had been guiding my idiocy; that the ensuing embarrassment, anger and drunkenness that had prompted me to embark on my quest were actually part of something much bigger.

As I called it a night, I glanced over at my bedside table, where Latte Girl and her beloved broadband package were continuing their romance. And for the first time, I felt happy for them.

CHAPTER THREE

The jogger moved quickly over the concrete path, the warm, early afternoon sun bouncing off her shoulder blades and the hiss from her headphones combining with the warbling of the park's more feathered patrons. As she rounded a couple of Saturday strollers and made her way towards the children's play area, I was transported back to an earlier time – about six months earlier to be precise (well, precise-ish). It was a lot colder then, a lot darker. A freezing, colder-than-a-pimp's-heart early evening in late November, actually, and far from reclining on a park bench unwrapping a sandwich, I was lugging four packed shopping bags about on the end of my aching arms as I lumbered my way back home from Tesco.

Reaching the busy crossroads that marked, roughly, the halfway point of my journey, I saw that the traffic lights on the road cutting through my pathway were just about to turn green, and so, rather than risk being flattened into the tarmac while half a dozen Braeburns and a can of skipjack tuna rolled poignantly past my head, I placed the two bags on the pavement in order to give my arms a rest and work out a suitable system of weight distribution for the next leg of my walk home.

I was, if I remember correctly, busy ruing the decision to include four litre bottles of sparkling water amongst my shopping when I heard quick, rhythmic footsteps and, from the corner of my eye, noticed a female jogger pulling up alongside me. At least I wasn't the only one exerting myself, I thought, rubbing some imaginary chalk between my gloved palms and bending down to pick up my bags. Returning to full height, I glanced to my left, where, back towards me and clad in a heather grey tracksuit, my fleet-footed neighbour was pushing forward on her extended left thigh to keep herself road-worthy. What kind of woman, I wondered to myself, was crazy enough to be out getting her Jane Fonda on in these frigid conditions? Then she swivelled around and stretched out her right thigh, and I discovered that the answer, quite categorically, was a woman so beautiful that my knees buckled and my breathing accelerated like I was the one who'd just run a couple of miles to get there. I mean, I couldn't vouch for her ears, which were covered by the alpine-ready headband locking in the earphones of her MP3 player, but unless they were the size of paperbacks I couldn't imagine them spoiling things.

The woman started to bounce gently up and down on the spot while, beneath my heavy winter coat, my heart pounded not-very-gently-at-all against my chest. I had to talk to her – but about what? It wasn't like I could just dip into my shopping bags and start bonding with her over a couple of freshly-baked cookies (or a handful of cherry tomatoes, depending on how far she was taking her health regime). No, what I needed here was an opening; something to get me started – but again, what? I was reluctantly reaching the conclusion that I needed her to be non-fatally (and, it was imperative, non-facially) knocked down by a car so that I could heroically call an ambulance and ride with her to the hospital, when, unexpectedly, a gift fell right into my lap. Or, more accurately, her pedometer – its hold on her elasticated waistband presumably loosened by all that bouncing – fell right onto the patch of pavement between us.

She motioned to retrieve her gadget, but for all her running and stretching she wasn't quick enough to beat me to the prize as, putting my bags back down again (read: dropping them instantly without a thought for their contents), I swooped down and came up clutching the small white object.

'There you go.' Placing the gadget in her gloved palm, I felt a spark as our fingers touched – although in all probability it was simply the static electricity from all that polyester.

'Thanks,' she beamed, decorating the pre-Christmas air with the white tinsel of her breath.

'No problem.' She clipped the pedometer back onto the waistband of her tracksuit trousers, then lifted her clasped hands to her impressively unchapped lips and filled the fleecy cocoon with hot breath. Shit. I had to build on this. But how?

Lame, half-baked conversation-starters rushed through my head as quickly and indistinctly as the cars rushing by in front of us. Could I get away with a demonstrative 'Brrrrr' or an affable 'You're brave'? It *was* exceptionally short notice, after all.

Above our heads and diagonally across the road, the traffic lights turned amber. 'Say something!' my mind shouted at me as the last, impatient motorists nipped through in their hurry to get home or wherever else they might be going. These people, it struck me, were go-getters; unafraid to take a chance, even if they were risking both their own and other peoples' lives (or at least a fine and points on their licence) for the sake of getting a microwaved chicken tikka masala down their neck three seconds faster. Could a little of that renegade energy rub off on me in the few seconds I had left? The traffic lights switched shades again. I was now on red alert. Say something. Say something NOW. Remark on how cold it was. Just say something. Just open your damn mouth and say something. I swallowed my inhibitions, parted my lips ... and watched helplessly as I filled the air only with a twisting cloud of frozen breath. It hung there like a screwed up bit of paper torn from a notepad and crushed into a ball in frustration at the unfinished, pathetic attempts at expression scrawled within its lines.

My rough workings hadn't even dissolved into the darkness when the green man stirred into life and the girl took off. Then, after a couple of seconds and without really thinking about it, so did I. My heavyweight brown boots had just hit the other side of the road when I realised I owed my impressive burst of speed to the lack of shopping in my hands, so – like a footballer running an intensive fitness drill – I darted back to retrieve my bags before once again tearing over the road and after this health-conscious cutie.

Ordinarily, I was naturally rather nippy on my feet – but this was a struggle. It wasn't just the weight of the bags, but also the fact that, with my hands full, I couldn't form blades to optimise my aerodynamicism. And so, with Heather Grey peeling further and further away from me, I dropped the bags to the ground and kicked it up a gear – several gears, actually. Unencumbered by shopping and with my hands now offering a textbook illustration of bladeage, I was able to make up some of the distance, but still my winter coat, jeans and clunky footwear conspired to keep me from getting within ten metres of the hood that bounced up and down against my target's back.

'Excuse me!' I called out. Then again, 'Excuse me!' But I was fighting a losing battle against the combined noise of the rush-hour traffic and HG's motivational music, and when she managed to nimbly beat the lights at the next intersecting road, there was nothing left for me to do but trudge back, short of breath but heavy of heart, in the direction from which I'd just come. An elderly lady was busy surveying my trail of debris.

'You dropped your bags,' she informed me, helpfully pointing at one of them with her walking stick. My shopping wasn't the only thing I'd let escape my grasp, though, and while I stooped to retrieve my battered groceries, I added another face to the mental photo album of girls who'd gotten away from me. In this case, as fast as her legs could carry her.

But that was then and this was now, and here I was busy atoning for that missed opportunity and myriad others by making a run – if, thankfully, not one that involved bladeage or abandoned shopping – at my favourite children's TV hottie. Well, technically, at this exact moment I was having lunch on a park bench with Eddie while, beside us, a tramp – sorry, make that 'homeless person' – in a red-and-black lumberjack shirt rummaged through the cans in a litter bin. My morning, though, had been spent at Artemis Studios, where I'd sat in on my first live recording of *The Hangout*. It had gone well – really well, actually. *Cash and Carrie* had elicited giggles from the show's young crowd (and guffaws from the cameramen, who clearly appreciated the odd adult-aimed double entendre), Judge Jessie's justice-by-giant-back-mounted-magazine set piece had been a hit, and the two presenters had sounded pretty comfortable reading my snappy, if hardly revolutionary, links to camera. Liam had even managed those tricky bigger words and flowing turns of phrase.

'Nice one,' remarked Eddie after I'd finished summarising my morning. I was slightly underwhelmed by his response. Not because my inaugural episode of *The Hangout* had changed the face of children's television, or even warranted more than the 'nice one' which Eddie had at least delivered with warmth and sincerity, albeit through a mouthful of bread, cheese and pickle. There was, I had to admit, nothing wrong with Eddie's feedback at all, assuming, of course, that it was about my morning rather than the sandwich he was currently getting started on – and even then it wouldn't really have mattered. The thing is, Eddie's feedback wasn't what I was after. I wanted to give him *my* feedback on something. I was dying to tell him what Jessica was like, but I didn't want to offer this information voluntarily. I wanted him to ask me about her first.

A blind man and his golden Labrador retriever walked past us. Eddie took a bite of his sandwich, then patiently chewed and swallowed it before finally coming out with the question that had evidently been playing on his mind.

'Do you think there's such a thing as a bad guide dog?' I paused for a moment, midway through unwrapping my own sandwich. It wasn't the conversational gambit I'd expected, but it had my interest all the same.

'What d'you mean?' I asked. 'Bad as in inept?'

'No, bad as in malevolent,' clarified Eddie. 'You know, a guide dog that deliberately stitches up its owner when it gets pissed off.'

'Oh, OK ... So for instance it might squeeze under a bench and out the other side while its owner's holding the lead?' Eddie cracked open his can of drink.

'Yeah, or lead them over an open manhole cover.'

'Or do a poo on the street and make sure they step in it,' chimed the homeless fella, his hand emerging victoriously from the bin with a crushed-but-apparently-not-quite-empty beer can.

'Yes!' exclaimed Eddie, touching cans with our fellow

deep thinker, who then promptly shuffled off to the next bin, swigging on his excavated dregs. 'Actually, I think they must weed out the undesirables at the training stage,' he speculated, a note of slight, back-down-to-Earth disappointment creeping into his voice.

'Yeah, you're probably right,' I agreed. 'It's probably quite easy to spot the dogs with the bad attitudes. They'll be the ones who won't wear the fluorescent bibs in case it damages their street cred.' With the flames of this burning question now seemingly reduced to embers, Eddie broke for another mouthful of sandwich before sparking a new subject into life.

'So anyway,' he began, his voice wavering a little but his eyes locked firmly on the concrete in front of his feet. 'About the wrap party. I'm sorry about, you know ... Well, I mean, it was me who kind of coaxed you into ...'

'Don't even say anything,' I insisted, giving my friend a gentle slap on the shoulder. 'It wasn't your fault. Besides, if anything, that little episode turned out to be a fitting, very definite conclusion to a particular period of my life. A period that I like to call The Gift and the Curse.' Eddie looked at me quizzically.

'The Gift and the Curse?'

'Yeah. When you fancy someone who's unattainable, it's like The Gift and the Curse. That was Joy. She's brought me happiness, sure. But she also brought me pain in equal measure.'

'Ah, The gift and The Curse,' pondered Eddie, stroking the thick goatee that he'd cultivated since I last saw him. 'I know exactly what you mean. For as long as your infatuation lasted, Joy to you was like a really good, hi-tech rucksack that has a lot of hidden compartments inside.' Now it was my turn to come over all quizzical.

'How so?'

'Well, you can keep all your valuables safely tucked away inside, but with so many hidden compartments, there's also a chance that you might actually lose them.'

'Yes,' I concurred. 'A hi-tech rucksack with hidden compartments. I knew that she reminded me of something.'

'She was like a quality birthday card with a slightly waxy finish inside,' continued Eddie. I thought about it for a few seconds before conceding defeat.

'Nope. Nothing.'

'The finish looks and feels good and creates an overall air of class,' explained Eddie. 'But if you write inside it with one of those nice metallic or glittery pens, or really anything other than a biro, it's liable to smudge.'

'Mmm,' I mused. 'Spot on. Hell of a comparison.' Clearly enjoying himself, Eddie tore off another mouthful of his sandwich, quickly scarfing it down in his eagerness to unveil the masterpiece he'd been building towards.

'She was like chicken fajitas.'

'Wait.' I leant forward on the bench and pressed my fingers against my forehead before triumphantly snapping them, bolting upright again and pointing at Eddie. 'Ooh, I've got this one! It's a delicious meal but you need lots of different plates, you're constantly having to construct your dinner while you eat it, and on top of all that you tend to get the contents all over your fingers and face and down your clothes.'

'Yes!' shouted Eddie as we enthusiastically bumped fists. 'Actually, I hadn't even thought about the different plates thing. It's even more apt than I thought.' Pleased with our work, we sat in silence for a little while until Eddie, following his final chomp of sandwich, came up with the question I'd been willing him to ask since we'd sat down on this bench.

'So what's she like?' I waited until I'd finished my own bout of chewing (which I prolonged slightly for dramatic effect) before responding.

'What's who like?'

'*What's who like?*' Eddie leant across the bench and shoved a palm into my shoulder. 'You know who I'm talking about!'

'Oh, Jessica?' I asked, eyes widened as I gave my best

attempt at looking innocent.

'Yes. Jessica George.' Eddie enunciated each word like he was talking to a three-year-old: 'What … Is … She … Like?' I thought about it for a couple of seconds before offering my considered answer.

'She's nice.' Eddie postponed his first mouthful of the chocolate bar he'd just emancipated from its wrapper.

'That's it?'

'She's really nice.' To my surprise, that actually *was* it. I'd been waiting anxiously to field this enquiry, but now that it had arrived, I found that I didn't have a whole lot to say about it. Maybe I didn't want to jinx my burgeoning relationship with Jessica, or maybe I sensed that, to a third party, our interactions wouldn't make for interesting listening, but for whatever reason, I was happy to grab thirty seconds' quiet time with my sandwich – before Eddie decided to approach the topic from a different angle.

'So what's *it* like?' He asked.

'What's *what* like?'

'Being in the same room as your favourite reasonably famous babe?' I pondered the question while a mischievous breeze tickled the leaves on the tree overlooking us. For some reason, I felt more comfortable about answering this one, or at least taking a crack at it.

'Hmmm …' I began, unscrewing the lid on my bottle of water. 'Have you ever copied something you saw in the movies?'

'Oh, sure,' responded Eddie. 'You remember that scene in *Deliverance* where …'

'Alright, alright,' I interrupted, relieved to be halfway through a turkey sandwich rather than a ham one. 'Well, anyway, after I saw *Back to the Future* as a child, I distinctly remember copying Michael J. Fox.'

'What, you travelled back to the year 1955 in a defunct sports car?'

'No, I started hanging out with a crazy, white-haired

scientist at weekends and after school. He did show me his so-called flux capacitor, at which point the police got involved. But no, seriously ...'

'Ah!' interrupted Eddie excitedly. 'I bet I know what you did. You took up skateboarding.'

'Nope.'

'You wore a body warmer?'

'Already had one. My mum was very vigilant of my body temperature back then.'

'Got it!' exclaimed Eddie. 'You started learning the guitar with the express purpose of playing Huey Lewis and the News songs!' I took a swig of water, then screwed the lid back on the bottle, placed it on the bench and walked over to the grass on the other side of the concrete path. This was going to require a demonstration. I turned to face Eddie and raised my voice to cover the extra distance. 'Remember when Marty McFly first arrives in 1955, and he's completely bewildered by the whole thing? He's wandering around doing three-sixty degree turns, just trying to take it all in. Well, for about a month after I saw that movie I used to cross every road in pretty much the same way.' I started walking slowly across the concrete towards Eddie, looking around in pretend amazement at my non-existent, Hill Valley-in-the-1950s surroundings. I did a full McFly turn, deliberately stumbling slightly as I completed the gobsmacked circle.

'Oh yeah!' chuckled Eddie. 'He *does* do that!' Pleased with my friend's amused response, I decided to commit myself to another slow, awe-struck turn.

'So I'm basically crossing every road whilst spinning, stumbling and looking at everything but where I'm ...' WHAM! Something or somebody collided hard with my shoulder, interrupting my encore turn and knocking me comprehensively onto my arse. I looked up to see a bald, middle-aged roller blader doing some hapless twirling and staggering of his own in a forlorn attempt to maintain control of his sinewy, lycra-clad body, but he too concluded a less-than-graceful pirouette by acquainting his thinly protected backside with the sun-baked concrete. Attempting to get up, he tripped before he was even halfway to standing, but his second attempt saw him successfully, if gingerly, rising up on his blades and regaining his balance.

'Bloody idiot!' he yelled, sticking his finger up at me to really hammer home his distaste for my bloody idiocy before pushing off, somewhat limp-limbed, from the scene of the collision. I looked at the asphalt around me and noticed a violent burst of dark, wet fluid to my left. Still in shock, I checked my tingling palms, but miraculously they were no more than mildly grazed. It was only when I saw Eddie doubled up with laughter and wiping his mouth with the back of his hand that I realised the spattered liquid was nothing more alarming than his forcefully projected, blackcurrant-flavoured soft drink.

'I'm sure there was a point to that,' he gasped, coming up for air amidst his convulsions, 'but it doesn't even matter now.' I rose tenderly to my feet, checking my forearms for scrapes or cuts.

'I was trying ... ah ... to illustrate what it's like to be in the company of Jessica.'

'Bloody painful, by the look of it,' chortled Eddie, who seemed close to hitting the concrete himself.

'No,' I groaned, limping back over to reclaim my spot on the bench. 'I was trying to illustrate that being around Jessica, it's like ... ah ... I genuinely have that sense of wonder and disbelief that I was merely trying to replicate back then. It's like ... ow, ow ... I'm constantly in a daze.'

'I'm not surprised,' noted Eddie, 'if you're repeatedly being clobbered at twenty miles per hour by psychotic spandex wearers.' I shot him a stern glare, or at least my best attempt at one.

'OK ...'

'I'm sorry,' he squeaked. 'So tell me what ...'

'No, no.' I waved a dismissive, still-tingling palm at

Eddie. 'I'm not talking about me anymore. It's too dangerous.'
I paused for a couple of seconds, looking deep inside myself to
summon up a banal but effective conversation-changer. 'How's
your music going?' I asked. Eddie's rock band was one of his
more enduring extracurricular activities.

'Pretty good,' responded Eddie through a mouthful of
chocolate. 'Actually, I was gonna say, we've got a gig at The
Crevice on Wednesday. There's a sticky bit of floor in the
basement of a cramped and grotty Camden pub with your name
on it.'

'OK. I'll see what I'm doing.'

'You'll see what you're doing!' mocked Eddie. I hit him
with a half-set stoneface that was quickly cracked by my own
mirth.

'What?' I laughed. 'You can't let me *pretend* I might have
a full and healthy social life? You can't even humour me on
that?' I screwed my sandwich wrapper into a ball, bounced it
off the side of Eddie's head and retreated into a pretend huff.
'Alright, I'll be there.'

'Thanks, man.' Eddie lifted his can to his lips before
breaking down as if taking a hit of laughing gas rather than a
swig of fizzy drink. 'Just do everyone a favour and look where
you're going when you cross the road, Marty.'

'Hey, what you saw there was my most faithful recreation
of *Back to the Future* yet,' I contended, inspecting my palms
and elbows one last time. 'That guy actually knocked me into
the middle of next week.'

It was Wednesday morning. Early Wednesday morning – or
early for me, at least. Sat in Fresh Coat's video research room –
in essence a small, nondescript lounge furnished with a
miniature sofa, a TV, DVD player and micro hi-fi system – I'd
come in to work a whole half an hour ahead of schedule. On the
face of it I'd done so in order to plough through the videos
submitted for *Highly Strung*, a contest designed to find the
viewer with the best air guitar wizardry at (literally) their

fingertips. Still, it wasn't the first time I'd got a head start on the action, and as I pointed the DVD remote and pressed play, I couldn't help wondering if subconsciously there was an ulterior motive for my excessive punctuality. My friendship with Jessica was progressing way too smoothly, way too quickly. Was I up with the larks in the hope of catching someone out; of surprising the crew of special effects wizards rigging up the smoke and mirrors behind this whole illusion? Maybe, but it turned out that on this occasion I was the one receiving the surprise as Jess entered the room carrying a plate piled high with toast.

'Morning, Ricardo,' she beamed. 'Watcha doing?'

'Just looking at some of the entries for *Highly Strung*,' I answered, placing my palm on the stack of DVDs sat at my side. On screen, and with some choice emo blaring in the background, a young, bespectacled boy with a blonde, pudding bowl haircut had hoisted his invisible guitar up under his chin and was wriggling his fingers about so frenetically that his hands looked like albino tarantulas on ecstasy. The overall effect was like watching The Milky Bar Kid channelling the spirit of Jimi Hendrix at Woodstock, and Jessica was instantly caught in his spell.

'Wow, look at him go.'

'Yeah, he's grinding that axe alright,' I concurred. 'So, what are you doing in this morning?'

'Well,' began Jessica, plonking herself down on the sofa, 'I'm going out with Greg and Yeti to film that piece at The Young Animators Awards in Leicester Square, but I came in extra early to check if Kate was still coming to a party that I'm going to tonight.'

'Oh, really? What are you two crazy gals getting up to?'

'Nothing, at least not together. It turns out she's getting an award at her slimmers club, so there's a plus one going spare.' By now on his knees, Milky Hendrix slowed his fingers down to a halt, and there was a backdrop of silence in place as Jessica spoke again. 'Would you like to go? I mean, I know it's short notice and everything but, you know … if you fancied it ...'

'Errr ... I don't know,' I lied, wandering over to the telly. A party with Jessica George? Of course I bloody wanted to go, but I was trying to play it cool (traditionally a struggle for me at the best of times), and at any rate, I'd already told Eddie that I was going to let him and his motley band of musos forcibly remove my hearing that evening. I crouched down, popped the DVD out of the machine and replaced it with another disc simply labelled, with a childish scrawl, 'Colin'.

'You'd like it,' continued Jessica, going for the hard sell. 'It's a party for Charlie Carter from *Tachbrook Park*, and if she's not your type, two of my other mates are going with me.' I turned to face her.

'They don't have slimming awards to pick up?'

'No, they're absolute monsters. Combined weight: thirty-one stone.' Jessica maintained her straight face for a second before breaking into a broad smile. 'I'm joking, they're both gorgeous. So whaddya say?' Chomping into a triangle of brown toast, she fixed me with her best puppy dog eyes and I knew there and then that, sometime that day, Eddie was going to be receiving an apologetic text from yours truly.

'OK, OK,' I conceded, making the return trip to the sofa. 'I'll go. But first you've got to do me a favour.'

'What's that?'

'Give me a piece of that toast, you fat gannet.' I grabbed a slice from the stack and sunk back down into the sofa. Jessica gave me a playful dig in the ribs as, using my toast-free hand, I grabbed the remote and hit play. 'So where's this party, then?'

'It's at Precario.'

'Precario? Is it done up to resemble a Costa Rican shanty town or something?'

'That's the one.' I contemplated risking what fragile credibility I had by asking Jessica whether or not she was serious, but before I made a decision, I found myself transfixed by the latest *Highly Strung* show reel.

The screen filled with the image of a shabby, hopelessly

dated living room as the opening strains of 'Pour Some Sugar on Me' blasted out from a shabby, hopelessly dated midi hi-fi system. Suddenly, a naked man bounded into view, throwing his skinny frame about, shaking his lank locks and stringy beard and looking for all the world like a mental patient in a cell plastered with repulsive 1970s floral brown wallpaper (Anoglypta, for that extra padding). While he'd forgotten to put his clothes on, this hard-rocking mentalist had at least remembered the purpose of *Highly Strung*, and was thus furiously playing air guitar in time to the music. Except that his imaginary guitar wasn't composed of air, but rather something more tangible. And infinitely more dodgy. Jessica put down her toast and looked disbelievingly at the screen.

'Is he playing Van Halen on his genitals?' she asked incredulously.

'No,' I replied, my lips – which were going to have to wait indefinitely to receive the bit of toast suspended mere inches beneath them – barely moving. 'It's Def Leppard.'

Showing a grasp of the theatrical as firm as his grasp of his gonads, this clothes-averse clown proceeded to magic up a container of sugar before emptying its contents into his greasy barnet. I'd have commended him for his keen sense of literalism were it not for the fact that, on closer inspection, his 'sugar' was actually a jar of Canderel. Sure, dietary awareness had certainly become more acute since 1987, but even so, 'Pour Some Calorie-Controlled Artificial Sweetener On Me' lacked both that certain ring and, more crucially, any feeling of caution-to-the-wind rock rebellion or sexual adventurousness. Still, if I thought that the nutter's penchant for sugar substitutes pointed to an innate conservatism, I was to be proven sorely mistaken as he turned down the volume on his stereo and peered into the camera lens. 'Hi Jessica,' he breathed in a harsh, slightly nasal voice, his extreme close-up revealing a pallid complexion and twin thickets of nose hair as wild and unkempt as the thatch on his head. 'Colin Thunder's the name, and I'd love to make beautiful music with you. Now, watch as I build to a thrilling climax!' Stepping back from the lens, he turned the volume back up and, as the muscular, joyously yobbish bridge of the song kicked in, began to, well, work his instrument. At that moment, time slowed down to a crawl like a scene from *The Matrix*. Jessica dived towards me, sending jagged triangles of toast (my own included) flying everywhere. Like Keanu Reeves, I somehow shifted my body in reaction to both her falling limbs and the shower of jagged toast fragments, and, as the passing second stretched itself out, managed to squeeze the off-button on the remote, letting off an infrared blast that immobilised Colin Thunder before, thank heavens, he had the chance to make his guitar gently weep.

I opened my hand and my weapon fell to the carpet in what appeared to be real time. Not much else about the situation felt real, though. Just days ago I would have given five pounds and my left testicle to be able to stand within half a mile of Jessica and not foam at the mouth. Now I was laid on a sofa with her on top of me, and all I could think about was a hairy man and his cock.

I placed my beer bottle on the uneven, artfully decrepit table and checked one last time that I hadn't imagined my surroundings. A collision of crumbling concrete, weathered wood and mangled metal, Precario, it turned out, really was a bar combining the nightmarish poverty of Costa Rico's slums with the nightmarish drink prices of London's West End. On this evening, at least, it was also suitably overcrowded, with minor celebs and wannabe minor celebs exchanging hip banalities over the Afrobeat shaking this shanty town to its presumably flimsy foundations. It was the most tasteless thing I'd seen since … well, since Colin Thunder's performance the day before, although I didn't express this to Jessica as she'd been genuinely quite shaken by Mr.T's todgertastic audition tape, now in the hands of the police.

Seated with me and Jessica were her friends Jaz, a buxom Indian lass from Leeds with a bubbly personality and bright blue eye shadow, and Hayley, a proper cocker-ney with a two-tone, brunette-and-blonde bob reminiscent of one of those seahorse-shaped, praline-based Belgian chocolates. Since making my disbelieving entrance a couple of hours earlier, I'd joined my fellow slum dwellers – who, I quickly realised, had got a significant head start on the evening's drinking – in making sarcastic cracks about the clientele and providing from-a-distance voiceovers for their vacuous interactions. Our dubbing skills were getting pretty sharp by the time we clocked Brett Scott trying in vain to tempt preternaturally blonde three-piece girl group Aniston onto the small but perfectly swarmed dance floor, and the comedy flowing from this too-perfect tableaux – much of it hinging on Brett's rhubarb-and-custard-coloured Argyle sweater – only stopped when Jessica (ably, if somewhat surprisingly, portraying Aniston member Leah as a rampant sex addict) suddenly broke character.

'Shhhh! I think Brett just looked at us. Suspiciously.'

'So?' shrugged Jaz. 'I thought you said he was a knob.'

'He is,' giggled Jessica, 'but I'm supposed to be hosting a charity function with him next month.'

'Yeah, Knobs in Need.' muttered Jaz.

'He's definitely onto us,' hissed Jessica.' Can we *please* talk about something else?' Jaz took a brief sip of her cocktail, a charming little potion called Coca Cholera, before complying.

'OK. So have you had sex with Liam recently?' Jessica flicked two fingers up at her friend. I felt sick to my stomach. Dangerously, life-threateningly sick to my stomach, like an authentic South American slum dweller.

'Liam who?' I asked. Please let it be another Liam, my mind screamed. Just not Liam Barton. Or Liam Gallagher, come to think of it, but definitely not Liam Barton.

'Liam Barton, of course,' confirmed Jaz. 'You didn't know?' No, I didn't know, and I didn't want to, either. I opened my mouth but nothing came out. Instead, it was Jessica who spoke next.

'Liam told a friend of mine that he'd slept with me, the

lying little shit.' Now something did come out of my mouth. I just hoped the music and crowd noise were loud enough to mask how forcibly I exhaled. I felt like my doctor had just told me I had three months to live, before looking at the name on the front of his brown envelope and revealing that, no, apologies for the mix-up – that was actually some other poor sap.

'Have you confronted him about it?' I queried. Jessica shook her head.

'No. It was back when he was a singer, after I interviewed him for *The Non-Stop Pop Shop*. He was a jumped-up, hormone-addled little kid.'

'Does he know that you know?'

'I don't know.'

'What a knob,' observed Jaz, bringing the conversation full circle. 'Just the thought of him having sex with you is ...'

'Alright, alright.' Jessica threw up both palms in submission. 'You can all go back to taking the piss out of Brett Scott.' I couldn't think of a better way to spend my suddenly not-quite-so-finite time on Earth, and so I decided to take Jessica up on her generous offer. Across the room, the Diamond-Breasted Tosser's mating rituals were now being performed exclusively to Aniston chanteuse Leah, whose hirsute ensemble – a fluffy cream gilet hooked up with a suede miniskirt and fur-trimmed Ugg boots – lent her the appearance of a prehistoric glamour model enjoying the notoriety earned from posing for sexy cave paintings.

'He's absolutely desperate to get into her gilet,' I observed, causing Hayley to splutter hysterically on the last mouthful of her Diphtheria Daiquiri.

'Her *what*?'

'Her gilet,' I repeated. Hayley wiped a dribble of pink liquid from her chin and gave Jaz a look of puzzled amusement that seemed to ask, 'am I the only one hearing pure gobbledygook coming out of this guy's mouth?'

'Her furry thing,' I elaborated, eliciting a fresh, if mercifully fluid-free, chorus of raucous laughter from the girls.

'That's what I was afraid you meant,' giggled Hayley. 'Is that a Midlands slang term?'

I rolled my eyes, then patted my chest and stomach with my palms by way, I hoped, of innuendo-avoiding clarification. 'Her waistcoat. Her body warmer thing.'

'I can tell him what he'll find inside that,' offered Jaz. 'Some unsightly scars and two big fat handfuls of silicone.' While Hayley nodded her Guylian 'do in wholehearted, choc-headed agreement, Jessica gave Jaz a friendly shove.

'Ooh, you bitch!'

'Oh, aye?' exclaimed Jaz, nudging Hayley. 'Looks like someone's already planning a trip up Harley Street.'

'Shut up!' laughed Jessica.

'There's nothing wrong with your breasts,' insisted Jaz, placing a pretend-sympathetic hand on her friend's shoulder. 'Tell her, Rich.'

'Uhhhh ...' I began, as Jessica stirred the ice cubes bathing in the remaining blue puddle of her Shanty Town Slammer. I wasn't sure I was allowed to have an opinion on her breasts, although for the record I did agree with Jaz that they were very nice just the way they were.

'Don't worry,' interjected Jaz, rising to her feet and hitching up the shiny, bright blue mini dress that, whilst a perfect match with her eye shadow, was struggling to contain her own generous quantities of feminine fat. 'I'm not going to force an answer out of you 'cos I'm going for a boogie.'

'Me too,' chimed Hayley, getting up to join her pal. 'You two coming?'

'In a little while,' said Jessica.

'It *better* be a little while,' warned Jaz. 'Some of us have got proper jobs to go to in the morning. How about you, Rich?'

Me? I'd much rather have continued fielding awkward questions about Jessica's breasts. Dancing an activity I liked to studiously avoid unless I was absolutely prepared, and by 'absolutely prepared' I mean 'blind drunk'. Unfortunately, it was my experience that any social group had amongst its members a number of Dance Floor Gestapo. Almost always female, these ruthless enforcers of shape-throwing would charm, coerce or even drag you onto the dance floor, refusing to accept 'no' for an answer on the basis that sweatily gyrating and flailing in close proximity to you was fun for *them*. This, in my book, put them in the same category as rapists as well as just the Nazi secret police. Jaz, it seemed was a card-carrying, badge-wearing member of the DFG (and by extension, then, tantamount to a Nazi rapist – just so we're clear) but with Jessica having already dodged her sinister grasp – at least for the time being – I reckoned I could too.

'Aaah, I don't want to spoil everyone's evening,' I reasoned.

'You'd be *making* mine,' said Jaz. Her brassy Northern style was strangely alluring, but I held my ground. After all, I enjoyed drawing, but I didn't go around thrusting sketch pads and pencils into people's hands and forcing them to knock up impromptu self portraits.

'Maybe later. Someone's got to keep Jessica company.' Jaz shook her head.

'I dunno. These TV people are so boring. Come on, mate.' She grabbed Hayley by the arm and the two of them goose-stepped off towards the dance floor.

And so, with her likeable gal pals having vacated their wonky wooden seats, there I was one-on-one with Jessica. I *still* couldn't quite believe this. We weren't in the Fresh Coat meeting room, the Artemis Studios canteen or even on *The Hangout*'s purple sofa. In fact, never mind *The Hangout*, we were hanging out as friends – a fact that suddenly made me feel a little nervous. It didn't help matters that Jessica, dressed in a wraparound kaftan top (thanks, Grattan, even if you fucked me over with that whole gilet thing) and with her dark hair rising up from her forehead in a smooth, impressive quiff, looked unbelievably hot. You know how hot a slice of tomato gets inside a toastie? Jessica looked as hot as one of those molten red discs feels on your tongue or against the roof of your mouth. Whether through hypnotic attraction, rigid, unblinking fear or perhaps a combination of both, my eyes could have stayed glued to her all night, but I realised I needed to get my mouth in on things, so instead I sent my peepers out into the crowd, where they moved over a grab bag of whispy-chinned boy banders, early hours quiz show presenters and assorted reality TV detritus before alighting on the curly blonde head of Charlie Carter, twentysomething soap starlet and the hostess-slash-honouree of this evening's slum-centric soiree.

'Why's she throwing this party, again?' I asked.

'I told you already,' said Jessica. 'Charlie's been named Spectacles Wearer of the Year.'

'Oh, OK. I guess what's throwing me is the fact she's not wearing glasses.' Jessica shrugged.

'No. She doesn't wear them all the time.'

'So let me get this straight. She's being recognised for having a minor visual impairment which she combats by occasionally wearing glasses for close work? My uncle sometimes wears a verruca sock when he goes swimming, but he doesn't get an official title or a big party with celebrity guests.'

'Ah, yes,' countered Jessica, tapping the rough and rugged table with her finger, 'but I'll bet your uncle hasn't helped make wearing a verruca sock cool and sexy.'

'Au contraire. All the teenagers at his local leisure centre have got them, in most cases purely for fashion. In fact, the really cool kids have two verruca socks: one for the pool, one for the streets.'

'Oh, really?' laughed Jessica, her smile providing more illumination than anything Precario's appropriately ineffectual lighting could muster. Yep, this definitely beat having Eddie and his friends prison-rape my ears.

'Anyway,' I continued, 'if they're opening things up to sporadic specs wearers then they should have given you the title. You look good in your glasses.' Jessica tilted her quiff to one side.

'You think so?

'Yeah. They suit you.'

'Awwww. Thanks, Rich. Well, just for you ...' Jessica encircled her eyes with her thumbs and forefingers, wiggling her remaining digits in the air. I wanted to lean over the table and kiss her until she tapped three times on my arm to come up for air, but instead I used my own thumb and forefinger to pinch my chin, narrowing my own, unencumbered peepers as I scrutinised her decidedly non-prescription eye wear.

'I've got to be honest. Your other frames look better on you. Actually, Judge Jessie's frames look better on you.' Jessica laughed and I laughed at her laughing. Then removed her knuckle-rimmed specs.

'I'm a little bit smashed,' she revealed exclusively.

'And yet you hide it so well,' I teased, getting up from my seat. 'Listen, hang tight and I'll get you some water.'

'Thanks, hon.' Jessica gave me a wave that almost made parting company with her worthwhile.

Precario's feeling of sweaty overpopulation was, it turned out, at its most authentic in front of the bar.

'We could have *gone* to Costa Rico, the time we've been waiting,' scoffed a man stood to my left. Clad in a tan suede jacket, he had luxuriant (if noticeably dyed) chestnut hair and a matching moustache, and I immediately identified and acknowledged him as one half of TV detective duo *Art and Kraftz*.

'*Thrust and Parry*, actually,' he corrected rather tersely. I'm Thrust, he's Parry.' He pointed to the other conspicuously middle-aged man in the room, who was perched awkwardly on a battered sofa staring at a young woman's bare shoulder blades. I waited for an announcement of the pair's real names, but Thrust, perhaps hoping I'd learn their fictional monikers before I troubled myself with anything more ambitious, instead grilled me on my occupation.

'I write for *The Hangout*, the children's TV programme. It's funny; we're actually doing something called *Cash and*

Carrie. It's kind of a good-natured send-up of what you guys do on your show.'

Thrust murmured something about 'dumbing down', then, to my bewilderment, pushed back the hem of his jacket and grabbed the walkie-talkie that was mounted on his stone-washed hip. He pressed down on a button and spoke into the mouthpiece.

'Thrust to Parry, Thrust to Parry. I forgot – Coke or lemonade, over?' There was the rough crackle of static, followed by a male voice. I turned around to see the balding Parry speaking into his own walkie-talkie.

'Parry to Thrust, Parry to Thrust,' replied his relayed, muffled voice. 'Coke, please. That's Charlie, Oscar, Kilo, Echo. Over.' Clearly, this pair was nuts (November, Uniform, Tango, Sierra. Over), so when I felt a tap on my shoulder, I was relieved to turn around and see Jaz and Hayley back from their boogie.

'Oh, hi!' I exclaimed. 'Can I get you two another drink? Each?'

'Each?' laughed Jaz. 'You *are* generous. Unfortunately, though, we've got to go.'

'Oh, really? I was just coming for that dance.'

'Liar!' Jaz prodded me in the shoulder. 'Next time I see you, you won't get away so easily, though. Anyway, nice to meet you, love.'

'And you. And you too, Hayley.'

'Yeah, it was wicked,' shouted Hayley, hoisting the strap of her handbag up over her shoulder. 'Now, make sure you take care of Jessica. I haven't seen her that merry in a long time.'

'I'll look after her,' I promised, securing warm smiles from my two new acquaintances.

'We could have *gone* to Costa Rico, the time we've been waiting,' yelled an already all-too-familiar voice. Next to us, Thrust was treating an elfin girl in a peasant top to his favourite off-the-cuff witty reflection. Jaz looked at me, her eyebrows squeezing down on her blue eye shadow

109

'Is he ...'

'Yeah,' I confirmed, rolling my eyes and tapping my temple. 'Mental.'

Five minutes later and I was weaving my way back through the crowd, a tall, icy glass of water in each hand and – oh, alright then – a sneaky shot of Tequila in my system in preparation for any impending hip-wiggling. I may have narrowly escaped the Jaz-Hayley double team, but I feared I'd be helpless if Jessica so much as hinted at taking a trip to Precario's dance floor. Matter of fact, I could already feel the booze daring me to rise to the challenge, pointing me to the heaving heap of limbs currently doing their best to raise Precario's rickety roof and assuring me that I could spazz out as gracefully as any of these fools. Besides, it wasn't as if, in her current state, Jessica was going to be scrutinising my every manoeuvre. She was, as Hayley put it, 'merry' – providing, that was, she hadn't snapped back into an impatient state of sobriety whilst I'd been brushing up on my phonetic alphabet with The Cowhide Kid.

I needn't have worried. At our table, my kind-of-sort-of-date for the evening was laughing heartily at the rapier wit of Brett Scott, who had graciously stepped in to keep my seat warm. Upon seeing me, Jessica stifled her giggling and did the intros.

'Brett, this is Richard. Richard, Brett.'

'How's it going?' I enquired, placing Jessica's water next to a couple of empty shot glasses that, like her new companion, had sprung up almost magically in my absence. Evidently the question was either too hard or too boring for Brett, who responded by squinting suspiciously at me. His face exuded as much warmth and friendliness as the cocktail stick that perched on his bottom lip, presiding over the cliff face of dark stubble that plunged into a lurid cashmere sea of pink-and-yellow diamonds. It was as if Clint Eastwood had showed up at the saloon in Jimmy Tarbuck's golfing gear.

'We were just talking about the charity thing,' announced

110

Jessica, taking up the conversational slack. It seemed I was going to have to feign interest.

'Oh yeah? What are you raising money for?'

'It's for muscular dis … muscular discjock …' While Jessica struggled to name that illness, Brett removed his cocktail stick (a prop whose pretensions of coolness and rebellion were undermined somewhat by its associations with cheese and pineapple), and fixed a smug grin across his eminently punchable face.

'It's for muscular disc jockeys? Oh, thanks, babe.' He flexed his sweater-swathed right biceps, placing a kiss on it before draping his arm around Jessica, who playfully pushed him away.

'Ha!' snorted Brett. 'You won't be shoving me when I break into movies.'

'Break into movies!' mocked Jessica. 'Eleanor says she'll see what she can do and suddenly you're Prad Bitt.'

'Who's Prad Bitt?' sniggered Brett.

'Who's Eleanor?' I asked, not interested in the slightest, yet desperate to cling onto some last, pathetic scrap of Jessica's increasingly elusive attention.

'Who's this guy?' grunted Brett, tipping his dark cow's lick in my direction.

'Shut up!' Jessica gave him an elbow to the ribs. Brett fell back clutching his side in an exaggerated picture of agony, while Jessica tended to my question in surprisingly near-coherent style. 'Eleanor's our agent. We're both on her box. Er, her books. So's Charlie, actually – that's how I know her. Anyway, Brett's asked Eleanor if she can get him some acting work.' She looked down at the budding thespian, who was still writhing like a flurry of buckshots had pierced through his cosy leisure wear (if only). 'As you can see, she should probably concentrate on getting him some acting *lessons*.' Brett snapped out of his near-death routine and rose up fully healed in his seat.

'You say I can't act,' he recapped, stabbing his cocktail

111

stick into the all too finite airspace between himself and Jessica. 'But put it this way, right? I'm acting ...' Bracing for what he obviously thought was an important point, he swirled his rebel-without-a-fork accessory around in a circular motion before triumphantly pointing it at Jessica. 'I'm acting like I'm enjoying your company.' One thing was certain: I *couldn't* act like I was enjoying the company of this idiot, who, at this point, could not have exuded any greater degree of smugness had he been one of those 'hot or not?' style barometer things in a broadsheet weekend style supplement. In fact, I could barely pretend I was enjoying Jessica's company anymore, at least not with this prize bell-end in her vicinity.

'I need the toilet,' I said, abruptly getting up.

'Well hurry back,' instructed Jessica, cupping her hand around the corner of her mouth whilst raising her voice a notch. 'I can't stand this guy.' Shit, I thought, the alarm bells in my head now going crazy. Playground Relationship.

After beating a path through to the opposite side of the room, I pushed through the ragged strips of plastic hanging from a battered door frame, then through an unlacquered wooden door labelled 'hombres'. Inside the toilets, I splashed some water on my face and stared at my reflection in the mirror. I looked pissed off. I *was* pissed off. Pissed off with Jessica for getting pissed up and flirting with that prick. Pissed off with myself for being pissed off with Jessica, who was, after all, allowed to flirt with whichever prick she wanted to, regardless of whether or not they took their fashion cues from a slice of Battenberg cake. Pissed off that I'd gone from cosying up with Jessica to staring at my pissed off reflection. Pissed off that, in a bar tasteless enough to style itself on a slum village, I was stood next to a man who, in a few seconds time, would expect me to put a pound on his little silver plate as payment for him handing me a couple of paper towels.

Still, if an ill-tempered tête-à-tête with my reflection was going to cost me, I might as well aim for a return on my investment. This whole thing, I reasoned with myself, was a quest, and like all quests it was going to require a bit of hard work and no little resolve. I could either lie down and surrender Jessica to Brett, or I could go back to that ramshackle table and show a bit of fight while Jess was still semiconscious. Plus, even if Jessica did manage the unlikely feat of getting any drunker, there was always the chance she'd add another vibrant colour or two to the front of Brett's jumper, and that had to be worth watching.

I emerged through the plastic strips a man reborn. Moving with renewed purpose, I saw gaps opening in the crowd ahead of time and passed through them with swiftness and agility – until a girl with a head full of blonde highlights and a metallic handkerchief for a top turned my through-road into a cul-de-sac.

'Hi, I'm Mandy,' she yelled over the music, which had just been turned up a level. 'I saw you talking to Desmond Simms and Ian Beecroft earlier.'

'Desmond who and Ian what?'

'You know, Thrust and Parry.' Her pale green eyes – roughly colour co-ordinated with the drink she was clutching – lit up. 'Are you a producer?'

'No, writer.' She looked disappointed. And like her eyebrows had been drawn on with a felt tip.

'I'm an actress.'

'Oh, OK. Anything I might have seen?'

'I was a prostitute in an episode of *Romsford Beat*.'

'I don't think I saw that,' I admitted. Mandy eyed me up and down before curling her sticky top lip into a sneer.

'Drop dead, you tosser.'

'I'm sorry,' I stammered, 'I wasn't being condescending, I just don't watch a lot of ...'

'No, no,' giggled Mandy, her narrow features softening as she grabbed my arm. 'That was my line.' We stood in silence for a few seconds before a light bulb (forty watts, by my reckoning) went off above Mandy's streaky head. 'So you could, like, write stuff to make me sound really intelligent and witty and that.'

'Yeah,' I replied vaguely, not knowing whether the best writer on Earth was capable of such an accomplishment. 'Sorry, I don't mean to be rude, but I've got to go and check that my friend's alright.' I was about to desert her when suddenly I had a brain wave. 'Actually, how would you like to meet Brett Scott?' Mandy's felt tip eyebrows leapt upwards.

'Really? He's fit *as*.'

'Oh, believe me, he's ever fitter in the flesh,' I promised, grabbing Mandy's hand and hurrying her through assorted partygoers towards our table. 'And he's right ...'

'There?' Mandy pointed to the dance floor, where Brett was getting his ill-defined groove on. With a gyrating Jessica.

As a deflated Mandy tutted and tottered off, I breathed in, breathed out and took a moment to assess the situation. Let's see: the girl I'd been sharing laughs with just minutes earlier was now sharing her pelvis with the tool we'd been sharing laughs at the expense of. And right now he was laughing at *me*, or at least he would have been if he wasn't so unrelentingly focused on Jessica's very nice, not-in-need-of-surgery breasts. Clearly, there was only one thing I could possibly do in these circumstances, so I did it. I spent half an hour brooding like a posse of ninjas had just gang-raped my dog, then disappeared out of Precario's front door without saying a word to anyone.

If I'd been a character in a Spike Lee movie, sorry, joint, the bespectacled Brooklynite director would, I'm certain, have portrayed my state of mind as I proceeded through the cool night air with one of his trademark double dolly shots. My pissed off face and confused head would, to the audience, have stayed static while the world and its inhabitants continued to move on, oblivious to my inner turmoil. I'd dollied my pissed off, confused way down several side streets when a sudden change of heart caused me to bring my tour-of-brooding to a halt. I thought back to earlier that evening. I'd promised Jessica's friends I'd take care of her, and even if I hadn't, it was still irresponsible and inconsiderate of me to just vanish into the night like a diarrhoea-stricken Cinderella. And because of what? Jessica – a single woman, let's not forget – had committed no more heinous an offence than dancing with a fuckwit TV presenter. Besides, I thought as I turned around and headed briskly back towards Precario, there was nothing worse than an insecure, possessive idiot who couldn't stand to see a girl he fancied having fun with another guy. And if Brett was going to have to learn this the hard way, then so be it.

Now resolved to snatch victory from the self-satisfied, stubble-coated jaws of defeat, I broke into a gentle jog, gathering speed – and almost flattening a pair of snogging lesbian goths – as I rounded a corner. Three more later (that's three more corners, not three more pairs of snogging lesbian goths) and I was slowing back down from a bladeage-equipped sprint for the final few metres of my journey. Precario's sweltering South American slum theme notwithstanding, I surely wasn't going to impress the establishment's neckless, fist-faced doormen by rolling up sweat-soaked and out of breath. Arriving, for the second time that evening, outside the club's self-consciously shitty facade, I was greeted first by the sultry, muffled sound of Afrobeat emanating from inside the club, and then by a familiar voice cutting clearly through the evening air.

'Brett!' A few yards up the street, Jessica shrieked the name of the man whose palm had just slapped hard against her left buttock. She turned around and used her handbag to playfully return fire on his shoulder while he hurried her into the back of a taxi.

'Jess!' I called out. Brett turned around and gave me a cocky shrug before disappearing into the cab, which started off down the road. 'Fuck!'

'Ah, The Bard,' slurred Thrust, joining me on the pavement. 'Tell me, have the events of the evening got your creative juices flowing? I ask, because it appears my, ahem, creative juices will definitely be flowing tonight.' He glanced slyly at the young, green eyed, blonde haired girl clinging to his suede-covered arm.

'Hello again,' said Mandy, offering a slightly embarrassed grin. 'Is everything alright?'

'No,' I replied, anxiously scanning the street for another taxi. 'My very attractive, very drunk friend Jessica just got in that cab with Brett Scott.'

'Lucky cow,' muttered Mandy, looking slightly dejected as she sized up her moustachioed, middle-aged consolation prize.

'What, that stubble-faced little shit in the Argyle jumper?' fumed Thrust, tapping insistently at a stain on his shoulder. 'He spilled a Jack Daniels and Coke down my jacket. And this is real suede.'

'There's not another taxi in sight,' I huffed.

'Taxi?' scoffed Thrust as a spotless black Land Rover pulled up to the kerb. 'You don't need one of those. Get in! You too, Mary.' Mandy and I piled into the back of the car, while Thrust assumed his position riding shotgun.

'Kidnap in progress,' barked Thrust at his partner in fictional crime-fighting. 'Follow that cab!'

'Typical,' moaned Parry, 'I'm trying to make your night easier for you and you repay me by ...'

'Did I mention possible date rape?' snapped Thrust. 'Step on it!'

'OK, buddy,' replied Parry, squeezing his foot down on the accelerator, 'but you owe me one.' He peered into the rear view mirror and rolled his eyeballs over Mandy's cleavage.

'Nope, not that one,' said Thrust sternly while the Land Rover picked up speed. Pointing at the back of his seat, I incredulously mouthed the word 'why?' at Mandy.

'He promised I could be in the show,' she explained meekly.

'I think we're in it right now,' I said as we veered, in fourth gear, around the sharpest of corners and onto a shop-lined street intermittently dotted with spindly trees. Brett and Jess had got off to a significant head start, and already there

116

were fifty metres and a Renault Megane between us. The latter proved to be of little impediment to Parry, who made use of the opposite lane to leave his fellow motorist in the dust, sliding back onto the correct side of the road just in time to avoid a head-on collision with an oncoming transit van, if not a huge, ear-piercing shriek from Mandy.

'Yes!' roared Thrust over a blitzkrieg of irate beeping from the van driver. 'Make the road work for you! Now, how about a spot of music?' He tapped at an iPod connected to the stereo and I was only mildly surprised when the *Thrust and Parry* theme tune filled the vehicle.

'You alright?' I asked Mandy.

'Serves me right for getting in the car with a nutcase,' she conceded. I was about to offer a sympathetic shrug when she added, 'does Jessica George know you're stalking her?' Rather than remind my fellow passenger that she was about to trade her body for a two second TV appearance, I turned to look out of my window. With Parry's loafer-encased foot clamped down on the pedal, launderettes, takeaways, phone boxes and the odd drunkard quickly – fifty miles per hour quickly – became vividly daubed details in a modern day Matisse painting. To my horror, it was mere seconds and one T-junction before, accompanied by the sound of a siren wailing, an evocative splash of blue was thrown onto the canvas.

'Nice one,' muttered Mandy, craning her neck to check out the company. Mumbling something at Thrust, Parry eased off on the accelerator then pulled up to the kerb while my heart sank down into my stomach. Watching the pin pricks of the taxi's tail lights fade to black, I couldn't help thinking that I should have stuck with Latte Girl. She may have been made of cardboard, but at least an evening with her wouldn't have landed me in trouble with the law.

'Relax,' instructed Thrust, switching off the stereo and reorganising his glossy, conker-coloured fringe in the rear view mirror. 'Leave this to me.' Behind us, a pair of car doors were slammed shut. Parry rolled down his window and a fortysomething policeman centred his balding head within the frame.

'Evening, people. Any idea why we've pulled you over?'

'Is it to notify me that your wife is anxious for my company?' enquired Thrust, a smirk developing beneath the plentiful cover of his moss-textured 'tache. 'If so, you've shot yourself in the foot because that's exactly where we were heading now.' I slumped down in my seat, burying my brow in my hand. Best case scenario: I spent the night in a different cell to this moustachioed clown. The policeman flicked on his torch and a beam of light danced over the deluded duo's facial features.

'Oh my life!' exclaimed our inquisitor. 'Take a look at this, Paul. It's only Thrust and bleedin' Parry!' Great, I thought as a squinty, acne-riddled lad poked his nose into the car. I was going to be in a cell *and* the tabloids.

'No word of a lie, mate,' enthused Paul. 'I had a naked upper lip until your show came out.' Lubricating his thumb and forefinger with his tongue, he proudly smoothed down his thin, threadbare attempt at a moustache before prodding at Parry's arm with his spittle-soaked digits. 'Guiggsy here was already starting to lose his hair, though, so don't be taking credit for that.' Parry offered up an unconvincing 'heh' while Guiggsy elbowed his precocious young charge out of the way.

'I'd give you a smack for that, mate, but I don't want you having a black eye in the photograph.' He held up his mobile phone and shone the torch directly onto my eyeballs. 'You don't mind, do you mate? If we go under that lamp-post over there we might have just enough light.' Suddenly, Mandy caught his eye.

'Here, weren't you a prostitute in *Romsford Beat*?' he queried, caressing her pale, goose bump-covered contours with the torch beam.

'That's me,' replied Mandy, flashing a smile that, without warning, abruptly metamorphosed into her set piece sneer. 'Drop dead, you tosser.'

'Watch it, darling, or you'll be feeling my hard, shiny truncheon,' chuckled Guiggsy. 'Alright everybody, if you'll kindly step out of the iconic, TV classic vehicle ...'

Five minutes later, we'd wrapped up a photoshoot that, for its ambitious finale, had culminated in four shaky-limbed men holding a horizontal, maniacally grinning TV prostitute in mid-air.

'Good work.' Arms now free of Mandy's arse, Guiggsy took back his phone in exchange for a patronising pat on my back. My work this evening, though, had been anything but good. It had, in fact, been fucking atrocious.

'Keep making those streets safer,' exhorted Thrust as the two real-life rozzers clambered back into their real-life Fiat Panda.

'You too,' replied Guiggsy. 'In the first instance, by driving sensibly.'

'Ten four,' confirmed Thrust, throwing in a casual salute for good measure.

'Coppers. They bloody love us,' reflected Parry as the police car disappeared into the night. Thrust turned to me.

'Well,' he sighed, 'it looks like our adversary has given us the slip. Need a lift?'

'No thanks. I'll get a taxi.'

'OK, well, good luck with the writing.' Thrust gave me his own, suede sleeved variation on the Patronising Back-Pat while Parry popped open the doors of the Clinically-Insanemobile.

'For God's sake,' I murmured to Mandy as she returned to the mobile, four wheel drive casting couch, 'just make sure you get a speaking part.' The Land Rover vanished into the night, too, the *Thrust and Parry* theme tune lingering around for a few deeply irritating seconds longer.

I couldn't say for certain whether it was guilt that motivated me to point the taxi driver towards Camden and The Crevice or rather the sudden, selfish urge to see someone I'd known for more than a fortnight in a place that was shitty and unkempt by default rather than by design. Probably it was a lamentable combination of both, because if I'd genuinely wanted to support Eddie in his artistic endeavours, I'd have been there feigning enthusiasm from his first, strangled vocal rather than dropping by belatedly after an evening of prefabricated shanty towns, high speed car chases and photo shoots with TV prostitutes. Whatever the case, though, there was definitely something pulling me past the throng at the bar and down the flight of stairs leading to the building's basement, and it wasn't the music rumbling up from down below.

Sticky with spilled drinks, the wooden stairs weren't particularly wide to begin with, but my descent into the bowels of The Crevice was made even tighter by the thick layer of flyers and posters that spread across the walls on either side of me like an uncontrollable fungal growth, screaming out the names of Yeast, Arse Gravy, Wrong In Every Way and the countless other once-obscure bands who'd heaved their guitars and amps up and down those very steps as they started out on their long and winding journeys to further obscurity. Forging my way downwards, I clocked a flyer advertising the forthcoming (well, it had been forthcoming half a year earlier) performance by The Backgammon Cowboys, one of Eddie and his friends' previous incarnations, although they'd long since dumped the name owing to a) the country connotations of the word 'Cowboys' and b) the fact that none of the band members liked, or even knew the rules of, backgammon. It wasn't the only name jettisoned by the group, either. Since initially forming – albeit with a slightly different, much hairier roster – as throwback metal troupe Portcullis, Eddie and his ragtag assortment of musically inclined misfit mates had also performed as Grapefruit Suicide, Fuck Me! They Cleared It (a reference to Christian Slater's BBFC-censored exclamation from *Robin Hood: Prince of Thieves*) and, well, Eddie and his Ragtag Assortment of Musically Inclined Misfit Mates. In addition to wielding these monikers, not to mention that of their still-in-existence glam rock side project Captain Bouffant and the Volumisers, they'd also had a brief, controversial stint as Abused From Childhood, a name dropped after it proved contentious with several of the band members' parents – not least those of Jason, the drummer, who'd bought their little boy his first drum kit at the age of seven and paid for his lessons well into his teens. Hardly, I had to admit, the kind of behaviour to have social services beating down the door.

Anyway, the band, at long last, seemed to have found themselves a permanent name in the rather splendid Burlap Ball-Sack, and as I peeled my trailing foot from the beer-varnished bottom step and wandered into the basement, I had to concede that their latest handle was an apt one. Every note of the song that Eddie and his three dishevelled band mates were belting out – the title track, it seemed, from their debut album 'In The Bag' – was struck with the sort of itchy irritation that, presumably, would result from having a scrotum made from the same material as a scarecrow's face. Not that the 'Sack were short of a charismatic frontman, mind you. Sporting newly-bleached tresses and jeans so tight I could almost hear his sperm – burlap-wrapped or otherwise – screaming for mercy over their master's own pained-sounding vocals, Eddie certainly had enough presence and lunatic energy to fill the stage. Although in fairness the stage, modestly sized to begin with, was already submerged under the thick white carpet of dry ice being pumped out from behind one of the group's amps, so you could argue that there really wasn't that much of it to be filled in the first place.

And if the musical stylings of Eddie and his three flailing friends weren't *quite* abrasive enough to smooth the edges off my bad temper, they at least furnished it with an appropriate soundtrack. Indeed, the volume at which the guys were torturing their instruments was loud enough to accommodate my own, impromptu excursion into the world of the singer-songwriter.

'Fuck Jessica,' I murmured. Then again, 'Fuck Jessica.' It was catchy enough, and so, with the Burlap Boys ratcheting up their racket to a speaker-shuddering high, I cranked up my own volume and let those two words fly, with added force, again and again: 'Fuck Jessica. Fuck Jessica. Fuck Jessica.' In hindsight, it doesn't sound like the most profound of lyrics, especially considering I'd collaborated with two co-writers, Alcohol and Self-Loathing, to come up with it. Nevertheless, it was deeply personal to me, and as the forty-strong throng in front of me bounced enthusiastically up and down, the only part of my body in motion was my suddenly slightly wobbly bottom lip.

The corners of my eyes got watery and, already wrapped up in BB's increasingly rampant machine-made fog, the block of bouncing bodies started to further blur around the edges. Meanwhile, in the slightly clearer centre of the picture, a girl in a green cardigan – one of the few in the crowd not abandoning her limbs to the crew's signature song 'You Got Me (Acting Like A Spazz)' – turned around, craning her neck as her eyes scoured the back of the room. Shit! It was Beth. Instinctively, I ducked behind the dirty blonde dreadlocks of the guy in front of me, and, content that I hadn't been spotted amongst the shadows, smoke and students that separated me and my sometime colleague, headed for the exit. That was it. Time to call this whole, sorry evening a write-off.

Two burly security guards stood on either side of the door frame that, with the bravest tendrils of dry ice attempting a breakout from the basement, now evoked the foggy portal that transformed plebs into celebs on *Stars in Their Eyes*. Tonight, Matthew, I thought as I gave the chap on the left a quick, upwards head flick, I'm going to be getting the fuck out of here.

I was about halfway up the steps when the clouds parted and a female figure came down towards me, the light from above tracing a golden loop around the thick ring of fake fur encircling her face. A pristine white T-shirt clung to her torso from beneath her runner bean body warmer while some perfectly worn-in jeans effortlessly slid over the space between her calf-hugging brown leather boots and the thick, studded brown belt that nonchalantly encircled her hips. As she got closer, the features of the young woman conveying two plastic cups of cranberry-coloured liquid towards the basement came into focus.

'Joy.' I tried to move up a step but found that my legs were stuck in place. Someone was really in for a job cleaning these stairs.

'Richie Rich.' The ice cubes in the drinks bumped shoulders while Joy slowly took another step downwards. 'How long have you been here?'

'Um, for a while. Actually, I was just leaving.' I wrenched my right foot from its sugar-coated backing board and affixed it to the step above.

'No, you're not.' Joy stepped directly into my path. 'If I'm seeing it through 'til the bitter end then so are you.' I wanted to say 'no', but I didn't have an ounce of fight left in me, and as the sounds on stage momentarily faded out, there was something strangely calming about the way the clinking of those ice cubes combined with the clopping of Joy's heels. I peeled my shoes off the steps for a weary one-eighty.

'Ears or hair?' I asked, pointing at Joy's hood.

'What?'

'Ears or hair? Which are you protecting?'

'Both.' Joy resumed her clinking and clopping. 'So, Eddie said you told him you were out on a hot date with Jessica George tonight.'

'Well ...' I began wearily.

'I told him you were talking bollocks,' related Joy. As we moved through the fog and back into the basement, I was about to respond, but a) the opening chords of the 'Sack's final number drowned me out, and b) I wasn't sure that Joy was particularly wrong.

CHAPTER FOUR

Jessica flew through the air. My eyes followed her as she climbed upwards, her outstretched arms assuming the role of wings while her pigtails leapt up above her head, jostling to see which one of them could reach the highest before gravity found them out and pulled them both back down to Earth again. Their playful contest resumed as they accompanied Jessica on her next journey upwards, then her next one and the one after that.

From my vantage point across the studio floor – slunk back in a beanbag on a metal seating platform – I watched as Jessica put a trampoline through its paces, and as the sight of her bouncing up and down combined with the sound of creaking springs, I realised that an Argyle-clad, chain-smoking male was the one missing component from the tableaux that had plagued my dreams for the last two nights. Indeed, as I looked down at the yellow shooting script at my side, I wondered how I'd ever managed to finish it the day before, when thoughts of Brett and Jessica getting together and getting it on had been getting in the way of my child-friendly banter and knockabout, wig-intensive sketches. At least, it seemed as Jessica addressed a crane-mounted camera, my all-consuming jealousy hadn't prevented me from scripting thematically appropriate – if not exactly taxing – quiz questions.

'So if you want to win this trampoline *(crunch!)* along with all the great stuff you see beside it *(crunch!)*, then just tell us which of these Australian animals is known for jumping up *(crunch!)* and down *(crunch!)* Is it A, the koala *(crunch!)* B, the kangaroo *(crunch!)* or C, the duck-billed platypus? *(crunch!)* Give us a call *(crunch!)* on the number you see on your screen *(crunch!)* but remember to get permission *(crunch!)* from the person who pays the bills *(crunch!)* Now what are you waiting for? *(crunch!)* Jump to it!'

'And cut!' called Michael, the director, as Jessica put in one last *crunch!* to round things off. 'Nicely done, Jessica.

Graham, how was that for you?'

'Looks great,' affirmed Graham the cameraman from aboard the crane.

'Alright, good stuff,' said Michael approvingly. 'We'll take a quick break there, everyone.' Jessica clambered down from the trampoline and retrieved her bottle of water from the giant stuffed gorilla who'd kindly been safeguarding it for her. I didn't know what I was going to say to her, but as she headed directly towards me, pigtails now winding down with a gentle bounce, it struck me that I was about to find out. I reached for my own bottle of water and raised it to my lips in an attempt to appear casual and preoccupied. Then I unscrewed the cap, as that seemed like a good way to heighten the illusion.

'I'm glad I wasn't doing that yesterday morning,' reflected Jessica, pulling up a pew – or rather squashing into a beanbag – next to me on the platform.

'Yeah. Pretty energetic stuff,' I noted. Jessica unscrewed the cap on her bottle and took a swig of water. Thirst quenched and vocal chords lubricated, she then got straight down to business.

'So I'm sorry about the other night. I kind of lost touch with you.'

'No, no. It was my fault. I wasn't feeling too good, so I left in a bit of a hurry.'

'Oh.' Jessica's brow hunched slightly. 'You seemed fine when I was with you earlier. I mean, from what I remember.'

'Yes, well, they were taking the whole shanty town theme pretty seriously in there. I may have been bitten by a tse-tse fly in the toilets.' Jessica smiled and squished back further into the exceptionally soft furnishing.

'I must admit, I felt pretty ill myself yesterday and it had nothing to do with a tse-tse fly.'

'Yeah ... You were a little bit tipsy when last I saw you.'

'A little bit tipsy?' echoed Jessica from inside her bean-filled nest. 'I ended up leaving with Brett Scott.' I swallowed hard.

'Really?' If my surprise upon hearing this information sounded genuine, it was because I hadn't expected Jessica to volunteer it, let alone drop it into the mix so casually.

'Yeah,' groaned Jessica. 'I was pissed and he wanted to have sex, so we ended up leaving pretty early, too. Apparently he couldn't wait 'til closing time.'

'What?' I whimpered, shrinking back further into my beanbag in the forlorn hope that it would swallow me up before spraying a geyser of blood, entrails and crispy polyester chips up at the studio ceiling, Freddy McKreuger-style. Even if Jessica was presenting Wednesday night's thrilling finale as a booze-fuelled error of judgement, did she have to be quite so candid with the details?

'Yeah,' she continued. 'He hooked up with Leah from Aniston. I got sandwiched between the two of them for the cab ride home. They were reaching over and pawing at each other the whole way. It was gross, but I guess it serves me right for making fun of her.' I pushed myself up by my elbows, although with Jessica's repulsed recollection having lifted a huge weight off me, it felt like I could just have easily floated my way up towards the studio lights.

'Oh. It was *her*. Cave Girl. One Million Years V.D. The one you portrayed as a nymphomaniac.'

'Yeah, and I was spot on,' asserted Jessica, emerging to meet me above bean level. 'The two of them couldn't dump me on my doorstep quickly enough. Yuck.' She screwed up her face, then took another swig of water as if attempting to wash away the bad taste incurred by the image. 'Anyway,' she sighed, 'I just wanted to check that we were cool.'

'Of course. Why wouldn't we be?' Jessica was quiet for a couple of seconds before cautiously venturing an answer.

'I hate to say it,' she began, squirming slightly in her seat. 'This sounds really awful, but I thought that me being friendly with Brett might have made you ... I don't know if jealous is the right word ...' Now *my* bum was the one putting the polystyrene through its paces. Were my feelings for Jessica really that transparent?

'Jealous? What? Why would I ... It's up to you who you want to ...'

'If it's any consolation,' Jessica interrupted, 'I think you guys are better off without him on your team.' I stared back at her, completely clueless.

'What guys? What team?' Jessica pressed on her bottom lip with her finger, a look of awkwardness suddenly seizing control of her features.

'You're not gay, *are* you?'

'Not that I know of.'

'Oh. Someone told me you were.' Jessica tilted her head in the direction of Liam, who was busy sliding a computer game from the prize table into his jeans pocket. 'In fairness, I didn't believe him – at all – until you started talking about gilets.' I thrust my arms open in protest.

'You couldn't have come to the conclusion that I was *French*?' Jessica laughed.

'So are you offended?' she asked. 'You know, that I thought you were gay?'

'Not at all. I'm offended that you thought Brett Scott would be my type. Believe me, if I were gay I'd have much better taste in men.' I glugged down some more water to cleanse my own put-out palette.

'Alright,' called Michael, back on his grind. 'Here's the plan: Fighting Fit have just arrived, so we're going to give them a few minutes to set up before we run through their performance, followed by the interview. In the meantime, Liam, if you could put that game back in its original place, that would be great.' Offering up an uncomfortable, I-was-only-joking chuckle, Liam returned the stolen item to the prize table, then, trying in vain to reassemble his fractured air of cool, walked across the studio floor and past the platform on which Jessica and I were slouched.

'Busted,' laughed Jessica under her breath, earning us both a darting, pissed off glare from our sticky-haired, even stickier-fingered colleague. 'Ooops,' she whispered, sinking back another inch and a half into her beanbag. I reached over and delivered a playful shove to the side of her squashy shell.

'Now *we're* busted.' Jessica rose to her feet.

'I've gotta go. So we're definitely cool?'

'Definitely,' I replied, throwing in a double thumbs-up for emphatic physical confirmation of our irrefutable coolness. I probably should have gone with the more reserved single thumber – while Jessica hadn't actually got busy with Brett Scott, she had, albeit drunkenly, been receptive to his distinctive brand of smarmy anti-charisma. But sod it, I thought; we all do stupid things when we're drunk (I'd once spent five minutes snogging a Bratz Magic Make-Up Styling Head in an all-night supermarket, although in fairness it *was* Sasha, in my opinion the fittest of the Bratz gang). Besides, it was worth it to see Jessica mirror my corny gesture before heading off to the production office, leaving me to watch a couple of burly gentlemen – one black with dreadlocks like gym ropes, the other white with a pearl light bulb for a head – setting up Fighting Fit's drum kit on the stage. The duo was just about done when a gentle crunch signalled the arrival of someone else's bum in the other beanbag.

'Ah, Richard,' observed Liam. 'Or should I call you Dick?'

'It's up to you. If Dick's what feels most natural coming out of your mouth ...' Liam's eyes narrowed and I could almost hear the cogs turning beneath his tufts and tramlines as he tried to work out whether or not I'd just insulted him. In the end he simply nodded towards the Fighting Fit lads, who, sauntering towards the stage, were busy greeting Fresh Coat crew members whilst simultaneously sweeping the studio floor with the frayed hems of their ill-fitting jeans.

'Takes me back, watching them,' reflected Liam. 'To my music days, I mean.'

'I'll bet,' I muttered. 'How many days were there, again?' Liam had some imagination comparing his short-lived musical career (which in reality had been more like a fortnight's work experience placement) to that of this week's guests. Fighting Fit's inoffensive brand of pretend punk wasn't to my taste, but Sam, Ben and Giles had already been in the game for two years, during which time they'd scored six number one singles and two number one albums, not to mention several high profile endorsement deals and their own range of wildly inaccurate dolls. Meanwhile, since sending an ominous warning shot to the rest of the pop world with a debut single that reached number eight, Liam had racked up a number twenty-six follow-up and an early elimination from *Celebrity Glass Blowing,* although in fairness he'd accomplished the whole lot in half a year before embarking on his current vocation.

'We all have pasts,' continued Liam, ignoring my crack. 'You know about my past; everyone does. But see, I know about your past, too. Here.' He leant over and handed me a folded up piece of paper. Suddenly, I felt my heart-rate quicken. What did Liam have on me? I wondered. I unfolded the paper and surveyed its contents.

'Tanning salons In South London?' Liam snatched the paper from my hand.

'*Obviously* I've given you the wrong thing, there.' He hurriedly folded it up again and crammed it back into the breast pocket of his skin-tight cowboy shirt. There followed a solid half-minute of creaking and crunching as, hand jammed first in one pocket of his jeans, then the other, Liam wriggled about in his beanbag in search of whatever it was he'd wanted to portentously present to me. He stood up and tried his two back pockets, but again came up with nothing.

'Shit. I must have left it in my dressing room,' he huffed. 'Don't go anywhere.' He stepped down from the platform and hurried across the floor, oblivious to the friendly 'Wotcha, Liam!' that came his way from one of the Fighting Fit boys.

I was busy pondering what undermined the crew's pretence at rock rebellion more – the fact that their devil-may-give-a-fuck haircuts had undoubtedly involved heavy salon price tags, long waits and, almost certainly, the use of tin foil, or that lead vocalist Giles had just sent the group's assistant off to find him a mozzarella and sun-dried tomato panini – when Liam returned brandishing a fresh sheet of A4. Keen to get this bizarre exercise over with, I held out my hand, only to be kept waiting a little bit longer as he folded this second piece of paper in half. Then into quarters, eighths and, finally, sixteenths.

'We all have pasts,' he recapped in the exact same tone that had already failed to make much of an impression. 'You know about my past; everyone does. But see, I know about your past, too. Here.' He slapped the paper into my palm, then continued to loom over me while I went about the laborious process of unfolding it. The thoroughly creased-up sheet, it eventually transpired, was a printout from an internet TV database, showing the details of *TTP*, the show that had given me my not-terribly-big break in the industry. There, beneath a brief synopsis (the programme was an 'irreverent late night sketch comedy show taking a sideways glance at the fast paced world of popular culture') and amongst a list of writers who contributed to the programme, was my name, helpfully highlighted with a fluorescent yellow marker.

'It's amazing what you can find out about someone by scouring the deepest darkest corners of the internet,' gloated Liam.

'Or alternatively by simply reading their CV.'

'Yeah, well I don't have access to that, do I? Kam keeps them locked up in her bottom drawer. Anyway, you're missing the point.'

'Yes, I am,' I agreed. Then, after about ten seconds of blank-faced silence from Liam, I asked, 'What *is* the point?'

'The *point*,' hissed Liam, 'is that *TTP* featured a number of jokes at my expense.'

'Oh. Well I don't really remember all the ...'

'I do,' interrupted Liam. 'I remember the snidey one-liners and I remember the stupid little sketches and I remember a full-blown piss-take of my song "Get Set" which showed me as a washed-up pop star working in a call centre.'

'Headset, telesales my best bet ... ' I sung under my breath. I'd forgotten about that one; it was classic. Well, unless you were Liam. 'Look,' I said, tapping at the printout with my finger. 'As you can see, there were eight writers on the show and I only did one series, so ...'

'So you're saying you weren't responsible for any of the jokes about me?' harried Liam. Now, this was a tricky one. Obviously, common sense demanded that I answer in the affirmative and hope that he believed me, but wow, now that I remembered it, I was really proud of that 'Headset' video – I'd written all the lyrics, kicked in with the choreography and even cameoed as one of the impostor Liam's fellow call centre workers-slash-backing dancers. Forced to make a decision, I let out a sigh and, against my better judgement, offered my interrogator an approximation of the truth. 'Look. I probably did write a couple of those jokes, but it was nothing personal. I didn't know you then, so it's not like ...' I was cut short by the sound of thrashing guitars, quickly joined by whining, cod-Californian accents as Fighting Fit launched into their latest three minutes of child-friendly gurn-rock, their elastic limbs colliding in mid air as they bounded about the small stage like gibbons in mating season. 'Well, anyway,' I shouted, 'if I contributed to hurting your feelings in any way back then, I'm genuinely sorry.'

'Hurt my feelings!' scoffed Liam. 'Yeah, right.' He sloped off, leaving me to reflect in bewilderment on what had just happened. It was confusing. I never wanted to upset anyone in life, so if Liam truly believed that I didn't care about hurting his feelings, he was wrong. Yet at the same time, there was undoubtedly a small part of me that really wouldn't have objected to hurting his face.

Jessica flew through the air, again. My eyes, as before, followed her as she climbed upwards, her outstretched arms assuming the role of wings while her pigtails leapt up above her

131

head, jostling to see which one of them could reach the highest before gravity found them out and pulled them both back down to Earth again. Their playful contest resumed as they accompanied Jessica on her next journey upwards, then her next one and the one after that.

This time, however, I wasn't observing Jessica's aerodynamics from a beanbag on the studio floor. Those plum seats were all occupied by the young audience members currently sat watching the week's edition of *The Hangout* unfold while I perched higher up than them – higher, even, than Jessica's jumping, jostling pigtails or the bright lights shining down on them – on a couch in a first floor green room at Artemis Studios. I'd already christened it The Players' Lounge the previous Saturday, and while that was probably overstating the room's level of luxury (complimentary chocolates and bottled water notwithstanding), its three couches, coffee table and big screen TV at least made the 'lounge' bit applicable, and as I didn't have one of those back at home, it seemed pretty damn luxurious to me. In fact, the only complaint I had about my surroundings concerned my cohabitants, two squealing, mini-skirted blonde girls in their early twenties who'd parked their arses on the couch opposite mine. I'd gauged from their loud, high-pitched conversation that they were the girlfriends of two thirds of Fighting Fit, who, now that Jessica had concluded her own bout of bouncing, were taking to the stage to jump, thrash, whine and gurn as if their energy levels alone were responsible for keeping every child in the audience alive.

Not that I was going to let this pair put a dampener on my morning. Unwrapping a sweet, I thought back to all the Saturdays I'd spent at home watching Jessica on a poor quality portable TV. Now look at me. I was ... well, technically I was still watching her on a TV, albeit a really nice big flat-screen, High Definition one, but I was doing so in the same building that she was actually in, and with the privilege of being able to drop by her dressing room and say hi afterwards.

I popped the sweet into my mouth and contemplated how I

was going to spend my afternoon. Maybe I'd go to the cinema and catch a matinee, or perhaps I'd mainline exorbitant amounts of caffeine and sugar whilst flicking through a stack of freshly purchased magazines. More than likely I'd do both, but there was one thing I didn't feel like doing and that was writing anymore of *Crushed*. Maybe not for a while, actually. In fact, I was starting to feel that perhaps I should give up on it altogether. Giving up on something, in my experience, could be extremely liberating. I still remembered, for instance, the immense feeling of freedom I felt at thirteen, when I gave up karate lessons after twice failing my blue belt exam. Had I just passed my second Dan black belt, I swear I could not have felt prouder and more at peace with myself than I did at that moment. It was like an even better version of the feeling I'd experienced five years earlier, when I'd packed in my increasingly joyless keyboard lessons (although for the record, I had both 'Guantanamera' and 'Dancing On The Ceiling' down pat, chord changes and all, so by that time there was precious little left for my teacher to impart to me).

Anyway, whatever impetus I had when I'd started writing *Crushed* no longer appeared to be with me. If a psychiatrist, rather than two shrieking undercover girlfriends, had been sitting opposite me as I sprawled on the sofa, he'd probably have surmised that, in his expensive, overvalued opinion, the project was my way of justifying my failed encounters with women. That, by spinning my romantic ineptitude into art (or at least a succession of words on a computer screen), I was conveniently absenting myself from doing something practical about the problem. I'd have responded by giving him a slow, sarcastic hand clap and requesting that he tell me something I didn't already know if he expected to be paid for this session with more than just a couple of miniature Mars bars and a glass of fizzy water.

My quest for Jess, on the other hand, would surely have had that same shrink nodding in approval while scribbling enthusiastic notes about 'vast improvement' and 'giant steps' on his clipboard. This was positive. This was pro-active. This was the brainchild of a man – alright, a nutjob – genuinely looking to rebound from all past setbacks by snatching up the big prize. I wasn't sat hunched over a laptop, I was positioned with just a carpet, a floor and a studio lighting rig between me and Jessica George, who right now was supplementing her trampoline skills by joining Liam on the sofa for a post-performance grilling of the slightly sweaty Fighting Fit lads.

'Natalie from Didcot wants to know if any of you have girlfriends,' relayed Jessica, reading from a card in her hand. 'Let's start with you, Ben.'

'No, to be honest with you, we don't really have time for girlfriends,' mumbled Ben into his chest.

'Oh, well, I suppose you won't have time for a shag tonight,' noted one of the girls sarcastically. It was great that they felt able to express themselves so freely around me.

When the show finished, I made my way down the stairs, Fighting Fit's latest catchy-like-Chlamydia ditty lodged firmly in my head. Pushing through some double doors on the ground floor, I was wondering whether anything was capable of dislodging it before the end of the day when I noticed Jessica, head poked around her dressing room door, concluding a conversation with Denise.

'Rich!' she called out as Denise walked towards me. 'Come and meet my boyfriend.'

Boom. The song disappeared from my head and I stopped in my tracks. Denise was still moving, but she was doing so in slow motion, her every step transformed into a Godzilla-like thud that seemed to reverberate through the corridor, shaking the framed photos on the wall. And so it ended here. The whole stupid scheme came to its sorry conclusion on this spot, in this corridor. And all it had taken was one word. The B word. Why hadn't Jessica told me she had a boyfriend? More to the point, why hadn't I asked her? Why hadn't I woven the question into one of our conversations instead of banging on about gilets and verruca socks and deep-fried Scottish child murderers? Was it possible she'd just hooked up with someone in the past few days? Oh, for fuck's sake, what did it matter when they'd hooked up? The point was, it was a wrap for me. A pathetic end to a pathetic plan.

'You'll love him,' promised Denise while the world around me returned to regular speed.

'Come on, Rich!' Jessica beckoned me in. Oh, well, I thought. Might as well make this official. Let's at least hope this dude wasn't doing up his flies when I walked in. Was Jessica even fully dressed? All I could see was her head and her impatiently flapping hand. All told, this was looking like it could feasibly surpass the Red Button wrap party in terms of sheer humiliation and heart-crushing disappointment.

I took a deep breath and stepped into the dressing room, bracing myself for a strapping, tousle-haired pretty boy in an extra-extra-medium T-shirt. Instead, a young blonde-haired lad in a wheelchair sat looking admiringly at Jessica through thick, coke bottle glasses, his small, fragile frame swaddled in a bright red fleece jacket and thick brown corduroy trousers. 'Richard,' began Jessica, placing a hand on the lad's shoulder, 'this is Josh.' I let out a huge, cathartic laugh, then, realising that it probably didn't look good to be guffawing at a boy in a wheelchair, quickly plastered a polite, pleased-to-meet-you smile onto my face.

'Hi, Josh. Did you enjoy the show?' Josh shifted in his seat and lowered his corn-coloured curls before speaking in a shy, quiet voice.

'I liked it when Jessica was on the trampoline.'

'Oh yeah? That was my favourite part, too. You give good bounce, Jess.' Jessica smiled and gave me an impromptu curtsy.

'Why, thank you.'

'So, Josh, have you ever been on one?' I asked. Jessica looked at me oddly and I realised what I'd just said. 'Er, I mean one of these backstage visits. Have you ever been on one before?'

'Oh, Josh comes to see me a lot,' said Jessica. 'Isn't that

135

right, Josh?' Josh nodded vigorously, his jumbled, jagged teeth posseing-up to form a broad, disorderly grin. 'Listen, Rich, Josh's mum is outside making a phone call and I'm desperate to use the little girls' room.' She squeezed both her palms and her thighs together to illustrate the severity of her predicament, 'Could you be a sweetie and hang out here with Josh for a minute or two?'

'Uh, yeah, of course. No problem.'

'OK, great. Back in a mo, Josh.' Jessica waved at her young pal and headed off for the ladies'. I smiled pleasantly at Josh, throwing in an affable raise of my eyebrows for extra value. Having exhausted this killer combo at such an early stage, I then proceeded to scratch the back of my head whilst scanning the mostly blank walls of Jessica's dressing room, less in search of inspiration, more as a way of filling up a chunk of time. It soon became clear, however, that a baby-sitting technique comprising only head-scratching and eye-shifting wasn't going to do either myself or Josh a lot of good, and that I therefore had no choice but to attempt to strike up a conversation with my fellow VIP and mate-of-Jessica.

'So,' I began awkwardly, 'how old are you, Josh?'

'Eleven.'

'You're good friends with Jessica, then?' Josh shook his head and sent a short blast of air through his nostrils.

'What was *that* about just then?' he asked. I could have been mistaken, but his tone sounded, frankly, a little aggressive.

'What was *what* about? When?

'Oh, don't give me that crap,' hissed Josh. 'That shit about Jessica giving good bounce. You were cock blocking me.' I looked down at the cute, curly haired little lad in the wheelchair. Then I looked around at the walls I'd already given the once-over. Then I looked at Josh some more. And then, finally, I spoke.

'Did you just accuse me of *cock blocking* you?'

'Yep,' replied Josh without hesitation.

'You're eleven years old,' I pointed out.

'I've still got a cock,' reasoned Josh rather sourly. 'Maybe you got yours later in life, or maybe you're still waiting for one.' I scanned my surroundings once more, this time looking for a hidden camera.

'Let me get this straight,' I said, unable to feel one hundred percent certain with what my ears seemed to be telling me. 'You think you've got a chance with Jessica?'

'More than you,' he snorted. 'We've already established you don't have a cock.' Once again, I paused to play Josh's words back in my head before continuing. Of all her adoring viewers, why oh why had Jessica been suckered into forming a bond with this venomous little toad?

'So this is quite the scam you're running here, pretending to be all sweet and innocent.' I leant in a little and turned up the heat. 'Do you even *need* this wheelchair?' I could almost hear Josh's blood boiling the second the words left my lips.

'I'm paralysed from the waist down, you insensitive prick.' His face was now as red as his fleece, but I wasn't finished yet.

'Well, technically, if the term "insensitive prick" is applicable to either of us ...' I know, I know. It was an awful, wicked, indefensible thing to say and the thought shouldn't even have flitted through my sick, depraved mind, much less passed my lips. Still, it was either dispense that off-colour crack or wheel Jessica's little pal out of the building and into the oncoming Wembley traffic, and the crack seemed like the lesser of two evils. Either way, it was now Josh's turn to look disbelieving.

'Did you just make fun of my disability?' he gasped, his eyeballs swelling up to fill his formidable lenses. He was quite intelligent, I had to give him that. I was certain that not every eleven-year-old would have understood my (literally) below-the-belt innuendo. Then again, I still held out hope that not every eleven-year-old was au fait with the term 'cock blocking', so what did I know?

'Uh, yeah,' I mumbled, looking down at my feet and

feeling at least a little guilty. 'I'm sorry, I shouldn't have ...'

'Don't apologise to me,' Josh snapped, his eyes retreating into sharp slits. 'Just give me a tenner.'

'A tenner?' I balked. 'You expect me to give you a tenner for that remark?' The devil child fixed me with a sly grin.

'Nope. I expect you to give me a tenner not to tell Jessica about that remark.' He held out his clammy, blackmailing little hand. Shaking my head, I delved into my pocket, pulled out my wallet and reluctantly withdrew a crisp ten pound note. I handed it to Josh, bottom lip tucked firmly under my front teeth before I said something that landed me with a further financial penalty. At any rate, however, the door opened before I even had a chance to rack up another fine.

'I'm back,' chirped Jessica. I thrust my wallet back into my pocket while Josh shoved his ill-gotten gains down the front of his jacket.

'Hiiiiiiii,' we responded in unison.

'You two chaps getting along alright?'

'Like a house on fire,' I reported. 'This is a, er, fine young friend you've got here.'

'Boyfriend,' corrected Jessica. Josh shot a sickening little smile at me, then reached into the pocket of his fleece.

'Jessica, I've got something for you,' he revealed in that meek little voice of his, handing her a piece of A4 paper folded into quarters.

'Oh, wow. Thank you.' Jessica enunciated each word whilst she unfolded the paper. 'Ohhh, look at this,' she cooed, voice wavering slightly. 'Is that me ... and you?' Josh nodded coyly.

'It's us on our wedding day,' he explained, squirming a little in his mobile throne of evil. I wanted to be sick. On him.

'Rich, look at this.' Jessica held up Josh's masterpiece, which depicted a bespectacled, tuxedo-wearing young fellow sat in a wheelchair whilst holding the hand of a smiley woman with flowing dark hair, big eye lashes and a white dress. The crayon version of Josh was smiling too, although I read it more as his trademark punch-provoking smirk-cum-demonic grin. In the background, a church steeple reached up towards the bright yellow sun that was busy rounding off the picture's trilogy of smiles. Attached to Josh's wheelchair were a 'just married' sign and a string of tin cans, which, I begrudgingly had to admit, were a couple of nice touches – although the picture as a whole still showed a horrible ignorance of human anatomy and basic perspective. 'Aaaaawww, this is lovely, Josh,' gushed Jessica, bending down and throwing her arms around Prick-asso. I imagined Josh was getting a pretty sweet view of Jessica's chest through those inch-thick specs of his. Meanwhile, I was getting a perfect view of Josh's small but distinctly upright middle finger, which he'd kindly hoisted up behind Jessica's back. All in all, I'd had more than enough of this young man.

'Alright, well listen, Jess, I've got somewhere I need to be, so I'm going to leave you alone with your charming young boyfriend.' Jessica emerged from the embrace, hair slightly ruffled.

'Husband,' she corrected, holding aloft the marital scene.

'Husband,' I affirmed, studiously avoiding eye contact with the little fucker.

Kam's elbows were on her desk, her palms were clamped against her temples and her forehead was facing the six stapled sheets of A4 laid down in front of her. Stood at her side, I had no idea whether she was immersed in deep concentration or wobbling on the edge of despair. She hadn't laughed yet, despite being on the sixth and final page, but I took solace in knowing this wasn't anything out of the ordinary. With Kam, I'd already learned, you were looking for a wry half-smile (her equivalent of a gut-busting, eye-watering, thigh-slapping fit of uncontrollable laughter) as validation, yet with her face hidden from view, I had no choice but to wait until she unclamped those hands from those temples, lifted that forehead and turned to deliver the verdict.

'Yep, that should work,' she predicted, and at last I let go of the air I'd been holding hostage in my chest. It was late Wednesday afternoon and I'd just finished feverishly bashing out a short-notice sketch assignment following an emergency meeting an hour earlier. You see, Aniston, who were supposed to appear on *The Hangout* that coming Saturday, had been forced to pull out due to a scheduling conflict (presumably they'd been tipped off about a sale on hooker boots at Miss Selfridge), but had, by way of compensation, agreed to let the show instead record some stuff with them during Thursday morning's Docklands-based rehearsals for their live show at the Waterfront Arena. Specifically, this meant a backstage tour and interview and, to help pad things out a little bit more, an extra special location episode of *Cash and Carrie*. This sketch was to be a doubly star-studded affair as, in addition to Aniston themselves, I had been told I could equip my already glittering spoof franchise with a cameo appearance from Carmen Clark, the twenty-one-year-old British R&B singer who, despite routinely ducking accusations of divadom from the tabloids, was the girls' vocally superior support act on their UK tour.

The premise of my hastily conceived sketch was that, with less than an hour to go until they hit the stage, Aniston had had a set of key outfits half-inched from their dressing room. Naturally, rather than notify the relevant authorities before sourcing alternative attire for the routine just to be on the safe side, the girls had pinned all of their hopes on Cash and Carrie tracking down the culprits and returning the stolen garments ahead of showtime. Hilarity, as you might imagine, ensued. Less predictably, so did an appearance by yours truly, as, in order to keep costs down, the four parts not being filled by celebrities were to be essayed by myself and my fellow classically untrained thespians Yeti, Greg and a likeable enough Fresh Coat runner called Tim. Only one of us was going to get roughed up by Jessica, though.

I ran down the corridor, puffing and panting. The puffing and panting had started out fake, but they were getting ever more authentic as, holdall in hand, I dashed across the same stretch of floor for the fifth time in a row. Hot on my tail with, respectively, the steadicam and the boom mic, Yeti and Tim were also slightly short of breath as the door at the end of the corridor opened once again and, clad in a brown leather jacket and blonde afro wig, Jessica stepped into my path brandishing her I.D. card. The effect was still very much *Coffy* meets Bet Lynch.

'Police!' she barked, and I dropped the holdall in surprise (the surprise part was actually getting more difficult to feign). 'Hold it right there, mister.' I squinted at her card.

'That's a coupon for money off toilet rolls.' On the previous take, I'd be unable to resist replacing 'toilet rolls' with 'Canasten Ultra', but with the clock ticking on the team's Docklands mission I was now professionalism personified. Jessica, too, was hitting her marks with precision, squinting at the card for long enough to accommodate the studio laughter that would doubtless greet the mention of a lavatory-related product (trust me: I'd got the hang of giving my new audience exactly what it wanted).

'Oh, yeah,' conceded Jessica. 'I must remember to pick those up on the way home.'

'OK. Well I guess I'll just be ...'

'Not so fast, scumbag!' she snapped. 'I know you've got Aniston's outfits in that bag.'

'What? No! The bag's full of ...' Jessica grabbed me by the lapels of my jacket and pulled me in so close to her that I could feel her wiry blonde curls brush against my forehead.

'SHUT UP!' she yelled, 'Or I'll wallpaper this corridor with your face!' The combination of the tickling and Jessica's super-serious line reading had tripped me up on at least two takes, but I reckoned I was going to get through it this time if I could just maintain my composure through Jessica's next command. 'Mister, you better open that bag up right now,' she ordered. There. I'd done it. Now, leaning down to unzip my holdall, I knew that I had a couple of seconds to wrestle my burgeoning smirk into submission before I had to face her again.

'Biscuits?' exclaimed Jessica. 'Who *are* you?' I rose back to 'fro-level.

'I'm Carmen Clark's personal assistant,' I revealed in the tremulous, weedy and, for no real reason, slightly Northern voice I'd been perfecting since my experimental second take. 'She gave me exactly two minutes to go out and get her twenty boxes of assorted biscuits.' The door swung open and Carmen stepped into the corridor brandishing a stopwatch. Her smooth black hair was wrapped around rollers, her petite frame smothered by a thick white towelling dressing gown.

'Two minutes, three seconds,' she observed, her voice dripping with fury and her pretty features tensed up like a clenched fist in a vodka-fuelled high street catfight. 'You're fired.' Tucking her stopwatch into her dressing gown pocket, she peered into the unzipped holdall, then leant down and pulled out the uppermost box of biscuits. From over my shoulder, Yeti zoomed in on Carmen's face as her eyes darted over the contents of the box, then pulled out again to capture her explosive reaction. 'These have got custard creams!' she fumed, raising the offending biscuit box above her rollers. 'I told you, NO! CUSTARD! CREAMS!' With each of those three words, she belted me over the head with the box. By the time she'd hit 'CREAMS!' for the fifth time (my fifteenth smack on the head overall – actually, make that sixteenth, as, arms starting to flag, Tim had accidentally dropped the boom mic on my head during the last take), I was beginning to wonder whether the rattling sound I was hearing was being made by broken biscuits or fragments of my battered skull. Stickler for authenticity that I was, I'd insisted against emptying the box so that the sound of my bonce being bashed with a Fox's Big Value Variety Pack rang – or rather crunched – true. That, though, was back when I deludedly thought we'd nail the scene in three takes tops.

'And ... cut!' called Yeti. 'Perfect. That's a keeper.'

'Are you alright?' asked Carmen, reaching up to stroke the top of my abused head. She certainly didn't seem much like the spoilt diva image she was gamely sending up.

'I'm fine,' I assured her. 'I'm just glad it wasn't a *tin* of biscuits.'

'Thank fuck that's done,' cheered Greg, appearing from around the corner clad in the same outfit as Yeti and Tim. 'I've got major chafing going on here.'

It was a line, I sensed, deployed by the big man more for comic effect than out of any genuine discomfort. While the transparent macs being modelled by the lads weren't the most comfortable-looking garments I'd ever laid eyes upon, the white sports bras they had on underneath, co-ordinated to perfection with their miniskirts and knee-high boots, at least ensured that their nipples weren't pressed up against the clear plastic. That said, Greg's decision to button up his mac meant that the rings of fat comprising his formidable belly most assuredly *were* pressed up against the plastic, his attempt to tuck in his distinctly un-Aniston-like midriff instead lending it the appearance of a boa constrictor stuffed into a goldfish bowl already containing the sweepings from a barber's floor.

I must admit, I'd been nervous about telling Greg he had to dress up in the outfit popularised by Aniston in their 'Love Monsoon' video (I'd been nervous about telling Yeti and Tim, too, but at least neither of them looked like they could force-feed me my own kneecaps), but it turned out that Greg quite fancied himself as an actor, specifically a comic one, and was savvy enough to realise that comic parts didn't come much juicier than that of a big hairy guy in sexy women's wear and a see-through mac. Primed for a role set to make him the Laurence Olivier of hirsute, overweight extras, he'd bantered away with me during the car-ride over, the two of us bonding in the back seat of Yeti's battered Vauxhall Astra while Tim fiddled with the radio. I felt like a tremendous weight had been lifted from my shoulders (and also that I'd dodged the threat of a tremendous weight hitting my face), and, if anything, my unforeseen alliance with Gregory had edged out my rough treatment at the hands of both Jessica and the biscuit-brandishing Carmen as the morning's most enjoyable experience. It made me feel as warm and fuzzy as, well, the big man's PVC-wrapped stomach.

Even Liam was refusing to make a fuss about the baggy, chunky-knit cardigan that drowned his prized – if not actually very impressive – biceps under a tide of oatmeal-coloured wool or the sticky-backed lamb chop sideboards which, against all odds, actually pushed his 'do to dizzying new levels of ludicrousness. Earlier, I'd overheard Leah from Aniston pointing out to her giggling bandmates how 'Liam and Leah has a wicked ring to it', so I thought I could guess the reason for his sunny disposition, but in fairness we were all reaping the benefits, as Liam had been knocking down his scenes like the consummate pro – and not merely those involving the fair-haired, thin-voiced threesome. Before I'd embarked on the first of my sprints down this corridor, he'd nailed a shot in which, hot on my tail, he'd run past the three waterproofed crooks before giving an exaggerated comedy double-take and – yes! – stepping back to ask the supremely shifty-looking gang which way I'd gone. Perhaps even more gratifyingly, at least from my point of view, he hadn't at any stage halted filming to dramatically hit me with a printout of my past misdemeanours in the writing world.

With *Cash and Carrie* in the can (the comic denouement, which saw the three eventually apprehended thieves forced to perform on stage in their stolen gear by way of punishment, had been filmed first by *The Hangout*'s stalwart cameraman Graham to accommodate Aniston's sound-check) and Carmen congratulated, the boys hurried off to record Liam's backstage pow-wow with Leah, Holly and Martine. For Jessica and I, though, our morning out at the Waterfront Arena was up. I had to return to Fresh Coat HQ to finish up the week's script, while Jessica was all set for an afternoon interview-stroke-audition with the producers of *Wow! Voyager*. Except that, as we headed for the exit, it transpired that she wasn't all set at all.

'This is going to be bad,' she forecast. 'They want me to do a five minute, scripted piece to camera. You know, about a holiday destination.'

'So?' I responded with a shrug. 'You'll read something off an autocue. You can do that in your sleep.'

'That part, yeah,' agreed Jessica. 'But see, when I say scripted piece, I mean scripted by *me*.'

'Oh.'

'Yeah. I guess it proves that I have a genuine interest in travelling. It's a smart, journalistic show.'

'Oooh, a smart, journalistic show,' I teased as we exited the building. 'So, you're not happy with your script?'

'What script?' asked Jessica. I stopped in my tracks.

'You didn't think to maybe get something – anything – down on paper?' Jessica looked down at the pointed toes of her boots.

'I would have worked on it last night but I was out.'

'Out travelling?'

'I went for a Chinese,' she offered with a timid grin. I couldn't tell whether this was intended as a travel-themed joke or not. I wasn't even sure whether Jessica knew, but it did, on the other hand, seem pretty obvious that she was fishing for my help here. I probably should have felt irritated or annoyed or at the very least irked. I probably would have, too, except that a) clad in a clingy, red-and-pink striped cardie and with her dark locks unleashed from beneath Carrie's spherical blonde bubble perm, Jessica was positively glowing against our grey East London backdrop and b) I was too busy being struck by my own luminous flash of inspiration.

'D'you like Egypt?' I asked. It wasn't a chat-up line I generally had much call to use.

'I suppose,' ventured Jessica. 'I mean, I don't know. I mean ... What? Are you taking me?' I pointed up the street, my finger carving out a path through our nondescript surroundings.

'Not quite, but if you're willing to walk with me just

145

round the corner there, to the Red Button Tower Of Power, I can furnish you with an informative but accessible, pocket-sized and fully illustrated book on Egypt. More importantly, it comes with a couple of free A4 sheets of Egypt-themed puns, quips and links from yours truly.' Jessica looked puzzled.

'Why would you have all this?'

'You never saw *Hieromaniacs*, Red Button's pyramid-based adventure game show?'

'No.'

'Is the right answer. It never made it to air, it was bloody awful. Don't worry, though, the puns are great. So what d'you reckon?' Jessica's stripy shoulders pushed her loose curls upwards.

'OK. Sure.'

As we set off on our mission, I reflected on my morning's acting work.

'You know what? I never knew that being repeatedly smacked over the head with a box of biscuits could be so much fun.'

'Blame the writer,' suggested Jessica.

'No, really,' I insisted. 'It was great.' Jessica reached into her handbag and pulled out a small pot of lip balm.

'I can't always tell if you're being serious or not,' she said, unscrewing the lid and gently circling her fingertip in the cherry-scented balm.

'Yeah, I get that quite a lot,' I admitted. 'It's a bit of a curse. It saddens me to know that I'll never be able to tell a girl she looks spellbinding and have her take me seriously.' Jessica massaged the balm into her lips and pressed them together.

'Spellbinding? Alright, now you're definitely being sarcastic.'

'No. I'm not.'

'Oh. Well, I can see how "spellbinding" would be a tough one for you to pull off.'

'Yeah,' I sighed. 'Maybe I'll try "enchanting" first.'

'I'd start with "half-decent" and work your way up from

there,' said Jessica, screwing the lid back onto her lip balm and returning it to her handbag. I laughed, and we continued a few metres up the road before Jessica, lips fully rehydrated and protected against the elements, spoke again. 'So, d'you know any girls like that?'

'Like what? Half-decent?'

'No. Enchanting. Spellbinding.'

'I don't know,' I answered, a little bit surprised by the question. 'Uh, maybe. Yeah, I guess I've known a couple. Plus, sometimes I'll just notice a girl who seems to fit that category.'

'And?'

'And what?'

'What happens when you notice a spellbinding girl?'

'Um, not much, usually. I mean, it's not like they ever notice *me*.'

'Awww, that's sad.'

'No, no. I don't want them to notice me when I'm in the tree outside their bedroom window under the cover of night. Actually, it's kind of imperative that they don't.'

'OK, I know this one,' enthused Jessica, squeezing her fingertips into her palms and shaking her wrists in the style of an overexcited game show contestant. '*Not* serious. I think. I *hope*.'

We walked onwards. A few metres ahead of us on the other side of the road, a huge billboard somehow managed the impressive feat of wrestling my attention from the top-of-her-cuteness-game Jessica. On it, a pretty, mixed-race woman with a buoyant, bouncing head of corkscrew curls was captured in profile, eyebrows raised, eyes wide open (sorry, *eyebrow* raised and *eye* wide open – the other side of her face could have burnt to a crisp in a freak chip pan accident for all I knew) and lips parted in amazement as a rainbow of different coloured waves washed over her smooth, sculpted cheekbone and flawless forehead.

Relinquishing my gaze, I noticed a woman walking towards us hand-in-hand with two young girls. As our two parties drew nearer, the children looked wide-eyed at Jessica then conferred excitedly with each other across their mum's legs until, game-plan settled, they flapped their free paws about whilst calling Jessica's name. By now, the penny had clearly dropped with the girls' mum, who smiled and informed Jessica, somewhat superfluously, 'They love you, they do.' Jessica smiled back, then used both hands to wave in exaggerated, circular motions to her young fans.

'I see you went for the double-handed wax-on, wax-off wave, there,' I noted as the girls cooed and cor-ed their way up the street.

'Hey, it did the job.'

'I'll say. The kids were looking at you like that.' I pointed across the road to the woman with the Technicolor kisser.

'Oh, right,' scoffed Jessica. 'Of course they were.'

'No, seriously. Your star power was actually washing over their awestruck faces in the form of a magical rainbow.' Jessica tutted and rolled her eyes.

'Just don't bother telling me I look spellbinding.'

'Ahhhhh, I've done it again,' I lamented, slapping my forehead as the aggressively plain architecture of the Red Button headquarters shambled into view. 'When will I ever learn? Seriously, though, the school holidays must be a nightmare for you.'

'No, the kids are fine, mainly. I mean, except for the odd cocky little sod. It's the men who shout filthy comments and the teenage girls who give you the evils because they've already prejudged what you're like.'

'Yeah,' I sighed as we stopped to cross the road, 'but people do that to me, too.' Jessica gave me a funny look.

'The rude comments or the prejudging?'

'Both.' We paused at the kerb to let a couple of cars go past. 'The other day some guy in a white van yelled "wanker" at me out of his window. And he'd only seen the back of my head when he shouted it, so it wasn't like he'd even made an educated call based on my face.'

148

We crossed over the road and into the Red Button courtyard. My heart was moving pretty quickly now, but in a good way; an excited, bring-it-on-now kind of way. Not that I was letting my excitement show. Nope, an air of do-this-every-day cool was going to be essential upon hitting those coffee-stained carpet tiles on the first floor. Actually, never mind the carpet tiles, it was going to be essential *now*, because I'd just noticed Beth heading to the Red Button entrance from reception, located in the building next door. Oddly, she seemed to be struggling with a cocoon-like object roughly her own size. Getting nearer, it dawned on me that the object giving her so much trouble was, in fact, a still, stiff body whose lifeless limbs and torso were mummified in bubble wrap. Its bulbous head was on full display, though, and as Jessica and I got closer still, its glazed black eyes stared at me from atop high, tight-skinned cheekbones. Its pallid, shiny complexion was a sickly-looking hue midway between green and grey. Pausing for rest and, presumably, a bit of a rethink on how best to transport the thing, Beth was just propping the body against the front of the building when Jessica and I rolled up behind her.

'Bethany,' I said cheerily. Appearing at Red Button with Jessica already had me in a good (if somewhat nervous) mood, but to be greeted by the sight of Beth wrestling with a fibreglass alien was the thick, luxurious icing on a particularly sweet, moist and decadent cake. Beth turned around. She could barely have looked more surprised if Mulder and Scully themselves had interrupted her close encounter, but she quickly slapped a look of nonchalance onto her flustered features.

'Oh, hi,'

'Beth, this is Jessica. Jessica, Beth.'

'Hi,' said Jessica, flashing her pearly whites from between her freshly balmed lips.

'Hi,' responded Beth. 'Good to meet you.'

'Aren't you going to introduce us to your new fella?' I enquired, nodding towards the bald, bug-eyed gent with his bubble-wrapped back against the wall. Delivered affably, this was nevertheless the type of line that was traditionally touch-and-go with Beth, who had a tendency to be a tad humourless when it came to cracks about her love life, or, come to think of it, any crack of which I was the author. Still, maybe in the struggle the alien had managed to get in a few ray gun blasts to her head, because it seemed suspiciously – disconcertingly, even – like Beth was taking my remark in the light-hearted spirit in which it was intended.

'This chap's going to be helping us promote our new show *Gross Encounters*,' she explained, 'and as the lift's broken again, you can get to know him better as you help me carry him up the stairs. You take the head, I'll take the feet.' She fixed me with a grin, and, as I grabbed my designated end of the alien, I wondered what this rare sighting of her gums was disguising. Was she irritated to see me arrive out of the blue with Jessica at my side, or was she trying to mask the fact that, deep down, she was secretly impressed? Actually, it was probably both. She was probably irritated to find herself impressed; peeved with the revelation that the pathetic fool she'd rolled her eyes at on so many occasions wasn't so pathetic and foolish after all. 'What's the matter?' she asked. 'Are you too big to remember the security code?'

'No, no, I've got it,' I assured her, punching those magic four numbers into the keypad and deftly holding the door ajar with my backside. 'I just assumed you'd have had it changed before I came back.'

'Yeah, that was a missed opportunity,' conceded Beth with another grin. Maybe I was mistaken. Was it possible that my absence had made her heart grow, if not fonder, then at least a shade more tolerant?

'You go first,' I instructed Jessica, gallantly bouncing the door open for her with my bum. 'The stairs are through that door just there. It's the first floor; we'll be right behind you.' Jessica squeezed past me and through the door to the stairwell, holding it open while I wedged my backwards-moving body into the door frame. Jessica had rounded the first short flight of stairs when Beth came to a stop a mere three steps into our journey upwards. The alien's head was the weightiest part of its not-really-that-heavy frame, so I was slightly surprised that the wiry Beth was already out of puff. Except it turned out that she wasn't.

'So what's this visit about, then?' she asked under her breath.

'We've come to get my Egypt book. Jess is auditioning for a holiday ...'

'Is this your way of getting back at Joy?' interrupted Beth. I didn't know what to say, but before I could say anything, Jessica, who'd just conquered the second flight of steps, filled the conversational void.

'Are you guys alright?' She called down.

'Beth just got poked in the eye,' I called back. 'Turns out aliens have got really pointy toes.' Beth employed both of her perfectly functional eyes in shooting daggers at me, while Jessica peered over the hand rail.

'Are you alright, Beth?'

'She's fine,' I assured her hastily. 'The other eye's working perfectly.'

'D'you want me to hold the door open?'

'Er, no, I can manage the door. Go on in. Mine's the first desk you see, right next to the coffee area. You can't miss it.'

'You certainly can't,' agreed Beth.

'OK,' Jess murmured timidly. I waited until I heard the door shutting before returning to Beth's out-of-nowhere interrogation.

'Getting back at Joy for *what*, exactly?' I asked, forcing Beth back into motion as, holding the alien's head up so as to clear the railings, I reversed around the corner

'Getting back at her for not fancying you,' replied Beth matter-of-factly. Now it was my turn to put our ascent on pause.

'If she doesn't fancy me,' I said, tersely enunciating each word, 'then how is this getting back at her?'

'Whatever,' sighed Beth. We started up again.

'Thanks for bringing up your little theory at this particular time,' I huffed while we lugged the alien up the remaining flight of stairs. 'Jessica's probably going to be feeling weird right now standing at my desk.' With one hand holding the alien by his bubble-studded collar, I pushed open the door and, with Beth in tow, forged headfirst across the office floor. There, at my desk, I saw Jessica. Or rather I saw several Jessicas. In fact, quite a lot of Jessicas. All of them were smiling – or at least looking happy – except for one. The life-sized one in the middle, who instead looked shocked, confused and frankly a teensy bit scared. Oh, shit, I thought, dropping the alien's head against the floor. My desktop decor.

'I can manage from here,' reckoned Beth, and she was going to have to, as, leaving otherworldly cranium on carpet, I walked, in a daze, to my desk. I felt short of breath, as if someone had just punched me in the stomach. Then, before my respiratory system had even had a chance to get back on its feet, I felt as if someone had just punched me in the arm. Which they had.

'Gotcha, Rich!' exclaimed Joy, materialising from out of thin air – or at least the break area – with her World's Greatest Aunt mug. Blow landed, she took a sip of her pink brew, then turned to face the bewildered TV presenter at her side. 'Sorry, Jessica. We were just trying to wind Richard up. Every time we run into him he can't stop going on about how nice you are. We always say it's like he's in love with you or something, so, in preparation for him coming back in a few weeks we, er, started compiling this.' She threw open her arms and proudly surveyed the gallery.

'I found the one with the crocodile,' chimed Eddie from over by the printer.

'Obviously we didn't know you were coming,' continued Joy, 'but as your presence here has only added immeasurably to Rich's embarrassment, I'd like to personally thank you.' She grabbed Jessica's hand and began to shake it vigorously while I watched, my body as rigid with fear as Jessica's arm was limp with stunned disbelief. At first, her face remained equally lifeless, her dark almond eyes as wide yet blank as the fibreglass alien's and her full-lipped mouth only half as expressive as its thin, functional slit. Then, after this (literally) shaky start, something happened. Something peculiar and a little extraterrestrial in its own right. It was if Joy had managed to send some kind of electric current up the arm of her ailing patient, because suddenly Jessica's eyes sparked into life and a smile began to flicker across her lips.

'You are looking a little bit flushed, Richard.' She placed her well-shaken hand, freshly released from Joy's resuscitating grip, on my left cheek. It was true that I'd felt, in all senses, a lot cooler as recently as two minutes earlier.

'Oooh, hold on, I think this one's actually hotter,' marvelled Joy, eclipsing the other side of my burning face with her palm. In different circumstances, being sandwiched between Jessica and Joy as they pawed my face might have been a fantasy made flesh, or at least it would have if, for the sake of, er, realism, my fantasies weren't divided by a velvet rope into those involving celebrities and those involving normal people. At this moment, though, I was actually willing the temperature in my cheeks to raise up just a couple of degrees more so that the spontaneous combustion of my head might bring an end to my squirming and – by way of posthumous revenge – leave Jessica and Joy with the arduous and unenviable task of cleaning charred flesh from my keyboard (Red Button's so-called cleaners didn't even wipe dust off the desks so it wasn't like they'd do it).

'This is my friend Joy,' I informed Jessica, desperately hoping that a formal introduction would bring down the curtain on the girls' burgeoning comedy double act. 'As you can see, she's quite the practical joker.'

'Hi, Joy.' Jessica removed her hand from my still-glowing cheek while Joy beamed back at her.

'Hi, Jessica. Right now I'm gonna leave Richard to cool

off, but it was nice to meet you.' Joy gave me a parting four-fingered double-tap on the cheek, then took her hand and headed back to her neck of the woods, her ponytail bouncing gently against her neck.

'Alright, that's us done,' I said. I could feel every eye in the office looking at me and my friend from behind their monitors.

'Haven't you forgotten something, Richard?' asked Jessica. What, I thought, besides the fact that my desk was a psychopath's shrine to her? Jessica held out her palm. 'Um, the Egypt stuff?' Ah, yes, the Egypt stuff. I slid open the middle drawer beneath my desk, only to be instantly greeted by a picture of Jessica in a white cotton vest. I'd taken that one down from my gallery after Beth argued that the vague suggestion of Jessica's nipples prodding at the form-fitting fabric amounted to sexual harassment on my part.

'Guys,' I announced, waving the offending picture above my head at my still-gawking audience, 'this stuff on my desk is one thing, but going in my drawers is taking it a bit too far.' I found the book and handed it to Jessica. No sooner had it touched her fingertips than Eddie, arm wrapped around Red Button's new intergalactic employee, arrived at her side to volunteer his expertise.

'I studied Egyptology a few years back,' he revealed, patting his extraterrestrial pal on his bubble-wrapped chest. 'You know him and his mates built the pyramids ...'

'Er ...'

'I'm Eddie, by the way, and this is my mate Ross Well. You know, like Roswell, where the American government performed their top secret alien autopsy back in 1947.'

Leaving Jessica to receive a lesson in complete nonsense from this pair of space cadets, I walked over to Mitch's desk and, through gritted teeth, quizzed him as to why my exhibition of Jessica photos had had its run extended.

'We thought you'd be back in begging for extra work, so we sat the work experience bird somewhere else,' offered

Mitch with a shrug. He lowered his voice and motioned towards Jessica with his eyes. 'We thought you'd pussy out after a week of 'aving to speak to 'er.' He pointed at a bit of paper, pinned up at his desk, which showed a list of Red Buttoners and their estimates. 'Actually, most of us said a day.' Rifling through his in-tray, he nodded to Rohini, sat next to him. 'Looks like Rohini here wins the money. She was the only one who thought you'd go the distance.'

'Thanks, Ro,' I said, placing my hand on my heart.

'Thank *you*, Rich,' replied Rohini as Mitch handed her a clinking brown envelope.

'I'll give you this,' said Mitch. 'She is actually pretty fit in real life.' He raised his hand to give me a congratulatory high five, but I left him hanging.

Before prying Jessica away from Egyptologist Eddie, I sheepishly made one last pit stop, at Joy's desk. Sat on top of Joy's monitor, Honey, her small soft hedgehog, was, as usual, clutching a felt 'J'. I'd seen this cuddly critter, a gift from one of Joy's little treasures, countless times before, but right now there was something different about Honey's expression. Even when I'd encouraged her to hook up with André, the monkey who held down the spot next to my telephone, her snout had maintained a look of carefree neutrality. Now, though, that same terry towelling schnozz seemed slightly more elevated, slightly more crinkled, while her normally flaying whiskers looked taut with tension and the plush fur on her back assumed a genuine prickliness.

'Thanks, Joy,' I murmured. 'I owe you one.' Joy prodded at a couple of keys, whacked her spacebar decisively, then looked up and gave a wry smile.

'You think?'

Back on the street outside, I took a deep breath of not-so-fresh Docklands air and paused to consider what had just happened. Any sense of triumph, of escaping a catastrophe by the skin of my teeth, was being wrestled to the floor by a heavyweight tag-team of guilt and shame. I hadn't come to

155

retrieve an informative but accessible, pocket-sized and fully illustrated book about Egypt (with a couple of free A4 sheets of Egypt-themed puns, quips and links) at all. I'd come to walk my sexy, immaculately groomed dream girl down Red Button's frayed, coffee-stained catwalk, pausing to strike a nonchalant pose in front of Joy before turning on my heels and striding backstage with even greater swagger. Instead, I'd tripped on my trousers, fallen on my arse and floundered helplessly as Joy – instead of pointing and giggling, as, perhaps, she rightfully should have – instantly leapt onto the runway to rescue me. To make matters worse, cashmere-clad crooner LaMont had, once again, set up shop on the side of a nearby bus shelter, seemingly with the express purpose of smirking at me. I looked anxiously at the traffic coming down the street, desperately willing the appearance of a taxi to whisk me and Jess away from Red Button Land.

'Your friend Eddie knows a lot about aliens,' announced Jessica all of a sudden. 'He said you and him had seen a classic grey whizzing through the streets in a spaceship early one morning.'

'Did he mention that the creature parked its futuristic craft outside the post office?'

'No.'

'His classic grey was an elderly woman in a mobility scooter. Eddie was going through his clubbing phase and he was still high on something from the night before.' Jessica laughed.

'Well, he spoke very passionately on the subject.'

'Oh, I'm sure. Eddie doesn't do things by half.'

'It doesn't seem like any of your Red Button mates do,' mused Jessica. 'At least not when they're playing a joke. I don't even remember any of those photos.' She paused. 'Except the one with the white vest. That shoot was bloody freezing.' I managed to cobble together a brittle, makeshift smile.

'Yeah. Quite the gallery they'd assembled there,' I noted, still scrutinising the oncoming traffic for any sign of our getaway vehicle.

'So,' pondered Jessica, 'you're going around saying nice things about me.' She flashed me a smile that somehow, at least for that moment, made me forget that I had just locked down the award for Twat of the Year.

'No, no. I swear, I would never ever say anything nice about ...' Without warning, Jessica grabbed me by the front of my jacket. Elevating on the balls of her feet, she pulled me in towards her until we were nose to nose.

'SHUT UP!' she yelled, shaking me as she had done during those five takes inside the arena. 'Or I'll wallpaper that bus shelter with your face!' She held me there for a couple of seconds, trying in vain to look intimidating before the corners of her mouth gave way and we both started laughing. As a taxi pulled up to the kerb, she let go and I smiled to myself. Jessica clambered into the back of the cab and I took a quick glance at LaMont to make sure he was getting this.

'West End, please,' Jessica instructed the cabbie. We buckled up, then she reached into her handbag and pulled out the Egypt stuff.

'Thanks for this.'

'Did I come through for you?' I asked as the cab pulled away from the kerb. 'Did I?'

'You did,' admitted Jessica, leafing through my pages of hand spun puns. Then she went quiet, looked down at her watch and looked up at me nervously. 'So, I feel terrible to even ask, but any chance you could ...'

'Bash it into a cohesive five minute script in the time it takes us to get to the West End?' The way Jessica bit her bottom lip told me I'd hit the jackpot. 'But I don't even have ...'

'Paper and a pen?' Like a magician pulling a rabbit from a top hat, Jessica reached into her handbag once more, this time producing a spiral bound notepad and a biro.

'Did you just take these off my desk?' It was a somewhat rhetorical question given that the back of the notepad featured the results of my office-wide straw poll on the all-time sexiest animated characters (my vote was with Pocahontas. I liked her taut, long-limbed body, vertigo-inducing cheekbones and bone-straight black hair) and the pen had a pretty distinctive, furry-maned plastic lion sat on a spring at its end.

'Yes,' submitted Jessica with an apologetic-but-still-very-disarming grin. Right now, she certainly didn't look capable of wallpapering a corridor, a bus shelter or any other surface with my face, but as I looked at my notepad and the bushy-bonced big cat wobbling away on the end of my pen, I realised that she was still far from powerless. Unlike me. The cab came to a stop at some traffic lights, and from the corner of my eye I could sense a billboard-sized LaMont looking down at me. I didn't look back at him, though. For one thing, I didn't want to give him the satisfaction. For another, I had a bloody script to write.

CHAPTER FIVE

As luck – not to mention the cross-promotional machinations of the television and record industries – would have it, LaMont was still on my mind the following Tuesday morning as I lit up his printed-out biography with a yellow highlighter pen and racked my brains for ways to have fun with him on that week's show. Yes, after continuously taunting me from bus shelters and billboards, the limber lothario of R&B's ringtone generation was, as part of a whistle stop UK charm offensive, dropping by *The Hangout* for a song, a chat and a punchy, unique little showpiece that I'd yet to dream up. Resolving that inspiration would hit me when it was good and ready, I had just turned my attention to *Tricky Trousers* (a regular game in which contestants tried to ascertain the celebrity owner of a pair of strides based on the contents of the pockets) when I felt a vibrating in my own jeans. On any other day I'd have headed for the kitchen as quickly yet discreetly as possible, but with Kam out of the office on some sort of reconnaissance mission with Greg and Yeti, I instead reached into my pocket, pulled out my mobile – which was showing, on its screen, an unfamiliar number – and flipped it open.

'Hello?'

'What's up, Arseface?' came the response. As filtered through my phone, the female voice on the other end wasn't instantly recognisable, but the caller's distinctive brand of jovial rudeness (and, specifically, the whole 'Arseface' thing) gave her identity away.

'Miss Bennett,' I deduced. 'Great. Now I've got to change my number.'

'Blame Eddie,' suggested Joy. 'He gave up the goods.'

'Getting my number off a third party, Bonita? That's a little stalker-ish.'

'You should know. Listen, I've got today off and I'm in your neck of the woods.'

'You're in my neck of the woods? Now you're really starting to scare me. What am I wearing? Can you see what I'm doing with my hand?' I waggled my fingers for the sake of, I dunno, full commitment to the joke, eliciting across-the-room smirks from Kate and Denise.

'I don't want to know what you're doing with your hand,' deadpanned Joy, 'and I don't need to see you to know that it's a Tuesday, so you're almost certainly wearing your favourite petticoat-and-high heels combination. Listen, d'you wanna meet up for lunch? If you're still hanging out with regular people, that is.' I leant back in my chair and, giving myself a push-off from my desk, rolled back a metre over the carpet.

'Well, I like to mix it up with the plebs every now and then just to keep myself grounded, so what the heck? Let's do it. You know where Garcelle's is?'

'Mmm-hmm. To be honest I thought you'd suggest somewhere a bit ritzier, but I do like the cakes there.'

'OK. Well, can you meet me there just after one?' I looked over at Kam's empty seat. 'Actually, I'll meet you at one o'clock on the dot.'

'Alright,' agreed Joy. 'See you then.'

'Cool. See you in a bit.' I snapped my phone shut, dug my heels into the carpet and, bit by bit, dragged myself back to my desk. With nothing to push off from, the return trip was, in my experience, invariably far bumpier and less graceful than the outward journey, but I spent this one lost in thought and slightly puzzled. For all our banter, the only times myself and Joy had ever conversed over a phone line was whilst making crank calls to each other's desks, so I was curious as to why she'd been bold enough to hit me mobile-to-mobile, let alone with the purpose of hooking up a lunchtime rendezvous. Most likely she wanted the opportunity to rip the piss out of me following my cringe-crammed trip to Red Button, which was, I supposed as I reopened my phone and retrieved Joy's number from the 'received calls' list, the least I could afford her. I pressed the letters 'J', 'O' and 'Y' on the keypad and hit 'Store' before sliding the phone back into my pocket and returning to work. I'd added about three more words to *Tricky Trousers* before I fished my phone out again, flipped it open and scrolled swiftly through my list of contacts until I landed on my newest entry. There they were, those three letters – capital 'J', small 'o', small 'y' – standing strong on the display screen next to the little sim-card icon. I stared at the letters for a moment, then folded my phone up once more and squeezed it in my palm. Joy was in my phone and I was in hers and for some reason that felt like a big thing.

It was ten to one when I put my jacket on and made for the door. Sure, a seventy minute lunch hour was a bit cheeky, but Kate and Denise had spent all morning giggling at what was apparently The Word's Funniest Private Joke, so it wasn't like I was the only one taking advantage of Kam's absence. Indeed, the pair of them were still laughing when Kate halted my escape to request a favour.

'You couldn't get me a copy of *Gab*, could you?' She pushed a two pound coin into my palm.

'Sure,' I said, letting them get back to their giggling as I hustled through the double doors. I knew for a fact that Joy, like me a stickler for punctuality, had 'Where the fuck are you?' stored as a quick note on her mobile, and would doubtless be more than happy to make this my inaugural text should I be even a minute late for our rendezvous.

As it happened, I arrived at Garcelle's a whole three minutes early. Peering through the window, I could see no sign of my lunch date either at one of the tables or slavering over the pastries, and so for the next couple of minutes I staked out a couple of paving slabs in anticipation of her arrival.

'*Bonita Applebum, you gotta put me on, Bonita Applebum I said you gotta put me on,*' I rapped under my breath. Outside a pub on the other side of the road, a blackboard showed Homer Simpson ogling one of the establishment's speciality subway sandwiches. Well, I say Homer Simpson, but in truth this shoddy 'likeness' had little in common with the character beyond his yellow complexion and bulging, spherical eyes. I shook my head (cack-handed reproductions of cartoon characters being a personal bugbear) and squinted up the street. With one o'clock rattling swiftly into view but Miss Bennett nowhere in sight, I was limbering up my own eyeballs in readiness for rolling them and / or staring disbelievingly at my watch when a familiar voice piped up to deprive me of the opportunity.

'I'd know that unwashed smell anywhere.' I turned around and there, bang on time, was Joy. A sleek side-parting corralled her black tresses into a ponytail and she was wearing jeans and a dark brown top-cum-mini-dress with a polar neck and cap sleeves (sorry, my girl in the Grattan catalogue obviously never modelled this exact style – it looked nice, though).

'Unwashed? I'll have you know I have a hands-and-face wash every morning and a full shower every Sunday night.' Outrage over, I couldn't keep from breaking into a broad smile. 'You alright?'

'I will be when I've got some cake in me,' predicted Joy as we made our way inside the coffee shop. Garcelle's was quiet but getting busier, with about eight people and four laptops decorating its tasteful, mahogany-heavy interior.

'Is here OK?' I asked, gesturing towards a sun-drenched table by the window.

'You really like showing your women off to the world, don't you?' Joy hoisted her ponytail over her cap sleeved shoulder, her cheeky grin lighting up the space between the glistening, oversized gold hoops that hung from her ears. Alright, I thought as we settled into our chairs, so I was going to get a little stick about my visit to Red Button. I'd known that in advance and I also knew that I deserved it. Still, I couldn't help but breathe a sigh of relief as a waitress arrived, and when she departed to fetch our coffee and cake I looked to the passers-by outside for a further stay of execution. Salvation came in the form of two identical, twentysomething female

162

twins striding in perfect unison – not to mention perfectly unified pinstripe trouser suits – across the pavement on the opposite side of the road.

'That's uncanny. Even their boobs are synchronised,' noted Joy, zooming in for a close-up while I pulled back to look at the bigger, philosophical picture.

'Could you ever go out with an identical twin?'

'I don't know. I take it you wouldn't.'

'It just seems like you're heading for trouble. Wouldn't you automatically fancy the other twin?' Joy rolled her eyes.

'Yeah, of course. I mean, it's not like there's any chance of them having different personalities or anything.'

'S'pose,' I conceded. 'But even if my charming, hilarious girlfriend's identically beautiful twin sister had the personality of a rawl plug, I still wouldn't like it.'

'Why not?'

'Ehhhh ... I'd just feel like someone else had the same thing as me.' Joy slowly shook her head.

'Well, thankfully for identical twins everywhere, I don't think it's something you have to worry about right now.'

The waitress – a friendly, slightly equine brunette – returned to grace our table with two tall glasses of foam-topped coffee and two generous slabs of cake (the components of our well-balanced lunch). I forged through the decadent-looking passion cake with my fork, then levered one of the resulting halves onto Joy's plate while fifty percent of the equally mouth-watering chocolate cake travelled in the opposite direction. We plonked lumps of brown sugar into our drinks, and for about half a minute the only sound between us was the clinking of metal on glass as we got our collective stir on. With the last granule dissolved, I found myself staring longingly into my own foamy caffeine vortex in search of a new talking point. Telling Joy that I'd been on screen with Jess three days earlier would only unleash that ever-imminent avalanche of mockery, so that was out. What I wanted to do was complement Joy on her 'do, but looking at it, and indeed Joy as a whole, I was suddenly reminded of another humiliating embarrassment, namely the last, ill-fated time I told her that her hair looked gorgeous. Instead I took a different tack.

'So, how are things with you and Matt?' Joy stopped stirring and withdrew her spoon from her coffee, then placed it down on the saucer with a gentle clink.

'Wow.'

'Wow? Things are that good, eh?'

'No. I mean "wow" as in "wow, you're really not going to say anything, are you?"'

'About what?' I asked, doing my best to convey an air of genuine bewilderment.

'Hmmm. Let me see ... About you, Jessica and your, shall we say, picture perfect day out?' I placed my glass down on my saucer, then picked up a napkin and wiped the froth off my top lip.

'Ah, yes,' I sighed, screwing up the napkin in my palm. 'Picture perfect. Good play on words, Joy. Well, again, thank you, because without you coming through for me that day, things could have turned out very differently.' Joy cringed.

'Well, why don't we skip any details about how things did turn out, and instead recap the bit where you said you owed me one?'

'I meant it. If there's anything I can do for you, ever ...' Feeling a little embarrassed, I busied myself with my first mouthful of passion cake. When I looked up at Joy again she was staring directly into my eyes, a broad, slightly apologetic but mainly mischievous grin stretched across her face.

'You know, it's really funny you should say that. See, I kind of promised my niece Constance, and her friend Kelly, that they could come and see *The Hangout*.'

'Oh, did you, now?' I paused for a couple of seconds to weigh up the logistics. 'Well, I think I can make your overly presumptuous – some would say morally questionable – promise a reality.' Joy topped up her favour-collecting grin and leant in ever so slightly.

'What if I said that I'd also promised Constance ...'

'And her friend Kelly?'

'And her friend Kelly, that they could come this week, when LaMont's going to be on.'

'How did you know that?'

'I didn't, but Constance did. She loooooovvess him.'

'Ahhh … This week?' I winced. 'I mean, it's what, Tuesday now and ...'

'See, it's her birthday on Saturday,' continued Joy, 'and this would be the best present ever, Rich. The *best*.' I thought back to one of the photos Joy had at her desk; one that showed her surrounded by an assortment of genetically linked pipsqueaks.

'So Constance is the cute one? Not that evil-looking thing with the unibrow.' Joy narrowed her eyes.

'All my nieces and nephews are cute,' she insisted, 'just like their aunty.' Putting her eyes back on full beam, she tilted her head to the side, the hoop in her left ear kissing her shoulder while its opposite number – glinting slightly in the sunlight that streamed through the window – lay down lovingly against her smooth, cocoa-coloured jaw. Somewhere in-between the two, her lips parted to deliver a solitary, seductive syllable. 'So?'

'Yeah, I'll see what I can do,' I sighed. 'Provided, that is, we can put all this Jessica picture stuff to rest.' Clearly content with the results of her charm offensive, Joy plunged her fork into her thick chocolate cake like an explorer triumphantly planting their flag into previously undiscovered soil.

'Deal,' she agreed. 'And thank you. You really are a special friend.'

'Don't mention it. You're sure this little rug-rat hasn't grown all gangly and awkward since that photo was taken?'

'Oh, please. Five minutes with her and you'll want to be a father.'

'No chance,' I asserted with equal conviction. 'I'm never having kids.' Joy paused her forkful of chocolate cake midway between her plate and her mouth.

'Why not?'

'Two words, Bonita. Dead animals.'

'Dead animals?'

'Dead animals. If the children's pet rabbit dies, whose job is it to scrape its cold, flat, lifeless body up from its hutch and bury it? Daddy's.'

'Not necessarily,' argued Joy.

'*Yes* necessarily,' I insisted, jabbing the air with my fork for cake-encrusted, four-pronged emphasis. 'In any two-parent household, the responsibility for disposing of deceased animals invariably and without fail falls to Daddy and Daddy alone.'

'So don't let your children have pets, then.' Content, it would seem, that she'd solved my dilemma, Joy hit play and hoisted her hunk of cake into her mouth.

'Fine. But what happens if there's a dead bird in the garden? Or a mouse?' Joy chewed and swallowed her cake.

'Don't let your children have a garden,' she suggested, showing me the ends of her own four prongs. 'Live, with your family, in a flat.' Conceding defeat, I laid my weapon down to rest on the china.

'Joy, you've cracked it. I'm doing a complete about-face. I'm having kids.'

'Please,' she groaned. 'Not while I'm eating.'

'Oh, thanks! You don't mind me talking about dead animals ...'

'Even my iron stomach has its limits.' Joy clamped her smirking lips around her fork and stripped it clean of icing before running her tongue over her teeth and hitting me with a brief but full-power flash of her gnashers. She may just have stuck me up for *Hangout* tickets, but it was her arsenal of smiles and grins – from sarcastic to semi-sincere to suspiciously sweet – that was starting to make this scheduled get-together feel strangely like an out-of-nowhere ambush. Suddenly, without warning, I found myself transported back to those days BWP, BMJ (Before the Wrap Party, Before Meeting Jessica), when just knowing that Joy was in the same room as me – that sooner or later she'd be passing by my desk – was enough to make me feel like writing the voiceovers for third-rate docusoaps was, despite my intermittent bitching and belly-aching, actually the greatest job in the world. True, this bygone period of my life had only ended a couple of weeks ago, but it already felt like a lot longer. Or at least it did until now. I looked down at my chest, then foraged around in my pocket. Damn. I must have left my security tag on my desk.

Some people are addicted to drugs, others to alcohol or cigarettes or gambling or any number of different, often debilitating vices. Back in the BWP, BMJ era, I'd been addicted to Joy. Our desk-side exchanges had frequently given me a heady buzz and the Grade A hits of banter we had in the coffee area made me feel happy and excited and at times even giddy, but after these soaring highs there invariably – and sometimes even immediately – came the gutter-level lows when I realised these encounters had only left me gasping insatiably for more Joy. Quite simply, I'd been a Joyaholic, and while I was certain I'd kicked my addiction, I now found myself wondering if I wasn't teetering perilously on the brink of a relapse.

Before woozy nostalgia sucked me all the way under (and transformed my tall, smooth glass of delicious coffee into a small, ribbed plastic cup full of unappetising IBS), I mentally fast-forwarded to the wrap party, sharpening the picture and turning up the sound so that I could feel all that pain and embarrassment in precise, High Definition detail. Ah, that was better, I thought, training my mental camera on the man who had, in the nicest possible way, administered the final, fatal blow to my hopes of hooking up with the woman opposite me.

'So, *now* can I ask you how things are going with Matt?'

'Oh, fantastic,' enthused Joy. 'He's great. I mean, you know us. We're not the type to start groping each other in the street but, I dunno, I feel like we've got something special.' She shovelled a hunk of passion cake into her mouth and groaned appreciatively. 'Mmmm ...' came the rather muffled verdict.

'Speaking of special ...'

I heaved some cake into my own mouth and reflected on how, having already managed to blindside me, Joy had now landed a solid blow to my head. If I thought that hearing about her and Matt's domestic bliss would inoculate me against Joy's charms, I was wrong: it only made me more aware of them. Still, it seemed that Joy didn't want to elaborate any further, which was fine by me except that suddenly I didn't know what I was going to say next. My eyes frantically scanned the street outside for a posse of emo kids or a plus-sized velour tracksuit model – anything to kick-start a new thread of conversation and prove my mouth's worth for something beyond simply chewing cake and sipping coffee. I sensed that Joy's eyes, too, were on the same mission. Though it seemed more like an hour, an agonising thirty seconds or so elapsed before our prayers were answered and Darth Vader drove past in a Ford Focus. Or rather, a small child wearing the Dark Lord's unmistakable black helmet and cape combo rolled by in the back seat of his mum's car.

'You think he's taking his cape to Sketchley?' asked Joy, her eyes leading mine to the name-brand dry cleaners across the street.

'Possibly,' I mused. 'You know, he seems smaller in real life. All that black gear's really slimming.' I could swear the crockery rattled slightly as Joy and I both exhaled, although in hindsight it may simply have been trembling in Vader's wake.

En route back to the Tube station, we passed by a newsstand and, thankfully, I remembered Kate's request.

'Hold up a sec.' I grabbed a copy of *Gab* from the jam-packed wall of magazines and Joy rolled her eyes at the selection of usual suspects whoring every pitiful fibre of their fame-crazed, dead-eyed beings on the glossy front cover.

'That's really sad.'

'It's not *for* me,' I pointed out, digging in my pocket for Kate's two pound coin.

'Your mum?' queried Joy.

'If you must know, it's for a girl in the office.' Joy rolled her eyes.

'God, she's got you under the thumb.'

'Like you with these tickets, you mean?'

'Hey!' Joy shoved my arm so hard I nearly dropped the money. 'You owe me, remember?'

'I know, I know.' I paid the vendor. Joy's earrings jingled as she shook her head disapprovingly.

'I don't know how people can tolerate the type of prats they have in there.'

'Me neither,' I agreed, pocketing the change and rolling the magazine into a celeb-coated cylinder which I waved at my friend as she headed underground.

Back at Fresh Coat HQ, it turned out that sweet-talking Denise for Saturday morning beanbag space wasn't that hard after all. She'd just managed to wangle a mate of hers – a jobbing stand-up – a gig warming up *The Hangout*'s young crowd before the show kicked off, and, whether through a desire that I should witness firsthand the calibre of comic she rolled with or simply because her handiwork had put her in a good mood, she was more than willing to accommodate me, even at such short notice. Of course, my late booking fee took the form of some gentle ribbing.

'Obviously you think you've got some sort of clout around here now,' she joked whilst tapping away on her keyboard to ensure that Constance, her friend Kelly and a backstage-bound Joy would be my motley crew of guests come Saturday morning. It was funny – one sketch appearance and I was being lampooned as a demanding diva. 'I hope you're not too pally with this Joy girl, though. We don't want any cat fights kicking off backstage.' I looked back at her with a kind of default half-smile, not really understanding this particular quip. 'Oh, OK,' chuckled Denise. 'I guess maybe *you* do.'

I was still clueless, but, buoyed by my ticket-nabbing

success and noticing that Kam was back at her desk, I went straight over and hit *The Hangout*'s head honcho with the killer LaMont idea that had eluded me all morning before hitting me like a sock full of snooker balls to the face the second I'd parted ways with Joy.

'Do I think LaMont could sing Happy Birthday to *who*?' asked Kam at the end of my garbled pitch.

'My friend's niece. It'll make for great television.' Kam didn't look so convinced.

'What other ideas have we got for him?'

'Well, there's *LaMontable Behaviour*, where we grill him about his favourite sexual fetishes and recreational drugs; *The Full LaMonty* – that one's pretty self-explanatory; *LaMonty's Python*, which might involve a snake or might simply require LaMont whipping out his ... well, now that I think about it, that one's essentially the same idea as *The Full LaMonty*.'

'Right,' interjected Kam, putting the brakes on my stream of nonsense-ness. 'This girl of yours, is she cute?'

'She's adorable,' I assured her, trying my best to look adorable – or at least trustworthy – myself. 'I'll stake my professional reputation on it.'

'Oh, well, in that case ...' said the gaffer sarcastically. 'Alright, I'll get someone to run it by LaMont's manager.'

'Thanks, Kam. You're the best.' I was about to return to my desk when Kam stopped me.

'Hold on a moment. I've got a favour you can do for me in return.'

'Certainly.' I knew what was coming, and with Kam so obligingly putting the wheels in motion on Constance's birthday surprise, I was already more than willing to sacrifice the cheeky anal sex reference I'd slipped into Liam's *Cash and Carrie* dialogue.

'Now,' began Kam, her voice dropping to an almost-whisper as she beckoned me to come closer, 'speaking of your professional reputation, I know this is none of my business, but whatever's going on with you and Jessica, I'd appreciate it if you could be a bit more discreet about it.'

'Um … Sorry?'

'It's nothing to get upset about, but I am a little wary of where this is heading. I know I can be a bit of a taskmaster, but I'm just trying to run a children's programme, without all this other stuff.'

'What other stuff? What have I done?' I scrunched up my brow and nervously pushed Kate's *Gab* – still rolled into a stiff tube – up under my bottom lip, awaiting enlightenment.

'OK,' said Kam with what appeared to be a wry smile. 'Well, we'll say no more about it. Just go and put some of that winning charm of yours into this week's show.'

Confused and, to be honest, a little upset, I trundled slowly towards my desk. I couldn't help but feel slightly pissed off with Kam. Was my friendship with Jessica really that much of a distraction? Was it the two of us talking that was threatening to derail *The Hangout* or was the show only thrown into jeopardy when these exchanges ended in laughter? Oh, sod it. Kam was probably just jealous that, after only a couple of weeks on the job, I'd already struck up a firmer friendship with her leading lady than she'd managed in all her time as the show's sinewy, caffeine-powered producer. I wondered if it would be of any consolation to her that the programme's other presenter apparently hated my guts?

This question and all of the others evaporated from my mind as soon as I reached my desk. There, pinned around my work station, were eight or so identical photocopied pictures of a girl in a stripy cardie who, even captured from the side in grainy black-and-white, I instantly recognised as a Jessica. I was slightly slower in identifying Jessica's male companion; the man whose jacket she was grabbing as she stood on her tiptoes and – or so it appeared – went in for a kiss. Then it hit me. That man was me.

'Page twenty-seven,' giggled Kate, appearing at my side and tapping the gossip-filled baton in my suddenly sweaty hand. 'Could you sign it for me please?' I opened up the

171

magazine and frantically thumbed my way to the twenty-seventh page. There we were again, myself and Jessica – smaller but this time in full, glorious colour – in *Gab*'s *Word on the Street* section. I studied the caption next to the photo: *'Up close and personal: The Hangout presenter Jessica George gets to grips with a special friend.'* Feeling, all of a sudden, slightly wobbly, I put the magazine down on my desk and sunk into my seat. Now I got it. Now I understood Kam's warning, Denise's celebrity remark and Joy's coffee shop cracks. Every detail fell chillingly into place like the last five minutes of a *Saw* movie. Well, not quite everything. I stared dumbfounded at the picture. Who the hell had snapped us on the street outside Red Button? More to the point, was a snapshot of a children's TV presenter and me, a complete nobody, really the starriest sighting *Gab* could manage? I'd just seen Darth Vader, for fuck's sake.

'Liam's going to be fuming,' predicted Kate, 'He's been trying to get in *Word on the Street* for months. He paid me twenty quid once to snap him leaving a Starbucks in Notting Hill with a mystery blonde.'

'And they never ran the photo?' queried Tim from across the room.

'It never got sent in,' giggled Kate. 'His bird bumped into him on their way out the door and he ended up with his frappucino down the front of his jeans looking like God knows what. I still have the photo, though, so if I'm ever strapped for cash I can always blackmail him.'

The idea of accidentally putting one over on Liam was of surprisingly little solace to me as the post-snap analysis continued with excruciating vigour. Good-natured wisecracks rained down on my ears from the team's more vocal members, while those unarmed with gags peered, not as discreetly as they thought, over their partitions to see me squirm.

'It's nothing,' I insisted, reaching across my desk and taking down the photocopies at a pace just leisurely enough to suggest that I could take a joke; that I wasn't fazed by my sudden notoriety. 'I can see it *looks* like we're about to kiss, but it was nothing like that. In actual fact, Jessica was manhandling me.'

'Oh yeah? Is that how you like it?' chuckled Trevor, a researcher who, up to that point, had said maybe three words to me. 'We're finding out a lot about you two this ...' His crack was snuffed out as Nina purposefully entered the room clutching her very own rolled-up copy of *Gab*. Kate hurried back to her desk while the meerkats ducked down behind their partitions and the room's talking heads stopped talking, their screens and sarnies suddenly more gripping than the week's top showbiz story. Shit. It was one thing being joke fodder for the Fresh Coat foot soldiers, but another to incur the wrath of the biggest, ripest and smoothest-textured cheese in the office. With her Botoxed brow meeting with minimal wind resistance, Nina was at my desk before I'd even had time to whip up a plan of defence. Then, while my heart got dragged into my stomach's spin cycle, she leant in close and spoke quietly so as to remain outside of the eavesdropping radar.

'Top work, Richard. Jessica's a great girl but God knows she could use a shag.' She gave me a sly flash of her bathroom tile teeth and an approving tap on the shoulder with her magazine, then disappeared as quickly as she'd arrived, leaving my gob even more emphatically smacked than it already had been.

Still, if the Series Producer's congratulations didn't have me bursting with pride and my colleagues' quips hadn't exactly split my sides, the irony of the situation wasn't lost on me. I'd whisked Jessica through the Red Button office in the hope of looking like her boyfriend, and now that's *exactly* what I looked like – in the nation's biggest-selling showbiz magazine, no less. And there was me thinking the entire thing had been an embarrassing failure.

At home that evening, I logged on to the internet and accessed my e-mail account. I hadn't checked it since before lunch, partly because, after Kam's talk with me, I'd been keen to knuckle down, slave over the script and generally play the part of diligent and professional Fresh Coat employee, and also because after discovering the nationally circulated impetus for Kam's consternation, I was in too much of a daze to remember how to use a mouse. Now, though, I saw that my inbox contained eight new messages, seven of which were from friends amazed that I'd apparently pulled my favourite celeb cutie (the eighth was an offer of penis enlargement from a company who obviously didn't get *Gab* in their corner of the world). I sifted through the various cracks and congrats – mostly from people who ordinarily swore they never touched *Gab* – but didn't respond to any of them, instead typing an e-mail to the girl who'd been first to clock my moment in the spotlight.

Dearest Bonita, I began. *So I've actually seen inside the latest super-soaraway edition of Gab, and now I know what you were on about this morning. Actually, although it pains me to say it, it's not what it looks like.* I paused, wondering how best to phrase my explanation before deleting the last sentence altogether and replacing it with a subtly revised version: *What can I say? When you're hot, you're hot.* Yep, that definitely conveyed the same information but more economically. I tapped the return key, then hit Joy with the good news: *Anyway, using my hotness, I've got audience seats for Constance and Kelly, plus you have the privilege of sitting on a couch with me behind the scenes. All you need to do is get the three of you to Artemis Studios for 7.30 sharp on Saturday and I'll meet you there. Love, Rich xx.* OK, that ought to do it. Joy knew where Artemis Studios was from her days as a researcher on daytime quiz show *All Bets Are Off*, so all that remained for me to do was cap things off with a cheeky postscript: *P.S. I know it's going to be hard for you, but try to keep your hands to yourself. If Jessica sees you pawing me, there's a chance she might not have full sex with me this weekend.* For good measure, I dipped into my pictures folder and found a pic of Jessica flashing a

Tipp-Ex-coloured grin as she gave the cameraman a double thumbs-up straight out of the Paul McCartney pose-book. Perfect. I copied and pasted it onto the bottom of my e-mail and hit 'send'.

Instantly, I felt a little, well, bad. Somehow I doubted Jessica was giving the thumbs-up (double or even single) to the already infamous *Gab* grapple. More surprisingly, perhaps, I didn't feel like holding aloft either one of my two stubbiest digits, either. Who knew that being pictured in a playful tussle with my favourite TV hottie would feel so ... un-fun? Perhaps in years to come, when Jessica and I had been photographed attending various movie premieres and other functions as an official couple, I – no, *we* – would look back on this snap as the one that started it all. For now, though, I just wanted to get through the week with as few people as possible witnessing my unrequested moment in the sun (well, except that cocky little shit in the wheelchair – I hoped he got a good, long look at it through those brick-thick glasses of his before promptly wheeling himself off the nearest tall building). The phone rang. I wandered into the kitchen and picked it up.

'Hello?'

'So your sister showed me this week's *Gab* magazine,' said my mum.

'Oh, yeah, well, the funny thing is ...'

'Your wallet's sticking out the top of your jeans pocket,' she interrupted. '*Anyone* could have stolen it.'

If I imagined that Friday's rehearsal was going to provide me and Jessica with the opportunity to talk about – and hopefully laugh off – our tabloid-teasing adventure, I was to be proven wrong. With the week's guests sorely lacking in the testosterone department, my sofa-filling thespian abilities were cruelly overlooked in favour of Kate's ample arse. Instead, I spent the morning entrenched in (what else?) a beanbag and, apparently, enveloped in some sort of force field that rendered me invisible to Jessica's eyes. I felt certain that, had I hauled myself out of my crunchy, shape-shifting seat and positioned my face directly in front of the teleprompter, she would still have looked straight through it and read the words scrolling down behind my head. If those words lacked their usual zing (which in itself hardly set record new levels of zinginess), it was because, once again, the troubling image of Jessica being tactile with a man had hindered my ability to fully focus on my work – not least when some wag had hilariously taped said image to my screen. With another copy taped underneath that one for good measure.

What, I wondered, was going through Jessica's mind? Embarrassment? Shame? The dim flicker of hope that one day the advent of time travel would enable her to reverse history and ensure that she never met me? Lunchtime brought me no closer to finding out, my partner in page-filling disappearing off site and leaving me to prod at my lunch in the company of Kate.

'You're quiet, today, Richard,' observed Kate in-between mouthfuls of salad. Stalling for time, I took a swig of water, swirling it around my mouth before resolving to probe my dining partner for inside info.

'Not as quiet as Jessica. Do you know whether she's upset about ...' I trailed off, assuming that Kate would fill in the rest.

'About what?'

'You know, the picture. In *Gab*'

'Oh, that.' Kate put down her cutlery, picked up her full-to-the-brim glass of water and downed every last drop before continuing. 'I don't think so. I think she's just got a lot on at the moment, you know, what with the *Wow! Voyager* job and everything.'

'Oh. She got the gig, then? I didn't know.' Kate skewered a plum tomato with her fork.

'Yeah, she got it, so it's probably just that. I wouldn't worry about it.'

But I *was* worrying about it, and I was still worrying about it when, with five minutes left of the lunch break, I headed to the gents for a wee. Walking down that photo-filled corridor, I was shooting extra-sharpened daggers at Hannah Thornwell when a figure clad in swishing black robes emerged from the ladies' and, in her hurry, nearly sent me flying.

'Sorry,' offered Jessica from beneath a mortar board hat (rehearsals, I should point out, were about to restart with a run-through of new, school-themed quiz *A Touch of Class*). OK. Here was my opportunity to find out where Jessica's head was at. Other than underneath some novelty headwear, I mean.

'Are you alright?' I asked.

'Yeah, but it's a good thing you're not a foot shorter or I'd have taken your eye out.' Jessica rotated her hat around ninety degrees to safeguard against future high speed impalements.

'No, I meant ...' As I spoke, Liam, looking supremely ill-at-ease in full school uniform, appeared at the end of the corridor.

'Catch you later,' said Jessica, swishing away in the opposite direction to her pupil. I pushed open the door of the gents and trundled in, more convinced than ever that the latest edition of *Gab* had (pun fully intended) snapped my relationship with Jessica in two. Handling my business at the urinal, I tilted back my head and looked up at the ceiling, inwardly hoping, perhaps, for some sort of guidance from above. As it happened, the wisdom I was praying for came at me from my side, and was delivered in a voice higher, surlier and considerably more irritating than I imagined The Lord's to be.

'If you want my advice,' muttered Liam from beneath the peak of a cloth cap balanced so delicately atop his barnet as to be practically levitating above the highlighted tips of his wayward tufts, 'you'll stop trying to get into Jessica's pants.' He unzipped the polyester shorts that finished just above his knees and threw his low-hanging, navy-and-gold striped tie into the urine free zone over the shoulder of his navy blazer.

'If *you* want *my* advice,' I responded, zipping up the flies on my own, resolutely full-length leg-wear, 'you'll get all your homework out of the way this evening. That way you'll have the whole weekend free to do whatever you want.'

My own evening was spent hunched over my laptop. Don't worry, though – I wasn't so sad or boring as to be simply spending my Friday night surfing the internet for movie news and sports highlights. Nope, far from it, as, having done all that already, I was busy using the sticky sides of a series of address labels to pick up the grime from in-between and underneath the keys. Meanwhile, up on my TV screen, Brett Scott was sat at a laptop of his own as, dressed in a *Reservoir Dogs*-style suit, situated in a *Reservoir Dogs*-style abandoned warehouse and, as always, practically screaming out for a *Reservoir Dogs*-style ear slicing, he smugly buffered the succession of wacky, out-of-focus internet clips that comprised the low-cost, low-laughter content of his new gig, *LMFAO!!!* I pulled the edge of my latest label up from underneath my spacebar, revealing a bumper haul that included a couple of hairs, some biscuit crumbs and what appeared to be a shard of cashew nut. I looked up at the telly, where two American lads were detonating gateaux while the captions 'WTF?!!!' and 'LOL!!!' (not to mention a trail of laughing emoticons) emphasised the gravity of their actions. It was genuinely a toss-up as to whether myself or Brett was presiding over the least interesting assemblage of crap found on somebody's computer. In keeping with the theme of the programme, I gave a stoneface followed by an SMH to the antics on screen, then SMHed myself for the EPIC FAIL of not having hit the off button sooner.

A few more hairs and a slither of fingernail later and my keyboard cleaning was finished. My fun-packed evening, on the other hand, was just getting started, as I still had to charge up my new digital camera and acquaint myself with the instructions booklet. I opened up the drawer beneath my bed, shuddering slightly as I saw my soft rock shoe box, and pulled out my still-in-its-package camera. Since getting the gadget a couple of weeks earlier I'd done little more than fondle its sleek curves, but the following day, I thought, might see this thing getting its first bit of action.

On the box, a scuba diver with a stubbled jaw and wandering blonde hair was putting the very same camera through its paces, although it seemed doubtful he'd spotted anything in those aquatic depths as vivid as his own scarlet swimming trunks, especially considering that he was surveying the LCD screen through a clunky, fogged-up scuba mask. Unlike Red Snapper, I didn't imagine I'd have cause to get my point-and-press on underwater, least of all within the distinctly landlocked confines of Wembley's own Artemis studios. Nonetheless, I couldn't help wondering – and worrying – whether the next day might find me in over my head all the same.

'Alright: another bottle of the good stuff.' I watched the bubbles rush to the top of our glasses as I poured refills for myself and Joy. We hadn't finished the previous bottle, but then that was half the point. It was Saturday morning at *The Hangout* and the two of us, clad, as it turned out, in his n' hers khaki combat trousers and denim jackets, were living large in The Players' Lounge: sipping free sparkling water, eating free sweets and watching the show on the big screen TV. As usual, the parents of *The Hangout*'s youthful audience had been herded into a separate hospitality area downstairs, leaving the lounge and its complimentary consumables at the disposal of myself and the woman who now sat at my side with a bowl of Celebrations in her lap. Well, us and a shaven-headed black gentleman whose XXXL frame, kitted out in a black leather jacket the thickness of a fourteen tog duvet, occupied the sofa opposite ours.

Consumed by the events unfolding live from the studio below, our fellow VIP had barely averted his eyes from the screen and certainly hadn't uttered a word to us, but that was fine with me. Small talk with strangers was the last thing on my mind as that man LaMont bounced, slid and spun across the stage, his ornately embroidered brown shirt billowing from his action figure torso while a pair of silver dog tags leapt about recklessly atop the tight white vest that shrink-wrapped his formidable chest. Meanwhile, the elasticated outbursts taking place between LaMont's hefty gold belt buckle and his gleaming, white-on-white Air Force Ones suggested that a dozen or so ferrets were running riot beneath the Japanese selvedge denim that encircled the singer's legs – certainly that would help account for some of the high notes he nailed as his goatee-framed lips pushed out the lyrics to his new tune, 'Step To You'.

Not that LaMont's considerable stage presence – or even, for that matter, the gyrations of his two midriff-baring female backing dancers – had me transfixed. Nope, as the pounding of my heart overpowered the tune's speaker-shuddering bass, suddenly the issue taking centre stage in my mind was whether Constance's imminent birthday surprise would turn out to be the masterstroke I'd thus far confidently assumed it to be, or whether it might yet supersede my set piece at the wrap party as the biggest fuck-up since records began.

Once again finding myself cruelly unable to enjoy the simple comforts of a quality sofa (and remember, I didn't even have a living room at home, much less a settee), I left the reclining to Joy and instead set about composing a quick mental character study of her niece using what little information I'd accumulated so far. As luck would have it, Joy had spied me coming out of Wembley Tube station earlier that morning and pulled over to scoop me up off the street. During the brief car journey from station to studio, Constance had overcome her initial shyness of me to exhibit a chirpy personality, chatting excitedly about the prospect of being in the audience at her favourite show and, better still, seeing first hand her favourite heartthrob in the whole wide world.

So far, so good, but Constance's birthday surprise – delivered by her favourite heartthrob in the whole wide world, don't forget – was going to take place on live TV rather than the back seat of her aunty's Peugeot 206. What if she went to pieces? Worse still, what if my once-in-a-lifetime surprise actually scarred her for life, plotting out a pathway that would see her shun all human company en route to finishing up her existence as an elderly recluse who lived in a darkened room with only her sixteen salamanders for company? What if she didn't make it that far? Was it possible, I wondered, for a nine-year-old to die of a heart attack?

At that moment, I received a shock of my own as Joy jolted forward in her seat, detonating a cluster bomb of individually wrapped chocolate miniatures.

'There's Constance!' she exclaimed, as, orbited by two plump afro-puffs, the birthday girl's head fleetingly filled the screen from its location (along with the rest of her body) mere inches from the on-stage action. 'If she gets any closer to him she'll faint!' Fishing a scaled-down Bounty from my crotch, I snuck a glance at the big fella in the leather jacket and wondered if it was too late to initiate contact. He might, it occurred to me, be my only lifeline if this all went wrong and Joy started stabbing me in the neck with her keys. With LaMont's vocal chords finishing their duties and his dog tags coming down to rest in the gentle, cotton covered valley between his pecs, I instead initiated Plan B, edging my arse an inch further away from Joy and nearer to the door.

'Wow!' Wielding a mic and wearing a Pepto-Bismol-coloured 'GIRLS ROCK!' T-shirt, Jessica strode into shot as the audience showed LaMont some E-number-enhanced appreciation. 'Thanks, LaMont. By the sound of it you've got a lot of fans in here this morning. But more importantly you've got one super-duper mega-fan, and that's who I need to find.' Ushering a handful of hair back over her shoulder, she took two steps down from the stage and into the pool of preteens. 'I'm looking for a young lady called Constance.'

From the corner of my eye I noticed Joy slowly rotating her neck. Then I felt her eyeballs pan across my face while the camera panned across those of the young tykes surrounding the stage. Getting nothing from me, she refocused her gaze on the screen just as the camera settled on her niece, who, despite some impressive arm-tugging from flame-haired partner in crime Kelly, had both hands clamped over her mouth, eyes open wide in amazement. Tapping into some emergency reservoir of strength, Kelly managed to pry her mate's left hand from her gaping jaw and wrench her arm up into the air.

'Hello, Constance,' began Jessica, taking her by the hand and leading her up onto the stage. 'Now, a little bird told me that you're a big fan of this gentleman here.' Joy grabbed hold of my thigh while Constance, looking up at her idol in awe, took a big gulp of air – nearly swallowing Jessica's mic in the process – and nodded vigorously. 'And the same little bird also told me that today is a very special day for you.' Joy sunk her nails hard into my thigh, which, like the rest of my body, was too numb with fear to really feel it.

'It's your birthday,' prompted Jessica.

'Yes,' Constance confirmed shyly. I breathed a sigh of relief and wondered if Joy was drawing blood.

'Fantastic,' beamed Jessica. And how old are you today?' Constance nervously kneaded her forehead with her fingers.

'Um ... nine.'

'Nine!' repeated Jessica. 'A lady of advanced years. Well, happy birthday from everyone here at *The Hangout*, but never mind us, I think LaMont's got a few words he wants to say. Isn't that right, LaMont?' The singer took hold of Constance's hand and spoke into the small, streamlined mic that swooped down from the side of his head and around his chiselled jaw.

'A-yo, no doubt, no doubt. Check this here: I'm live on *The Hangout* and I want to say a little something to my special girl Constance.' Placing his left hand on his heart, LaMont launched into a soulful, acapella rendition of 'Happy Birthday', letting his voice take flight as he hit the newly nine-year-old's name. Constance beamed in wobbly amazement. Joy (as far as I could gather from my peripheral vision) dabbed something from her eye.

'Riiich.' Joy's voice wavered with what I suspected might possibly be emotion.

'You didn't know?' I shrugged, popping a sweet into my gob. 'Me and L are boys.' On screen, it transpired that my boy had one final surprise up his sleeve, or, to be precise, around his neck.

'This is for you, little lady,' said LaMont, removing one of his dog tags and lowering its chain over Constance's head. 'Now we got one each to remember today by.' With the chain catching one of Constance's afro-puffs on the way down, it was a manoeuvre slightly lacking in the singer's signature smoothness, but this didn't dim the smile on Constance's face as, clutching her metallic keepsake, she gazed up adoringly at her man.

'Riiich,' repeated Joy, this time tempering the emotion in her voice (if, indeed, that's what it was) by landing a blow to my shoulder. 'You arranged that?'

'Well, it came at a price,' I related as Jessica cued up *The C-Syde* and the stunned, hyperventilating face of Joy's niece gave way to the animated antics of 8-Ball and his aquatic pals. 'So if you'll excuse me I have to go to LaMont's dressing room and have sex with him.' I motioned as if to get up from the couch when Leather Jacket Man leant forward and spoke in a gravelly, bass-filled American voice that, I swear, made the bottles of sparkling water on the table rattle ever so slightly.

'I'm LaMont's manager,' he growled, his eyes drilling a pair of holes in my face, 'and I don't remember that arrangement being made.' I froze dead in my tracks, my buttocks suspended motionless an inch and a half above the sofa cushion while my heart pumped at double speed. 'I'm just messing with you, mate,' he revealed, this time delivering his words in a broad Brummie accent. 'I'm Kevin, the warm-up guy.'

Kevin the Warm-up Guy may have taken his time in debuting his voice (or, indeed, voices) to myself and Joy, but when the show finished and our VIP viewing party moved out of The Players' Lounge and down the corridor leading to the stairs, the noise coming from him was incessant. Technically, mind you, it wasn't Kevin but rather his black leather jacket that was doing all the talking, creaking away boisterously in response to his every movement and replicating, pretty faithfully I imagined, the sound of an insomniac elephant struggling to get some shut-eye on a bouncy castle. As we descended the stairs I stole a sneaky glance at Joy to see if she was picking up on this – I didn't see how she couldn't be. Joy didn't make eye contact but was definitely smiling to herself about something.

At the bottom of the stairs we continued along another corridor, in this case the one festooned with pictures of Hannah Thornwell and friends. As we forged onwards, the racket from the jacket began to mingle with the murmur of excitable audience members streaming past the double doors at the far end. By the time we'd passed another six or so wall-mounted celebs, the murmur had become a palpable rumble. Then the doors opened and, like prison inmates making a mid-riot break for freedom down some hidden underground tunnel (albeit one decorated with myriad soon-to-be-forgotten stars of light entertainment), Denise, Kelly and Constance came towards us.

'D-Nice to the rescue!' I exclaimed. 'Thanks for picking up the kids.'

'Pick them up?' Denise chuckled. 'I had to pull them down from the ceiling, especially this one.' She smiled down at Constance, who had already set to work tugging on Joy's jacket sleeve.

'Aunty Joy! Did you see?'

'I saw it,' laughed Aunty Joy, sending a warm look in my direction. 'I couldn't believe it, but I saw it!'

'Look!' Constance held aloft the dog-tag that hung down low enough to touch her tummy. 'Look what LaMont gave me!'

'Wow!' marvelled Joy. 'You keep that safe, young lady.' Denise slapped Kevin on his squeaky, pumpkin-sized shoulder.

'So, Kev, you wanna come and get that pic for your web site?'

'LaMont's cool with it?' asked Kevin.

'Yeah, totally,' insisted Denise. 'He's a super-nice guy.' Sensing the opportunity to really put the girls' outing over the top, I pulled my camera out of my pocket and started to polish it demonstratively with the bottom of my T-shirt. Naturally, Denise took the bait. 'Is that a hint, Richard?'

'You think he'd be alright with us all cramming into his dressing room?'

'Yeah, of course.' Denise nodded at Constance, now showcasing her formidable sleeve-tugging skills on Kelly's pink hooded sweatshirt. 'You're rolling with his new best buddy, don't forget. Come on, let's go.' With Constance and Kelly bouncing and Kevin resuming his creaking, Denise led us through the doors and the still-flowing stream of children and parents, then down a couple more corridors until we arrived outside a door with LaMont's name stuck on it. Denise patted the tops of her twists and gave two sharp knocks on the door. An elfin American woman with an eight-year-old boy's haircut, artfully distressed clothes and a conventionally distressed manner opened the door and beckoned our six-strong party inside.

'L, honey, we gotta go do radio in like a half-hour so let's make this quick,' she instructed as Denise, Kevin, Constance, Kelly, Joy and myself trooped into the small but comfortable dressing room that LaMont was already sharing with both her and the two buddies squeezed into the room's compact sofa. One of his mates, a lanky-limbed, shaven-headed chap in untied Timberlands, sagging jeans and a bulky, navy blue body warmer, sat tapping away on a laptop while the other, a heavyset fellow in a pristine white T-shirt that simultaneously billowed around his torso and hugged his meaty neck, twirled a fitted baseball cap on his chubby finger. Both of them cracked smiles when they clocked the vertically-challenged contingent of my own crew shuffling into their beige-and-white holding cell. Nor did Constance's arrival go unnoticed by the boys' internationally known buddy, who was getting ready in the mirror and clicked into entertainer mode as soon as he spotted the reversed version of his erstwhile muse.

'Aww, there's my girl!' he exclaimed, securing a twinkling, acorn-sized cluster of karats in his right earlobe before hastily buttoning up his fresh, baby blue shirt in preparation for his Kamikaze photoshoot.

First into the viewfinder was Kevin, who gripped hands with LaMont and feigned an expression of laid-back confidence while Denise backed up across the carpet to meet the compositional demands of her pal's formidable frame and capture the historical meeting of these two born showmen. Next, and following a quick introduction from Denise that billed me as 'the brains behind the birthday surprise', it was my turn to get to work. I began, of course, by immortalising Constance and LaMont's encore embrace, the flash from my camera almost rendered redundant by the birthday girl's megawatt smile as, against the exotic backdrop of a snacks table laden with water, soft drinks, barely touched fruit and heavily hit boxes of chocolates and doughnuts, the crooner leant in and squeezed his arm around her. Constance was short of words but quite clearly thrilled by how her birthday was turning out.

More than conscious that LaMont's PR girl was in danger of bursting out of her vintage AC/DC T-shirt if this session went on much longer, I hurried Kelly in to fill LaMont's other arm before managing, with a little help from the singer himself, to coerce Joy (who'd been sneaking in a few snaps herself with her mobile) into joining the action. Mission accomplished, we left Team LaMont to continue its whirlwind tour of London's media outlets, and, while Kevin and Denise went off in search of Kam (Kevin, it turned out, had inside his squeaky jacket a DVD show reel he thought she'd be interested in), myself, Joy and the girls headed for the exit. We'd just passed through the second set of doors on our route when we ran into Jessica – or rather she ran into us.

'Oh, hi,' she said, apparently quite surprised to find our motley crew roaming the corridors. 'You haven't seen Kam anywhere, have you?'

'No,' I replied, 'but Denise and her friend are after her, so if you hear the sound of heavy breathing and a squeaking leather jacket you're probably on the right track. Hey, Jess, that was unbelievable this morning. You know, what you did for my friend Constance, here. Thank you.'

'Don't be silly. I was just carrying out your master vision,' insisted Jessica. 'Besides,' she added, landing a gentle tap on Constance's denim-shrouded shoulder, 'the birthday girl here was the real star.' Joy looked up at Jessica and gave a smile that was at once both proud and a little bashful. They were both stars as far as I was concerned, and so, keen to capture this corridor-based constellation, I reached for my camera. The gadget was barely halfway out of my jeans pocket when Jessica noticed and reacted, it seemed to me, as if I'd just flashed at her the cold, hard steel of a gun. 'So, er, anyway,' she stammered nervously, 'I've got to dash. Nice to meet you, Constance, and you too ...'

'Kelly,' I volunteered.

'And you too, Kelly. And nice to see you again, Joy.'

'Yeah, thanks for ...' began Joy, but Jessica was already halfway down the corridor. Raising a finger, Joy half-pointed at the space vacated by the presenter and gave me a quizzical look that said, 'is it just me, or ...' It wasn't just her, though. Jessica had definitely seemed nervy and in an awful rush to wrap things up. In fact, I wondered if she hadn't managed to shave a second or two off our last, amicable-but-awkward corridor encounter, although in fairness she'd been wearing a mortar board hat and flowing robes then, which was hardly the most streamlined of get-ups. Either way, as I slid my Glock, sorry, my camera back into my pocket, there was a more pressing question on my mind.

'So Joy, you know how I owed you one?' Joy balled up a

fist and gently bounced it off my shoulder.

'You know what? I think we might be quits.'

'Uh-uh. Not quite. Who's for a slap-up birthday lunch?'

Clearly, mixing it up with fresh-faced R&B royalty was hungry work, because the answer, it immediately transpired, was 'everyone'. And so we clambered into Joy's car and headed for an artery-hardening early afternoon lunch at Angela's, a family oriented, American-themed eatery known for its tasty, no-nonsense grub and hearty portions. As we exited the Artemis car park, Joy shot a quick glance into her rear-view mirror, then reached across and pressed a button on the CD player. The feel-good opening keys of 'You're the Inspiration' by Chicago filled the car. I smiled to myself. Or so I thought.

'Oh, what?' asked Joy. 'You think a black girl can't like music by middle-of-the-road white boys?'

'On the contrary,' I laughed. 'Everyone should listen to the classics.' Joy peered, again, into her rear-view mirror.

'Constance usually complains, but I don't think she's too concerned about the in-ride music at the moment.' She was right. In the back seat, Constance and Kelly were practically bursting out of their seat belts as, impervious to Joy's playlist, they buzzed about their unforgettable morning.

The buzzing continued apace at Angela's, where, amidst mouthfuls of burgers and fries, the two girls excitedly relived LaMont's serenading of Constance before hitting rewind and, amidst mouthfuls of ice-cream and brownies, reliving it all over again. The post-show analysis paused briefly when, following a discreet, en route-to-the-toilet tip-off from yours truly, our waiter brought a birthday cake to our table (and I persuaded a strangely self-conscious Joy to join me and Kelly in singing 'Happy Birthday' somewhat less tunefully than the R&B dreamboat), then assumed another dimension when the girls spotted a classmate settling down with her parents at a table across the room and scuttled over for a third party perspective.

'I've got to hand it to you,' said Joy, smiling as she

watched her niece excitedly model her new jewellery. 'You've had quite a run with the ladies lately.' This, I decided, was my cue to address Joy's apparent misconception about me and Jessica, something that, looking at the girl Bennett from across a table full of ice-cream-smeared bowls and screwed-up serviettes, I now suddenly felt compelled to do.

'That photo in *Gab*, it's not what it looks like. That was like a fraction of a second of us larking around. Well, of Jessica larking around, actually. There was no larking on my part. Total, across-the-board lack of larkage.' Joy looked sceptical.

'Well you two seemed pretty friendly when you came by the office.'

'Friendly,' I echoed as our waiter arrived to clear our table. 'Exactly. That's it, that's all we are. Friends ... Well, not even friends, really. We're colleagues who happen to be friendly. Friendly colleagues. Frolleagues. That's what we are: frolleagues.'

'Really? I assumed you'd come in to show your girlfriend off.'

'Well, to be honest, that's what I *was* doing,' I confessed sheepishly. 'Except she's not my girlfriend.' Eyebrow raised a notch, Joy pondered my revelation while the waiter – young and gangly with floppy, centre-parted blonde hair and the biggest Adam's apple I'd ever seen in my life – scooped up our crockery. It wasn't until he and his king-sized throat-fruit had disappeared to get our cheque that she spoke again.

'OK. Well, while we're being honest, I have something to tell you, too. But first you have to promise not to kill me.'

'Alright,' I agreed. 'But only because your untimely death would undo all of my good work by putting a minor dampener on Constance's birthday.'

'Well you see, that's the thing,' said Joy, stretching a nervous, slanted grin across her face. 'It's not actually her birthday today.'

'Oh. So it's tomorrow, then?'

'No.'

'Monday?'

'Not quite. Her birthday isn't for another two months. I just told you it was today to make double sure you got her in.' I paused to take stock of the news. I was quite amused by Joy's duplicity, although naturally I went for a reaction somewhere between 'aghast' and 'outraged'.

'What the hell? Are you two like an aunt and niece con team or something?'

'It's pretty bad, I know,' admitted Joy. 'But guess what? I've got another confession.'

'Don't tell me. That girl over there isn't really your niece.'

'Nope. My confession is that, right now, I should probably feel bad that I lied to you. I *should* … but I don't.' I was about to ask Joy what she meant when Constance came bursting over.

'Aunty Joy,' she gushed. 'Meena saw us on TV!'

'Wow!' exclaimed Joy before tempering her tone slightly. 'Well, Little Miss Superstar, I'm sure Meena and her mum and dad want to order their food, and we're going now, anyway, so go and get hold of Kelly.' As Constance scurried off again to retrieve her sidekick, a smile played on Joy's lips.

'Can I make one final confession?' she asked.

'Go ahead. Cleanse your soul.'

'Well,' she began, placing her palms on the table and leaning in towards me. 'The thing is, I'm kind of glad you and Jessica aren't an item.'

'Why?' I asked, suddenly feeling nervous without really knowing why. Joy looked around, leant in a little further and lowered her voice to a near-whisper.

'Because then I wouldn't be able to unveil my new name for her.' She paused for a second before the grand unveiling. 'Jessic-whore.' Beaming from hooped ear to hooped ear, she fell back in her seat, clearly thrilled with her verbal ingenuity.

'Oh, that's genius,' I noted as my man Adam Sapple brought us the bill and a small bowl of after-dinner mints. 'You've actually made the word "whore" a fully integrated part of her name.' I changed my voice from one of mock admiration to mock admonishment. 'And after she was so nice to both you and Constance. *On her birthday.*'

Lying on my bed that evening, I looked into Joy's eyes, then studied the contours of her rich brown cheeks. She looked happy and I knew I was. In fact, a full four smiles were staring back at me from the screen of my laptop, although Kelly's was slightly obscured by the elasticated cuff of her pink sleeve as she tended, a split second too late, to a stray smidgeon of chocolate cake. As captured by the multitasking Mr. Sapple, it was a great photo; the perfect memento of a perfect day, although as I scrolled through the handful of other photos I'd taken, I suspected that Constance would be rather more made-up with the snap of her hugging her new mate LaMont in his dressing room. Scrolling onwards some more, I studied the group shot I'd put together with the singer's help. Expert lensman that I was, I'd managed to capture Joy's mouth ajar as she turned towards LaMont, but while the photo gave the impression that she, like her niece, was in awe of the smoothie in the baby blue shirt, she'd actually been boldly correcting his assertion that, in the character doing the (in this case largely inept) pointing and pressing, she had 'a good man'. LaMont, it struck me, was a good man himself, and with all previous bus shelter and billboard beef now officially squashed, I reckoned that I might even download his album or, better yet, pick up a physical copy if I saw it at a decent price (eight quid or less). It was a shame that I hadn't managed to get a snap with Jessica in it, but now that I thought about it, it had been pretty boneheaded of me to even contemplate pointing a camera in her direction. Amateur photography had caused her enough embarrassment recently – that had been made pretty clear by the speed with which she'd bolted from me in the corridor earlier. And, for that matter, the day before, too.

I double-clicked the internet icon at the top left corner of my screen. The funny thing was, the slight twinge of sadness I was starting to feel wasn't because Jessica's awkwardness around me had in any way spoiled the day – not at all. No, it was because I'd just had a day that *nothing* could have spoiled, and in my experience days like this didn't come along very often; not in my world, at least. I probably wouldn't have a day this good for another two, two and a half years – if ever. This, quite possibly, had been the greatest day since records began, and in a strange sense that really sucked. The day on which I'd eaten Thai chicken with Jessica had been great, but compared to today, that had been like a rainy Monday's work experience at the abortion clinic. I was still trying to figure out why that was the case (it couldn't all have been down to the larger portion sizes at Angela's), but one thing I knew for certain was that the incredible high I'd been experiencing ever since LaMont crooned to Constance (actually, since I first sat down in the passenger seat of Joy's car) couldn't last much longer, and that the grim, shadow-cloaked figure of anticlimax was just around the corner waiting to punch me in the face while a group of mates with camera-phones gleefully recorded the incident for internet broadcast. Still, I thought as I checked into my e-mail account, I'd take that happy slapping tomorrow. For now, I was going to keep today's fun and frolics alive and well by sending Joy my action-packed pics.

Before I got a chance to do so, I noticed that Joy had got in there with a reply to my earlier, ticket-confirming, hotness-touting e-mail from Tuesday. I opened it and read the contents:

Dearest Arseface, sorry, Rich,

Thanks a million for today. You gave Constance the best (fake) birthday ever! The good news is that my sister wants to marry you, so if you see an angry-looking black man with a lazy eye following you about, it may be my brother-in-law. Oh, and by the way, and before I change my mind, I think you've earned this ... But if you show it, or speak of it to a single soul, I'll rip your head off, scoop out the innards and fill it with flowers to make a hanging basket.

192

Love always, Joy xx

I scrolled a couple of inches down the screen and there, beneath Joy's charming words, was the 'this' that, at long last, I'd apparently earned. 'This', to my delight, was a scanned reproduction of the image I'd been longing to see for months; an image that, in my mind, had acquired an almost mythic, Holy Grail-type status. And now that it was there, in front of my eyes, it not only met my sky-high expectations but surpassed them. There, as per the legend, was a fresh-faced Joy, who, together with two mates, was modelling the type of gear and attitude that was straight from the cover of, well, TLC's 1992 debut album, *Oooohhhh on the TLC Tip!*

One of the crew, a slightly chubby, light-skinned black girl, was crouched on the floor in a manner that was half-B-girl, half-squatting-to-pee girl – although if nature had been calling, she'd have had to work fast to unfasten the spacious, canary-yellow dungarees that enveloped her doughy frame (actually, on second thought, the dungarees were so generously cut she could probably have let loose without fear of soaking fabric or flesh). At the other side of the picture, a white lass whose blonde, tomboyish haircut made her the default T-Boz of this tribute band stood strong in frayed denim shorts and an enormous multicoloured T-shirt, mature enough to have tended to any toiletry needs before the shoot but brandishing a baby's rattle nonetheless. And there between them was Joy, arms spread wide and the grin on her youthful features spread even wider.

Red was the predominant colour of her ensemble. Bright, eyeball-throttling crimson red. It was the colour of the baggy, billowing shorts that hovered around her thighs and the Cincinnati Reds baseball cap whose brim leant over the side of her head as if seeking out a different, hopefully conclusive view of the fashion catastrophe it couldn't quite believe was taking place below. A pair of braces were the only thing keeping the shorts up, although without them Joy's dignity, such as it was, would at least have been preserved by the plaid boxer shorts which reached up towards the twisted tendrils of black hair flowing from beneath that crimson cap. Conversely, by strapping down a white T-shirt large enough to double as a wedding marquee, the braces were also, it seemed, the only thing that would have kept Joy earthbound had a sudden gust of wind crept up one of the sagging sleeves that hung down past her elbows.

The devil, however, was most definitely in the details. Above her shiny black combat boots and the scrunched red socks whose fabric piled up like icing from a piping bag, one of Joy's knees was encased in a fluorescent pink, green and yellow kneepad while the calf of her other leg bore a couple of sticking plasters. The effect was like looking at the before and after photos of a BMX safety campaign. Then there was the piece de resistance; the very reason why Joy's decision to get on the TLC tip had, she'd told me, proven so controversial. Hanging down nonchalantly from the elasticated waistband of Joy's not-so-underwear was that most fashion-forward yet practical of accessories: a strip of condoms. I counted four yellow circles staring at me from against their white backing, and I wondered if the four-week grounding Joy had received from her mum had been decided upon using a one-week-per-visible-rubber ruling.

You might imagine that Joy could have avoided any punishment whatsoever had her friends simply told her what she looked like, but clearly they too had wholeheartedly embraced this exciting new wave of Sheath Chic. Indeed, Squatting Girl had, with the help of some plastic joke shop glasses, secured one of the condoms in front of her right peeper à la the late Lisa 'Left Eye' Lopes, so in fairness she probably had a very limited view of Joy's appearance. How times change: these days most mothers would probably be thrilled to know their sixteen-year-old daughter was equipped at all times with a generous supply of Durex.

I clicked 'reply' and, one by one, attached my own photos

before typing my response:

Dearest Chilli,

Awesome, just awesome. Can't wait to get this printed on a T-shirt. Good to see that, even as you embarked on a lifetime of promiscuity, you were already aware of the importance of protection. Attached are some R&B superstar-themed photos of my own – enjoy!

Love, R xx

P.S. I think I saw your blonde friend at Kings Cross the other night. She still carries a lot of condoms about her person.

That ought to do it, I thought, hitting 'Send'. There was no point expending all my wit in the written word when I could derive hours of future fun from ridiculing the grown-up version of Prophylactic Girl in the flesh. *If* I decided to go back to Red Button, that was. In the meantime, I went back into Joy's e-mail, then reached over to my bedside table and grabbed the cable hanging from my printer. I plugged it into my laptop and sent the e-mail to print. It wouldn't hurt to grab myself a physical copy of Joy's early-nineties masterpiece – you know, for comedic inspiration. Lying back on my mattress, I listened to the whirring and shuddering of the printer, followed by the sound of two sheets of paper dropping down to join the three spiral bound *Crushed* episodes already lining my carpet. Since arriving home in the afternoon, I'd actually resumed writing the abandoned fourth episode. It was odd, but for the first time since I made the exhilarating decision to jack in my infatuation-themed opus, I'd felt the urge to do some more work on it, even if my new photos had somewhat distracted me from the task. I yanked the printer cable out of my laptop and dropped it to the floor with the rest of the debris, then clicked off Joy's e-mail. A page of my resurrected comedy classic took its place, but before I could even try to make a concerted run at three consecutive words, the sound of my buzzer practically jolted me off my bed. Tripping over one of my shoes, I stumbled into the hallway and pressed down on the intercom.

'Hello?'

'Hi. It's me,' announced a crackle-encrusted female voice transmitting live and direct from my doorstep. I didn't recognise who 'me' was, but it definitely wasn't Mrs. Quinn from down below. 'It's Jessica,' clarified the voice. Jessica? What the hell?

'Um, OK … Come on up.' I pushed down on the button then tore back into my room, picking up the paperwork from my floor, shuffling it together and ramming the resultant pile together with the other scripts residing in the magazine rack on my desk. Order was restored just as Jessica appeared in my door frame wearing a cream-coloured top, jeans and a nervous expression. She had a bright orange handbag tucked under her arm. 'How did you ...' I began.

'Sorry,' offered Jessica, hands clasped together as she stepped into my room. 'I copied your address from Kam's Blackberry after I saw you today. I hope you don't mind. It's a little stalker-ish, I know.' I gave a shrug.

'Well, yeah, now I'm gonna have to move out, but as you can see, that won't be too much of a shame.' I was trying to sound cool, but inside I was more than a little unnerved by this surprise visit.

'Nah, it's cosy.' Jessica turned around to observe her surroundings, coming to a stop with her back now facing my bed.

'Cosy? I was going to offer you the tour but that little on-the-spot, one-eighty turn you just did is pretty much it.'

'Ooohh, she's cute,' remarked a suddenly distracted Jessica. I followed her eyes and noticed that they'd alighted on my broadband box , now basking in the glow of the angle-poise lamp on my desk. I squinted at Latte Girl as if stumbling upon her charms for the first time.

'Yeah, she's alright,' I concurred. 'She looks vivacious, I'll give her that.' Jessica leant in for a closer inspection of Latte Girl's floodlit features.

'You're right. She *does* look vivacious.'

'To a fault. She looks vivacious to a fault.'

'Yep,' agreed Jessica, nodding vigorously. 'To a fault.' After a few more seconds of prolonged piston action, her neck muscles gradually ground to a halt, at which point she vacuumed up every breath of air in my bedroom and clasped her hands together under her now-steady chin.

'So listen,' she exhaled. 'I came to apologise.'

'Apologise? For what?'

'I thought you'd be pissed off with me.'

'What? Why would I be pissed off with you?' Jessica let her hands fall back by her sides. Behind her, on my bed, my *Crushed* script faded out in deference to a screen saver of – ohhhhhhhh, shit! – Jessica herself.

'You know, the picture.'

'The picture?' I repeated anxiously, looking over her shoulder and directly into her eyes.

'The picture in *Gab*.'

'Oh, *that* picture,' I squeaked as the picture on my screen gave way to one of Jessica snuggled up in a polka dot-covered hooded zip-up. 'I thought *you* were pissed off. Or embarrassed or ashamed or something.'

'What? Come here!' Jessica flung her arms around me, sending the smell of shampoo rushing up my nostrils. Now *this* was a cosy set-up, or at least it might have been were I not desperately wondering how to avert the disaster of Jessica turning around and finding herself the star of a second shrine. Joy wasn't here to save me now, so instead I sent my right hand – the one not clamped rigidly against Jessica's back – on a do-or-die mission into my pocket.

'Uh, it's just that, you know, you've got a reputation to uphold,' I reasoned, stalling for time while my fingers scrambled frantically over a screwed-up tissue and onwards

197

into the darkest, most lint-infested depths of my jeans.

'Shut up!' laughed Jessica. Behind her, the slideshow continued apace with a picture of her cuddling a saggy-faced basset hound. 'You know, I'm pretty sure you didn't take this job with the dream of becoming my boyfriend.'

'True,' I lied as my fingers came up for air clutching one of Angela's finest after-dinner mints, 'but I still say you got the rough end of the dog. Er, the deal.'

'It could have been worse,' reasoned Jessica, 'I could have been photographed drunk leaving Precario with Brett Scott.' I laughed but it was nervous laughter. This was it, I realised, squeezing my sugar-based lifeline into my palm. My entire future with Jessica was to be determined by my hand-to-eye co-ordination and a foil-wrapped palate-cleanser which had, until now, been conserving its energy in a bed of tissue and crumpled-up till receipts. I cocked back my wrist and, with one fluid but truncated underarm swing, sent the sweet flying through the air. The moment it left my hand I knew I had overthrown it. As the sweet reached the peak of its trajectory about three quarters of the way across the carpet-covered canyon between me and my bed, I realised it was going to fly straight over the laptop and ... No, wait ... It was just possible ... I held my breath, cutting off the Pantene aroma while, in agonising slo-mo, the mint curved downwards. My heart pummelled Jessica's collar bone. The mint clipped the top of the screen and, after holding its pose for what seemed like an eternity, fell down onto the keyboard, banishing my visitor's digital likeness (by now she was cheesing it up at a children's movie premiere) from sight. My script returned to the screen and the smell of shampoo returned to my nose while Jessica's ears – or at least the one not pressed against my chest – pricked up. She broke the embrace and looked around.

'What was that?'

'Probably just a paparazzo's camera going off,' I joked. 'There's a slight gap in the curtains.'

'We should probably stand at opposite sides of the room,'

suggested Jessica, smiling slyly. 'Joy'll probably kill us both if we hit the newsstands for a second time.'

'Joy? What d'you mean?'

'Well, I wouldn't want to see *my* boyfriend plastered across the gossip mags with another woman.'

'Joy? No, she's not my boyfriend,' I babbled. 'I mean girlfriend. She's not my girlfriend.' Jessica looked surprised.

'Oh. I just thought …'

'She's got a boyfriend,' I pointed out. 'Who she lives with.' Jessica hoisted the strap of her handbag, which had fallen down her arm during our embrace, back up onto her shoulder.

'Oh, well, good for her. And him. Good for both of them.' She looked at me curiously for a second. 'Right?'

'Yeah, they're a good couple,' I reflected, stepping across the carpet to attend to my laptop. 'Excuse me while I just ...'

'Sorry. I've interrupted your ...'

'No, no,' I insisted, scooping the sweet up from the keyboard and hastily folding the laptop shut. 'I was finished anyway. I was just sending an e-mail to ... I mean, I was just doing some writing, but I wasn't really having much J ... uh, I wasn't really getting anywhere.'

'Oh, well, if you're absolutely sure.'

'I'm sure. Besides, now that you've infiltrated my hideout, the least I can do is get you something to eat or drink. Or both.' Jessica smiled sweetly, letting that orange leather strap ease its way a couple of inches down her arm again.

'I wouldn't say no to a cup of tea. Milk, no sugar, please.'

'Coming right up.' I headed out of the bedroom door before briefly poking my head back around. 'Make yourself at home.'

In the kitchen, I opened my tightly clenched fist and placed my aerodynamic breath-freshener down on the sideboard. Now *that* had been a narrow escape. Even narrower than the narrow escape at Red Button. Adrenaline still flowing through my body, I rinsed my kettle out three times, then filled it with water, placed it in its base unit and switched it on. As if

Jessica popping in unannounced hadn't been enough of a shock.

'So what were you writing?' Jessica called out.

'When?' I called back.

'Just now. Before I came.'

'Oh ... um, just a little script I'm working on. Just some stupid stuff.'

'I'd love to see some of this stupid stuff sometime.'

'Hmmm ... Well, if you're really desperate to sample my oeuvre, there's a stack of scripts in that rack on my desk. Next to Latte Gi ... uh, next to the vivacious lady.'

'Where?' Jessica called back. 'Oh, yeah. Here they are.'

There they were and there she was. Never in my wildest fantasies had I imagined Jessica George being in my bedroom, although that was mainly because, as a general rule, our imaginary sexual gymnastics had tended to take place in a room with at least a double, rather than a single, bed and without bubbles in the wallpaper. Still, I thought, opening the cabinet overlooking my sink, even if my humble abode wasn't a *Cribs*-ready fantasy pad, the least I could do was extend to my guest the very best level of hospitality available. I pulled two mugs out of the cupboard and placed them down on the sideboard. Jessica was getting my finest item of crockery – a lovely, vibrantly coloured vessel decorated with leaping lambs (as well as the arguably superfluous words 'leaping lambs') and capped off with a pearlescent finish. It had come with an Easter egg and a small cuddly lamb tucked inside, too, so you know this thing could hold some serious liquid. For myself, I selected a faded promotional mug from Red Button's canine athletics competition *Britain's Fittest Butcher's Dog*. When your favourite television hottie was waiting for you in your bedroom, it was good to remember where you came from.

With the kettle doing its thing, I wandered back into my bedroom and found Jessica leafing through *Flexi-Bill and Ioan Lung*, an absurdist superhero comedy in which, following a free onsite company health check, two office workers combine their newly discovered talents for flexibility and respiration to fight crime in and around their place of work.

'When did you first decide you wanted to be a writer?' she asked, looking up from the duo's adventures. 'Do you remember?'

'I remember it clearly,' I replied, locking my arms behind my back and lifting my jaw as my mind transported me back in time. 'I was twelve and in my last year of middle school, and my epiphany took place during a particular lesson.'

'An English lesson?'

'Actually, a French lesson. As I recall, we had to write these little plays to act out with classmates. I wrote myself the role of a difficult restaurant customer who is perturbed to be given snails when he in fact ordered crepes.' Jessica closed *Flexi-Bill and Ioan Lung* and placed it back on my desk so as to give my flashback (which, even at this early stage of its narrative, had already wrong-footed her expectations) her full attention.

'Well, yeah, I suppose you *would* be put out.'

'Oh, I *was* put out,' I related, turning on my heels and proceeding – in as much as the limited floor-space allowed it – to pace across the carpet. 'I, or rather my character Jean-Claude Cristophe, was *très* put out. So put out, that, in his indignation, he furiously bellowed, "Pour l'amour de Pete!"'

'Pour l'amour de what?'

'Pour l'amour de Pete!' I encored, spinning back around and thrusting a triumphant finger towards my ceiling. 'Or, in English, "For the love of Pete!"' Jessica looked back at me, vaguely bewildered.

'Shouldn't that be "For the love of *Pierre*?"'

'No,' I said firmly. 'The phrase specifically says "Pete", and besides, when Pete Sampras played on French clay, nobody temporarily called him Pierre Sampras, did they? Anyway, the look I got from Madame Warburton, the French teacher, when I deployed that particular phrase let me know that I was pushing boundaries with my writing.'

'You mean you were using a phrase that French people

don't use,' posited Jessica. 'That *English* people don't use.'

'Well, I can assure you that, on this particular day, the phrase leapt effortlessly from the Gallic lips of Jean-Claude Christophe,' I said, staring proudly back into the past (or at least at my putrid wallpaper). 'Meanwhile, the question I was asking myself was, if I could create this kind of magic within the format of the three-minute French language vignette, was there any limit to the greatness I could surely accomplish in my native tongue?' Jessica held up her hand.

'Did nobody ask the question of whether you needed mental help?'

'Hey!' I protested. 'From what I hear, my script-writing skills have served you pretty well, Little Miss Travel Show Presenter.' Jessica looked surprised.

'Oh, you heard about that?'

'I keep my ear to the street. Congratulations.' I paused for a second before adding, 'You deserve it.'

'And you deserve this.' Jessica dipped into her handbag and came up with a neatly wrapped, square-shaped present. 'That's kind of the other reason I've hunted you down like a madwoman tonight. You did me that script at like a minute's notice and I never got the chance to thank you. I mean, I did get the chance, but ...' She paused to take a deep breath before handing me the present. 'Well, anyway, thank you.'

'Oh, wow. Thanks. You didn't have to.'

'Oh, I did,' insisted Jessica as I tore open the wrapping paper to reveal a copy of 'Give You My All', Liam's album. I laughed out loud at the sight of our colleague, hand pressed over his heart, looking up longingly from beneath the strands of his slicked-down pampas grass fringe.

'Awww, you shouldn't have. *Really.*' Jessica gave me a cheeky grin.

'You don't have it already, do you?'

'Other than Liam, I'm pretty sure that *nobody* has this already.' I opened up the jewel case and slid out the glossy inlay booklet. Flicking through it, I was met with half a dozen shots of Liam preening, pouting and posing. 'Thanks to all my fans for the support,' I said, reading aloud from his 'Special Thanx' section. 'Wow. He really jumped the gun on that one.' I flicked over another page and landed on the money shot. 'Do you think Liam would sign this for me?' I asked, holding up a picture of the would-be dreamboat sporting a tight-fitting plaid waistcoat with nothing underneath, his skinny naked arms locked in a praying position. Jessica gasped and made a gagging face. I took the CD out of the case, walked over to the micro hi-fi system on top of my chest of drawers and popped it in. 'I'm sorry, but track number seven's called "Lost In Your Lips."' I hit play on the tune in question and Liam's dire, rice paper vocals – spread to levels of near-transparent thinness over a piss-weak synth beat – filled the air.

'Oh, God,' I groaned.

'Hey, don't knock it just yet,' teased Jessica, returning to my magazine rack and rifling through my scripts. 'I haven't finished sifting through your back catalogue.'

'Don't mention my writing in the same breath as his so-called singing or I'll put bleach in your tea,' I warned, returning to the kitchen.

Forgotten during the excitement caused by Jessica's present, the water in the kettle had already long since boiled, but I wanted my surprise guest's cuppa to be perfect, so I pressed the button down again. The water quickly returned to peak temperature, its bubbling becoming progressively more boisterous until steam billowed from the kettle's spout and, content that its work was done (again), the red light clicked off. I took two tea bags from their box, dropped them in the mugs and drowned them in hot water before grabbing a container of milk from the fridge and lacing the liquid with some meandering semi skimmed clouds. Into my own brew I added a shaking of artificial sweetener and contemplated how jealous Colin Thunder would be if he could only see my current house guest.

My smugness was short-lived as I examined Jessica's

pallid potion and realised that despite (or perhaps because of) her allotted mug's considerable capacity, I'd gone overboard with the milk. Sending my teaspoon on a rescue mission, I hauled the teabag from the insipid depths and pressed it up against the side of the mug in a bid to turn the off-white mixture brown. Nothing doing. I dropped in another tea bag and squeezed it, too, up against the side of the mug but it was no use. As weak as the whining coming from my hi-fi, Jessica's tea looked set to peak somewhere between 'Slipper Satin' and 'Crisp Linen' on the Dulux colour chart. Desperate times called for desperate measures, so I poured the wannabe tea into the sink and, using the remaining hot water in the kettle, started from scratch. Content, at last, that Jessica's beverage was back on track and worthy of flowing through her luscious lips, I decided to offer her my appraisal of the tea-brewing soundtrack she'd so kindly provided me with.

'You know, this might be the worst, most spiteful gift anyone has ever given me,' I called out. Jessica didn't answer me. Either she was lost in my writing or Liam's crooning had prompted her to strangle herself with my printer cable.

I fished the teabag out of the mugs, tossed them into the sink and gave the drinks one last stir, satisfied that Jessica's had reached a hue pitched perfectly between manila and clay. 'Make the most of this,' I advised, carefully carrying the two piping hot cuppas across the hallway and into my room, 'because when I'm living in a mansion in Holly ...' I stopped mid-sentence. Jessica wasn't there. Hmmm ... Maybe she'd gone to the bathroom. It wouldn't have taken her long to find it by process of elimination. Then I saw something that told me everything I needed to know. There, lying on my floor, were the two pages comprising my printout of Joy's e-mail. The first page, the one that showed her younger self on the TLC tip, wasn't the problem. The problem was the second page. The one that featured a two-thumbs-in-the-air picture of Jessica and my tongue-in-cheek remark about having full sex with her.

I dropped both cups of tea and the hot, just-the-right-shade-of-brown liquid bled across the carpet and into the corner of the Jessica page. A thump sounded from underneath the puddles and the pictures.

'Pack that music in!' shouted Mrs. Quinn.

'Fuck off, you dusty old cow!' I shouted back. It wasn't much consolation, but it seemed I probably *would* have better days than this after all.

CHAPTER SIX

I shovelled a handful of M&Ms into my mouth, then wiped my chocolate-streaked fingers on my silky polyester shorts. The midday sun was doing its best to soften up my weighty cache of confectionery, but the prolific rate at which I was dipping into the plastic bag at my side meant that, even burning as hot as it was, it still had its work cut out. That said, it wouldn't hurt to get a little assistance with my chocolate chomping, and besides, it was only polite that I offered some of my goodies to the friend who'd kindly allowed me to share the park bench with him, and to whom, for the last ten minutes or so, I'd already been talking.

'You want some?' I asked, holding out the king-sized bag and giving its contents an enticing shake.

'Thanks,' said the tramp, sorry, homeless person – the same chap who'd contributed to mine and Eddie's malevolent guide dog conversation a couple of weeks earlier – from somewhere behind his straggly grey beard. He formed a makeshift bowl with his hands and watched as an assortment of vibrant, sugar-shelled pellets landed on the matted navy fabric of his fingerless gloves. 'I'd offer you some of my refreshments but it appears I've finished them.' I looked over at the crumpled beer cans twinkling from within the crinkled plastic folds of his own less-than-luxury luggage.

'That's alright,' I said, throwing back another handful of highly addictive, brightly coloured pills. 'I'm all set.' I cracked open one of the cans from my own six-strong arsenal and chased the chocolate down with a lengthy swig of the carbonated, caffeinated hard stuff. My head was buzzing now, thanks, it seemed fair to assume, to the lethal cocktail of sleeplessness, sunshine and shit-loads of sugar that I'd prescribed myself to help soothe my heartbreak. Truth be told, it hadn't numbed the pain at all, nor dulled my acute awareness of the fact that I was without question the biggest, most worthless piece of excrement to ever foul up this park or any other environment, urban or rural. I felt devastated. I felt worse than devastated. I had hurt someone I really liked, someone who I had come to think of as a real friend, and what's more I'd done it through a moment of complete and utter carelessness. Not that how I'd done it made any difference. The bottom line was that I'd hurt Jessica and there probably wasn't much I could do to put things right. I'd try, of course, when I saw her, but for now there wasn't much I could do beyond scarfing down chocolate and guzzling fizzy drinks. In fact, prior to embarking on my sun-baked bingeing session, the only halfway productive thing I'd done was pick up my computer and drag my photographs of Jessica – all of them – into the wastepaper bin at the bottom right corner of the screen. The computer speakers had relayed the sound of paper being scrunched into a ball and nonchalantly tossed into a metal trash can. I didn't need that noise to let me know I'd screwed this one up.

I looked over at my fellow benchwarmer, who was busy trying to displace a shard of chocolate from his molar. Maybe I'd grow a beard (as it happened, I'd already started), say a tearful farewell to basic hygiene and opt out of society altogether – it seemed like it might be the best thing for both parties. Indeed, given that I'd left the house wearing navy flip-flops with black socks (a combination shown off beautifully by the shimmering silver basketball shorts that sagged down past my kneecaps), it could be argued that I was already giving the middle finger to society's rules and regulations.

I lifted the can to my lips and tilted back my head, closing my eyes as the sun beat down on my face and the sticky brown liquid cascaded down my throat and into my sickly sweet bloodstream. I was definitely starting to feel odd, so it came as only a mild surprise when 'Greensleeves' started to ring in my ears. The contents of my can duly drained, I pushed forward my head and pulled back my eyelids to see Tweety Bird and Tinkerbell flying about in front of me. I closed my eyes again and opened them once more, this time realising that I was looking at an ice-cream van whose side panels were adorned with wonky, unconvincing renderings of copyright-protected cartoon icons – an industry standard from my experience of these vehicles. I crushed my can and tossed it into a nearby bin, where a posse of wasps set to work on it like Sunday bargain hunters hitting up a car boot sale.

'Ice-cream?' I asked my furry-faced neighbour, who himself was attracting a considerable share of attention from the wasp community.

'I'd prefer booze,' he admitted. I rose to my flip-flop-rocking feet, sending a couple of stray M&Ms ricocheting off the concrete like rainbow-coloured hail stones.

'I can see if they've got a cider lolly, but I'm not sure they're in vogue these days.'

'Hang on. I'll give you the money.' The tramp reached under the frayed outskirts of his trademark (and presumably sweltering) red-and-black lumberjack shirt and rummaged in the hip pocket of his cords, which were similarly heavyweight though generously insulated in several places. 'I'm taking the piss,' he laughed, flashing a collection of teeth that, whilst markedly incomplete, nonetheless spanned the entire colour spectrum of an overripe banana.

I trooped over to the ice-cream van, where a compact, powerful-looking chap with gelled hair and a hoop earring sorted me out with a pair of his finest ninety-nines. Back at the bench and following a quick chorus of Toto's '99', I handed my new mate his generously stacked, Flake-augmented cornet.

'What's your name?' I asked.

'Morris,' he replied.

'Hi, Morris. I'm Richard, by the way.' Resuming my spot on the bench, I got to work customising my own dessert, studding the thick white ice-cream with some M&Ms before using my teeth to unwrap a king-sized Snickers and plant it opposite the Flake that came as standard. True, this was probably a rather decadent snack to be preparing in front of a homeless person, but I'd already hooked Morris up and besides, he'd said himself he preferred booze to the sweet stuff.

'Morris, do you ever feel like you just fu ... excuse me, messed your entire life up? To the point where you've thrown away everything you've had and now you're left with ... nothing?' Morris wiped his mouth with the cuff of his checked sleeve while his close-but-deep-set, flinty brown eyes stared back sternly at me from within the folds of his chamois-skinned face. Almost immediately, I realised that my enquiry could possibly have been construed as an ill-mannered rhetorical question, and as a hole formed in Morris' ice-cream-daubed beard, I half-expected a beer scented gale of abuse to blast out. Instead he spoke softly and, to my surprise, with startling perceptiveness.

'It's about a girl, isn't it?'

'Is it that obvious?' I enquired through a mouthful of chocolate, ice-cream and more chocolate.

'Let me guess. You formed a wonderful friendship with a girl you'd idolised from afar – some would say your dream girl. Then, owing to a moment of stupidity and carelessness, you threw it all away. It's like you ripped the relationship apart at the seams.' My jaw dropped at Morris's powers of deduction. Actually, my jaw was already open to receive my next mouthful of ice-cream, but I was extremely surprised by Morris's powers of deduction nonetheless.

'How did you know?' I asked.

'You've mentioned it a few times now,' related Morris. He paused to employ his tongue in apprehending a trickle of ice-cream that was rapidly escaping down his cone before adding, 'A lot of the more personal things you've been thinking, you've actually been saying out loud, too.'

'Oh. Sorry,' I murmured, feeling suitably embarrassed. 'That bit about ripping the relationship apart at the seams. Were those my exact words?'

'Yeah.' I clamped my free hand against my forehead.

'Urgghh,' I groaned. 'That's awful. I mean, that's really horrible. I apologise for subjecting you to that, Morris.' While I returned to ravaging my ice-cream, Morris looked at me. Kind of soulfully, I thought.

'Sometimes I feel like I'm lucky to be living rough,' he sighed. I nodded appreciatively at his wisdom.

'Yeah, you know, I can see that. I guess, in a funny way, life is less complicated for you. You don't have to deal with these heartbreaks.' Having apparently used most of his ice-cream to decorate his beard, Morris took the first crunch of his cone, then chewed and swallowed before answering.

'No,' he corrected. 'I mean because, as a general rule, I don't have to listen to people like you whining on like women having their periods.' His milky whiskers parted and I was once again treated to his ramshackle grab-bag of yellow, brown and black fangs. Wow. A tramp was making fun of me. At least I could say I was spending my Sunday helping the homeless.

'Well, the good news for you is that I'm going to fill my whining mouth with more ice-cream,' I announced, polishing off the sharp end of my cornet and getting up from the bench. 'You want another one?'

'No, thanks.' In fairness, Morris hadn't actually finished his current one.

'Yeah, I guess you don't want to spoil your appetite. You're probably having soup later on.' Well, if he was going to rip into *me* ...

'Bastard,' chuckled Morris, flicking two grubby, half-covered fingers up at me. At least if I did decide to opt out of society, I thought as I trundled over to the ice-cream van for seconds, I'd have someone to help smooth the transition by providing the insults I'd previously received from Joy.

'I'll have a ninety-nine, please,' I told the man manning the pumps.

'Blimey. Someone's hungry.'

'Yeah,' I confirmed with a half-arsed smile. Feeling, considerably too late, a twinge of guilt over my gluttony and sensing someone behind me, I turned to see who had gathered to witness The Incredible Ice-cream Consuming Man – and, to my surprise, found myself face to face with a Fresh Coat colleague. There, floating in front of me and filled with as much helium as I was sugar and self-hatred, was 8-Ball, his tentacles tickling the air between him and the clenched fist of his owner. 8-Ball, the guy who'd helped get me psyched up for my first foray into the Fresh Coat meeting room; the guy who'd smiled goofily at me after I'd emerged acquainted with Jessica. The guy who, right now, as I offered him a wobbly-lipped smile, was twisting around awkwardly in mid-air to avoid eye contact with me. I swallowed hard and plonked some extra shrapnel down on the ice-cream man's counter.

'Better make it a double.'

Returning (again) to the bench with my double-barrelled desert, I flung myself back into the throes of conversation with Morris, who'd just popped the pointy stub of his cornet into his gob.

'So, in all seriousness, these soup kitchens, then. I've always wondered: do they serve up a lot of different flavours or is it mainly just your bog-standard tomato?' His understaffed team of pegs having completed their work, Morris swallowed his final mouthful and answered the enquiry.

'Actually, you'd be surprised. They vary it up a bit. What was it we had yesterday? Um, spicy parsnip.'

'Nice. Carrot and coriander?'

'Yeah, we have that sometimes. Lentil, too, but I don't like that so much.'

'It's a little bland,' I agreed, 'but then I guess something like mulligatawny isn't to everyone's taste.' Morris added a few more furrows to his already multi-furrowed brow.

'Mulliga-what?'

'Mulligatawny. It's like a curry-based soup. Probably a little spicy for some tram ... uh, some homeless people's palates.'

'Well you say that, but carrot and coriander can have quite a kick to it.'

'That's true,' I conceded. 'You're right about that. It's the cumin.' So that was my sparring with Joy and now my inane conversations with Eddie successfully replicated. If I could get a confirmation on the local soup kitchen serving mulligatawny it was officially a hobo's life for me. For now, though, it was still sweets rather than savouries on the menu as I wolfed down the remainder of my ice-cream and chased it with a pack of jellybeans. Then, after talking some more tripe with my main man Morris, I headed back to the van for another re-up. By now, a small queue had formed and I found myself waiting behind three children and, up front, a rotund, thirtysomething woman in a black vest who was making heavy work of her selection.

'Does that one contain nuts?' She asked, pointing at the illustration of a chocolate-coated number clearly both covered in and stuffed with nuts, and which, for the record, was called Choc Fulla Nuts. 'I'm allergic to nuts. They make me swell up.'

'You must have swallowed a couple of bird-feeders on the way over,' I muttered, tugging the front of my damp white T-shirt up from my chest. Dragging my palm back over my sweat-slicked forehead, I let my eyelids drop, plunging the green, leafy world around me into darkness. Well, dark redness, actually. With the midday sun burning down from above, the nothingness in front of my eyes was more like maroon than black, as if a pair of thick cinema curtains had, at long last, been hauled across the fantasy world in which I'd been living. Like that moment hadn't already happened the evening before. My stomach was churning, not because of all the sugar-laden crap inside it, but because I'd just cast my mind back to *that* moment. The moment at which I'd walked into my bedroom to find my incriminating e-mail on the floor. I hadn't stopped replaying this moment in my head. I couldn't. I just kept travelling back in time to those horrible few seconds. If only I could go back further. If only I could lift my lids and arrive, turning and stumbling like Marty McFly, in a world where the worst thing Jessica had discovered about me was my inability to separate real fruit from plastic replicas. I breathed in,

212

breathed out and opened my eyes. Perhaps inevitably, it appeared I hadn't gone back in time, although with the same chunky, nut-intolerant customer still deliberating her choice, it seemed like I'd inadvertently arrived upon a way to pause it.

'Hurry it up, will you?' I called out. 'You're choosing an ice-cream, not a wedding dress.'

The woman swivelled her flabby neck to face me, hoisting up her stubby middle finger so that its tip faced the burning midday sun and hitting me with a look that could have stripped the gaudy unlicensed paintwork from the side of the van. I noticed that her vest bore, in white letters, the legend 'D*CK MAGNET' (with a down-turned magnet representing the 'A'), a title that I suspected wasn't backed by much evidence either statistical or scientific.

'Drop dead!' she huffed. I didn't respond (either to her or the kids, who alternately gasped and sniggered at the beef suddenly simmering on either side of them), instead choosing to consider the woman's forthright suggestion while she, praise the Lord, finally got her shit together and made a selection before waddling away spitting swear words at me. If I could, I probably would have. Dropped dead, I mean. I was pretty sure it was a course of action that wouldn't meet with too much disapproval from Jessica and besides, if my antics had consigned me to spend a lifetime in Hell, it couldn't be that much different to my current situation: standing in baking heat staring at badly drawn cartoon characters while a tramp (whose pungent aroma, incidentally, I could still smell from five metres away) waited to resume making fun of me.

In front of me, the two lads had proven to be more decisive customers than their portly predecessor and were now racing off with their lollies. Stepping up to the window, I raised my sun-touched brow affably at the man in the van. 'Hello again,' I began. 'I'll have one of those nut things that the Dick Magnet didn't understand, please.'

'Sorry,' he replied with a slow shake of his gelled head. 'No can do.'

'Oh, you're sold out? Well, in that case, I'll have ...'

'No,' he corrected firmly. 'I mean I can't serve you.'

'What d'you mean, you can't serve me?' The man placed his palms on the counter and leant in towards me.

'You've had enough, mate.'

'No, no. I haven't. I know it probably *looks* like I've had enough, but I actually haven't.'

'You're wearing a shirt you've borrowed from a tramp,' he pointed out. I looked down and discovered that, true enough, I was wearing a tatty, red-and-black lumberjack shirt over my T-shirt. I lifted the cuff of the right sleeve to my nose. It certainly *smelled* like it belonged to my new pal. I looked over at the bench, where Morris was showcasing a thick thatch of chest hair that, like his beard, wore a glistening coat of melted ice-cream.

'You wouldn't take no for an answer,' he recounted with a bare-shouldered shrug. 'You'd given me the chocolate and the ice-cream so I thought, what the hell?'

'See? He's fine about it,' I reasoned with the ice-cream man. 'He's got darker skin than me, so he's less liable to burn. True, it's mainly a layer of dirt, but I mean, I burn up *quickly*. I get sun-burn at the cinema if the movie's set in a hot place. And if it's a *long* sunny movie? Oh, man. My mum made me wear factor 30 to watch *Dances With Wolves*.'

'Seriously,' he interrupted, impervious to my attempts at affability. 'You're scaring off my customers.'

'Oh, what?' I laughed. 'The big woman? Trust me, you haven't lost her custom. She'll be back again in five minutes.' My opponent snorted at me.

'Like *you*, you mean? Listen. How's this, mate? I'll give you a free bottle of water, then you go and find yourself some shade somewhere and just chill out.' In hindsight, it actually seems like a pretty fair and reasonable offer. In hindsight.

'I want to speak to your manager,' I demanded.

'Sure,' responded the ice-cream man, wiping his hands with a flannel and fixing me with a humourless smile. 'I'll just nip upstairs and get him.' I squinted up at the top of the van, not because I was looking for a first floor, but because I now needed to know the name of the insolent mobile desert provider who was refusing to provide me with my desert. Information gathered, I placed my own clammy palms on the counter, narrowed my eyes and went nose-to-nose with my new adversary.

'Listen, Chief Whip, if that is indeed your real name ...'

'Clearly it isn't.'

'A-ha!' I declared triumphantly, spinning around in time to catch the attention of a couple of elderly women. 'See how he revels in his own deception? He's a fraud, a phony, as fake as the artwork on the side of his van.' I thumped a lime green impression of Top Cat (or was it Top Rat?) in his way-too-pointy nose, letting the resultant metallic thud punctuate my point. Apparently startled by the noise, the passers-by veered sharply (well, doddered as quickly as their decrepit legs could carry them) away from me. I turned back around to find that, by contrast, Chief Whip had positioned himself even further and more squarely in my face.

'Oh, you've got a problem with the artwork now?'

'No. *You've* got a problem with the artwork,' I informed him. 'I think the Walt Disney Corporation would be very interested to know about some of these colourful characters you've got here. Warner Brothers, too – we've got Bugs Bunny there, I see ...' I began pacing up and down the hot concrete, scrutinising the bastardised cartoon icons gallivanting in the sun. 'Hmmm ...' I continued, lowering my eyebrows and raising a ponderous finger to my lips. 'I don't remember Fred Flintstone ever having a mullet, but then apparently Barney Rubble also sported a bubble perm at some stage, so let's hope the good folks in the legal department at Hanna Barbera don't make me look too foolish when I speak to them on the matter.'

'You're making yourself look pretty foolish right now,' sneered Chief Whip.

'If you want to offer me your opinion on something,' I

215

countered, rapping a knuckle against another of his shockingly drawn spokespeople, 'you could start by telling me who you think this yellow, spiky haired character might be. The one right here, brandishing one of your signature ninety-nines.' Cradling my chin with my fingers, I took a step back in search of a more enlightening vantage point. 'See, at first glance I thought that maybe it was Bart Simpson, but now I see that he's gripping said flagship ice-cream with five digits rather than Bart's usual four and staring at it with eyes disproportionately large, even by the exaggerated standards of Matt Groening, who, by the way, I'll also be adding to my list of phone calls.' While I paused to regain my breath, the Chief fixed me with a smile icier than any of the lollies he was refusing to serve me and spoke in slow, measured tones.

'Well, while you're compiling that list, I suggest you put down the number of your nearest mental health specialist, because you, my friend, are a bloody psycho.' Even with my head buzzing, I could see pretty clearly that this guy was pissed off with me, and that I was going to have to call time on my career as an art critic if I was to stand any chance whatsoever of him supplying me with my next fix. So, letting a bizarrely anorexic-looking Pooh Bear off the hook, I pushed out a deep, cathartic breath and offered Chief Whip a reconciliatory shrug-and-smile combo.

'Alright,' I chuckled, 'I can see we've got off on the wrong ...'

'No, really mate, I don't know if I can put this any clearer. Fuck off before I step out of this van and twat you so fucking hard you'll ...' He stopped before he'd brought his threat to a bloodcurdling crescendo (although I think I nonetheless got the gist), his eyes seemingly occupied with something going on behind my red-and-black checked shoulder. I looked around to see a woman with two small children pulling an abrupt U-turn away from the van.

'Come on, we'll get them somewhere else,' she squeaked over the groans of her frustrated brood. I turned back to find

Mr. W looking so incensed that I half-expected to see cartoon steam clouds blow out of his ears (terribly drawn cartoon steam clouds, obviously), but over on the bench, it was Morris who decided to divest himself of some hot air.

'Tell him if he doesn't serve you, you'll give him a whipping,' he croaked excitedly. 'A *whipping*!' I looked over at my most unattractive of cheerleaders.

'I appreciate the support Morris, but everything's under ...'

'Tell him that if he doesn't accept your lolly, you'll cream him!' advised Morris, his voice now as saturated with confidence as his breath was with alcohol.

'Very good, Morris,' I called out through gritted teeth. '*Two* puns, there!'

'And you'll stick a Flake up his arse!'

'Alright,' I sighed, turning to issue my would-be gag writer with a glance that was half-weary, half-exasperated. 'That's not even a play on words, you're just being vulgar.' Looking confused by the distinction, Morris returned his attention to an M&M that was melting away in the folds of his flies (at least I hope that's what he was doing) while I returned mine to the man melting away behind the counter. 'Sorry about my friend over there,' I began, 'and sorry for kicking off in front of your customers. Listen, I'll compensate for those lost sales. Just let me buy three ice-creams and you'll be all straight.' I don't know why, when he'd already adamantly refused to sell me one ice-cream, I thought Chief Whip would be willing to sell me three. Still, maybe he saw the business sense in my proposition or maybe he just realised that quelling my desperate appetite for more sugar was the only way to get rid of me, because, to my complete surprise, he pulled a fresh ice-cream cone from the stack at his side. 'Thanks, man,' I exhaled. 'And listen, once again, I'm really sorry about ...' I trailed off as Chief Whip crushed the cornet in his hand before releasing an ominous shower of orangey-beige shards and splinters onto the counter. Maybe I was being paranoid, but I got the distinct feeling that the cone was probably being used to portray me in ten seconds' time.

'That's you in five seconds' time,' he growled. Seemed he was going to reach out and pull me over the counter rather than waste time getting out of the van. The way I saw it, though, I still had at least two seconds left to switch up my approach one last time and appeal to The Cornet Crusher's better nature with some good old fashioned begging.

'Pleeeeaaase, just give me a ninety-nine,' I groaned. You'd say I'd swallowed my pride, but as I was stood wearing a tramp's shirt, it seems safe to say that the last tiny piece of pride had already long since disappeared down my throat.

'I'll give you a one!' he barked, treating me to my second middle finger of the day. I boiled with anger, not at my foe's finger but at his forearm, which was etched with a chronically inept rendering of Speedy Gonzales. While I seethed, The Badly Illustrated Man pulled down the shutter, clambered into the driver's seat and turned the key in the ignition. As he drove off to a reprise of 'Greensleeves', the blonde Snow White on the back of the van ensured that he had the last laugh.

'Can I have my shirt back now?' called out Morris, who was using his hands to protect his naked shoulders from the sun. I noticed that I'd at least been kind enough to let him keep his fingerless gloves.

The Fresh Coat meeting room. It was the site of my hazy, nervous introduction to Jessica, and now, exactly four weeks later, I was sat in that same seat at the same table across which I'd originally laid eyes on her, watching her sift through her bag and smile improbably at my half-baked contributions to my inaugural Monday meeting. Except that now, Jessica wasn't sifting or smiling or even sitting – at least not in that chair or, for that matter, anywhere within those four white walls that seemed for all the world to be gradually closing in on me.

'Jessica's not feeling very well this morning.' That was the information that Kam had just conveyed to myself, Nina, Kate, Greg and Yeti – along with something about Liam doing voiceover work for a cheese singles advert – and truth be told, I'd felt better myself. I'd barely slept since Jessica's sudden exit (ironic, considering that the last forty hours had seemed like one big, uninterrupted nightmare) and her current no-show was only making things worse. Right up until Kam's news flash a minute earlier, I'd been bracing myself for the excruciating discomfort of sitting in a confined room with Jessica, but sitting in a confined room without her was, I now realised, even worse. While I didn't have to worry about where to position my eyes upon Jessica's entrance or whether to offer some sort of apologetic half-smile (or, indeed, whether I'd even have control over my eyes, my mouth or any other part of my body), I'd also been robbed of the opportunity to collar her after the meeting; to request a moment of her time so that I could work valiantly, and, in all likelihood, pathetically to apologise and try my best to set this whole thing straight. Instead, all I could do was sit in silence, staring at the slightly bobbled purple fabric on the back of that empty chair while Kam went on about ... about ... well, whatever it was she was going on about. With my mind completely preoccupied with this whole, horrible mess, I was catching the words coming out of her mouth only sporadically, like a deep sea diver intermittently coming up for air in-between surveying the battered, decayed remains of a once great and beautiful vessel.

Still, it was during one of these fleeting visits to the surface (my third, I reckon, as in addition to hearing about Jessica's illness, I'd also absorbed the fact that, incredibly, teenage talent vacuum Danny Waters was already back on the show's guest list) that I experienced a sudden, unexpected and wholly unwelcome moment of clarity.

'So this is it,' announced Kam, embarking on a new thread after talking at length about whatever it was she'd been talking about. 'The week we hastily decide, and announce, the winner of *Highly Strung*, although it's safe to say that one Mr. Colin Thunder has ruled himself out of the running.' That's when it hit me; the exact moment at which a horrible, inescapable truth raised up, pulled back its fist and punched me square in the face. As I retreated back under the waves and Kam's words faded out once more, I realised that I was Colin Thunder: a sad, pathetic stalker, albeit a sad, pathetic stalker without even Colin's undeniable talent for genital-generated stadium rock. Yep, the facts were clear: I was the poor man's Colin Thunder, and as a result the chair opposite me was empty.

Despite her absence in the meeting room, Jessica's presence was inescapable when I returned to my desk, and for the rest of the day and all of Tuesday and Wednesday, her eyes burned down on me from the wall above, daring me to look at her. Every so often I'd accept the challenge, and each time it felt horrible, like I'd fluffed the final, all-or-nothing question on a game show and was now being forced to view footage of the exotic holiday destination I'd exchanged for a T-shirt and gold plated roller-ball. Liam's grinning, fist-beckoning face wasn't helping matters, either.

By the time I came into work on Thursday morning, that damn picture had broken me to the point where I could no longer even throw a glance in its direction, so it was while looking up from my computer but away from the dreaded canvas that, at around 9.30am, I saw Jessica – the real one – conferring with Kam over at her desk. Immediately, my heart started pounding. What was she doing in the office? Was Kam now receiving the news that her latest recruit was a demented sex pest who'd come onboard the show with the sole, deluded purpose of having his wicked way with Jessica? I got up from my desk and, head bowed and ears pricked, moved slowly over to the water cooler, from where Kam's voice became audible.

'Believe it or not, I just spoke to Liam and he's on his way, which hopefully also bodes well for next Wednesday.'

'Oh yeah, Wednesday. The inner city sports initiative thingy.' Jessica, too, was coming through clearly enough. 'What's the address of this school we're going to? I'll be coming from a business lunch up here.'

'Ooh, a business lunch – get you!' mocked Kam. The barrel bubbled and rumbled and cold water filled my cup. 'Well if you can be here for two, you can share a taxi to Bethnal Green with Marcus.'

'Perfect. You'd probably better tell Liam to be here at one, though.'

'Actually, he's making his own way down there. He's filming an episode of *Celebrity Shelves* in the morning. But I will drum the Bricks and Balls thing into his head today.'

'OK,' said Jessica. 'Well, I'm gonna grab myself some breakfast before he arrives. Alright if I leave my stuff here?' She plonked her handbag on the end of Kam's desk and turned to leave the room. As she did so, our eyes met for a split second of staggering awkwardness before hastily parting company, Jessica's disappearing through the double doors and mine returning to my fake business at the water cooler. Atop his rumbling, clear plastic barrel, 8-Ball was also having difficulty looking me in the eye. Slumped forward and focused on the carpet beneath his blue-tinted throne, it was as if he knew what was going through my mind but didn't have the heart (and certainly not the spine) to declare his misgivings. No matter, I thought, lifting my cup to my lips and glugging the water down in one chest-chilling go. I was doing this with or without his help.

I crunched the empty cup in my fist, dropped it into a nearby wastepaper bin then set off across the carpet and through the double doors. It wasn't that I didn't understand the doubts of my tentacled buddy. For starters, I wasn't thrilled that the encounter that was about to go down was about to go down in a kitchen. After all, if I'd actually suggested Jessica accompany me into my own kitchen on the previous Saturday evening, I wouldn't be standing there feeling sick to my stomach as I looked at her through a thick pane of glass. Still, this was my opportunity to speak to Jessica one-to-one; to clear the air. I took a deep breath and pushed open the door. Jessica was leant against the sideboard, monitoring the progress of two slices of bread sunning themselves in the toaster while a teabag luxuriated in a bath of piping hot water and milk.

'Jess, can I talk to you for a minute?'

'Go away, Richard,' said Jessica quietly. She didn't look at me, but then she didn't need to. Just those three words, spoken softly, deliberately and at that low volume were enough to pretty much snap my heart in two. I couldn't quite pinpoint why, but I was certain I would have preferred a loud 'Fuck off' to a quiet 'Go away, Richard.'

'I just want to ...'

'Fuck off,' instructed Jessica loudly and I was interested to learn that, actually, that was just as bad after all. If, at that moment, I'd have suspected Jessica of possessing a super-power, it would be the ability to absorb and assume the physical properties of any object or material she touched, because at that moment her usually bewitching facial features seemed to flicker with all the emotion of the inch-thick Formica against which her palm was pressed. The slices sprung up from the toaster to excitedly compare tans and Jessica lifted her hand from the sideboard, presumably mere seconds before her face took on a faux marble finish. She laid the slices of toast down side by side on a plate, ripped the lid off a margarine tub and delved into the cutlery draw for a knife. Satisfied that her weapon of choice wasn't sharp enough to fatally wound me, I forged ahead with a mouth as dry as Jessica's breakfast.

'That e-mail you found, it was really nothing. It was just something I typed in a moment of ... I mean, it's not in any way a reflection of how I look at ... What I ...' Realising that a compendium of half-thoughts and unfinished sentences wasn't going to help my cause, I changed gears and tried my best to get straight to the heart of the matter. 'I have a problem,' I blurted out. 'I have a problem in that I can be incredibly stupid.' Jessica furiously scraped margarine across the toast, her wrist becoming a blur and her face becoming the cold, hard steel of her knife.

'That makes two of us,' she hissed through serrated steel

teeth. At that moment, the kitchen door opened and Kate bounced in sporting a new, tomato soup-coloured bob and a similarly bright and zesty joie de fucking vivre.

'Hi guys,' she beamed from beneath her thick, freshly installed fringe.

'Your hair looks fantastic!' exclaimed Jessica, effortlessly snapping into effervescent presenter mode as if someone, unheard by me, had just shouted 'Action!'

'Yeah. It's really now,' I offered, as if someone had just shouted 'Be impossibly lame!' Kate proudly patted the back of her new (and, indeed, 'now') barnet.

'Oh, thanks. My hairdresser said it would complement the shape of my face,' she rabbited before backtracking for a snip-by-snip account of the masterpiece atop her head. Quite what it entailed I couldn't say, as, pissed off by Kate's untimely interruption, I was too busy trying to make her freshly decorated head explode via my hitherto untested telekinetic powers.

'Well, I haven't come in here to talk about my hair,' said Kate, who didn't seem to have come in to *not* talk about her hair. 'I better get back to my desk. I'm waiting on a call from Danny Waters' manager. For a change!' She opened one of the cabinets and pulled out a packet of rice cakes, then, with a cheery 'see you later,' headed back to base. Inaudible to me over the click of the door, someone called 'Cut!' and Jessica's thawed-out features instantaneously froze over once again.

'I said go away.' She placed one slice of toast on top of the other and forged a forceful diagonal path through them with her knife.

'And you also said to fuck off,' I reminded her. 'And I'll do both of those things, but first I want you to know that I'm really sorry that I've hurt you.'

'Fine.' Jessica dropped the knife into the sink with a clank, put the lid back on the margarine tub, stormed past me and put the tub back in the fridge. She didn't quite slam the fridge door shut, but I wouldn't say she closed it gently either.

Sensing futility, I let out a dejected sigh and changed gears once again.

'The good news is that after Friday you won't have to put up with me.' These words were genuinely intended to offer some glimmer of solace, but as they left my lips I realised too late that they probably sounded sarcastic and self-pitying.

'Oh, well.' Jessica picked up her plate of toast with one hand, using the other to lift the saucer beneath her cup of tea. As she approached the kitchen door, it became apparent that, in her haste to leave, she hadn't thought her exit through, and with her cup rattling frantically against the saucer, it became equally apparent that she wasn't going to be asking for any assistance with her departure.

'At least let me help you get away from me,' I pleaded, striding across the room to open the door.

'Thanks,' she muttered blankly, and as she stepped out into the corridor I noticed that the colour of her tea was midway between manila and clay.

I hung back in the kitchen for two minutes, staring at the Formica and the floor tiles until they started to blur and wobble slightly. I walked over to the work surface, grabbed a square of kitchen roll and cut off any waterworks before they had the chance to properly get going. At this stage, the least I could do for Jessica, the very least, was to get through my remaining few days on the job without drawing red-eyed, wobbly lipped attention to our bust-up. I screwed the tissue up and tossed it into the bin, then took a deep breath and headed out of the kitchen and down the corridor. I couldn't say how Jessica looked at me, or whether she looked at me at all when I entered the office. I knew where she was – back at the end of Kam's desk – but I kept my eyes trained forward on the journey back to my base. The best thing I could do was get my head down and crack on with the week's script, although as I reached my destination, it appeared that someone was already doing their best to hinder me in that aim.

'Morning,' sneered Liam, spinning around in my chair to

face me. Shit. This was all I needed.

'Alright?' I replied flatly.

'So, mate,' he began, idly flicking a bit of fluff off the shoulder of his distressingly scoop-necked T-shirt. 'It looks like the wheels have finally fallen off your little ...' He trailed off, searching for that elusive right word. 'Car.'

'What?'

'Yep, you've been well and truly rumbled. Found out for what you are.' Oh, this was just perfect. Not only had I wrecked my friendship with Jessica, but now Liam knew all about it too.

'Look,' I sighed wearily. 'I don't know what you've heard, but ...'

'Oh, it's not just what I've heard,' interrupted Liam, holding aloft my mouse. 'It's what I've *seen*.' I waited nervously for him to elucidate – perhaps Jessica had spilled the beans to her co-presenter via an email – but instead he simply stared back at me, a glint in his eye as he gently rattled the mouse like a bomb-toting movie bad guy with his finger on the detonator. Anxious to get my latest humiliation over with, I let out an impatient sigh.

'What have you seen, Liam?' Liam swivelled into screen-facing position, placing my mouse back on its mat.

'It's amazing what you can find out about someone by scouring the deepest, darkest corners of the internet.'

'Yeah, you said before.'

'So I was looking on YouTube ...' he revealed.

'That's not one of the deepest, darkest corners of the internet. It gets about a billion hits a week.'

'Nevertheless,' asserted Liam. 'I was still looking at it.' He clicked on a window that he'd minimised and a web page touting competitively priced back, sack and crack waxing filled the screen.

'Amongst other things,' I noted while Liam hastily cleared his latest bit of consumer research and sifted through the three other minimised windows lurking at the foot of the screen. Unfortunately for him, these turned out to be the script I was working on and a couple of pop-ups.

'Must have clicked off it altogether,' he muttered, logging back on to the internet. The Google home page filled the screen, and while Liam prodded laboriously at the keyboard, I snuck a sombre look over to the other side of the room, where Jessica was still conversing with Kam. Once again, her eyes, whether by chance or as a result of her stalker-sense tingling, met mine momentarily before she quickly looked away. It was awful. Really, really awful. I shifted my focus back to my computer screen – unless Jessica had blessed YouTube with a venomous, direct-to-camera address about how much she hated me, there was surely no way that Liam's newest web-based discovery was going to make me feel any worse about myself than I already did.

So it proved as Liam pressed play on a video entitled 'Headset – Liam Barton Piss Take.' Within the confines of the familiar YouTube rectangle, a pair of lips stirred into life and a weedy, would-be lover-man voice oozed pure Camembert into a face-mounted mic and through the computer's tinny speakers, setting into motion the *TTP* skit that I'd masterminded two years earlier.

'Hey girl,' said the lips, which, along with the voice, belonged to comic Rhys Jeffers. 'I just wanted to let you know ... that if you sign up for double glazing by the end of this month, you'll get a whole twenty percent off the total cost.' The opening bars of Liam's uptempo pop confection 'Get Set' kicked in – actually, they were the opening bars of a song *just* different enough from Liam's sole almost-hit to nimbly sidestep copyright infringement – and the camera pulled back to reveal Rhys-as-Liam as one of the button-bashing minions in a busy call centre.

'Bringing back any memories?' asked Liam.

'Yes,' I responded, pulling up a chair from the vacant desk beside mine and settling down for the show. 'It takes me back to those halcyon days when you hit the dizzying heights of a UK number eight.'

'Seven,' corrected Liam tersely, 'and that was before downloads, back when singles sales actually meant something.' He circled the mouse around on its mat, bringing it to rest with the cursor hanging over the YouTube pause button, and turned to face me while, on screen, I made my musical debut as one of the comedy Liam's call centre crew. 'You know, it's funny. A few days ago, you seemed a bit foggy about your involvement with this so-called sketch, but wait ...' He hit pause. 'What's this?

'Someone's elbow?' I observed accurately.

'Yeah, obviously,' hissed Liam, clearly miffed to have bungled his show-stopping moment of revelation. 'But *whose* elbow?'

'Well it's not mine. If you noticed in the previous frame, the one you *meant* to freeze, I was actually wearing a short sleeved shirt.' Growing more irritated by the second, Liam hit play, then pause, this time successfully freezing my gurning face. '*Now* do you still deny that you were a part of this video?' I stonefaced my interrogator.

'I just described what I was wearing.'

'Right, well that's that sorted, then. Now, what have you got to say about it?' I leant back in my chair and stroked my chin ponderously.

'Well, from what I remember it was a pretty hectic day's shooting, not helped by the fact that, believe it or not, Rhys, the guy so brilliantly, hilariously portraying you, hadn't fully memorised his ...'

'Well I'm glad you find it funny,' snapped Liam. I leant inwards to read some of the viewer comments posted beneath the video.

'Evidently I'm not the only one. Laffman Jonas 83 says, and I quote, "it's funny as fuck", and it made Fitgirl LOL.'

'Saddoes,' scowled Liam. 'Nothing better to do than sit at a computer watching this crap.' That was it. I didn't mind Liam insulting me (although so far he'd failed miserably to do so), but I'd be damned if I was going to let him talk trash about my

227

audience.

'Liam. You were a crap pop star. There, I said it. You were terrible, absolutely awful. You came second to Danny Waters and he himself is shit, so that right there says that ipso facto you were worse than shit. I held that opinion throughout your entire twelve seconds of musical notoriety, and so did a large section of the general public. Now, that doesn't reflect at all on the job you currently do as a television presenter – and in fact I think you're moderately talented at that provided you're not coming unglued by some of the longer words on the autocue – but, to reiterate, you were a shit, laughably bad pop star and if anything this video paints a flattering portrait of your meagre abilities in that field.' Liam stared back at me, soaking in my career appraisal for a few seconds before he spoke.

'You're calling *me* meagre?' he sneered. 'That's rich.' Passing behind us on her way back from the printer, Denise stopped when she caught sight of my frozen ugly mug.

'Is that you?' she asked excitedly. 'Let me see!' I looked at Liam.

'Go on, Liam. Let Denise see.' Liam muttered something inaudible but definitely abusive at me and pressed play, sending my slightly blurry on-screen self back into motion and bringing his own digitised doppelganger preening and prancing back into the frame. Denise let out a surprised laugh.

'I didn't know you two had worked together before.'

'That's not me,' huffed Liam.

'It's a parody version of Liam's song that I was involved with,' I explained. 'He actually found this and showed it to me. I thought he might be upset about it but he's being a really good sport.' Denise gave Liam a hearty pat on his shoulder.

'Well, you *were* shit, Liam, weren't you?' Liam's fingers tensed around the mouse while Kate, curious to see what it was that was keeping us entertained, came over and took a peak. She quickly descended into hysterics as, captured in split-screen, the call-centre Liam sung lasciviously about accident insurance to an elderly woman enjoying a bubble bath in the comfort of her own home. 'Classic!' she shrieked. Liam rose up from my seat.

'I've got to get to this meeting,' he said, beating a hasty retreat across the office floor. Little did he know that, in this heavyweight clash of the morons, it was actually he who'd emerged victorious. Operating at the cocksure, swaggering and utterly self-deluded peak of his powers, Liam had boldly set up shop at my desk with the express purpose of embarrassing me, leaving instead with his tail between his legs and with his own blimp-sized ego thoroughly deflated. It was just the type of encounter that I would dearly have loved to share with the girl now shuffling off to the meeting room with him and Kam.

That Friday at Artemis Studios I got what I wanted – a sit-down with Jessica. Well, kind of. I'd run into Jess in the corridor earlier that morning and she'd crunched her eyeballs into reverse gear the second she saw me (I knew by now that it was possible for someone to look away from you with the same focus and intensity as if they were shooting daggers directly at you). Now, though, there was nowhere for either one of us to hide. At the behest of Kam, I had returned to tread the boards – or rather fill the sofa – as I reprised my classic, star-making role as pop sensation Danny Waters, back already to hawk his new *Feel My Way to Your Heart* live tour DVD. If this was a case of history repeating itself, however, then Jessica seemed pretty anxious to consign this encounter to the past before it had even begun.

'Can't we skip this bit?' she called out to Kam, who, Styrofoam cup in hand, was monitoring proceedings from the studio floor. 'It seems a bit pointless rehearsing it.'

'Well, we need to see how the segment looks in Hangovervision,' replied Kam bluntly, 'so let's get on with it, shall we?' Clearly unimpressed with Kam's misreading of her below-par demeanour, Jessica heaved out a sullen sigh, slapped on a brittle grin and got down to business.

'So, Danny, lovely to have you back,' she began.

'It's lovely to *be* back,' I assured her unconvincingly. I certainly didn't feel like someone with a Phwoar Factor of ninety-one percent.

'Now, you've got your new *Feel My Way to Your Heart* live tour DVD out,' noted Jessica, holding up a copy of said masterpiece. 'Why don't you tell us about that?' I swallowed hard and nervously began the breakdown.

'Well, it basically gives people the chance to join me on tour,' I explained, fighting against the dual threat of a turbulent stomach and an arid mouth. 'You'll see me performing on stage, chilling out on the tour bus, backstage in the dressing ...'

'Great stuff,' interrupted Jessica, hauling a small, sawdust-stuffed metal dustbin up onto the table in front of us, 'and I'm delighted to say that you're going to be performing your next single, "Blowing Up Your Inbox", for us a little later. In the meantime, though, we're going to play a little game. I'd like you to try and feel your way – geddit? – to the hearts buried in this bin right here.'

'Who comes up with this stuff?' I enquired, hoping that a little impromptu self-deprecation might help thaw the ice.

'An idiot,' replied Jessica, demonstrating her own, under-her-breath flair for improvisation before getting back to my uninspired script. 'So, if you'd kindly dive in ...' I rolled up my shirt sleeve and plunged my arm into the sawdust, rummaging around for a few seconds before deciding to freeze my foraging forearm and affect a startled grimace.

'Shit!' I exclaimed. 'I think I just found a dead hamster.' There was a smattering of laughter from some of the more easy-to-please members of the crew but absolutely nothing from Jessica. 'OK, this is more like it,' I remarked, fishing one of the heart-shaped cards out of the bin. I blew the sawdust out of the ridges in the thick, corrugated red cardboard, then opened up the card and proceeded to read the question printed on the square of white paper stuck inside. 'Let's see ... Angellica from Ealing asks, "Where's the most romantic place you've ever taken a girl on a date?"' I paused, nervously running my hand over the top of the head. This, I realised too late, was a mistake, as I now had flecks of sawdust running through my hair. Oh, well, it wasn't like a spot of wooden dandruff was going to lower me any further in Jessica's estimations, even if it did bring that ever-plummeting Phwoar Factor down to around the three percent mark.

'Spud-U-Like,' I said, getting on with the question at hand. 'I bought this girl a ring from Clare's Accessories, and when she wasn't looking I hid it under the cheese in her baked potato. The look on her face when she realised was a picture. Unfortunately, that's because it was in her throat.' This time I couldn't even tell you whether there was any laughter from the studio floor. I had blocked out all forms of human life in the studio except for myself and Jessica, and at this moment the only reaction I cared about was hers. Except that I could hardly bear to take it in. It had been bad enough seeing Jessica looking sad, angry and upset back in the Fresh Coat kitchen, but seeing those same emotions illuminated by the hot studio lights was maybe even worse. It suddenly occurred to me that in all my time watching *The Hangout* for the girl who now hated my guts, I'd never seen that purple sofa accommodating a Jessica who looked anything other than happy. Until now. Even perched on these cushions, she couldn't muster up a strictly professional flash of her gnashers. And who could blame her? In one fell swoop I'd fucked up both our friendship and our working relationship and now what was I doing? Trying to be funny.

Alright, that was it. Three strikes and out for my lame attempts at humour. As my hand burrowed through the sawdust in search of a second cardboard organ, I decided my best bet (in the event of not finding a gun in the wood shavings and blowing my brains across the sofa – which, to the best of my knowledge, would be another first for this iconic piece of furniture) was to ditch my ill-advised comic stylings and weather the rest of this stormy segment with sensible, efficient, straight-to-the-point responses. Coming up with another heart, I read aloud its contents.

'"You get all the girls and kiss all the girls, but I'm too shy to speak to girls. What advice can you give me about how I should act around girls?" And that's from Kevin, aged ten, in Leighton Buzzard. Um, well, Kevin, don't be fooled by my videos. I certainly don't get all the girls, let alone kiss all the girls and definitely not all the ones I really like ...' I could feel beads of sweat forming on my forehead, so I ran my hand over it. Excellent. Now that was covered in sawdust, too.

'You're very modest today, Danny,' observed Jessica with a smile that probably looked sweet and light-hearted to everyone but me. 'So do you have any advice at all?'

'Uhhh ... advice?' I nervously tapped my thigh with one of the card's curves whilst staring at the cold hard metal of the dustbin. 'OK, well, yes I do, actually. I would say, first of all, you're ten years old. You've got a lifetime of heartbreak ahead of you, my man, so I don't know why you're so eager to get started now. But that said, if there's a girl that you like, I do know one thing: You shouldn't act anyway at all around her. You should be yourself and always, always be honest.' My metallic focal point shook from side to side as Jessica rattled the base of the bin against the table top.

'Last question,' she prompted solemnly. I ventured into the bin for the third and final time, then paused when I opened the card and saw the question inside. The studio lights burned down on my sweat-speckled brow. I swallowed hard and proceeded.

'Shelley from Basingstoke asks this,' I said, leaning forward in my seat and pausing for a supplementary swallow. 'She asks, "What type of girl would it take to win your heart?"' My mouth was so dry, it might as well have been filled with sawdust too. Not that Jessica was exhibiting much in the way of sympathy.

'Well?'

'That's a good question,' I reflected, staring down at the toes of my boots as if the answer was contained deep within the creases of the leather. 'Hmmm ... Well, a nice girl, I guess. She'd be, um, good-hearted; a total sweetheart.' With my eyes probing ever deeper into the darkest reaches of those leather folds, I listened for the sound of Jessica wrapping up the segment.

'Is that it?' she asked. Damn, suddenly Jessica was going all Paxman on me.

'OK,' I continued, 'I can't lie. I'm a little bit shallow so she'd be beautiful. Stunning, even. Definitely sexy. But, and this is important, she wouldn't walk around like she knows it.' Again, I listened for the sound of Jessica wrapping things up. Again, nothing. I picked a stray piece of sawdust from the hem of my shirt, rolling it up with my thumb and forefinger before dropping it to the ground. Then I slowly raised my head and looked my inquisitor dead in the eye. If Jessica wanted more, she could have more. 'She'd be fun,' I said, my voice faltering slightly. 'And funny. I mean ... just ... just the type of girl where you live to make her smile, you know? Where that's like your whole life's work. Because one little smile from her is enough to completely turn things around if you're having a shitty ... er, sorry, kids ... a bad day.'

'Wow,' responded Jessica as expressively as if she'd just heard me announce that there was three pence off sweetcorn at the local supermarket. 'Some heartfelt answers from Danny, there, who'll be doing his thing for us live on stage a little bit later. Now, though, it's time for a fellow who's got more than enough heart for any challenge as our ring-tailed renaissance man Lawrence adds another stripe to his already eye-straining tail ...' And with that, Lawrence's signature sting music struck up while, on the screen behind us, he prepared to try his paw at cheerleading.

''Scuse,' requested – or rather ordered – a voice from my side. Liam had come to reclaim his seat on the sofa. Rising to my feet, I looked at Jessica. She was focused on the screen behind her, watching Lawrence categorically demonstrate that brandishing a pair of pom-poms only heightened his proclivity for the pratfall. I brushed some final flecks of sawdust from my jeans then slowly walked off the stage and across the studio floor.

'Good job,' remarked Kam. At least she didn't have to worry about Jessica and me acting too friendly any more.

Her dark eyes stared right back into mine from beneath her jagged jet black fringe. Though I hadn't noticed from across the room, a small, glistening stud nestled in the right side of her nose. She wasn't really my type, but there was definitely something about her. Doubtless she would have looked even better with a complete jaw and two ears.

'Oh, you like Annette?' Eddie placed a hand on my shoulder.

'She has a certain edgy charm,' I admitted. 'You know this girl?'

'No, at least not in the physical sense. Annette's a product of my fecund imagination,' explained Eddie, ushering me on a couple of steps to the next drawing. 'Some of them are real girls, though. For instance, Lauren here's a French exchange student who came on my course at Uni for one semester.' As captured by Eddie, Lauren was alluring enough, but the fact that he'd immaculately shaded the contours of her top lip with various soft pencils whilst leaving her bottom lip untouched gave the unfortunate impression that, in the late 1990s, French girls – or at least those in tertiary education – favoured thick, dark moustaches.

I glanced around at the thirty or so women lining the walls of the gallery, or 'space' as Eddie insisted on calling it (either way, there was no disguising the fact that this was a disused scout hut). The pictures, most of which were black-and-white line drawings, comprised his curiously titled 'Conclusion' exhibition, the latest in Eddie's seemingly endless array of creative projects, and one which had managed, on this Friday evening at least, to pull in a pair of viewers other than the artist and myself. Across the room, sorry, space, a young couple were looking, well, baffled by the images around them, although in fairness they weren't benefiting from commentary by The Master himself, who was busy giving me a post-work, pre-pub insight into his artistry.

'Now, Valeria here *is* my dream girl,' he announced, gesturing towards a full-length picture of a sexy brunette stood with her hands held assertively on her hips. Well, I say 'stood', but with only one leg emerging from the bottom of her clingy sheer dress, it was more a case of 'balancing.' Unsure of whether or not the girl of Eddie's dreams was an amputee, I decided to, er, tread carefully and not mention her missing limb.

'Your dream girl, eh?' I took a pew on the bench that Eddie had strategically positioned in the glow of his five-toed object of desire. 'Well, for your sake, I hope you never cross paths. Believe me, meeting your dream girl isn't all it's cracked up to be. Unless awkwardness and discomfort are your things.' Eddie sat down next to me.

'You two didn't look too awkward or discomfortable in the photo.' He paused for a second. '*Un*comfortable.'

'Ah, the photo,' I cringed, recalling the only existing documentation of myself and Jessica ever having been friends (it seemed *Gab*'s photo was even more of an exclusive than they knew). 'Didn't Joy give you the story behind it?' Eddie placed a hand on my shoulder.

'Believe me, I got the full report. In fact, she showed me the photos from the dressing room, too. That was a lovely thing you did for her little niece.'

'Oh. You're talking about Joy.'

'Well, yeah. Your dream girl.'

'My dream girl? So who the hell is Jessica?'

'A work crush,' shrugged Eddie, before softening his stance somewhat. 'I mean, what I'm saying is, she's not Joy. And Joy likes you. I mean, *really* likes you. She's head over heels.' I stared incredulously at my friend.

'Do you have *any* recollection of how things panned out

last time you told me this?' I asked, dumbfounded. 'I do, because it involved me going from giddy elation to pitch black depression in a matter of seconds. I don't know if you've ever had that experience ...' Eddie rose to his feet.

'Oh, I've been there.' He locked his arms together behind his back and squinted theatrically into the middle distance. 'It was 1987. July the fourteenth, to be precise – Bastille Day. Guess where I was.'

'Were you in France?' I asked impatiently. Eddie shook his head.

'No, I was at school with my classmates, celebrating French Day, as we called it, by eating crepes, playing boules and having longer French lessons than we would normally. Mind you, all of this was, at least from my point of view, peripheral to the authentic street art contest going down on the paving slabs outside the home economics block.'

'Wait,' I interjected. 'Do you know that in French, the phrase "For the love of Pete" is "Pour l'amour de Pete?"'

'Shouldn't it be "Pour l'amour de *Pierre*?"'

'No! Why would ... When Pete Sampras played in France, he wasn't known as Pierre Sampras.'

'Why d'you think he never won the French Open?' questioned Eddie. 'Because he refused to abide by the linguistic rules. Anyway, this street art contest: It was a competition that pitted me against the heavily favoured Naomie Conway. You know who that was, right?'

'Let me guess,' I sighed. 'Someone you fancied?'

'Urghhhh,' groaned Eddie, recoiling at the very thought. 'Get lost! No, she was widely considered the best artist in our year, if not the entire school. She was certainly the red-hot favourite to win the street art contest.' I stared at Eddie, bewildered.

'How would I have known that?'

'Anyway,' he continued, 'reputation proved to be for naught as my sweeping, four-slab rendering of Asterix The Gaul saw off her rote, soulless and overly literal depiction of the Eiffel Tower to take home first prize. Naturally, I was ecstatic, and indeed I was still on a high when I got home that evening and went upstairs to my bedroom. I took off my beret and the string of onions around my neck and placed them on my bedside table along with my prize, a paperback copy of *The Cool Kids' Guide to the Impressionists*. Preparing to flop down contentedly on my bed, I loosened the back of my right deck shoe with my left foot and joyously kicked it off. Well, my jubilation turned to horror as I watched my navy blue canvas plimpsol travel across the room and straight through my window pane.' He paused briefly, apparently transported back in time to that freshly ventilated boyhood bedroom, before soberly rounding off his tale. 'Suffice to say, no amount of plaudits for my Parisian street art could prevent my mum from wrenching my left deck shoe from my foot and creating an impression on my arse.'

'OK,' I conceded, 'so you experienced something, um, similar to me. Sort of. But with coloured chalk and deck shoes and, er, onions. Is there a point to this story?'

'There's a point alright,' insisted Eddie. 'The *point* is that after that calamity I faced a choice. I could either allow my artistic spirits to be crushed, just as Naomie's defeat at my hands prompted her to start sniffing spraymount in the art block stock cupboard, or I could brush off the stinging sensation in my backside and forge ahead, more determined than ever that one day I would eventually make my way in the world of fine art.' Arms outstretched, he slowly turned around on the spot, proudly surveying his portfolio. 'I'll let you be the judge of which path I chose.' As far as I could make out, the only path being travelled by this artist-slash-raconteur featured prominent signposts to the loony bin.

'Well, I'm still not entirely sure what you're going on about,' I admitted, 'or why you still think I'm infatuated with Joy, but I sense this is the part of the conversation where you gloss over her existing relationship with Matt by telling me it's not built to last.' Eddie gave me a puzzled look.

'Joy didn't tell you?'

'Tell me what?' I asked, rising to my feet.

'Her and Matt split up three weeks ago. Was I right or was I right?' I didn't answer, and for a few seconds our footsteps provided the only noise as we resumed our languorous trail around The Robert Baden Powell Gallery.

'Once again,' I noted at last, 'this is all eerily similar to information given to me by your good self shortly prior to the most heart-wrenching evening of my life. Well, until last Saturday, anyway.'

'What happened last ...'

'I'll tell you at the pub.'

'OK, well this *is* similar, yes,' conceded Eddie, raising aloft his forefinger. 'But on that occasion I told you that Joy and Matt probably weren't built to last.' He placed his palm on my shoulder. 'Now, granted, that was based on a hunch rather than actual, concrete information, but in hindsight that hunch looks eerily prescient in light of the actual, concrete information that I'm furnishing you with now, which is that they actually *have* split up. Their relationship is both null and void.' Eddie gave me a slap on the back. I couldn't deny that I was impressed with his spirited defence, particularly his use of the phrase 'eerily prescient', but I wasn't wholly convinced by it. At least not yet.

'So Joy's told you all of this?'

'Well, no, not exactly,' grimaced Eddie, 'but she confided in Beth, who instantly told me, and when I said to Joy, "I'm sorry to hear about your thing," she said "thanks."'

'Wait!' I demanded, revealing my missed calling as a hotshot lawyer. 'Did you say, "I'm sorry to hear about *your thing*," or something more specific like, "I'm sorry to hear about you and Matt" or "I'm sorry to hear about the break-up?"' Eddie looked at me quizzically and gave a shrug.

'What difference does it make?'

'A lot,' I contended, tucking my arms behind my back and pacing back and forth over half a dozen dusty floorboards.

'Something else bad might have happened to her that day and she assumed you meant that. Maybe her car failed its MOT or she lost an eBay bidding war. I missed out on a pair of Sanaa Lathan's flip-flops last month and I got pretty depressed for a moment – she'd actually worn them and everything.' I turned to face Eddie, unlocked my arms and thrust a forceful forefinger in his direction. 'So I ask you again to cast your mind back to that day and tell me, as you remember it: in expressing sympathy for Joy, did you refer to her rumoured break-up as "your thing" or something more specific?' Eddie pondered the question for a moment before solemnly submitting his response.

'I said "your thing." Yep, definitely, I have to admit that. I remember being wary of how to broach it because she had a pair of scissors in her hand at the time.' Noticing my face crumple into a frown, he instantly tried to assuage my doubt. 'Listen, this is reliable intel I'm giving you here. This is top class, CIA, FBI level intel.'

'Is it?' I asked. 'Or do you just like saying "intel" a lot?'

'Look, if I say it's good intel, it's good intel,' asserted Eddie, doing little to answer the question either way. I looked at him through narrowed eyes, not quite ready to conclude my cross-examination.

'And she's moved out?' I probed. Eddie shook his head.

'No,' he admitted soberly. I threw my arms up in exasperation, but no sooner had they fallen back by my side than he grabbed my shoulders and, excitedly rattling my torso, broke into a broad, jubilant grin.

'She never moved in with him in the first place. I think that's one of the reasons they split up. I guess her heart wasn't in it.' Presumably confident that, with this last revelation, he'd put his testimony beyond doubt, Eddie let my shoulders go and I let his words sink in, processing the information and thinking thoroughly about what it meant before giving the only response that presented itself.

'SHIT!' I shouted. The expletive rang out loud, clear and

239

with a slight echo. 'Sorry,' I whispered to my fellow art enthusiasts.

'Don't worry,' said the woman with a nonchalant laugh. 'We were just thinking the same thing. Come on, darling. Life's too short for this.'

'Naomie Conway?' I asked as the couple sniggered their way out through the door. Eddie smiled at me, unfazed.

'Perfect example,' he noted. 'Am I going to let those critics bring me down? No chance. You remember that story I told you, my friend. I'm not going to say anything about tendering offers or any of that, but you remember that story. Are you going to let a deck shoe through your bedroom window crush your spirit …' He held out his arms once more, his fingers spread apart as if each one was channelling energy from his various masterpieces. 'Or are you going to set up your easel and be an artist?' I couldn't help but crack a smile. Not because Eddie looked or sounded ridiculous (although he did indeed both look *and* sound ridiculous), but because I realised that I had genuine admiration for him. For his complete and utter self-belief and his complete and utter lack of self-consciousness. I was even willing to forgive the fact that the bench we'd been sat on had mud and grass clippings on its legs, as well as a plaque inscribed with the words 'In Loving Memory of Harold Elam.'

Eddie gently clipped my shoulder with the back of his hand.

'So, you like my work?' On the wall next to me, a Chinese girl cupped her naked breasts with her hands. Her right hand was – like her face, hair and collar bone – painstakingly (if imperfectly) drawn and shaded, but her hastily scribbled left hand looked like a burger with five sausages pinned to it with cocktail sticks.

'Yeah,' I said, hoping that my nodding would pass for enthusiasm. 'No offence, though, but all these women look, er, unfinished.'

'Exactly right,' responded Eddie. 'I drew every one of

these beautiful girls to stimulate my, um, senses. In each case, that stimulation reached its conclusion – hence the title – before I'd had time to finish drawing the subject. Each picture is a document of that individual sexual relationship.' I took a hasty step back from Burger Hand.

'You mean?'

'Yes,' confirmed Eddie. 'The supposedly incomplete nature of the work is in fact a raw testament to the power exerted by the female subject over both the male viewer and, specifically, the artist.' Good Lord. Eddie's imagination was fecund alright. I looked at the next drawing on the wall. The paper was blank except for one eye, a nose and a pair of voluptuous, provocatively parted lips.

'Obviously you liked *her* a lot, I observed, 'but I can't imagine she was satisfied.' Eddie laughed, then glanced at his watch.

'Alright. Closing time. Let's go and have that drink,' he suggested. 'Do us a favour and grab an end of that bench.'

I had to admit, it felt good to be out with Eddie on a Friday night, especially after the shitty day I'd had, along with the shitty few days preceding it. Having a few drinks with a mate was certainly better than enjoying a lethal cocktail of sugar and sunstroke with a cocky homeless person, and, after getting the subject of Printout-gate out of the way, the standard of intellectual discussion filling the air in clean-but-not-sterile, cool-but-unpretentious boozer The Jug had been reassuringly silly. From our location at a small round table in a shadowy corner of the room, we'd already discussed the prevalence of clear packaging in the flapjack industry, whether an aroused, slacks-wearing pensioner at Eddie's exhibition would have better concealed or rather inadvertently accentuated his erection had he worn cords (the heaviness of the fabric versus the added bulk factor) and how a top quality printer must be an essential tool in the armoury of the gentleman thief (as Eddie pointed out, going to your local office shop and asking for two hundred business cards reading, 'You've just been visited by The Fox. Thank you for your generous hospitality' would surely arouse suspicion). Each of these subjects and several more besides were enthusiastically, comprehensively dissected until, as our latest bout of laughter subsided, Eddie attempted to kick-start a less fruitful topic of conversation.

'So what are you going to do about you-know-who?' he enquired.

'I don't know who you-know-who is, but if it's a girl whose name begins with a "J", I know I don't want to talk about her right now. In fact, I know I don't even want to think about her.' My tone wasn't terse; I was just far more inclined to gauge Eddie's thoughts on, say, whether it would be more satisfying to shear a sheep or actually be the sheep having an all-over baldie on a sweltering hot summer's day. Eddie held aloft his palms like a police negotiator attempting to avert a potentially calamitous hostage crisis.

'Alright. I respect that.'

'Cool.' I reached across the table and flicked Eddie's near-empty bottle. 'Same again?'

The bar was doing a pretty brisk trade. Not Precario-level business, granted, but the two-guys-and-a-girl on the opposite side of the pine were certainly getting a decent workout as they scrambled to keep their punters lubricated and their till ker-chinging. Glimpsing a rare glimmer of woodwork amongst the backs and bums, I squeezed my way in-between a lanky lad in a rodeo shirt and a girl in a floral blouse and dug into my pocket for cash. Pulling my wallet out, I accidentally nudged my elbow into my female neighbour's upper arm. The collision of limbs was gentle, but enough to divert her attention from both the buzzing bar staff and the blonde girl stood to her right.

'Sorry,' I grimaced, apologetic palm already hoisted at half-mast.

''Salright,' she replied, allowing her lips to collaborate briefly on a polite smile before quickly ushering them away from me. There was a mirrored panel behind the bar, and I couldn't resist using it to take a sneak peek at the girl as she staked out the bar with her blonde pal, the two of them combining their feminine forces in an attempt to reel in one of the barmen. Shot through with caramel highlights, her chestnut hair was beautifully, methodically messy. Piled thick on top, it channelled into free-spirited, collar-kissing wisps at the back, while at the front it curved across her forehead just in time to avert a collision with her sturdy-but-really-rather-sexy eyewear. Actually, those glasses seemed strangely familiar, as did the lips, which were made-up but only minimally so. And that's when it hit me. Though her fringe, as it appeared in the mirror, swung to the left rather than the right, her facial features looked exactly the same in reverse as they'd appeared seconds ago during our brief, right-way-around exchange. Her face, it seemed to me, was perfectly symmetrical.

I tapped her gently on the shoulder and she turned around.

'Hi. Zoe.' Her eyebrows, which appeared to have lost a little weight since last I saw them, took advantage of their increased athleticism by leaping swiftly upwards before dropping down into tense, crouched positions atop her specs. 'You have no recollection of me, do you?' I deduced. Zoe's eyebrows remained flexed, so, by way of a clue, I tucked my jaw in against my chest, offering her a satellite picture of the top of my head. 'Don't tell me you don't recognise this distinctive double crown,' I called up. No response was forthcoming over the mid-volume indie rock filling the room. No response at all. I looked up, half-expecting to see either an empty space or a few fresh replacement revellers where Zoe and her friend had once stood. Instead, I witnessed Zoe's eyebrows relaxing and a perfectly symmetrical look of realisation spreading evenly across her face.

'Aaaah! Yes! I *do* remember! You lost your keys!'

'Yeah, that's me,' I confirmed. I wasn't thrilled with the legacy I'd apparently created for myself, particularly as I hadn't really lost my keys in the first place, but I was pleased that Zoe at least remembered making my acquaintance. Besides, in light of recent events, 'loser' seemed, now more than ever, like a pretty accurate character sketch anyway.

'Sorry. I, uh, don't think I got your name back then.'

'Richard.'

'Richard, this is my friend Kim,' announced Zoe. I offered her friend Kim a smile and a friendly flash of prime palm.

'Hi, Kim.'

'Hiya.'

'So I can't remember,' said Zoe. 'Did you ever find your keys?' I shook my head forlornly.

'No, I'm afraid not, I've been locked out ever since, just wandering the streets. Actually, I've only come in here to have a wash in the men's room, you know? Pick up a couple of crisp boxes from round the back for my bedding.' Zoe laughed and, on the spot, I decided to take advantage of her good spirits by conducting a little post-haircut enquiry of my own. 'Anyway, one thing *I* never found out – did you end up getting married to Tousled Guy?'

'Who?' Zoe looked perplexed

'The guy you gave your number to that day.' I didn't want to sound like a stalker by revealing that I remembered the idiot's real name was Rob.

'Oh, him.' Zoe's specs climbed a couple of millimetres as she scrunched up her nose. 'No, I gave him a fake number. He was too full of himself.'

'He seemed full of something alright,' I noted, sounding casual but secretly pretty excited to have discovered Zoe's finely honed twat perception skills. 'So didn't he come back to the shop to hunt you down?' Zoe gave a shrug. Her shoulders looked good wrapped up in that flower-covered fabric.

'I wouldn't know. I've got a job at a salon these days. I guess I probably won't be cutting your hair again. '

'Don't be so sure,' I cautioned. 'Recently I've been thinking of growing my hair out, getting some highlights, a little feathering action, you know?' Cradling her chin in her fingertips, Zoe nodded in approval of my proposed image

244

change.

'I think we could do that for you,' she said, breaking into a grin.

'I'm sure you could. I like *your* hair, though.'

'Oh, well, you can thank Kim for that. She's my colleague.'

'Good job, Kim. I like your work.' Kim flicked back a handful of her own, gently teased, honey-hued tresses.

'Well, you know, she's a walking advertisement for the salon. We can't have her going around with crap hair.'

'Very true,' I agreed. 'So can I get you both a drink?'

'Are you sure you can afford it?' winced Zoe. 'You know, being homeless and all.'

'Ah, don't worry about it,' I said, swatting the air with my hand. 'Busking keeps the money coming in.'

A couple of minutes later, I turned to pass the girls (who'd taken a step back from the frontline) their drinks and found both of Zoe's forefingers pointing directly towards me. 'Tight Fist!' she exclaimed rather loudly. I looked down at the drinks in my hands. Had I unknowingly bought Zoe some cheap, off-brand wine, or was it that she expected me to intuitively throw in some spur-of-the-moment bar snacks? I certainly didn't have her down as a pork scratchings or even Monster Munch type of gal, although in fairness I perhaps could have looked for Minstrels.

'Sorry?'

'You know – your show. The one with the guy who holds things tightly.'

'Aaah, *Firm Hold*,' I corrected, handing her and Kim their glasses before copping hold of mine and Eddie's bottles. 'Unfortunately, it didn't get past the pilot stage.' Zoe looked surprised, which surprised *me* considering what little faith she'd shown in my killer concept back at the barber's.

'Oh. What happened?'

'Spiralling production costs,' I said with a philosophical, seen-it-all-before shrug. 'Plus it was crap.'

'Shame,' said Zoe. 'What else have you been writing?'

'Well, I've just finished writing for *The Hangout*.' Kim's eyes widened and her lips instantly abandoned the straw protruding from the neck of her bottle.

'Is *The Hangout* that thing that comes on TV on a Saturday morning?'

'Yeah.'

'Oooh, I like the lad who's on that. What's he called? Lee? Leon?'

'Liam,' I said, trying my hardest not to look and / or sound incredulous and / or revolted.

'That's it. He's a bit tasty, he is. I wouldn't mind running my fingers through *his* hair.' She gave the front of her top a slight, cleavage-maximising tug, as if expecting Liam to show up at any second.

'Urrrghhh.' Zoe looked *and* sounded both incredulous *and* revolted.

'I know, I know,' cringed Kim. He's probably young enough to be my son. You know – if I'd been really slutty during my GCSEs.'

'It's not that,' insisted Zoe. 'It's the fact that he's so full of himself.' She clamped her hand over her mouth, then peeled it away, leaving an apologetic palm lingering in the air. 'Sorry. He's not a mate of yours, is he?'

'Nope. Nooooooo. Not at all. He's *overtly* not a friend of mine. He's barely even an acquaintance, really. I'd quite happily murder him if I was guaranteed that nobody would trace it back to me. I mean, *actually* murder him. I don't think I'd have the nerve to stab him, but I'd definitely hold a pillow over his face until he stopped breathing. In fact, that would be better, 'cos I could mess up his hair at the same time.' It was probably a more emphatic response than she required, but hey, Zoe had just dissed both Tousled Guy and Liam in the space of mere minutes. If I could get her to voluntarily call Hannah Thornwell a skanky, untalented, raven-faced little shit, I might have to propose to her on the spot.

'Well that all sounds perfectly reasonable to me,' surmised Zoe. 'So, are you just out with some mates tonight?'

'Just one, actually. I literally have only the one friend.' Zoe bundled up her brow, pursed her lips, and tilted the whole lot to one side.

'Awww. Well if you decide you need any more at any point, feel free to come and join us.'

'Alright,' I said, raising my bottle. 'Thanks.'

CHAPTER SEVEN

A small globule of drool crept slowly out of the side of my mouth. Its movement was clumsy enough to stir me from my slumber, but an emergency intervention from my swooping tongue still arrived a split second too late to stop the spittle from completing its defiant plunge onto the pillow below. Feeling the wetness taunt my cheek, I lifted my head from its suddenly soggy base and hauled my right hand up from my side to flip the pillow over. En route, my elbow cracked into my laptop, which had, it seemed, remained watching over my leaking face throughout the night – apparently, neither a few drinks with Eddie nor overwhelming apathy from the TV industry had prevented me from cracking on with *Crushed*. Eyelids sealed shut with sleep, I grabbed hold of the pillow ... and froze. That was odd. Maybe my semi-conscious mind was playing tricks on me, but my pillow felt as if it had shrunk overnight. I ran my fingers over the saliva-soiled fabric. That was odd, too. It felt like suede.

I cracked open my eyes. The colour that met them wasn't the rich, dark-red-and-terracotta combo of my pillowcase but rather a cool powder blue, and even in my current state just back from The Land of Nod, it dawned on me that I wasn't looking at a pillow at all, but rather a small, plump cushion. I sat bolt upright. There was no mattress underneath me and no duvet on top of me. I wasn't on my bed or, for that matter, any bed. I was on a couch the same powder blue colour and the same suede texture as the spit-hit cushion, albeit a little drier. The laptop at my side wasn't mine, either – it was bigger and newer and chromier and flashier than mine. At least the clothes I had on – a wrinkled white T-Shirt and some checked blue boxer shorts – were my own, although I would have felt considerably happier to see my trousers, shoes and the rest of what I'd been wearing the previous night somewhere in the vicinity of the sofa.

Actually, there wasn't anything in the vicinity of this sofa. There wasn't even a single window in the room and the pristine white walls simply stared back blankly at me, refusing to give up any clues as to my whereabouts. In fact, so pure and spotless was said whiteness that I couldn't make out where one wall turned a corner into another, or even where they met the floor. That, of course, was assuming there even was a floor. Or walls. I ran my hand over my confused, slightly scared head. Was it possible that the sofa I'd just woken up on was simply suspended in the middle of a white nothingness, and that if I attempted to remove myself from the sofa and stand in my new surroundings, I'd find myself falling through this infinite white abyss for ever more, arms outstretched and hands snatching aimlessly at fistfuls of thin air? In an effort to find out, I filled those same fists with the sofa's right arm and cautiously dangled my bare foot over the side until, to my relief, my toes touched a cold, hard surface and I knew I'd hit floor.

Equipped with this knowledge, I rose to my feet, all sorts of thoughts cart-wheeling chaotically through my mind. What had happened after Eddie and I hit that bar last night? This wasn't Eddie's sofa. It wasn't his front room, either – unless he'd radically redecorated it and jettisoned both his piles of specialist publications and those annoying window things. In fact, it didn't feel like *anybody's* front room. Maybe I'd died and gone to Heaven, and right now I was in some kind of waiting room while God scrutinised my CV and looked over a couple of character references to see whether I made the grade. Now I started to get really worried. If The Big Man had asked Jessica to pen a couple of paras I'd be overdressed, even in just my undergarments, for where I was headed next. I held out my arms and looked down at my body for cuts, bruises or a shard of license plate embedded in my belly. What were the odds that, if I *had* come a cropper last night, I'd spent my last spinning, staggering seconds on Earth entertaining Eddie with a post-pub performance of my famous Marty McFly impression?

Still, the *really* peculiar thing about this whole situation wasn't that I'd just woken up on a strange sofa with a strange laptop. It was the fact that, despite my trepidation, both of these strange objects appeared strangely familiar. Come to think of it, even the sofa's pure, spotless white backdrop seemed to ring a vague bell somewhere in the dustier recesses of my mind.

No sooner had I (just about) heard it than the barely-audible ringing of this distant, dust-coated and rather rusty bell was stamped out by another louder and more immediate sound. Well, 'stamped' is the wrong choice of word, as the footsteps coming from my right were light and elegant and seemed to involve a heel of some kind – more a 'clop' than a 'stamp', if anything. Looking towards the source of the sound, I noticed that the whiteness wasn't as featureless as I'd thought, a small door handle (admittedly white in colour) casting a subtle shadow onto the blank surface behind it. The footsteps stopped and the handle turned slowly. If this was indeed one of God's angels come to reveal the results of my application, would I be pushing my luck to point out that a solitary laptop didn't excuse the absence of a few recent edition magazines? Even the worst waiting rooms on Earth were capable of cobbling together a couple of *Take-A-Breaks* and a three-year-old copy of *Golfer's World*. The door opened and a woman entered. A beautiful black girl with a halo of curls. I couldn't be certain, least of all with a few crumbs of sleep remaining in my eyes, but she looked like she might be vivacious. Her slender fingers weren't wrapped around my CV or any other paperwork, but rather the handles of two tall, flared glasses containing the type of foam-topped, sexy stratified coffees I'd sipped on in Garcelle's with Joy a few days earlier. She didn't have wings and she wasn't even wearing white robes, having opted instead for jeans and a spearmint roll-neck. I'd probably have started speculating on whether God let his staff wear casual clothes when they worked weekends were it not for the fact that I now recognised the woman currently holding one of the sexy stratified drinks out towards me. It was Latte Girl.

'Morning,' she beamed, showcasing a set of perfectly

aligned teeth as white as the whiteness all around us. 'I brought you a latte.' Her smile got even whiter as she surveyed the look of surprise on my face. 'Well it's not like I'm Cup-A-Soup Girl.'

'True,' I agreed, accepting the drink with a nervous laugh. Latte Girl stepped past me and motioned to take a seat. I was using my free, non-coffee-clutching hand to pull together the flies on my boxer shorts when it suddenly struck me that I'd never actually completed my mission of flipping over the drool-draped cushion. Quick as a flash, I reached over and pulled off the manoeuvre a second before my host's pert, denim-wrapped rear came in to land. Posterior in place and with the base of her glass resting on her thigh, she served up a friendly smile.

'Soooo …' she offered, placing the conversational ball firmly in my court.

'I like what you've done with this room,' I ventured. 'Very clean … Minimalist.'

'Thank you.' Latte Girl took a sip of her trademark beverage while I looked around the room for a more bountiful source of badinage. Complimenting her on her comfortable sofa would, quite clearly, have been lame and boring, so instead I took a radically different tack.

'Nice laptop.'

'You like?' Latte Girl cocked her head to one side, arched an eyebrow and seductively stroked the computer's chrome curves in the style of a game show dolly bird showing off the star prize. 'It's even better now I've got wireless internet access. It allows me to surf the net from … Oh, what the hell am I going on about? You've already got the same package. It's how we met.' Her recollection was punctuated by a quick, electronic bugle blast coming from the laptop's speakers. 'Sorry to be rude, but d'you mind if I look at this? My friend Rainbow Face Girl sends me the most hilarious e-mails.'

'Rainbow who?' Latte Girl balanced her drink on the arm of the sofa.

'Rainbow Face Girl. You may have seen her. She's on the

billboards advertising another internet service provider whose name I'm not really supposed to mention.'

'Yes, I *have* seen her,' I enthused. 'She's stood gaping in profile while waves of different colours wash over her face. Similar hairstyle to you, actually. Don't you consider her a rival?' Latte Girl's shoulders sagged and she looked a little mournful.

'I only wish I could,' she sighed. 'Truth be told, the fact that she's got a rainbow on her face limits the amount of work she gets.' I looked down at my bare feet, then lifted my head back up and slowly shook it as I squinted into the white void in front of me.

'It's such a shame that in this day and age we still can't seem to get past skin colour.'

'Yeah,' agreed Latte Girl. 'So, anyway, as a result she has a lot of time on her hands to send me e-mails.' She glanced downwards at her trusty gadget. 'May I?'

'Oh, sorry, yeah, of course. Don't mind me. Go for it.'

Latte Girl may have been worried about breaching sofa-sharing etiquette, but as she swirled her slender fingers over her mouse pad and tended to the e-mail from her friend with the multicoloured complexion, I was grateful for the chance to take stock of what was going on. Dipping my top lip into the frothy crest of my coffee, I swivelled my eyeballs around to make double sure this was happening. Yep, apparently it was. Apparently I was sat on a sofa drinking coffee with the girl from the lid of my broadband box. I mean, that was her alright. Emphatically so, in fact, because at that moment, and with her coffee returned to her right hand, she threw her head back and laughed at whatever it was that Rainbow Face Girl had blessed her inbox with. Though I was viewing it from a different angle, it was exactly the image I'd seen immortalised on cardboard every day for the last month and a half. In fact, it was this history – my familiarity with the moment currently playing out in front of my eyes – that forced me, after taking another sip of impeccably brewed coffee, to ask the inescapable question.

'What's so funny?'

'Take a look.' She swung the laptop around on her knees. The screen was filled with a photo of a snowman receiving oral sex from his frosty but obviously far-from-frigid other half. I laughed, but my polite chuckling was undercut somewhat by the obvious look of surprise on my face. Latte Girl herself seemed surprised by my less than raucous reaction.

'What? You don't think it's funny?'

'No. I mean, yes, I do. It's just ... I would never have thought you were laughing at something so ... rude. I always assumed you were laughing at a picture of a bulldog in a nappy or your sister's kids with chocolate on their faces.' I flipped my wide, disbelieving grin into a school master's snooty frown. 'To be quite honest, I expected better of Rainbow Face Girl, too.'

'You want *rude*?' Latte Girl's eyes glinted as her fingers scurried double-quick over the mouse pad. 'You should see this picture of Wilma Flintstone with her boobs out while Dino ...'

'Er, that's OK,' I interrupted. 'Thank you.' Latte Girl smirked at me.

'Oooh, you don't want to tarnish hallowed childhood memories?'

'No, I'm just very fussy about unlicensed representations of cartoon characters.'

'Oh, of course,' she giggled. 'I should have known. Your little showdown with Chief Whip the other day was classic.'

'What? How did you know about that?' LG smiled cheekily.

'I'm inside your mind,' she reasoned with a shrug of her spearmint shoulders. 'We're both inside your mind.' While Latte Girl sipped on her drink, I pondered her surprising revelation for a moment before concluding that it actually made perfect sense.

'Well, at least I understand all the white now,' I said, looking afresh at my surroundings. 'It's to make it look bigger than it actually is.'

'Bear in mind that this is just one room,' Latte Girl pointed out. 'Although I must admit, the rest of the place *is* a bit of a state.' She looked down at her portable filth-storage unit. 'These pictures, though: they're like professional quality. They may even have been done by the original animators – you know, as favours to perverted friends without their prodigious drawing talents.' She teasingly caressed the mouse pad with her forefinger then double-clicked the button beneath it with her thumb. 'Sure I can't interest you?'

'I'm sure. Thanks.' I retreated to my coffee for a few moments before curiosity got the better of me. 'Just out of interest, you don't have anything with Pocahontas, do you?' Latte Girl swung her laptop around once more. On the screen, the beautified Disney version of the Native American heroine was busy making a decidedly non-Disney-approved use of a long feather. In fact, the look on her face suggested she'd actually been making use of it for some time.

'Wow,' I gasped, sinking my elbow between my legs just to be on the safe side. 'It turns out I may have been a little rash in my quickness to condemn all unauthorised likenesses of iconic animated characters.'

'I told you,' beamed the pretty, coffee-serving cartoon-porn peddler. 'Professional quality. All her features are in correct proportion to each other.'

'*Almost* all of her features,' I corrected. 'She's got the most incredible ...' My companion let loose another of those wonderful signature laughs, and her reaction to my reaction distracted me from the action on screen. 'And you have incredible teeth,' I observed. Latte Girl screwed up her face dismissively.

'Oh, please. You think I could throw back coffee all the time and still have teeth as white as these?

'You had them whitened?'

'Photoshopped.' I liked her honesty. It was another good thing she possessed in addition to her beautiful looks and that Pocahontas picture, and suddenly, without warning, I felt myself swooping in for the kill.

'Well, seeing as we both like coffee, could I take you out for one sometime? Or even something to eat? You could order something teeth-staining. Maybe some tomato soup washed down with a glass of red wine.' Latte Girl didn't laugh but instead smiled sweetly at me, the ends of her hair swaying ever so slightly as she pushed three of her fingers into the coin pocket of her jeans. She came up with a gold band, which she proceeded to slide onto her ring finger.

'Sorry,' she offered through an apologetic, computer-cleaned grin. 'They made me take it off for the photoshoot. They thought it would make the internet package look more desirable if it was being used by a single woman.' I was surprised. Not so much by the ring, but by the fact I didn't feel more stung by Latte Girl's revelation. It seemed the one positive thing about my fallout with Jessica was that it had apparently numbed me to feeling any freshly generated pain. Put simply, I couldn't feel any worse than I already did, and so I simply wiped off Latte Girl's rejection as easily as my tongue had the froth from my upper lip and, nodding at the laptop, kept the conversation moving.

'If they wanted to make it desirable they should have put Comes with a Feather there on the front. Could you turn her around now, please, before I embarrass myself for the second time in one minute?'

'Sorry.' Latte Girl grinned as she spun Poca-hot-ass out of my eye line. 'I suppose it's about time we got down to the reason you're here.'

'You mean I'm not here to look at obscene images of cartoon characters?' Latte Girl shook her curls.

'Alas, not. You're here because I wanted to tell you that, no matter what you might think, you can still iron out this whole situation with Jessica George.'

'How did ...' I began. 'Oh, yeah, I forgot. The whole "in my mind" thing. Well, I appreciate your support but you probably shouldn't even waste your time. I mean, Jessica won't talk to me – she'll barely look at me, in fact – so how am I supposed to ...'

'You know what us women are like,' interrupted Latte Girl. 'She's upset with you and right now she's letting you know that.'

'You're not joking,' I sighed, looking down despondently into the light brown depths of my glass. 'Message received.' Latte girl reached over and jabbed a couple of fingers into my thigh.

'Listen, though. When she's ready, she'll also let you know how you can make it up to her.' I smiled feebly at my host.

'Well, with all due respect, I think we can safely say you haven't spent too much time in Jessica's mind. The only thing she's likely to let me know is where I can stick my apologies.' I sipped on my drink, eyes staring straight into the white abyss in front of me.

'I'm telling you,' insisted Latte Girl, placing a hand on my shoulder, 'she'll let you know. You'll see.' From somewhere beyond the whiteness a door slammed shut.

'Shit!' exclaimed Latte Girl, springing up from the sofa. 'That's my husband!' She glugged down the remainder of her drink while I placed my still half-full glass on the floor, rose to my feet and appealed for calm.

'OK, let's not panic here. Can't we just tell him I'm a friend of yours and that you were giving me some advice on a personal matter? I mean, that *is* what you were doing ...' Latte Girl looked back at me, her face as blank as the pallor around us. For a moment I thought she was pondering my sound suggestion, until her eyes panned slowly down beneath my waist and I realised that my genius plan had failed to factor in my lack of trousers. Now it was my turn to start panicking. Latte Girl made for the door. I followed her, but, with one hand on the door handle, she turned and held up her free palm (the one that seconds ago had been holding an empty coffee glass) like the world's best-looking lollipop lady.

'No!' she insisted, eyes wide. 'It's too risky. I'll stall for time, but I'm afraid you're going to have to go out through the secret passage ...'

'The secret passage!' I laughed. Sure, my laughter was probably due in no small part to nervous energy, but I was still impressed by Latte Girl's ability to – momentarily, at least – diffuse the tension with a spot of playful humour.

'I'm serious,' she hissed. And that's when I realised she was, er, serious.

'OK, well, any hints on where it is?' Latte Girl folded up her palm and pointed at the wall opposite the door. The one as featureless as the other three.

'There's a small button on that wall.' I followed her finger. It *had* to be a small button, as I couldn't make out a thing. I was still squinting when Latte Girl's lips grazed my cheek and, after dispensing a quick 'See ya', disappeared, together with the rest of her component parts, around the door.

'Uh, LG?' I called out after her as quietly as I could. Preceded by the cusps of her curls, Latte Girl's head reappeared around the door.

'Yeah?' she whispered.

'You obviously know a lot about what goes on in here. In my head, I mean.'

'Yeah,' she agreed. Feeling embarrassed, I looked down at my toenails.

'Well, I'm sorry about the time I fantasised about me and you and that fridge full of ...'

'Ohhhh ... The whipped cream and maple syrup thing?'

'Yeeeaah,' I confirmed, feeling my cheeks add another rare splash of colour to the room. 'For what it's worth, I had no idea you were married.' Apparently mislaying her sense of urgency for just a moment, Latte Girl tilted her head to the side and rolled her eyes upwards while a sly smile crept across her lips.

'Don't worry. It was fun. Now go!' And with that, she vanished into the whiteness once more while I gave a small but

257

forceful fist-pump to celebrate the fact that our sweet sticky sexcapade (into which, after all, I'd put a considerable amount of thought) had been good for her too. Ill-timed, wholly inappropriate celebration concluded, I got down to the important business of pissing my pants. Well, not literally, although it was reassuring to know that if that situation did occur, all resulting yellow stains could at least be Photoshopped off the floor and / or out of the sofa fabric. Ditto the coffee that, at the prompting of my big toe and its four-strong team of henchmen, splayed across the floor as I rushed past the sofa and over to the allegedly button-bearing wall. Arms outstretched, I ran my hands across the spotless surface in desperate search of a protrusion so tricky and discreet that it continued to evade my eyes altogether. My fingers were no more successful, failing to come up with a speck of dust let alone a button. But while this wall seemed intent on keeping its secrets, the one opposite it – the wall surrounding the door through which Latte Girl had appeared and subsequently vanished – was leaking noise. As my fingertips thanklessly traversed every indiscernible inch of this featureless slab, a succession of thwacks (or were they slaps?) could be heard troubling the floor beyond the white cell. Were those footsteps? I wondered, and if so, what kind of brute had taken Latte Girl's mouse pad-clicking hand in marriage? The thwacking-slash-slapping stopped and a male voice entered into the mix.

'I've got some cracking photos,' the voice announced excitedly with what sounded like an Australian accent. 'Some real beauts. I'll load them onto your laptop so you can have a look. It's in here, right?'

'Uh, no. Actually I, um, think it's ...' stammered the voice of Latte Girl. 'Wait! Aren't you going to dry yourself off?'

The answer, it seemed, was 'no', as the slap-thwacks started up again, briefly growing in volume until, once more, they stopped. Next came the sound of the door handle being turned. With my palms still buffing up the wall beneath them, I cast a petrified glance over my shoulder and across the sofa.

The sight that met my eyes caused my jaw to drop and my hands to instantly shut down their rotations. There in the doorway stood a man clad, basically, in a pair of skimpy scarlet swimming trunks. A diver's mask covered his eyes, its thick elastic strap pinning down both a snorkel and the mop of damp, straggly blonde hair that reached down to lap against his glistening, stubbled jaw. He was clutching a digital camera which, I noticed, was the same as mine. Time, as was its wont around me, seemed to freeze for a few seconds, halting everything except the drop of water that made the bold leap from the guy's prickly chin and down onto one of the black flippers on his feet.

'Red Snapper,' I noted. He peeled the mask back from his eyes, dragging it onto a new perch atop his forehead.

'Who the hell are you?' he asked, squinting at me through piercing green peepers. It struck me that he looked a heck of a lot harder than he did on the front of my camera box.

'Just checking the place for rising damp,' I fibbed, giving the wall a final, satisfied pat and rising to my bare feet. 'But, as the only damp thing in here appears to be your good self – well, you and that puddle of coffee – I think I'll just be on my way.'

'Like hell you will, mate,' growled Red Snapper. He tossed his camera onto the sofa, but unfortunately for him it bounced off one of the cushions and landed, with a hard crack and a gentle splash, face down in the glistening brown coffee pool on the floor. He looked pissed off by this, so I decided it was in the best interest of myself and, specifically, my face to offer him some reassurance.

'I have that same camera,' I related. 'I've dropped it a couple of times – once on concrete, actually – and it's always been fine. It's waterproof, too, although, er, obviously you already know that.'

My sympathetic words apparently hadn't done the trick, because Red Snapper had gone from pissed off to steaming. I mean, literally steaming – his face was red and there was a sizzling sound as the droplets of water on his forehead and in his hair evaporated to form a twisting cloud around his damp blonde head and fogged-up goggles. Behind my back, the fingers on my increasingly clammy right hand frantically resumed their hunt for that elusive button.

'OK, I can see we've got off on the wrong foot, here,' I admitted, stalling for time. 'Or in your case the wrong flipper.' Red Snapper stared back at me, visibly unamused. 'Sorry,' I continued. 'Bad joke, but in all seriousness, me and your wife were just talking.' Red Snapper looked over at the laptop and his bronzed features tightened.

'Talking and enjoying pornography on her laptop, I see.' His goggles leant over his brow while his eyes squinted incredulously at the screen. 'Is that ... *Pocahontas*?'

'Um, yeah,' I confirmed gingerly. With that mythical button still a no-show, it looked increasingly like I was going to have to win over my soggy, sinewy opponent if I was to stand any chance of getting out of this room alive. 'Actually, this you *will* find funny. The irony is, when it comes to unauthorised pictures of well-known cartoon characters, I'm actually very particular about ...'

'Oh, I can see you're very particular, mate,' sneered Red Snapper. 'This is some specialist shit you two have been getting off on.'

'Alright,' I began, raising my voice in the hope of reaching Latte Girl's ears. 'I really think it's best if we ask your wife to come in here and clear things up.' My absentee host failed to enter, so I raised my voice some more and went for the direct plea. 'Uh, LG? Could you come in here for a second, please?'

'LG?' seethed Red Snapper. 'You're calling my wife by her initials?'

'It's just a shorthand,' I reasoned meekly. 'You know, for convenience. It's not an affectionate thing. I really wouldn't read anything into it.'

Red Snapper weighed up my advice for a second, then charged at me. Well, I say 'charged', but his choice of footwear meant that 'waddled' was probably more accurate, the slapping of his flippers against the floor giving him the aura of a demented penguin whose boss had just casually informed him that, after thirty years of loyal service, he'd been transferred to their Sahara office, effective Monday coming. Still, it was nonetheless more than enough to scare me into spinning back around, dropping to my knees and once again scouring the pure white plaster for that pesky release mechanism, my search losing none of its intensity as, behind me, Red Snapper tripped on his flipper and joined his camera in the coffee. Whilst he scrambled to get back on his amphibious feet, my fingers scrambled across the whiteness, but still to no avail. Nope, it was looking for all the world like the MIA Latte Girl had knocked back one too many cups of caffeine and hallucinated the existence of a ... Wait! What was this? In the centre of the wall, beneath my right hand, I could feel a raised, rounded bump. Could this be it? Could this be the button that Latte Girl had spoken of? That magical, mystical button which secured my escape seconds before Red Snapper beat me to a pulp and took a photograph beautifully contrasting the stark white floor with the pool of dark red blood around my head? I pressed down firmly on the button, but whilst I felt it squash beneath my fingertips, nothing happened. The wall refused to slide back and no hitherto-unseen portal threw itself open. I pressed down harder on the button, but again to no effect, and I was still hammering hopelessly on it when Red Snapper's hard, brine-covered hand landed on my shoulder.

I awoke to find myself jabbing one of the bubbles in the pale green wallpaper behind my headboard whilst simultaneously attempting to wriggle free of my non-existent, flipper-footed assailant. But while Red Snapper was gone, from over my shoulder and above my head I could nevertheless hear the voice of someone who, I was fairly certain, wouldn't have minded strangling me. Sparing the air bubble's life, I turned around to discover that, up there on the television that had apparently remained on throughout the night, Jessica was shooting the breeze with my sometime alter ego Danny Waters. There they were on that familiar purple sofa, carrying out a warmer, more civil version of the interview I'd rehearsed so torturously with Jessica the day before. And here I was back in the real world. I wondered whether being chased around by a psycho scuba diver with a passion for amateur photography wasn't, in fact, preferable to this.

Letting out a pained sigh, I flopped back down on my mattress and sunk my cheek into both my pillow and a small puddle of cold wet saliva. Things, I reflected solemnly, had been a whole lot different a week ago. Seven days earlier, I'd been sat in The Players' Lounge with a glass of sparkling water in my hand and Joy's fingernails in my thigh. Now, I was laid in my bed with a churning sensation in my stomach and an impudent bedspring in my side. Seven days earlier, I'd been paranoid Jessica was upset with me. Now, there was no paranoia about it. Seven days earlier, Jessica's every word and every smile, taking place a few metres beneath me, had been conveyed to me via a huge, pristine plasma screen. Now, those same words and smiles, unfolding several miles from where I lay, came to my eyes on a dusty, diddy-sized portable telly up high and out of reach

I'd blown it. My run on the show had finished, and, after spending four weeks in Jessica's company, my chances of hooking up with her were now approximately a million per cent less than when we'd never met, an outcome that I had somehow neglected to account for back when I'd hatched this idiotic scheme. That wasn't important, though. The self-pity that had sparked this whole thing into motion was nothing compared to how bad I felt at having upset Jessica. Back before that brainwave, I'd moped about because Heather Grey and Cagoule Girl and the Kerry Washington lookalike hitting the camping shop didn't even know my name. Now, though, I would have given anything for Jessica to be similarly deprived of this information.

Behind that grubby glass and at the end of those several miles, Danny Waters was sat on the sofa, delving into a sawdust-stuffed dustbin and answering questions about dates and talking to girls and so on and so forth. The same questions I had answered from that same spot on that same sofa the day before. I didn't hear Danny's answers, but whatever he was saying was enough to earn him a compendium of grins, giggles and 'ahhh's from his interviewer. It stood to reason that Jessica had a lot of reactions in reserve, though, having barely wasted a single facial muscle on me in rehearsals. Even sat a metre from her, her features fully illuminated to me by those same studio lights that had conspired with my stress and embarrassment to stick sawdust to my forehead, I couldn't have said for certain whether my words – the last words I'd said to her and, in all probability, the last words I ever would say to her – had connected in any way, but hers had pretty much let me know where I stood. Up above, on screen and in the here-and-now, Jessica looked directly into the camera and delivered the same words I'd heard her utter twenty-four-ish hours earlier, right before I vacated both the purple sofa and her life. Well, mostly the same words.

'Wow. Some heartfelt answers from Ri … from Danny, there,' she observed. I sat bolt upright. Had I just heard what I thought I had? Surely I couldn't have. No, I had – I was sure of it. I'd heard a 'Ri …' there. Not a 'Richard', not even a 'Rich', but definitely a 'Ri …' While my heart started pounding, Jessica certainly seemed like she was trying to compose herself from *something*. 'So, er, in case you're wondering,' she stammered, 'Danny will be doing his thing live on stage for us a little later. Now, though, it's time for a fellow who's got more than enough heart for any challenge as our ring-tailed renaissance man Lawrence adds another stripe to his already eye-straining tail …' That was it. The 'er' confirmed beyond doubt the 'Ri …' and that's when it hit me. That's when – just as Latte Girl had promised – Jessica's words let me know there was a way I could reach out to her; a way to draw a thick, indelible line under (or better yet *through*) the entire godforsaken mess. The sound of Jessica's words ringing through my hung-over head had got me into this whole, sorry mess and now it was going to get me at least some of the way out of it. There was a perverse but perfect symmetry to it, a symmetry that was only accentuated as I dived across the floor and heaved into my wastepaper bin. Rising to my feet and dragging the back of my hand over my mouth, I noticed that, from her vantage point on my bedside table, Latte Girl was, to her credit, resisting the temptation to shoot me a smug, told-you-so look. Instead, she was simply carrying on as usual, sitting on that powder blue sofa and flashing her Photoshopped gnashers at the action taking place on her computer screen. Another filthy e-mail attachment from Rainbow Face Girl, no doubt.

'Jess, we need to talk.'

'I can't hear you,' replied Jessica, and to be honest she wasn't coming through too loud or too clear to me either. Actually, just seeing her was proving pretty tricky, too, despite the fact I was sat right next to her. Back when we'd sat down at that canteen table and bonded over Thai chicken and rice and Freddy McKreuger and Liam's sub-par Top Trumps statistics, I'd joked about wanting to get inside Lawrence the Lemur and help him find his voice. Now, in a last ditch attempt to salvage my friendship with Jessica, I was doing a pretty terrible job of both, fighting against the combined noise of the taxi's engine, local radio (Earth, Wind and Fire's 'After The Love Has Gone' – I'd smiled grimly at its aptness) and the surrounding traffic to even make myself audible from beneath the character's cumbersome (and, truth be told, slightly smelly) dome.

'I don't know why you have to have the head on before we even get there,' commented Jessica. 'Is this your strange way of getting yourself into character?' Nope, it was my strange way of getting into a cab with her before she herself lost her head. To that extent, at least, my plan had gone off surprisingly smoothly. I'd caught Marcus, Lawrence's usual alter ego, starting his working day with a cigarette in the alley behind the Fresh Coat building, and after unburdening my wallet of twenty pounds (a further scrunched-up tenner had miraculously evaded his eyes) and a points-packed Nectar reward card, I'd secured access to both the costume and the sparsely populated corridors of Fresh Coat HQ. Emerging fully garbed from the thankfully barren toilets clutching my jeans, trainers and shirt, I'd spied Denise disappearing into the office and decided that she'd be a suitable minder for the civvies-stuffed plastic bag in my paw. I was going to have to bring my current duds back anyway, so I might as well leave my own gear in a safe place. It was kind of like when, stripped down to his Spider-Man suit, Peter Parker would swathe his street clothes in webbing and leave them stuck on an alleyway wall while he slugged it out with Doc Ock or The Green Goblin. Or at least that's what I told myself.

Moving, with considerably less grace and agility than Spidey, down the corridor, I paused outside the double doors and peered through one of the thin, rectangular glass panels. Thanks to the plentiful lunchtime options of Oxford Street, Tottenham Court Road and their various tributaries, the office was, to my relief, quiet, with Denise – who was now taking a seat at her desk – one of only four people on the shop floor. Reminding myself that this was the easy part of the task, I took a deep breath (not that it was much use – even at this early stage of the mission, oxygen was already at a premium inside Lawrence's head) pushed open one of the doors with my paw and walked, fur-of-foot on fur-of-carpet, towards Denise's perch.

'Lawrence!' called out Yeti. 'You should be able to help with this. Gluttonous beast, nine letters.' I stopped, there on the spot. I knew that one – it was 'wolverine' – but I couldn't risk betraying my identity for the sake of a compliment on my crossword skills and natural history knowledge (besides, why let Marcus get the credit?), so instead I simply dispensed a big, exaggerated shrug before continuing on to my destination.

Denise was using her left hand to grip a cheese and tomato baguette and her right to flick through the pages of a glossy fashion magazine, stopping on a double-page spread of brightly coloured ponchos and pashminas.

'Denise,' I said, pitching my voice loud enough to travel through the thick foam and fur fabric of Lawrence's muzzle but not, if I'd weighted it right, to carry any further across the office. Denise glanced up at me before returning her attention to a purple poncho. Or possibly pashmina.

'I can't help you,' she said flatly. 'I tell you every time: I don't smoke anymore.'

'Denise,' I repeated as she hoisted her baguette up towards her mouth. 'It's me.' Denise freeze-framed her fangs a centimetre short of piercing their target, her eyeballs climbing upwards over the insistent animal at her desk.

'Richard?' she ventured incredulously.

'Yeah,' I confirmed, a note of disbelief finding its way into my own muffled voice. Denise put her baguette down on top of a copy of *Black Hair* magazine and wiped her palms clean of flour.

'What the hell are you doing dressed up as Lawrence the Lemur?'

'It's a long story, but the point of it is that I messed up with Jessica and I really upset her and I need to say sorry to her and this, believe it or not, is the only way I can do it.' Garbled explanation over, I stared out through the eyeholes in Lorro's face, waiting for Denise to soak in the info.

'Awwwww, that's so sweet,' she cooed, a little too loudly for my liking. I raised a furry forefinger to the underside of my newly acquired muzzle, prompting Denise to turn down the volume, if not her level of excitement. 'Odd ... but sweet,' she qualified. 'Any way I can help, just let me know.' I held aloft my sack of garments.

'Any chance you could look after my clothes?' Before I was able to discover whether Denise was willing to accept the Lemur Laundry Challenge, we were interrupted by a voice –

which I instantly recognised as Kam's – calling out the name 'Marcus' from across the room. I froze on the spot, waiting for her to finish her business with this Marcus character before I could conclude mine with Denise and hightail it out of there.

'Marcus,' prompted Denise, reaching over the desk to relieve me of my clobber. 'You probably can't hear through that thing but Kam's talking to you.' Suddenly remembering that I was answerable (or at least gesture-able) to the name 'Marcus' as well as 'Lawrence', I turned to face Fresh Coat's commander-in-chief.

'You hear that sound?' Kam cupped her hand to her ear. Now she mentioned it, I could just about make out the sound of a car impatiently beeping its horn from the street down below. 'That's Jessica waiting for you in the cab.' I didn't need telling twice, least of all by Killer Kam, so I hit her with a classic military salute and Denise with a north-facing thumb (I was, at least, getting the hang of this body language thing) and hurried out of the office.

'Go, Lawrence!' Denise shouted after me.

'And don't let me hear about you having a fag break in front of the kids,' warned Kam, rather less excitedly, as the doors swung shut behind me.

Down on the street outside Fresh Coat HQ, a handful of nods and muffled grunts had been enough to get me into the back of the cab without suspicion, if not to prevent some impatient tutting from Jessica when I proceeded to close the door on my tail. Now, though, having spent the ensuing cross-town journey as a passive audience to the taxi driver's cracks about not usually allowing animals in his cab, it occurred to me that I was doing *too* good a job of concealing Lawrence's inner self. My nerves and the cabbie's insistence on regaling Jessica with anecdotes about other celebrity passengers he'd presumably also bored to tears meant that, as our destination grew near, I was no further forward in my own audacious mission.

Now, though, it was time for the moment of truth. I

clamped Lawrence's chubby cheeks between his padded paws and heaved his head up from around my own.

'Oh for God's sake,' sighed Jessica, as, hitting the cab ceiling, Lawrence's Lemur-ish face gave way to my own markedly sheepish features. It was a less hysterical reaction than I'd braced myself for, but the level of disgust on Jessica's face was very much as anticipated.

'I'm sorry, but the only way I could think to speak to you was ...'

Was to start stalking me disguised as a ring-tailed lemur?' interjected Jessica, by now very audible. 'Brilliant. Because this isn't creepy in any way at all.'

'Ten fifty, please,' chimed the driver. I remembered that, in the bag strapped to the side of my hide, my wallet contained the tenner which I'd been able to keep concealed from Marcus during the cash-for-costume transaction, but by the time my brute of a right paw had got to grips with the bag's suddenly microscopic plastic catch, Jessica had taken care of it.

'Let me give you some money,' I volunteered, finally cracking open the catch.

'Forget it.' Jessica pushed open the taxi door and planted her trainer-clad foot onto the street outside. Well, this was going well, I thought, copping hold of Lawrence's head and clambering out of the cab, tail swinging as my padded hind paws joined Jessica's cushioned kicks on the tree-lined pavement outside. I thanked the smirking cabbie, slammed shut his door and turned to survey my new surroundings. I'd almost forgotten that the venue for this afternoon's all-or-nothing rescue bid was a primary school playground in Bethnal Green.

'Shit. Better put my head back on before the kids see me.'

'Yeah,' muttered Jessica. 'You wouldn't want to shatter anyone's illusions.'

Even accounting for the difficulty I was experiencing in controlling my newly acquired lemur legs, I was still some way off Jessica's pace as she strode, head-down, through the school gates and across the asphalt towards the triumvirate of talent gathered beneath a brand new basketball goal at the far end of the playground. I suppose I expected her journey to conclude with a blurted betrayal of my identity or even a request that the shoot be called off, but instead Jessica politely introduced herself to the school's creaky-looking headmistress Mrs. Gibbs, stern-looking Bricks and Balls publicist Carly, and Dale, a photographer wearing a red satin baseball jacket, tweed combat pants and Velcro-intensive trainers (we'll go with twattish-looking). For my part, I offered the team a raised paw and, I'd hazard a guess, a creepily impassive, googly-eyed stare.

'By the way, gang,' said Dale, delving into a plastic bag, 'Liam's in the boys' toilets. Not that I could tell the difference, but apparently he messed up his hair putting on his T-shirt.' He tossed Jessica a T-shirt adorned with the Bricks and Balls logo. 'Hopefully your 'do's a little lower maintenance.' Jessica slid her arms out of her tracksuit jacket, placing it down on top of Dale's duffel bag before pulling her pink promotional garment over her own white tee. The top of her ponytailed head was just emerging through the collar when Liam jogged back into the scene, a snug-fitting, powder blue Bricks and Balls T-shirt on his chest and his hair apparently back at full strength.

'Alright, Marc?' he muttered. Just as I was wondering how he'd managed to confuse the name 'Dale' with 'Marc', Liam gave me a clip round the back of my gigantic head, knocking the whole carpet-covered structure forward and completely depriving me of the power of sight. 'Marcus, you deaf bastard!' he called through the fur. 'What's up, mate?' With one paw busy dispatching a fuzzy thumb-up in Liam's general direction, I used the other to push upwards on my muzzle until the sight of Mrs. Gibbs looking disapprovingly at Liam confirmed that my human eyes were officially aligned with the small holes on either side of my lemur snout. Testing my newly restored (if still somewhat limited) eyesight to the full, I panned across to see that, by contrast, Dale was trying to stifle a smile as he foraged once again in his bag full of threads. 'Ah, one more thing, mate,' he said, throwing Liam a pink towelling headband. 'I'm gonna need you to put that on your bonce.' Liam sighed and mumbled something inaudible before placing his palms together inside the headband and solemnly bowing his head. Actually, it's highly possible that he was appealing to the Lord to watch over his precious tresses, as he then proceeded to part his hands, stretching out the headband as far as the elastic would allow before slowly, painstakingly lowering it down around his crowning glory as if every chemical-soaked strand was wired with a 40,000 volt electrical charge. Happy, presumably, that he'd thrown enough clothing (and / or torment) Liam's way, Dale sized up my silhouette.

'Are you going to lose the messenger bag,' he enquired, 'or are we filming Lawrence Learns how to work in the media?' Using my paws as best I could, I hoisted the bag's strap (already adjusted to its loosest setting to accommodate my extra bulk) up over Lorro's bulbous head, and, with as much dexterity as I could manage, stowed my luggage alongside Dale's. It had my wallet and that tenner in it, and, having just had the genuine Marcus take me to the cleaners for the honour of inhabiting his stuffy second skin, I was in no mood to be robbed twice in one day.

'Mrs. Gibbs, if you wouldn't mind, I think we're about ready for the kids, now,' announced Carly. While Mrs. Gibbs headed off to the school building to unleash her young charges, Dale tossed Liam a basketball and ushered *The Hangout*'s fab three into place on the patch of concrete underneath the hoop. 'Let's kick things off with a group shot before everyone's too hot and sweaty,' he suggested. 'Lawrence, if you could get in-between Jessica and Liam and put your arms around them ...' I tentatively followed his command, shuffling into the space between the presenters and delicately placing my paws on their shoulders. 'Come on, guys,' implored Dale. 'Look like you mean it. Lawrence, bring your paws down where I can see them, and you two give Lawrence a hug. He's a great big cuddly lemur, for crying out loud!'

'Come on!' yelled a suddenly hyped-to-the-hilt Liam,

thrusting an arm around my back and slapping the basketball into my mercifully padded stomach. I couldn't tell whether his enthusiasm was sarcastic or if his trip to the toilets had seen him scoring some coke from an eight-year-old. Wherever Jessica's hands were, though, they hadn't landed with as much impact as her co-presenter's, or even assumed their positions with enough feigned affection to be felt through Lawrence's thick pelt. I prayed that Jessica was similarly numb to my touch as, placing my right paw down stiffly on her collar bone, I realised that the tips of my chunky, inflexible fingertips (uh, pawtips?) were levitating precariously over the outskirts of her right breast. The one thing creepier than a stalker dressed as a wild animal was, I felt fairly certain, a sexual predator dressed as a wild animal.

'That's the stuff!' shouted Dale. 'A bit more affection, please, Jessica. Lemur's aren't carnivorous, you know.' I sort of felt Jessica slide her rigid right hand across my chest, but it remained there for only two camera clicks and one 'Wicked!' from Dale before she absented herself from the sports-themed love-in.

'I have to sit this out for a second. I'm feeling a bit ill.'

'Are you alright?' asked an anxious Carly from behind her clipboard.

'Yeah, yeah, I'll be fine. I just need to take a time-out.'

'A time-out, eh?' repeated Dale. 'Well, at least you've got the basketball terminology down. Alright, let's get some hot man-on-lemur action going with you two. If you could maintain that loving embrace for just a few seconds longer ...'

'She's probably pregnant,' speculated Liam beneath both his breath and the sound of Dale's exhortations. 'Richard spent the last four weeks trying to stick his dick in her.' While Dale continued to click away, my own buttons were most definitely being pushed. Life inside Lawrence's skin suddenly got even hotter and less comfortable and I felt my arm tighten around Liam's neck.

'Oh, the headlock – I love it!' hooted Dale. 'Yeah! Give it

to him, Lorro!'

'Steady on, mate, don't kill me,' joked Liam before returning to his original train of half-thought. 'Thank God he's left, though. Richard, I mean. What a twat. Plus the new writer Natalie's pretty fit. You never know.' Alright, that was it – Liam had asked for this. Tightening my stranglehold further, I balled up my free paw and ground my hairy knuckles into his scalp.

'Yeah!' shouted Dale. 'It's the law of the jungle out here on Lawrence's court!'

'Aarrgh! Watch the hair, you bastard!' railed an at best half-joking Liam, wriggling free of my grasp.

'And you watch your language,' advised Carly, not-even-quarter-jokingly as, led (barely) by their headmistress, a swarm of twenty youngsters in pastel-coloured B&B T-shirts charged noisily across the playground and, in the case of at least two of them, painfully into my groin.

It was a couple of rowdy minutes before order – and the feeling in my nether regions – was restored. Carly corralled myself, Jessica, Liam and the kids into a huddle under the hoop, a momentous gathering that Dale snapped with the manic energy of someone who'd been given exclusive photo rights to a surprise reunion of The Beatles, John included. When, a roll of film later, the group unglued itself to gear up for some basic basketball drills, I watched Jessica talking to a girl with pigtails and for a moment I forgot the lamentable state of affairs that had led to me observing their chit-chat through the eyeholes of a smelly lemur suit. In fact, for those few seconds, it slipped my mind that I was even inside a smelly lemur suit, until Jessica looked in my direction and I realised I couldn't turn my head half as quickly as I wanted to; certainly not quick enough to evade her scowl. Here I was, then, floundering aimlessly in a pungent lemur suit and facing one very pertinent question: what the hell was I going to do?

'What you could probably do is stand on the sidelines and cheer on the kids,' directed Carly, perhaps unaware that

272

Lawrence plied his trade as a silent artist. As if to illustrate the fact, I simply shrugged before trundling over to park my soft bum on the hard bench. There, I bowed my head in solemn commemoration of my last shred of dignity while Carly went about the task of dividing the players into pairs.

By the time I looked up again, the drills were ready to begin. Almost. Tucked behind a yellow line on the ground, ten pairs of players, spearheaded by Jessica and her new, pigtail-rocking pal, were fondling basketballs and chatting excitedly. A couple of feet to the other side of the line, Carly was speaking to Mrs. Gibbs while, stood between them, a girl with her left arm in a plaster cast looked up and swivelled her neck from side to side as she followed the conversation. To the side of this gathering, a bristle-bonced, XXXL lad in a size S tee and similarly skimpy white shorts clumsily bounced his basketball against the concrete, anxiously awaiting the outcome of this playground power summit.

'Alright,' began Carly, breaking up the huddle to address the troops. 'As you all know, Maria here's nursing an injury, so unfortunately we're a player down.'

'No we're not,' objected Liam, thrusting a finger, to my complete surprise, at yours truly. 'We've got Lawrence.' Carly eyed me up and down, her face dripping with scepticism.

'I'm not sure Lawrence is dressed for basketball.'

'No, Lawrence is up for it,' insisted Liam. 'Haven't you seen some of the things he does?'

'Let Lawrence play!' pleaded a bespectacled Chinese girl from beneath a thick, decorator's paintbrush of a fringe.

'Yeah! Let Lawrence play!' agreed a gangling, twig-limbed lad with flaxen blonde hair. A twenty-strong chant of 'Let Lawrence play' began to swell up, causing Carly to cave. Mercedes, Liam's pretty but prissy-looking partner, dropped her shoulders and stropped to the back of the queue, clearly gutted that her trophy boyfriend had been snatched from her grasp. Jake allowed a sly grin to carve through his doughy, already sweat-glazed cheeks and a whispered 'yesssss!' to leak out from between them. I wandered, in something of a daze, back into the action, nodding sympathetically at Maria as she headed, with her headmistress, in the opposite direction, and wondered whether I was really any better equipped than her for sporting endeavour.

'Serves you right for messing up my hair,' laughed Liam as, somewhat bewildered, I joined him halfway along the two-abreast queue. The exercise, as outlined by Carly, was a simple one: one half of each pair would begin dribbling a basketball towards the hoop, their partner running alongside them until, halfway across the stretch, they were passed the ball, at which point they'd dribble the remainder of the way and take a shot at the basket.

Jessica and friend were the first to go. I watched as Jessica started off across the playground, dribbling the ball while, two metres to her left, her partner scuttled along sideways, expectant palms open wide like some kind of sports-crazy crab. Jessica had just angled a gentle bounce-pass into her partner's pincers when Liam nudged me in my side.

'Did she mention anything on the way over ... about her and Richard?' I shook my head, as much out of disgust as the need to maintain strictly non-verbal communication. While Jessica's buddy heaved a shot at the hoop, Liam surveyed the young heads around him and leant inwards, murmuring his words just loud enough to be heard through my fur and over the clank of oxygen-filled rubber bouncing off iron.

'I bet she did shag him, you know. Brett Scott said he saw her with some geeky twat at Precario. She probably had him in the toilets.' I bit down hard on my bottom lip and tried to concentrate on the pair of lads currently making heavy work of their trip towards the basket, but despite their classic odd couple dynamic (gangling beanpole and reluctantly uprooted couch potato), they were as ill-equipped to distract me as they were to execute the drill. I couldn't have felt any more hot and bothered if someone had filled the inside of Lawrence's head with itching powder. And flames.

'Don't speak about her like that,' I blurted out.

'What?'

'I said don't speak about Jessica like that.' Liam looked at me like he was trying to burn two new eyeholes into Lawrence's face.

'Guys,' Carly called out. It turned out that Liam and I were now at the front of the queue. Not that Liam was in any hurry to showcase his skills

'I should have known it was you, you psycho.'

'Guys!' repeated Carly somewhat irately. 'Let's keep the action going, shall we?' Tucking the ball under his arm, Liam chose to grant her request by going nose-to-nose with me, although the fact that Lawrence's coal black snout capped the end of his chunky white mound of a muzzle ensured that my enemy's attempt to get in my face was only halfway-successful.

'For the record,' he hissed through my left eyehole, 'I don't care what you've done with her. She's a slag, anyway.' He thumped the ball into my chest, which, it transpired, was considerably less padded than my stomach, and flicked his towelling-wrapped forehead in the direction of the hoop. 'Let's go.' I squeezed the Spalding between the palms of my paws. Never mind getting in my face, Liam was inside my head like air was inside this dimpled orange sphere. When Joy had, on numerous occasions, referred to Jessica as a slag, it had been funny. Hearing Liam use this description, though, was considerably less amusing, and as he broke into a gentle jog, I felt myself snap.

It took me roughly a second to discover that ballin' like Chris Paul wasn't that easy when your body was smothered in heavy, ill-fitting fur fabric and your head was encased in a settee. No sooner had I pushed the ball against the playground than it tried to veer free of my fat paw's scant control, and with my lower half emphatically voting 'no' to sharp lateral movement, it was only the sheer size of my mitt that enabled me to prevent it from heading for the railings.

But while my cumbersome clobber may have severely

diminished my speed, mobility and ball-handling skills, my irritation with Liam burned stronger than ever. Taking a single stride, I bounced the ball just once, this time catching it between both paws and briefly cocking it against my chest before whipping a perfectly weighted pass to my partner. When I say 'perfectly weighted', of course, I mean perfectly weighted to hit him straight in the noggin. The ball ricocheted off Liam's temple and bounced across the ground. Liam stopped and clutched the side of his head, although I couldn't be sure whether he was wincing out of pain or the grim realisation that I'd flattened one of his meticulously organised rosettes.

'Whatcha do that for, Lawrence?' yelped a young female voice. Clutching her basketball, Mercedes, who'd been standing at the back of the line, ran over to tend to her ailing idol while, back behind the yellow line, an approving Jake sniggered to himself and gave me the thumbs-up.

'It's alright, I'm OK,' Liam reassured his little groupie. 'Is it OK if I borrow your ball?' Taking the ball from her hands, he turned and hurled an eight panelled, rubber-coated cannonball at my head, but I stepped aside just in time to escape impact. I'd attribute my miraculous manoeuvre to my inbuilt lemur sense, but as the ball whistled past my cheek, towards the bench and straight into Maria's plaster cast, you could argue the extent to which sense of any kind played a part in it. The hard crack of plaster gave way to Maria's shrill, pain-filled wail, and, hurrying over to comfort her, the next shrill sound I heard was Carly's whistle piercing through all four of my ears as she too rushed to the accident scene.

'Alright, Lawrence,' she barked, pulling up behind me, the sobbing, injury-prone youngster and the gasping Mrs. Gibbs. 'I think that's enough from you.'

'Hear, hear,' seconded the fossilised head teacher.

'What?' I couldn't believe I was being made the scape-lemur.

'You've done enough,' insisted Carly over Maria's sobs. Never mind that, technically, it was Liam who had catapulted

276

the ball into Maria's mummified limb, and who was only now sauntering over to affect his best approximation of sympathy. Clearly it was Lawrence, rather than *The Hangout*'s pretty boy presenter, who was expendable where the afternoon's activities were concerned. Still, peering at Maria's tear-stained face through my eyeholes, I was determined that my impromptu P.E. lesson wasn't going to end this way.

'Let me sign her cast or something,' I suggested desperately. 'Maria, can I sign your cast?' Maria stopped crying for long enough to offer what I interpreted as an affirmative sniff. 'Has somebody got a pen?' I pleaded with the urgency of someone scrambling for a vial of antidote to a deadly, flesh-eating virus.

'Here you go,' sighed Carly, reluctantly reaching into her pocket and handing me her biro. After struggling to gain mastery of the pen, I scratched the nib against the patch of hard white plaster between a green sunflower and an impressive multicoloured rendering of the 6 Appeal logo.

'I think she might need an ambulance rather than your autograph,' huffed Mrs. Gibbs, but as I struggled in vain to coax any ink out of Carly's crappy writing instrument it seemed a safe bet that Maria wasn't going to be getting either anytime soon.

'It doesn't work,' I whined. 'It's not making a ...'

'Rest assured you've made enough of a mark this afternoon,' seethed Carly, snatching the biro from my paw and prompting a fresh bout of waterworks from Maria.

'But ...'

'Seriously, that's it.' Carly, whose face was by now the colour of Tandoori chicken, pointed her crappy biro at the world outside the railings while Mrs. Gibbs led the sobbing Maria back towards the school building. 'You're red carded.'

Had I been feeling facetious, I'd have pointed out to Carly that there were no red cards brandished in the game of basketball, and that had she done her research into the sport, she'd have instead told me that I was being 'ejected'. But I wasn't and I didn't. In fact, I didn't stick around to protest the contentiously worded call at all. It was indeed time for me to go before I dragged Lorro's good name (and, by extension, that of the entire lemur community) any further through the mud. Besides, my work here was done. I'd made my bed of shit, now I had to lie in it.

'Lawrence, mate.' I turned around to see Liam extending his hand to me, a look of fake compassion spread thickly over his face. 'Friends?' Naturally, my preference would have been to bypass his outstretched palm altogether and instead make a direct connection between my own, foam-clad fist and his smarmy little cheekbone, but a quick scan of the twenty, sorry, nineteen little faces anxiously awaiting my reaction convinced me that this wasn't the best course of action, so instead I swallowed my pride and enveloped Liam's hand in my paw. Liam pulled me inwards and flung his other arm around my back, speaking quietly into the fur over my human ear. 'I've known some cocks in my time,' he related while the youngsters cheered our seeming reconciliation, 'but you're undoubtedly the biggest of the lot.' In my head (the one inside Lawrence's), a thousand retorts wrote themselves, but as we broke up our touching embrace, I instead turned away without saying a word. I knew what Liam meant and he was right. The despairing look on Jessica's face provided final, unmistakable confirmation of the fact.

Unfolding beneath a sky that was by now as grey as the concrete under my big, clumsy feet, the journey to the school gates was a long one (not least because, halfway into it, I realised I'd forgotten my bag and had to awkwardly go back for it), and unfortunately it gave me plenty of time for reflection. More specifically, for the second time in as many weeks, I was forced to contemplate the soul-churning question: 'what the fuck have I just done?' On this particular occasion, the literal answer was that I'd tried to make amends with a woman I'd already freaked out by donning a lemur suit to play basketball – violently – with a group of school children; a scheme inspired,

278

lest we forget, by the advice of the woman on the front of my broadband box. In a dream. It was easy to say in hindsight, but now that I thought about it, I might well have been better off posting a letter to Jessica at the Fresh Coat office.

Every ounce of my disgraced and humiliated hide was weighing down on me as I eventually emerged through the school gates. Slumping onto a bench overlooking the kerb and opposite a newsagents-slash-general store, I let my bag drop to the pavement. I'd have taken Lawrence's head off and thrown it into the path of an oncoming mini-van were his unflinching yellow eyes not providing such effective shields for my own suddenly redder and more watery ones.

Across the road, a male-and-female police duo were making their way into the shop when the guy caught sight of me.

'If you're thinking of taking a dump, you better make sure your owner cleans it up,' he cracked as the two of them bundled through the doorway. I could have done without the copper's comedy stylings but a) he was a copper, and b) it seemed like he was trying to impress his female colleague, so personal experience told me he was probably due a fall sometime in the future. Besides, my attention was suddenly taken up by the figure emerging from the shop: a bearded guy in a long, tan raincoat that matched the paper bag he was clutching.

'Jessica!' he called out. There was something strangely familiar about both him and his harsh, slightly nasal voice, yet even as he arrived on my side of the quiet road, I couldn't remember where I'd seen – or heard – him before.

'Jessica!' he called out again. I followed the path being travelled by his flinty, deep-set brown eyes, over the railings and across the playground. Oblivious to his calls, Jessica was busy being piggy in the middle of two excitable young girls.

'Can I help you?' I asked, still trying to place this character. The lank hair flowing from his head and face was nagging me, but when I noticed the stuff sprouting out from inside the collar of his raincoat and covering his exposed shins, a grim realisation suddenly started to take hold. Then, as he pulled pack the brown paper to reveal a bag of sugar, my swiftly mounting fear became a reality.

'Colin Thunder's the name,' he announced while a gentle breeze sent a chilling ripple through the bottom of his coat. 'I'm here to see Jessica George.'

'There's no way in hell you're going anywhere near Jessica,' I informed him, stepping up from the bench and planting my body in-between his and the playground gate, 'or anywhere further than where you're stood right now.' Ever the maverick rock n' roll front man, Colin crumpled up the brown paper in his palm and defiantly dropped it to the ground.

'Says who, raccoon boy?'

'I'm a *lemur*. I'm Lawrence the Lemur. I thought you watched the show.' The sneer faded from Colin's face.

'I do,' he maintained somewhat defensively, before adding with a shrug, 'it's just that I tend to lose interest when Jessica's not on the screen.' In fairness, I knew where Colin was coming from (Liam was rubbish, I generally used *The C-Syde* as shower time, and as for Lawrence himself, his antics, prior to this afternoon at least, could undoubtedly come across as one-note), but a shared opinion wasn't going to get him past me, even if he'd just taken another step forward to situate himself firmly inside my personal space.

'Well I've seen *your* show, so I think I'll be taking this.' I clamped my right paw around the bag of sugar in Colin's hand, but before I could confiscate it he tightened his own grip. A brief tug of war ensued, ending with both of us clutching a shredded bit of wrapper and Colin's sucrose stash sprinkled across the pavement. We threw our shreds to the floor (I wasn't one for littering, but there were no pockets on Lawrence's hips and while the nearest bin was but a few metres away, going to it would mean abandoning my post as gatekeeper) and Colin, by now visibly pissed off, resumed his place within strangling distance of me.

'You've sabotaged my signature move,' he hissed through

his manky, mangy beard, 'but the show must go on. I still need to see Jessica.'

'You need to see a doctor,' I advised, whilst, beneath my fearless furry exterior, my stomach hit a spin cycle in anticipation of whatever the hell it was that was about to go down. At this moment, though, the only thing going down was Colin's bushy brow, gradually compressing his eyes into harsh, glinting slits while his lips rose up unchallenged under the formidable cover of his hooked nose. He looked, all of a sudden, very sinister indeed, but with Lawrence's lemon yellow peepers unhindered by eyelids, my aggressor's attempt to stare me down was to prove futile, and after a few more seconds' scrutiny, he unclenched his leathery face and spoke in a soft, defeated voice.

'Alright,' he sighed. 'Have it your way.' His head dropped, sending his greasy hair tumbling down the lapels of his coat as he slowly turned to leave. I was surprised that he'd capitulated so easily, although not as surprised as I was a second later, when, in one fluid (or at least greasy) move, he turned around and drove his fist into my stomach. I teetered back a couple of steps over the root-ruptured pavement. Owing to the padding in Lawrence's belly, I was only mildly winded, but in the few seconds it took me to regain my breath, I was able to reach one crystal clear, irrefutable conclusion. It was *on*. I uncrumpled my tummy, then curled up my right paw and, summoning as much force as I could muster, threw a punch that connected with Colin's jaw and sent him staggering back on the heels of his Doc Martens. Without thinking, I punctuated the blow with a high-pitched cry that may or may not have been an accurate representation of the sound an agitated lemur would make if provoked by a hirsute flasher. Either way, neither the sound nor my furry fist were enough to immobilise Colin, who, whilst I bounced gently up and down on my hind legs, was now sizing up the jungle-bred opponent he'd thus far badly underestimated. Slowly and deliberately, he began to untie the belt that was knotted around his waist, all the while squinting at me from across the pavement. I squinted back through my eyeholes, but only because I was trying to discern whether, beneath that belt, Colin's outer garment was buttoned up. To my horror, it wasn't. Colin fixed me with a sadistic smirk as he dragged the unfastened belt out from underneath the loops on his trench coat, holding it momentarily in his tightly clenched right fist before letting it fall to the floor. The implications could not have been graver had my opponent just dropped a live grenade rather than a length of tan coloured canvas, and he knew it. While I couldn't see Lawrence's face, it's just possible it was as awash with fear as my own. We held down our spots for a few seconds, the breeze shifting the sugar grains across the concrete and sending Colin's screwed up paper bag tumbling through the space between us. Then, suddenly and without warning, Colin charged at me, his mac flying open to reveal his flabby midsection and – yes, or rather, dear God, no – his prized Stratocaster. Time slowed down like 32x DVD playback, the horrific sight of my attacker's swinging instrument sending me into a state of fear-fuelled hypnosis, freezing my feet to the concrete until – Wham! – his body rammed into mine and I found myself on my back, sandwiched between Colin's balls and the grass verge in front of the playground fence. Feeling Colin get up from on top of me, I tried to find my feet, only for my assailant to reappear, right fist cocked back, into my line of vision. Then I felt a blow to the side of my head and my world was plunged into darkness.

My blackout, I quickly came to discover, hadn't occurred because Colin had knocked me out (indeed, the generous padding in Lorro's left cheek had offered ample cushioning against Mr. T's incoming knuckles), but because his blow had twisted my carpeted crash helmet ninety degrees around my head. Desperate to regain my sight before Colin hit me with any real impact or, worse still, marauded, knob out, through a playground peopled with innocent children, I pawed my way through the darkness to locate Lawrence's muzzle somewhere over my own right ear, then dragged his snout around until my lemur vision was once again fully restored.

The good news was that I didn't even have to lift my shoulder blades to locate Colin. The bad news was that this was because he'd clambered onto the fence and was now looming over me, his tackle taking on the ominous aura of a spectacularly gruesome (if fortunately not concrete) gargoyle. The really ugly news was that this horrific sight was edging into sharper focus as my nemesis bent his knees in preparation for lift off. Calling on every ounce of my innate lemur agility, I rolled over just as Colin and his tackle went airborne, leaving both of them to slam straight onto the patch of flattened grass I'd briefly been keeping warm.

Hearing a commotion from behind the railings, I rolled onto my belly and rose up on my knees in time to see an army of vertically challenged ballers stampeding over the asphalt for a better view of the action. Next to me, Colin Thunder remained face – and genitals – down on the ground, his open coat giving him the appearance of a bird shot down from the sky. Twitching from beneath the water-resistant canvas revealed that there was life in this particular grubby pigeon yet, though, and after letting out a pained groan, my underdressed, indestructible foe pushed his chest up from the turf. Instinctively, I dived on top of him, taking advantage of my added bulk to keep Colin contained from the cluster of young faces that, apparently oblivious to Carly's frantic whistle-blowing and the croaky cries of 'come back!' from Mrs. Gibbs, were peering through the railings.

'Get him, Lawrence!' implored my main man Jake, squeezing his chubby fist between the iron bars and pounding at the air beyond the playground while, behind him and his pipsqueak peers, a row of adults formed. The whistle abandoned Carly's bottom lip as she placed a hand over the camera lens Dale was surreptitiously preparing to point, while Mrs. Gibbs used her bony, liver-spotted hands to cover the four young eyes nearest to her and Liam demonstrated another of those smug head-shakes he was getting so good at. Then, at the end of the line, there was Jessica. I was almost surprised to see Jessica looking shocked. At this stage, I'd have thought a look of weary resignation would be her default reaction to my antics, but then I remembered just who it was I had pinned underneath me.

'Jessica!' Colin called out. 'Jessica, it's me!' Jaw in freefall, Jessica looked at him, then up at me, then up a few feet more at something going on behind the two-deep heap of hairy psychos. Feeling a hand land firmly on my shoulder, I twisted my neck to see that its owner was the wisecracking officer from over the road.

'Does one of you two young lovers mind telling us what's going on?' he asked, while his colleague screwed shut the lid on her freshly purchased bottle of juice.

About twenty minutes later, the duo were sufficiently up to speed, whisking Mr. Thunder away for further grilling whilst I thanked my lucky stars that I was currently picking up my enemy's shredded sugar packet rather than sitting thigh-to-thigh with him en route to the local police station. Fortunately, my insistence on ensuring that the underage crowd was cleared before I let Mr. Thunder rise to his feet had, it seemed, been construed as an act of community mindedness rather than bobby-baiting dissidence, but while this unprecedented demonstration of good decision-making had got me off to a reasonable start, it hadn't got me off the hook. Nope, from what I could gather – and to my complete surprise – I owed my freedom to whatever testimony Jessica had given Five-O whilst Colin and I shared the back seat of the cop car, him muttering under his breath and me staring down at the cuffs cutting into my furry wrists and wondering how a crush on a children's TV presenter had led me to this place, this situation. For that matter, I'd wondered, where was I now headed? Was a public punch-up with a wacko flasher a prisonable offence? I remembered once watching a documentary about a minimum security prison and coming to the conclusion that it was an environment I'd thrive in. Working to a regimented timetable and free of distractions, I'd be able to get in plenty of writing everyday whilst still taking breathers to play unparalleled amounts of table tennis, a sport that I enjoyed but seldom got the chance to play. There in that car, though, it was suddenly very clear to me that free in the outside world was where I wanted to remain. I could draw up a formal timetable for myself and take a more disciplined approach to my writing, and besides, there had to be a leisure centre near me with table tennis facilities.

Thankfully, these options were available to me now that I was once again free to wander the streets, or, more specifically, clean them – I'd been commanded by the Fuzz to pick up the paper or face a fine for littering, which seemed like a reasonable trade, especially as my task was unhindered by handcuffs. Depositing the last pawful of paper into a nearby bin and satisfied that I was presiding over a clean street (save for the sprinkled sugar and the legion of hungry ants now chowing down on it), I reclaimed my spot on the bench next to Lawrence's head. And there we sat, just two sets of eyes staring into the window of a newsagents-slash-general store. Until, that is, a third pair of peepers took up a pew alongside us.

'Hi,' said a female voice.

'Hi,' I responded, still looking dead ahead.

'You must really like that scratch-card poster,' observed Jessica.

'It's pretty vivid,' I remarked, focusing in on the item of window dressing in question, 'I like how they went with the pink lettering against the blue background. The message really jumps out at you.' Jessica took a deep breath and drummed her fingers on the arm of the bench.

'You know, I had you pegged as many things, particularly over the last week. But I never had you down as a fighter.'

'Me neither,' I sighed. 'Just my luck that the first time I throw a punch, I'm dressed up as a bloody ring-tailed lemur.'

'Well, anyway,' continued Jessica. 'Thanks for throwing

yourself in front of a set of naked male genitals for me.'

'It's the least I could do. I mean, all things considered … So, listen. Thanks for putting in a good word for me. You know, with the police. My parents would have killed me if I'd been expelled *and* arrested on the same day.' On the opposite side of the road, a pushchair-wielding dead ringer for the '91-era Alfre Woodard (*Grand Canyon* Alfre rather than the earlier *Scrooged* Alfre or the much later *Desperate Housewives* Alfre) did a double take as she clocked us, then nonchalantly looked away, as if a children's TV presenter and a half-man / half-lemur mutant hybrid were the exact cross section of society that typically occupied this particular bench. The gritty sound of the pushchair's wheels rolling over the concrete had almost faded out by the time Jessica spoke again.

'So, back in the cab you said you wanted to speak to me.' She was right, of course. I *had* said that and I *did* want to speak to her. Even if I hadn't; even if the afternoon's events had me ready to declare my fleeting friendship with Jessica a write-off, now more than ever I owed her some sort of explanation. It's just that now that I finally had the opportunity, I didn't quite know what to say or where to begin. It dawned on me that, for all the bizarre effort I'd put into achieving this one-on-one meeting with Jessica, I'd given remarkably little thought to what I was going to say to her should such an opportunity for reconciliation arise. I stared across into the space vacated by Alfre '91, took a deep breath and let the words spill from my lips.

'OK,' I began. 'So, I had a crush on you before I came to work on the show. A borderline infatuation, actually. Because of you, I watched more children's TV than any grown man has a right to. Between you and me, I even had a picture or two of you up at my desk.' I paused, not because I expected Jessica to laugh (she didn't), but because already I needed a moment to collect my thoughts and, hopefully, move the notch in my throat along before it started causing me trouble. 'So, yeah,' I continued, my thoughts hastily, haphazardly cobbled together rather than collected and that notch still loitering with intent, 'I had an ulterior motive for coming on the show, but it was never about, you know ...' I trailed off for a moment, wondering if there was any way I could continue my story without sounding like a complete mentalist. There wasn't, so I just got on with it.

'Alright, here it is. Make of this what you will. Every girl I ever really liked, that I ever really wanted, I always let them slip through my fingers. I never had the courage to do anything about it. The day before I asked to come on the show, I tried to tell a girl that I had feelings for that I, um, had feelings for her. Except that I couldn't get that message across to her. And, bizarrely enough, I chose to atone for this by putting myself in a position to ask out, well, you. I mean, what else would I do?' I stopped there. So far, it certainly wasn't the pithiest thing I'd ever put my name to. A few seconds elapsed before Jessica replied. Maybe I'd already spent too much time working in TV, but it felt like she was sat somewhere over the other side of the world speaking to me via satellite link-up.

'Wow,' she said slowly. 'That's a lot of information to process. A lot of really strange information.'

'Yeah, believe it or not, it kind of is for me, too, hearing it all in one go like that. The thing is, though, since I've met you, none of that ludicrous back story has had any bearing on the way I feel about you.' Again, I waited while my words bounced about through space, then waited a little bit more as Jessica's reply embarked via satellite on the return journey to my ears.

'The truth is, I never thought of you in that way at all, even *before* I thought you were a psycho. I'm sorry.'

'That's OK. That's OK,' I insisted. 'I just want you to know ... that I really like you.'

'Richard, don't ...' began Jessica, this time without the delay.

'No, no. I don't mean "really like" as in fancy. I mean, as in, I genuinely like you. I genuinely like the genuine you. The you behind the sometimes yellow-tinted woman on my crappy, wall-mounted portable TV. The you behind the many pictures at my desk, from the one with the inflatable crocodile to the one in the white vest where you can see your, er ... where you said you were really cold. What I mean is ... I think you're great.' I stopped while a car went by and the driver beeped their horn, then continued. 'Don't worry, though. At this point, I don't expect you to feel that way about me. In fact, you definitely shouldn't feel that way about me.' Jessica ushered a renegade strand of hair back behind her ear.

'How *should* I feel about you?' Hmmm ... That was a toughie. For someone who'd put so little preparation into her *Wow! Voyager* audition, Jessica was showing surprising signs of a future in serious journalism.

'I couldn't say,' I admitted. 'Honestly, at this point I'm just hoping that you like me more than Colin Thunder. That's all I want: to know that I'm higher than Colin Thunder in your affections.' Jessica held aloft a slither of thin air between her thumb and forefinger.

'I've got you slightly ahead.'

'I'll take that. Plus I've always got our photo in *Gab*.' Jessica looked around.

'You know we're gonna end up in there again, sitting out here like this.' I held up Lawrence's hollow head.

'I could get back into disguise if you'd prefer.' Jessica shook her head.

'Nah. I think I'd rather be linked to you twice than look like a slut being linked to you *and* another man. Besides, I don't want to end up being all awkward around Lawrence, too.'

'That reminds me,' I said, placing Lorro's disembodied dome back on the bench. 'Why didn't you reveal Lawrence's identity to Liam?' Jessica considered her answer for a second before coming clean.

'Don't go getting bigheaded now, but you're actually higher than *two* people in my affections.'

'Yes!' I whispered, pumping my paw triumphantly while, I'm pretty sure, a vague smile pestered Jessica's lips.

'Plus,' she added mischievously, 'I was halfway to

forgiving you back on the sofa last Friday. You looked so pathetic with that sawdust stuck to your head.' I bounced my spongy heels against the concrete.

'OK. Well, while we're admitting things about that little sit-down, I have something to confess, too. You know that last question, the one about what qualities your dream girl would have? I made that one up. It wasn't what was in the card.' Jessica raised an eyebrow.

'Oh, really? What was the real question?'

'It was, "they say the way to a man's heart is through his stomach. What's your favourite sandwich filling?"' Jessica screwed her face up.

'What a weird question.'

'I know. It would have been a lot quicker to answer, too, but I didn't think 'strawberry jam' would have conveyed to you all the things I wanted to say.'

'That's never your favourite sandwich filling.'

'No, but I'll wager it's Danny Waters'. Strawberry jam on white bread with the crusts cut off.'

'You're probably right. Mine's egg-mayo.'

'No way!' I exclaimed, nearly falling off the bench.

'Yeah. Why, what's wrong with that?'

'Nothing,' I said, indulging in another, more discreet fist-pump. 'It's a great answer.' We sat there on the bench in silence for a bit. Part of me wished I'd ascertained the egg-mayo situation back when I first met Jessica, but a larger part of me was just relieved to be, well, sitting on a bench with her staring into the window of a general store. A couple of cars passed between us and that oh-so-vivid scratch-card poster before, almost without thinking, I said exactly what was on my mind.

'Animal attraction.'

'Pardon?'

'That's what *Gab* will go with. Animal Attraction: *The Hangout* presenter Jessica George goes wild with a mystery mammal.' Jessica pondered for a few seconds before unveiling her own caption.

'Creature Comforts: Jessica George snuggles up with a tall, grey and furry stranger.'

'Jessica George reveals her latest bit of fluff,' I suggested. Jessica nodded approvingly and then went quiet. I assumed she was rummaging through her brain's pun department for a show-stopping, animal-themed caption, but instead she returned to an earlier topic.

'This girl you had feelings for. Do you still?' I let the question sink in. Now it was my turn to dish out a delayed response.

'Yes,' I eventually answered. 'But I'm pretty much guaranteed to never be with her, which, come to think of it, actually seems like a fair enough fate given this little episode I've dragged you through. There's a certain poetry to it.'

'So you told her, and she rejected you?'

'Uh, yes. Well, no, not exactly. The thing is, she didn't know I was serious.'

'Oh,' mused Jessica. 'So tell her again, and this time make sure she knows you are.' I contemplated her suggestion.

'OK,' I said, looking into her eyes, 'but what if this time, knowing that I'm serious, she *does* reject me?'

'What if this time, knowing that you're serious, she *doesn't*?' I stared across the road again. Perhaps sensing that her words had hit home, Jessica went in for the kill. 'I mean, even if she does say no, it's not like you could possibly make a bigger idiot of yourself than you have with me.' I looked down at the ground and smiled at the patch of concrete between my wide, spongy feet.'

'You make some compelling arguments,' I noted, stroking my chin with my paw. 'Someone needs to give you your own relationships show.' Jessica lifted a cautionary forefinger.

'If they do, promise me you won't tell me you've got some handy reference book in your desk drawer.'

'Ah, yes. Promise.'

'Good,' said Jessica, getting up from the bench. 'Well,

believe it or not, I've got to go and do an interview now with Carly for the Bricks and Balls web site; talk about how much fun it is to take part in sports. You know, when it doesn't involve deranged flashers or children getting their already broken limbs hit with basketballs. How are you getting back?'

'Jake's mum's going to give me a lift. I'm having tea at theirs tonight.' I nodded towards the bottom of our long, leafy road and the comparative hustle and bustle taking place at its vanishing point. 'Actually, I'm going to go and thumb a taxi, which, other than punching hairy naked men, is just about the only thing I can do with these paws.'

'Jessica,' called Carly from over the railings, the very sound of her abrasive voice bringing me to my feet.

'I'll be right there,' responded Jessica.

'Have fun with your interview,' I said, picking up Lawrence's head and cradling it under my arm.

'Have fun trying to get a taxi,' replied Jessica. Part of me wanted to chance giving her a hug, but it didn't seem entirely appropriate. Especially since Colin Thunder's tackle had been all over my fur. Better to quit while I was ahead.

'Take care,' I said.

'You too.'

'And sorry,' I added. 'Sorry about, you know, everything.' Jessica's face turned serious.

'Don't be sorry. Just promise me something else.'

'What's that?'

'Promise me you'll tell Joy how you feel about her.' Taken aback, I opened my mouth to say something, only to discover that I didn't know what. Actually, it turned out I'd already covered this one. 'Like you said,' Jessica reminded me, a half-smile playing on her lips, 'I should have my own relationships show.'

CHAPTER EIGHT

Jessica hadn't been joking when she wished me luck in hailing a cab. Well, actually she had been, but the point is that, in spite of my increased thumb size, flagging down a taxi was indeed proving easier said than done. While several of my fellow pedestrians were kind enough to acknowledge my existence with badly concealed sniggers or abusive quips, their cab-driving counterparts were united in their insistence on simply showing me their exhaust pipes. Although in fairness, one wag did at least lean out of his window to inform me that there were 'no animals in the cab'.

It was about twenty minutes before my furry-footed pavement pounding paid off and a benevolent cabbie at last stopped to pick me up. So glad was I to park my backside on his back seat that when, a few seconds into our journey, he informed me, 'I wouldn't normally allow animals in the cab,' I responded with a good, hearty laugh at his original, winning witticism.

'So I couldn't help noticing your tail as you got in,' said the cabbie. 'And your big, fat, bug-eyed head – I mean the one sat on the seat, there. You're Lawrence the Lemur, from that Saturday morning show. What's it called, again?'

'*The Hangout*. Yeah, that's me. For today, at least.'

'I knew it!' he exclaimed triumphantly. 'My daughter's mad about that programme. Can't say I mind it myself as long as that girl's on it. What's her name?'

'Jessica George.'

'That's it, yeah. She seems like a nice girl.'

'Yeah,' I confirmed, smiling to myself as I stared out of the window at nothing in particular. 'She's great.'

'Fit and all,' mused the cabbie. 'If I was a lesbian, I'd definitely want to do her.'

'Right. So as a straight male you don't want to, then?'

'Maybe, but it would be more sexy if *I* was a girl, too.'

I didn't stop to mull over the cabbie's logic – I had other things to think about. It was funny: this whole farce had been sparked because of an innocent, innocuous line Jessica had delivered to the nation's preteens; a line which, in my infinite desperation, I had somehow managed to interpret as a call to destiny delivered to me in my hour of need and residual inebriation. Well, this afternoon she'd actually given me an instruction direct to my face. The least I could do was follow it up. Yeah, definitely. I was going to do it. I was going to tell Joy how I felt about her. Again. I was going to tell her how I'd always felt about her; how I'd never stopped feeling about her, even during my four weeks away from Red Button and in the company of Jessica. *Especially* during those four weeks. I guess in my heart I'd always known. No, I *know* in my heart I'd always known. It had just taken an incredibly harebrained play for another woman to really hammer the point into my thick skull. Like I said, it was funny.

Still, if I'd put myself through the wringer to reach this realisation, then it was kind of fitting. A beautiful girl in the street or on the Tube could put a dampener on my day, but when it came to bringing the pain, they simply weren't on the same level as Joy. Just as these nameless cuties would disappear like ruthlessly efficient assassins into a crowd, so, over time, their faces would eventually fade away amidst all the other shit clogging up my mind's severely limited storage space. Not Joy, though. She was no clinical, cold-as-ice hitwoman. Popping a bullet in my brain from long range before blending instantly into a sea of bodies wasn't her style. That was too humane for her. No, Joy was a sadistic, knife-wielding psychopath stood leering and laughing over me as blood leaked from my trembling body and bubbled up from between my lips. Even as she threw her wet crimson carving knife onto the floor and walked away from her wide-eyed, still-twitching prey, her brisk, purposeful steps would ring out across the abandoned warehouse into which she'd lured me, her perfume crawling up into my nostrils as one final, fragrant 'fuck you'. I didn't think

I'd ever had such a beautiful connection with a woman before.

I'd been right all along: this *was* for Joy. I didn't quite know when I was going to tell her. I didn't quite know how, even. At any rate, I didn't have much time to ponder it, because at that moment I was interrupted by a shuddering from down by my side. I reached into my bag and, a few seconds of protracted fumbling later, I prised open my phone – which was flashing up Eddie's name – and buoyantly addressed my caller.

'Fast Eddie! What's going on, my man?'

'Riiich,' responded Eddie, his voice accompanied by a slight echo. 'How's things? What are you up to?'

'Things are good,' I informed him. I paused for a second, wondering how best to encapsulate the extraordinary events of the afternoon. 'Pretty average day, really.'

'Listen, mate,' said Eddie, his voice suddenly softer and quieter but still packing that slight echo. 'I just wanted to set the record straight about something. I think there's a chance that I may have misled you the other day.'

'Misled me about what?'

'About Joy.'

'What about her?' The tick-tock of the taxi's indicator filled out Eddie's silence before he summoned up the courage to continue.

'She's heading to the airport tonight, as soon as she leaves here at five.'

'What?'

'She's going to try and win Matt back. You know, stop him getting on the plane to go to work in Australia.'

'You never told me he was going to Australia.'

'He probably isn't, now,' Eddie pointed out. My stomach-within-a-stomach sunk. I couldn't believe it.

'But you said they were finished. You said that her heart was never really in it.' There were a few seconds of silence before Eddie responded.

'Some of that was guesswork.'

'*Guesswork*?' I repeated, unable to prevent a slight note of

anger creeping into my voice. 'You said it was intel. You said –
and stop me if I've misremembered this – that it was FBI, CIA-
level intel.'

'In hindsight, I think you were right,' conceded Eddie. 'I
think I just liked saying "intel."' Now it was my turn to provide
the dead air. I was floored.

'Alright, well ...' My voice cracked a little bit.

'Sorry, man,' offered Eddie meekly. Then I heard a
flushing sound.

'Where are you?'

'I'm in the gents. I had to go somewhere where Joy
wouldn't walk in on me.'

'You've been conducting this whole conversation sat on
the toilet?'

'No, I'm stood by the sinks. That's someone else who just
finished their business. Well, I say finished, but something tells
me the after effects of this one could linger on for some ...
Urgghh!'

'Who is it?' I demanded, anxious to know which of Red
Button's motley crew had been privy to what I'd naturally
assumed was a private conversation.

'Don't worry. It's just the bloke who's come to mend the
photocopier. I tell you, he might have fixed that but he's done
some serious damage in here.' I heard the sound of a door
unlocking, then a man muttered something tersely at Eddie,
who duly told him, 'I'm sorry mate, but it's true.' Over a
backdrop of water rushing into a sink, Eddie returned to our
conversation.

'So anyway, I just had to tell you, 'cos, you know, I didn't
know what had been going through your head after we talked
the other day.'

'Oh, yeah, that,' I said as casually as I could. 'Well, I
probably wasn't going to go for it, anyway. I'd pretty much
come to the conclusion that me and Joy are just ...'

'Sorry, hold that thought, mate,' interrupted Eddie. 'The
bloke's about to dry his hands and I don't want to miss what

295

you're saying.' There followed about ten seconds of complete silence before I decided to speak up again.

'Is he ...' I began

'He's just flicking off the excess water,' explained Eddie. After another ten seconds or so of stark nothingness, the hand dryer at last cranked into action, its gushing hot air interweaving with the crackling of Eddie's phone. Either Photocopier Guy was also running tests on the hand dryer or, as seemed more likely, he was now intent on winding up Eddie by sucking the natural moisture out of every pore in his rough, machine-mending hands, because for a solid minute this was all I heard, albeit with the intermittent percussion of the dryer's metal button being punched to renew the blast. Still, I used the time to try and tame the lump that was getting its weight up in my throat, and when finally there was quiet, I picked up where I'd left off.

'So, yeah, I was just saying that I think me and Joy are definitely just ...'

'Dry enough?' It took a moment for me to twig that Eddie wasn't talking to me but rather making a sarcastic enquiry of Photocopier Guy. The sound of Eddie's phone clattering against the hard tiles of the floor suggested that the question hadn't met with a particularly jovial response.

'We're in the gents!' yelled Eddie, that echo now in full effect. 'The *gents*! That means we're *supposed* to behave like gentlemen!'

'Fuck off!' came the flat reply, followed by the sound of a door slamming shut, footsteps approaching the phone and then, at long last, Eddie giving me his full undivided attention.

'Sorry, mate, what were you saying? Mate? Rich, are you still there?' I closed the phone. I didn't have anything more to say. What *was* there to say? At five o'clock, Joy was going to be hightailing it to the airport to declare her undying love for her affable, blandly handsome boyfriend. If, that was, I didn't get to her first.

'Change of plan,' I told the cabbie. 'Can you take me to

Docklands, please?'

Ten minutes later, and while the taxi driver was indeed taking me in the direction of the Red Button House of Dreck, he wasn't doing so at a pace anywhere near sufficient to satisfy my helter-skelter nerves, or, indeed, keep the journey within my strict ten pound budget. With my status as a star of his daughter's favourite TV show, I was confident that I could talk the cabbie into releasing me next to a Docklands cash point, but as he executed a much-hyped 'shortcut' that landed us on Liverpool Street and right at the rear of a possibly backwards-moving traffic jam, I realised that, at this rate, I was going to be punching in my four digit pin code while Joy and Matt were at MFI comparing shower curtains and squares of carpet fabric.

Surveying the distinctly static picture outside my window for the slightest sign of forward motion, my eyes landed on Liverpool Street station. With the meter already at £8.70, I decided to deviate from the play book. I thrust the cabbie my emergency tenner, crammed Lawrence's fat head into my bag as far as it would go (roughly snout-level) and bolted out of the door.

'Sorry, man – gotta go.'

Outside the Tube station, and with Lorro's eyes surveying the street from down by my side, I stopped to catch my breath. It had been past four on the cab driver's clock – was I going to make it all the way over to Red Button before five, or would I be better trying to head Joy off at the departure lounge? I didn't want to run into Matt, that was for sure, but it would be preferable to missing Joy altogether. Besides, in the worst case scenario of me getting into my second dust-up of the day, at least Matt was likely to be fully clothed. Oh, but wait a moment – what airport was Joy heading to? Heathrow or Gatwick? I cast my mind back to Eddie's call. Amongst the scuffling and the swearing and the extended hand-dryer solo, I don't think he'd included this information, so it looked like I was going to have to interrupt whatever toilet-based altercation he was currently involved in to get it.

Ignoring assorted cracks from a trio of teenagers whose Technicolor, all-over-print hoodies looked – unbeknownst to them, apparently – even more ridiculous than my own attire, I squeezed my hand into my bag and wrenched my phone out from underneath Lawrence's head, wondering how on Earth his paws were going to rise to the challenge presented by the phone's flat, metallic keypad. As it happened, they responded by promptly letting it, along with the rest of the phone, dive straight through a gap in the drain cover in-between Lawrence's feet. Red Button it was, then.

At the ticket machine inside the station, I opened my wallet and crammed as much of my big cloddy paw as I could into the small, slim, leather-bound pocket of air behind my bank card. Pressing my furry thumb hard against the card's front, I pulled it out and successfully slid it into the slot. Now I was cooking, or at least I was until I tried to enter my pin code using the machine's decidedly lemur-unfriendly keypad. Not even Lawrence's thumb was delicate enough to hit a button without also taking down one of its neighbours at the same time, so it was only as an absolute last resort that I squatted down and used my nose to punch in those fiddly four numbers. Success at last. Either my nose possessed the accurate touch lacking in my spongy mitts or the machine simply couldn't stand watching me embarrass myself any further, but either way, it regurgitated my bank card and spat out the ticket I'd been working so hard for. Grabbing the grey plastic and pink paper rectangles (at last, something I could manage), I turned around and came face to face with a twattish, twentysomething city kid with a lilac French collar shirt and a knot the size of a CD jewel case in his matching lilac-and-lavender striped tie.

'If you had asked me for a pen,' he hypothesised smugly, 'I would have lent you one and you could have tapped the correct numbers on the keypad so as to look slightly less of a prat.'

'Why don't you lend me one now so I can stab you in the

windpipe with it?' I asked, eyeballing him intensely for just long enough to make him wonder whether the loony in the lemur suit was really psycho enough to puncture his poncily attired larynx. Even if I had been, though, there was no time, so instead I bolted towards the turnstiles, my hind legs struggling for traction on the smooth tiles underneath them. After getting some well-earned use from my hard-won travel card, I half-ran, half-stumbled down the escalator, drawing irritated tuts, amused chuckles and baffled murmurs from the travellers I squeezed past or, alternatively, flattened. Skidding by a busker at the bottom, I tore down a couple of corridors, the rumbling of a train beneath me adding a shuddering bassline to my panting as I wove in and out of my fellow commuters. The bassline had just faded out when, seconds later, I hustled my way down a flight of concrete steps and onto the platform, where the train was waiting, doors open.

I leapt into an already packed carriage – nearly bouncing straight back onto the platform as my belly bumped into a giant rucksack on legs – and yanked my tail in through the doors just as they slid shut. Grabbing the handrail above my head, I tried my best to look inconspicuous while the resumed rumbling of the train stifled the sighs, tuts and sniggers of my fellow commuters. Then, with the train hitting full speed, I noticed my nearest neighbour, a squat, shaven-headed man whose faded Arsenal jersey concealed either an official Gunners football or a considerable beer gut, eyeing me up and down.

'Bet you're used to that,' he remarked, angling the apex of his stubbled, potato-shaped dome up at my paws, which were still wrapped around the handrail. 'You know, from gripping all those tree branches.' I dignified his comic stylings by reluctantly tugging the left corner of my mouth upwards and dispatching a truncated gust of air through my nostrils. Now I knew why I never saw lemurs taking the Tube.

I parted ways with my comedian pal and the rest of the carriage at Bank. The platform there gave me more room for manoeuvre, and with the board above informing me that the next train was two minutes away, I took advantage of the space by pacing anxiously up and down. Those two minutes were three more than I had to spare, and while my long lemur tail was swinging more freely, my whole human body was tense as I waited for that damn train. Moreover, it turned out that pacing anxiously up and down was harder work while wearing a furry romper suit (especially following an afternoon of running, fighting flashers and injuring already-injured children), so I cut it short and instead looked to the posters on the tunnel wall to distract me through the remaining sixty seconds.

There, staring back at me from beside an advert for some soulless West End confection, was LaMont. He was still clad in that clingy, cream-coloured cashmere number, his eyes once again set on 'smoulder' and his fingers, as usual, cradled beneath his robust jaw. It was, then, exactly the same picture that had plagued me for the last few weeks, but I was looking at it differently now. LaMont had come through for me in spectacular style a week and two days ago. He was my man now, not some airbrushed Casanova who hung around at bus stops and on billboards waiting to poke fun at my romantic failings. Hell, I didn't even begrudge him having two capital letters in his first name anymore.

This time, I thought, the look on *his* face was different, too. This time he wasn't smirking at me. Yeah, there was, as there had been on those previous run-ins, a slight movement in the corner of his lips, but it wasn't a smirk – even as he surveyed me in my ridiculous attire, it wasn't a smirk. No, this was an almost smile; an almost smile of encouragement. An almost smile that almost said, 'Go and get the girl – that one whose niece I serenaded on that show, you feel me?' I did. I did feel him.

Not a moment too soon, the train rumbled up alongside the platform and I absorbed LaMont's familiar-but-definitely-different facial features for a final few seconds. Was I reaching here, or was LaMont also radiating a look of pride from behind his granite cheekbones and every-follicle-accounted-for goatee?

300

Yeah, I was positive. That was pride written all over his sculpted, lady-killing face. Well, that and the word 'TWAT', which someone had taken the liberty of scrawling across his forehead in biro, but like I said, he was my man now so I ignored that.

Pumped up by LaMont's vote of confidence, I found a seat in a pleasingly underpopulated carriage, directly opposite a rotund, grey-faced woman and with a balding, fortysomething businessman snoozing away two spaces to my left. Maybe it was my unwieldy suit, but, curling my paws around the edge of my pew, I began to feel like an astronaut waiting for his shuttle to blast off. I looked around nervously at my fellow space cadets. Mr. Sleepy was hoovering up the hot underground air through his gaping gullet while Grey Face's occasional blinking provided the only indication that oxygen of any sort was entering her corpulent frame. Then I looked at my own ridiculous reflection in the opposite window. Yeah, this was exactly the sort of elite squad NASA assembled for their missions.

That said, we hadn't even reached the countdown stage yet, let alone ignition. What the hell was keeping us? I was starting to get really anxious again. What if I got to Red Button too late? Actually, with all sense of momentum quickly dissipating and doubt once again seeping into my mind, I was beginning to wonder whether getting there in time wasn't a recipe for greater disaster. I looked back at LaMont through the scuffed, scratched window. Nope, this was where I was meant to be: here with these misfits in this carriage, feeling sick to my fully carpeted stomach as I prepared to go and tell the real woman of my dreams how I felt about her. Properly. I just needed to get myself in the right mental state to rise to the challenge.

I looked over at my dormant travelling companion, slumped back with his briefcase laid on his lap, and wished I could reach even a quarter of his level of relaxation. I couldn't sleep on public transport at the best of times, but beyond simply pulling off that trick, he was also snoozing through the music that was currently escaping his ear buds at a volume just loud enough to soundtrack the action, or lack thereof, in the carriage.

I listened more intently. I was pretty sure – no, actually I was almost certain – that I could make out the song bouncing off his unreceptive eardrums. My eyes followed the thin white wire emerging from the right ear bud, momentarily losing it as it hooked up with its left-side partner over Mr. Sleepy's starchy white collar before the two of them, now united as one slightly thicker white wire, snaked through the tropical flora and fauna of his loosened, multicoloured tie, over the rounded hillock of his belly and across the smooth black leather of his briefcase into a glistening silver iPod guarded only by its owner's left thumb.

Edging carefully across the seating, I squinted at the screen and, sure enough, there it was: 'I Want to Know What Love Is' by Foreigner – confirmation that my thin-haired, loud-tied neighbour was in fact a messenger from God. No sooner had this realisation hit me than, at long last, the carriage doors slid shut and the train shuddered into motion, the sound of its grinding all but suffocating my soundtrack. Great. Now my mission had the momentum but not the message. I suddenly felt more ill-equipped than ever. Approaching Joy without any soft rocking sonic inspiration was going to be like lining up for the Olympic 100 metres sprint final without having done any gentle stretching exercises beforehand.

And then something strange happened. The carriage rattled slightly – nothing major, but just enough of a tremble to cause Mr. Sleepy's left ear bud to jump from his ear, bounce off his sagging shoulder and land on his briefcase. Now this was an invitation if ever I received one. Wasn't it? It wasn't like he was using it. At this stage, that ear bud wasn't even conveying sounds into his subconscious – why let it go to waste? I mean, I would have asked his permission but it seemed rude to wake him. After all, he'd probably had a really tough day.

With such sound rationalisation completed, my mind was

made up. I edged across the seat until my shoulder was almost touching his, and was just limbering up my right paw when I remembered I was being watched. Grey Face! I looked over at her impassive, concrete-coloured features and swallowed hard. I didn't want to scare her, but she was a liability and I couldn't run the risk of her flapping her trap before Foreigner had delivered their much-needed pep talk. Wracked with guilt, I nonetheless lifted a furry finger to my solemn lips, narrowing my eyes slightly to complete an expression that, I assumed, simmered with just the right amount of quiet menace. For her part, Grey Face replied with an unblinking expression that captured the exact emotion of a threadbare tennis ball, and so, surmising that she might actually be dead, I proceeded with my operation by taking a deep breath and cautiously reaching in over Mr. Sleepy's right forearm.

They say that in times of emergency it's possible to discover a reserve of strength you never knew you had. Well, I don't know about strength, but in that moment I found a level of dexterity that had previously eluded my chubby lemur digits, pinching the ear bud between my thumb and forepaw and – guided by some unseen force – slowly lifting it up towards my left ear. Its ascent was paused when I noticed a smidgeon of orange earwax clinging to its perforated metal foil and, discovering that the wire wasn't long enough to get the ear bud to the back of my seat, instead reluctantly brushed it off on my thick shoulder fur. In doing so, I must have yanked slightly on the wire connected to the other ear bud, as Mr. Sleepy stirred just a bit, making a gentle nibbling noise with his mouth and tightening his right hand's grip on the edge of his briefcase. Heart bumping, I froze in my seat for a few seconds until, satisfied that my neighbour was still out for the count, I transported the ear bud up an extra few inches and into my own ear – just in time to hear the song's final bars fading out. Shit! There was nothing else for it: I had to go back in. My thumb hovered over the iPod's scroll wheel while Mr. Sleepy's, which suddenly appeared to loom as large as my own super-sized digit, guarded the perimeter. Slowly but steadily, I brought my thumb downwards so that its tip was touching the 'rewind' side of the wheel. One ever-so-gentle application of pressure was all the situation needed. I breathed in, breathed out and softly pushed downwards. Hazy synths filled my ear and confidence started to ooze back into my body. I pulled my arm back from the airspace over the briefcase and victoriously, if delicately, pumped my paw. Now I was firing. Before I knew it, my scuffed-up reflection was murmuring the lyrics in time to the music.

'Gotta take a little time, take some time to think things over.
Better read between the lines, in case I need it when I'm older.
Now this mountain I must climb, feels like a world upon my shoulder.
Through the clouds I see love shine, it keeps me warm as life grows colder.
In my liiiife, there's been heartache and pain
I don't know if I can faaace it again.
Can't stop now, I've travelled so far, to change this lonely liiiiffee ...'

I was hyped to the hilt as, ably assisted by Foreigner frontman Lou Gramm, I hit the chorus:

'I wanna know what love is, I want you to show me.
I wanna feel what love is, I know you can show me.'

With that confidence continuing to build up so that it positively swelled at the seams of Lorro's skin, I closed my eyes and immersed myself in the second verse, my readiness for the task at the other end of my train ride increasing with every word. Indeed, so lost in music was I that it was only upon opening my eyes during the song's climactic, gospel choir-assisted chorus that I realised that two middle-aged black women, swaying from the handrails at the far end of the carriage, had wholeheartedly joined me on backing vocals. Likewise, it was only when the women – one of whom was using her free, non-handrail-holding hand to clench an emotive fist – abruptly stopped singing that I noticed my own soulful adlibs (*I'm feeling so much love ...*) were being performing acapella. Cutting off my crooning, I turned to see that the borrowed ear bud had been reunited with its owner, who was now very much awake. And, judging by the look on his face, very much pissed off.

'What the hell are you playing at?' he asked, quite reasonably if more than a little irately.

'Uhhh ...' came my cogent, well-articulated response. I cast a glance in the direction of Grey Face, who, I was interested to observe, was grinning like a maniac. Unlike Mr. Not-So-Sleepy-Anymore.

'Weirdo,' he huffed, gathering his belongings and storming off to the other end of the carriage. 'If this is one of those hidden camera shows I'm not signing the release form.' He might not have been impressed with me, but, psyched up from my stolen soft rock workout, I was impervious to his crimson-cheeked scorn. Indeed, so firmly had Foreigner's digitally imparted words of wisdom embedded themselves between my ears that I felt only warmth for their thinly-thatched conduit when, a minute later, he muttered an obscenity at me as he got off the train. With Grey Face also alighting (along with my backing singers, who, in contrast to Mr. Sleepy, gave me cheery waves on their way out), my carriage became dotted with an entirely new cast of supporting characters, although with my head now bowed in deep concentration, I acquainted myself only with their shins. Unfortunately, it wasn't long before the owner of two of those shins decided to intrude upon my preparation time.

'Look! He's playing with his willy,' narrated a coarse young female voice.

I looked up at the train's budding anthropologist – a vole-faced teenage girl in a satin bomber jacket, sat next to a braces-wearing friend – then back down at the tail whose tip was nestled in the palm of my paw. It was like I'd been caught standing over a strangled body clutching the end of the noose.

'Yeah,' sniggered her mate, taking up the narration through a mouthful of wire and dental cement. 'His big, black-and-white stripy willy.' I let out a sigh and dropped the incriminating appendage. This was exactly the sort of thing I could live without. I'd suffered enough wisecracks this afternoon. Enough wisecracks, enough hostility and definitely enough willies. Eyeing up an empty row of seats at the other end of the carriage, I silently rose from my seat in an attempt to rise above the vulgarity. Things were going well for about three steps until ...

'That raccoon's a wanker!' shouted Metal Martha. I froze in my tracks. Then, blood beginning to boil, I slowly turned to face my tormentors. Now they'd crossed a line. Nobody called me that and got away with it.

'I'm ... not ... a ... raccoon,' I growled.

'But you *are* a wanker,' argued The Vole, perhaps taking note of my hairy palms. I felt my lips part to say something, but then I realised – there was no need. Instead, I turned away, smiling to myself as I trod across the carriage and took up the seat I'd been heading for in the first place. The journey that had led me to this seat, on this train, had pitted me against mental make-believe coppers, prickish pretty boy presenters, lunatic scrotum strummers and, worst of all, my own unsurpassed idiocy, so I could certainly take the witless wisecracks of two aspirant teenage mums in my stride. Sure enough, the girls' abuse faded into the background and, five minutes later, I was so focused on my goal, so far beyond even the tiniest shred of bitterness or hostility, that it was as if they weren't even on the train. Actually, they weren't, having been forced to get off at West Quay when I'd snatched one of their rucksacks as the doors opened and thrown it across the platform and onto an escalator. Served them right, the gobby little shits.

Still, even if the pair had held megaphones to my ears and

taken it in turns to yell 'wanker', I still would have been resolutely, unshakably in the zone. See, there was one fact I just couldn't deny any longer. A fact that I'd previously tried to avoid and look away from, but which I was now pulling in close to my chest as the intimate climax to a convoluted but enthusiastic hip-hop handshake involving every muscle in my right arm. Though I'd subsequently tried to deny it, I'd been right at the wrap party. I *did* love Joy. In fact, I loved everything about her. I loved her soft brown skin, her dark brown eyes and her jet-black eyebrows, which were smooth and neat but thick enough not to look like they'd been drawn on with a biro. You know, like some girls' do.

I loved her hair whether short or long, braided, straight or curly. I loved the right middle finger she flashed at me so liberally and I loved the left middle finger she hit me with when the right one was wrapped around a cup of IBS or a mug of pink tea and thus unavailable for duty.

I loved Winter-Warm Joy in her bulky bubble coats and snuggly, figure-hugging jumpers and I loved Summer-Sexy Joy in her little denim jackets and clingy, figure-hugging vest tops. Speaking of denim, I loved that, like me, Joy adhered to The Fifty Percent Denim Rule, which dictated that a person should not wear denim on both the upper and lower half of their body simultaneously (see also The Fifty Percent Khaki Rule, of which we were also both disciples). True, Joy didn't own a pair of glasses, but I could always hope that, in later life, her eyesight deteriorated to just such an extent that she would require them for close work. Or possibly I could buy her a pair of plain glass ones, if she didn't find it too weird.

I loved the things that we had in common (we both liked coconut-based confectionery, Guy's first album, Pepe LePew and watching people run frantically to catch buses) and the things we didn't (she looked gorgeous in a camisole; I almost certainly wouldn't).

I loved that Joy didn't laugh at every joke that came out of my mouth. Of course, I loved it even more when she did laugh;

the way that her nose would crinkle and a small, vertical crease would cut through her brow as her soft, sumptuous lips (which, by the way, I loved in their own right) pushed in opposite directions to reveal that diastema of hers (yep, that too, although I think I've already covered that). Come to think of it, most of all I loved those fleeting moments in which Joy was trapped between 'not laughing' and 'laughing'; those moments when, having sustained a direct hit during an exchange of comic insults, she would try in vain to preserve the marble smoothness of her facial features as they fought a losing battle with the oncoming crinkling and creasing and lip-parting and diastema-displaying.

How strong were my feelings for Joy? Eddie had once asked me whether, if I befriended a gorgeous, charismatic, well-dressed girl who didn't eat egg-mayo sandwiches and just so happened to be called Judy, I'd want to go out with her in the face of certain, relentless piss-taking. At the time I'd given him a firm 'no', but now I knew I'd answered too hastily. If Joy's parents had given her a 'U' and a 'D' in place of her familiar 'O', I'd still want the two of us to be a twosome.

How strong were my feelings for Joy? Put it this way: if, by some strange alignment of the stars, she loved me too and one day we had a family (again: stars, alignment), I wouldn't just be willing to scrape the children's dead rabbit up from its hutch or lift a gone-too-soon sparrow from the garden lawn; I'd enjoy it. Alright, maybe I wouldn't actually enjoy that particular part of it, but I'd certainly enjoy looking over my shoulder and knowing that the woman who was nowhere to be seen – the one who'd delegated all animal corpse removal duties to Daddy – was the woman I'd been crazy for ever since she first limped her way across the coffee-stained Red Button carpet tiles and into my field of vision.

Now, however, it was the Heron Quays station that was looming into full view, meaning that it was time for me, like that grubby, graffiti-covered piece of pink luggage I'd made airborne two stops earlier, to vacate the train. Back in my jungle-tested, handrail-holding position and once again feeling nervous as hell, I hoped that a smoother fate awaited me on the other side of the train doors. Damn, this had the potential for disaster. Disaster on an epic, unprecedented scale that would both haunt and embarrass me for the rest of my life, even if, in real terms, the rest of my life only amounted to the couple of minutes it took me to throw myself, in full heavyweight lemur pelt, into the Thames. I tugged nervously at the shoulder strap of my bag and looked at my reflection. As sweeping, workplace-based romantic gestures went, me bursting in on Joy wearing a lemur suit was hardly Richard Gere arriving for Debra Winger in his crisp naval whites at the end of *An Officer and a Gentlemen*. Certainly, it was hard to imagine Joy playfully putting on Lorro's noggin while I scooped her up in my fuzzy arms and carried her out of the building to the strains of 'Up Where We Belong'. I pressed my jaw against my chest and realised that I could feel my heart punching at it from the other side. Then I felt a pulling sensation in my rear, and looked down to see a young girl tugging on my tail with one hand whilst holding the hem of her mother's coat with the other.

'Are you Lawrence the Lemur?' she asked, her eyes scaling upwards.

'Yeah, kind of,' I exhaled, relieved to at last be receiving a little recognition after a barrage of shit. It was, however, to prove fleeting as my inquisitor's saucer-like eyes slowly narrowed.

'Your face looks different,' she observed sceptically. While the train screeched to a standstill, I returned her crevice-eyed squint with interest.

'I shaved.'

The train doors parted and I leapt out, sprinting across the platform and beating an elderly Indian gentleman in a tweed suit and spanking new, technology-packed white trainers to be the first down the station's concrete steps and onto the street below. At ground level, a charity worker in a rather baggy and formless beige dog suit was stood on the street rattling a bucket of loose change. I was a couple of speedy steps past this individual when I suddenly felt compelled to stop and turn back. I didn't know for what worthwhile cause this floppy-eared fellow was collecting, nor did I care (although I imagined it was an animal-aiding charity and they generally do have my support). At that moment, exhausted from tearing across town under a shagpile second skin, I felt a kinship with my canine compatriot. To the other passers-by, or at least those who didn't need to reach up above their heads to clank change into his bucket, the pooch probably didn't look like the most expressive character to ever pound the pavement. To them, his big, Bourneville-brown eyes probably looked flat, unrevealing and, well, rather like they were made from felt. Not to me, though. I looked into those two swirling, simmering pools of raw emotion and I saw a kindred spirit. I saw an itchy-skinned, motor skill-impaired kindred spirit. Put simply, I *felt* the felt. Instinctively, I patted my thighs in search of some loose change, but of course the only thing between my hands and my by-now somewhat tangled and, frankly, slightly moist boxers was two layers of grey fur fabric, meaning that an apologetic shrug was the most I could offer. The pooch turned his palms skyward and tilted his head sympathetically to the side, his floppy left ear lying down flat on his shoulder. 'I've been there myself,' he seemed to be saying. Offering one last, appreciative nod, I turned on my heels and started off across the pavement, breaking into a run as, tail trailing through the air behind me and Lorro's head bumping against my hairy hip, I wove in and out of the pedestrians concluding their working days.

Seeing (or, more accurately, imagining) a gap in the traffic, I bolted across the road, but my human feet were working too fast for my lemur feet, causing me to stumble into the path of an oncoming people-carrier. It would be poetic to say that, as rubber screeched against concrete and my paws slammed down on the bonnet of this four wheel drive killing machine, I looked up and a frenetically paced slideshow of all my unrequited loves flashed before my eyes, but in reality the sight that greeted my widened pupils was that of a middle-aged woman mouthing the word 'wanker' at me through her windshield. While she superglued her enraged palm against the horn, I scrambled onto the pavement and, shaking off the shock of almost becoming roadkill (I hadn't even been doing the McFly Manoeuvre, either), resumed my fast and furry-arsed weaving through the bodies between me and Red Button. Ahead of me, a burly businessman and his lanky mate were making liberal use of the pavement's full width. Noticing a slender gap between the big fella's left shoulder and a length of railing, I accelerated through the slipstream, my tail whipping against the man's briefcase as I emerged triumphant ... and, unfortunately, straight into the shoulder of another, if markedly more slender, luggage-toting pedestrian: a young blonde woman who was busy rummaging through her densely packed handbag.

'Hey!' she shouted as the bag fell from her hands and its contents spilled onto the pavement. Tutting loudly, the woman stooped to usher a diary and a pack of travel tissues back into their monogrammed leather home while I fumbled with my chunky paws (which had already proved woefully inadequate in the bladeage stakes) to overpower an escapee Chapstick that was making a spirited break for the nearest drain.

'Sorry. I'm used to having opposable thumbs,' I panted, standing up and reuniting the Chapstick with its owner. It was Beth. She looked me over from head to toe, and I wondered whether she'd opt for a barrage of straightforward abuse, a catty quip or a simple question beginning (and perhaps also ending) with the words 'What the fuck?' Instead, she rolled her eyes and, to my complete surprise, volunteered exactly what I wanted to know.

'She was still at her desk when I left,' she sighed. 'But you'll have to hurry.'

'Thanks, Beth.'

'I'd say try not to make too much of a twat of yourself this time, but ...' She held an upturned palm out towards my furry

311

body and shook her head in weary disbelief. 'Just get a move on, OK?'

Beth didn't need to tell me twice. I turned on the jets and attacked the final stretch of my journey with the speed, agility and pure primal drive of, well, probably a ring-tailed lemur. If the pedestrians peppering the last leg were looking on in amusement or disbelief, I didn't know. I was hurtling by them too quickly and with too much focus on my goal. There it was: Red Button HQ. And, as I executed my second and final road crossing with my lemur life intact, there *she* was, emerging through the front door and into the courtyard.

Joy scrunched up her face as she felt the first spots of rain intermittently dropping from above, but her tense, tightened features collapsed in surprise as she saw six foot of grey fur jogging towards her. Drawing on every last ounce of her considerable skill and experience in ignoring my antics, she had just about managed to regain her composure by the time my hind legs finally came to a well-earned halt.

'I'm not even going to ask the obvious question,' she said, fastening up the buttons on her lightweight, military-style jacket. 'No, actually, I am. Why are you dressed as Lawrence the Raccoon?'

'What?' I panted. 'Why does everyone think I'm a raccoon? I'm Lawrence *the Lemur*.' Joy peered at the straggly appendage hanging down between my exhausted legs.

'Huh. You stripy-tailed folk all look the same to me.'

'A raccoon has a medium-length, bushy tail,' I explained, reaching behind my bum and grabbing hold of Lorro's trademark hooped body part. 'This is a long, prehensile tail.' Joy looked back blankly at me, so I continued with the natural history lesson. 'A prehensile tail is one that functions almost as a fourth limb. You know, it provides balance and ...'

'Alright,' interrupted Joy. 'Let's move on to the second question: What are you doing here? Wait, let me guess. You and Eddie are going to partake in a little bestiality-themed role-play.'

'Not today,' I said, clutching my cramped stomach with my paw. 'I wanted to catch you before you left.'

'Before I left work?'

'Before you left for the airport.' Joy looked puzzled.

'What? What airport? I'm not going to any airport.'

'You're not?'

'No.'

'You're not going to the airport to try and stop Matt from going to Australia?'

'What?' Joy looked even more puzzled. 'No. I was going to go round to his flat tomorrow to get my DVDs back from him ...' She looked down at her feet. 'We split up a few wee ... I mean, we split up recently. Who told you he's going to Australia?' As if on cue, Eddie appeared through the door. His attempt to look inconspicuous was unsuccessful, helped very little by the shiner encircling his right eye.

'Reverse psychology,' he whispered to me, arching the eyebrow that presided over the purple. 'Just make sure you make this worthwhile. That phone call from the toilets got me into a bit of a scuffle, plus our photocopier's now broken worse than it was before.' A sly smile cut through his bruised face as he zipped up his jacket, patted my padded shoulder and continued on his way. 'Night, Joy.'

'Night, Eddie,' said Joy. She waited until he was out of earshot before voicing her concern. 'Can you believe it? Apparently he walked into the hand-dryer. The one in the ladies is a lot lower than eye level.'

'Yeah, me and Eddie have been fighting for months to get ours lowered,' I lied, awkwardly rubbing the back of my head with the palm of my paw. 'Hopefully Eddie's accident will serve as some sort of wake-up call. So anyway, I'm sorry about you and Matt.'

'Don't be. I was never crazy about him in the first place. Plus it turned out that he was sleeping with a runner, so ...'

'Ouch.'

'Ouch for him. I punched him in the face. Anyway, what's

313

all this about him and Australia and airports?'

'Forget all that. I got all of that wrong. That's not what's important.'

'Oh. Alright.' Joy now appeared to have graduated 'puzzled' and moved on to 'baffled'. 'So what *is* important?' At that moment, three members of Red Button's contracted cleaning team – two stocky, unshaven men and a stocky, unshaven woman with violently scraped back hair – arrived for duty. Taking in my get-up, they muttered something in an Eastern European language that I couldn't pinpoint, but a tone I narrowed down to either 'derisory' or 'flat-out piss-taking'. The monkey noises the two men made while the woman punched the security code into the keypad were, on the other hand, clear in any language. Clear and incorrect.

'I'm a lemur!' I snapped as the door clicked shut. Meanwhile, Joy was growing impatient. Impatient and damp.

'Look, it's raining so can you just ...'

'I'm in love with you, Joy.' There, I'd said it. Again. I waited to hear Joy's thoughts on this, but as the rain pattered down and my heart made a concerted effort to split the seams of my outfit, she seemed intent on simply squinting at me. Then, after what seemed like an eternity, her pursed lips parted company and she spoke.

'Haven't we done this already? At the wrap party?'

'Yes,' I agreed. 'I think we have. From what I remember, it didn't turn out the way I'd hoped.' Joy cranked up her squinting to new and impressive levels of squintiness.

'I thought you were taking the piss.'

'No.'

'And you're not taking the piss now?'

'Do I look like I'm taking the piss?' I asked, holding out my paws. I was fearless now, largely because I was in no danger of looking any more stupid than I already did. I had the eye of the tiger – or at least the eye of the lemur, anyway. Joy stared at me. It was a straightforward, open-eyed stare, which was at least a change of pace from all the squinting.

'And you've run all the way over here to tell me this?'

'Yeah. I mean, I took the Tube, but yeah, I ran part of the way. Several parts of the way. Believe me, it's not easy getting up to top speed in this thing.' Joy reached out to my shoulder and pinched my pelt between her fingers.

'I'm not surprised. It must weigh a tonne.'

'It's heavy alright but it's not just the weight. It's the shape, too. You can't get any bladeage going.'

'Any what?'

'You can't form blades,' I explained, holding aloft my fat, rounded, decidedly non-aerodynamic paws. 'You know, to become streamlined and cut through the air.'

'Oh,' pondered Joy. 'So why are you telling me this now?'

'About the bladeage?'

'No, not about the bladeage. The other thing.'

'Ah, the other thing. Well, again, technically I *have* told you before. But I'm telling you again because I absolutely have to know, one way or the other, whether you have any of the same stuff going on.' I waited for a reaction. Whatever Joy had going on, her face wasn't giving any clues.

'You're pretty bold today,' she observed. I let out a nervous laugh.

'I just narrowly avoided arrest after fighting a bearded man with no pants, so I'm kind of living life to the full right now. Taking some chances.'

'What?' Joy's facial features hit 'perplexed', then immediately headed off towards 'completely bewildered'.

'Nothing. I kind of had some stuff to sort out with Jessica, and there were some obstacles along the way.' Now 'suspicion' was holding court on Joy's face.

'So what? Your little scheme fell through and now you're going with your fallback option? I'm second best to Jessica?'

'Nope. She's second best to you. Second best by a long, long way. She was always second best to you. I only asked Mitch to get me that gig on *The Hangout* after the wrap party when I tried to open my heart to you, and, well, you know ...'

Joy placed her inwardly turned palms a couple of inches from her chest and moved them in a circular motion.

'So you really did like my bits that night?'

'Excuse me?'

'The beads and sequins on my top.'

'Oh, your bits. Yeah. I loved your bits. You looked ... spellbinding.' I bit down on my lower lip and waited for Joy's reaction. I felt like a golfer watching a crucial putt trickle across the green towards the hole. No rolled eyes: it was looking good. No snort or wry smirk: the ball was still on course. Joy's lips parted in slow motion. Now came the moment of truth.

'Thank you,' she said. Yes! YES! I'd done it! I'd cleared 'spellbinding'!

'I love all your clothes,' I volunteered, anxious to keep the momentum going. 'I like that jacket you've got on now, actually.'

'Thanks,' murmured Joy, looking down at her garment, the khaki fabric of which was now spotted with droplets of rain. 'It's new.'

'It looks great on you. And you've hooked it up with jeans, not combats, I see.'

'Fifty-fifty. That's the rule. Even you know that.' Now I was really starting to feel bold.

'I could stand here and look at you all day.'

'Well you're not going to.' Joy placed a protective palm on her hair and glanced anxiously at the leaky charcoal clouds up above. 'It's about to piss it down and I didn't bring my brolly.' I grabbed Lawrence's snout with my paw and wrenched his disembodied head out of my bag.

'You want to borrow this?'

'Yes please.' To my surprise, Joy accepted my made-in-jest offer and took the emergency headwear from my hand. Then, just as I thought my *A Lemur and a Gentleman* fantasy was on the verge of coming true, she clouted me over the head with Lorro's hollow, spongy bonce. 'Thanks,' she said, handing the head back to me.

'Jeez. You try and help somebody ... I don't know why you're so worried about your hair anyway. I've seen horses standing in the rain before.'

'You cheeky fucker!' Joy made a lunge to retrieve Lawrence's head from me, but I whisked it out of her reach and up above my own head (yeah, *now* I had basketball skills), leaving her stood on her tiptoes and swiping in vain at the air around my wrist.

'I'm joking. I love your hair. I love everything about you, Joy.' Our eyes locked. Joy ceased her swiping and, as her hand retreated and her heels reconnected with the concrete, I pulled Lawrence's head down from the sky. 'I've been in love with you since my first day in that building. Since the very first time you were ever rude and unwelcoming to me.'

'How come you didn't say anything? I mean, before you did at the wrap party.'

'Well, there was the Matt factor,' I reasoned. 'But even before that, I was too scared of ruining what we had.'

'What did we have?'

'I don't know. I don't know what we had. What we *have*. All I know is that every day I ever spent inside that building ... I lived for it. I lived for every inane exchange we shared, every insult you threw at me. Every insult I threw at you.' Joy scrutinised me in silence for a moment before speaking.

'And you're not worried about ruining all that now?'

'Right now, I'd rather trample on everything we ever had than spend the rest of my life wondering whether I could have had a chance of being with you. So please, if you can find it in your heart to put me out of my misery one way or the other ...' I looked down at my bedraggled wet chest and let out a half-laugh / half-sigh. 'Because this shit is giving me grey hairs.' Joy didn't laugh. Or smile. In fact, I couldn't get any sort of reading from the impassive look on her face. I spread my arms out wide and presented one crucial last argument. 'Do you think I would have hurtled across town at rush hour inside this thing – without any chance of bladeage, don't forget – unless I

317

was absolutely head over heels in love with you? With gangs of teenagers out of school and on the Tube?' Now a smile flickered across Joy's lips.

'You ran into teenagers?'

'A few.' Joy's smile turned into a grin. Yes! We had diastema.

'Did they give you stick?'

'You could say that. It was mainly "wanker", although if memory serves, there was a "hairy grey twat" in the mix, too.' Joy hit rewind on her grin, turning it back into a smile before her face defaulted to 'serious' again.

'So, before I make a decision,' she announced, 'I need to know something.'

'What's that?' I asked.

'You've said some pretty slushy stuff to me there. If we're boyfriend and girlfriend, does it mean we have to be nice to each other?' I gave a shrug of my soggy shoulders.

'Not if you don't want to.'

'Good, 'cos I just want you to know you look like a fucking idiot right now.'

'Oh, well, maybe if I'd got a strip of condoms hanging off my arse instead of a tail ...'

'Like you'd even know what to do with a condom.'

'Do you always have to have the last word?' I asked.

'Yes,' said Joy. And then we shared a kiss that made the hairs on the back of my lemur neck stand on end.

ACKNOWLEDGEMENTS

Thanks to:

Andy Cowan, Lucy Beckett, Suki Gill, Robert Jones,
Ann McGruer, Phillip Mlynar, Sarah Murphy,
Niamh O'Carroll-Staton, Peter Simpson, Jim Staton,
James Thoo, Parby Tiwana and all my Tachbrook Park people.

Extra Special Thanks to:

Michelle Allbright, Monica Brown, Clay Lowe and my family.

www.ingramcontent.com/pod-product-compliance
Lightning Source LLC
Chambersburg PA
CBHW020336180626
46812CB00001B/234